# IN SHAME AND IN HONOR

**Paul Sheahan**

authorHOUSE®

*AuthorHouse™*
*1663 Liberty Drive*
*Bloomington, IN 47403*
*www.authorhouse.com*
*Phone: 1-800-839-8640*

*First published by AuthorHouse 2/2/2010*

*ISBN: 978-1-4490-6939-1 (e)*
*ISBN: 978-1-4490-6937-7 (sc)*
*ISBN: 978-1-4490-6938-4 (hc)*

*Library of Congress Control Number: 2009914356*

*Printed in the United States of America*
*Bloomington, Indiana*

*This book is printed on acid-free paper.*

# CHAPTER ONE:
# THE PLAYERS

Adeline was unlike the other girls, sometimes aloof, often silent, but never morose. If observed closely one could see the intensity of her thoughts; the wrinkled brow dealing with some problem, be it academic, social, or religious. Her lips were pursed, like a trap, symbolic of the thoughts she held to herself. No word was wasted in idle talk, by nature, life for her was innately a serious business.

In no way could she be considered asocial. Communication was a way to discover new insights into life, but she was not involved with the frivolous side typical of a growing young woman.

At that precious age girls can move from uncontrollable and frivolous giddiness to a floodgate of tears with the bat of another's angry eye. Their wrath can be furious, particularly if aimed at themselves or even their kin. Sensitive to a fault, they can rescue, mother, and defend any cause with passion, but they are a joy to those who have the heart to believe that one day each will, in her own way, become a graceful swan. They can mimic the roles of their own mothers and yet still need to hug a doll at night. To a father they can be the most unfathomable of creatures, angry one day, playing coquettishly the next, and loving unbearably by the third. They are a mystery sent by God to teach us that the heart is a fragile beauty for which the book of instructions is understood only by those who stand back and watch like the wise old owl perched on the branch of a tree viewing its nightly domain.

Adeline was the archetype of this mould. Her father worried about her incessantly. Was she normal? Her mother, in contrast, could remember her own growing years and those memories were carved into her memories like the work of a delicate woodcarver. Time would take care of all!

Adeline was not like the average girl, physically. Tall for her age, she possessed a set of broad shoulders topped with a head a head within which lay a brain of unfathomable depth. The head was fine, but strongly set. Deep dark eyes were perched slightly above high and prominent cheekbones. Her nose was lengthy and her jaw manly. She was not a part of the family heritage. Neither pretty nor striking she was statuesque and in a feminine way, handsome. Adeline knew all these things about herself, for after all, self-analysis was the road to growth.

Miss Plankard, her teacher for this time period, had only glorious praise for Adeline's unique spirit, for this mentor saw remnants of herself in this growing young girl. For Miss Plankard, Adeline was beyond the perfect student. School brought out one side of her. An 'A' student, she went beyond the expectations of excellence for a mere country girl. Practical skills like sewing and cooking were of little interest to Adeline. She did them to appease her parents.

Books were her path to understanding the world in which she lived and the world beyond as well. She came alive while reading '*Uncle Tom's Cabin*' and recognized a portrait of what was wrong with this nation where she lived, slavery. The local school trustees of Jenkins County, where Adeline resided, saw, in Miss Stowe's book the key to comprehending the Southern way of life and expanding their sons' and daughters' views on this malevolent evil. Thus in September 1853 grade eight students were encouraged to read this novel. However, they did not go as far as mandating its use, thus recognizing that views on slavery and blacks varied among the inhabitants of their county. Let the teacher absorb the anger if any should complain.

Miss Plankard was an emerging abolitionist and she thought that this book would be an excellent means to infuse her students with what she viewed as 'the new community values'.

The first to be given a copy was Adeline, of course. She read it three times and was beginning to wear some of its pages. To Adeline this book was akin to the Bible itself and presented the views that all should see in the hated institution. To her it was like a parable for all to hear and learn the lesson that it taught, namely, that the 'evil institution' must be abolished.

But in Jenkins County the war was still far away. Upon her graduation Adeline had the rare opportunity to attend Bartholomew College even though her parents were scarcely capable of funding such a venture. Once again Miss Plankard was to make her presence felt. Determined, the modern lady took it upon herself to have a meeting with the trustees. She proposed that the community bear the burden of the $300.00 annual tuition. With their approval Miss Plankard went from door to door soliciting whatever funds the community could afford. She particularly sought out homes with daughters. She even managed to eke out $10.00 from her tight-fisted merchant father. The small price Adeline would pay would be her frequent return to Jenkins County, and to speak to anyone interested on the state of America, politically, socially, and economically. She encouraged Adeline to find out more about slavery and search out its place in this expanding nation. As a result, Adeline was to become an eloquent speaker of note in the county.

Great excitement, at least for Jenkins County. While not a traditional route for a black escaping bondage utilizing the Underground Railway, the county experienced its first real contact with the Railway. Her name was Amelia. During her trip north she had become separated from the rest of her group and sought solace wherever she could. Miss Plankard had managed to make arrangements so that Adeline, who was off school at the time, could temporarily care for her.

In the first days of this new relationship conversation was light and focused more on Amelia's physical care and emotional well-being. She was in amazingly good condition despite her trials and tribulations. Amelia was almost six feet tall and appeared quite statuesque. Her face was attractive. Full lips and dancing brown eyes hid horrors Adeline could not imagine. Slowly her story unfolded. Family separation at birth, humiliation at the hands of the trustee, fourteen hours a day at field work, personal poverty, and the death of her adoptive mother........all of this made for a persona devastated by humiliation and loneliness. Adeline listened attentively during the frequent walks the two took around the ancestral property. Meanwhile, Miss Plankard was busy making arrangements with the Underground Railway to continue her journey northward to Canada. But this was far from the minds of these two young ladies.

There was no room for color differences with this pair, only the desire to learn from the experiences of the other. The topics were endless, the stories often heart rendering, and often ending in floodgates of tears as Amelia shed layer after layer of domestic abuse. On one such outing and based on mutual trust the generally unspeakable topic of sex was raised. Amelia dropped her head and became silent. Silence ruled the relationship for the first time.

Ominous clouds formed in the sky above, great thunderheads, foretelling of violent inclement weather. Neither girl noticed the sudden change. The swirling wind whistled, drowning out the hoof beets of two apocalyptic riders.

The men were upon them, quickly dismounting and facing the two females with nasty glowers revealing toothless mouths. Being downwind Adeline and Amelia were beset with the malodor of the two, making them feel they were in some human dung heap. Stubbled faces of grey and black were interspersed with pitted holes, the malingering effects of youthful smallpox invasions. Their clothes, if one could call them that, were almost colorless, and masked in dirt, like their minds. Smiles became grins, evil and malignant grins. Revolvers hung from each hip, but they weren't needed here

"Well, missy," slurred the shorter of the two, "After what we been through to find you we figure some kind of reward is due us before we head south with you. White girl you can watch or stay. It don't make much difference to us." Like two lions that had awakened from their regimen of relaxation, the two stripped Amelia naked in less than a minute. A handkerchief, embedded with ions of snot, was forced down her throat to silence her wailing protests. She tried to run, but it was wasted energy. The two were upon her. Broken fingernails covering fingers of dirt and sweat hauled this innocent girl to the ground. She hit the ground so hard one could hear the whooshing sound of air escaping her lungs.

Pants were dropped and each man fumbled with their privates. Penises were inserted in both her vagina and her anus as each man desecrated the girl. In further humiliation each urinated a dark yellow stream over all parts of her body. They seemed quite comfortable doing this. Catching slave runners must have bred these obscenities into their code of conduct. They had brought dishonor to themselves and the institution they represented. Blood trickled from Amelia's private areas. The rag was removed and stale water obtained from a nearby swamp was used to make Amelia presentable for her master.

"Get dressed, nigger!" barked the shorter of the two men.

And where was Adeline during all of this? Frozen like the ancient Neanderthal who had wandered too far up some ancient mountain. Her brain shouted to her as the men left her, ignoring her existence. Nothing! No movement! The Neanderthal stood, wanting to do something but unable to figure out what that should be. This phenomenon is not unique. Faced with the most terrible of crimes, man is capable of a silent stupor.

Amelia disappeared with the two riders, the two bounty hunters smugly hiding behind the ugliness of the "Dred Scott' decision. They did so confident in their conquest. They took their time, for the laws were on their side. Better still, each would earn $25.00 for their conquest. Now Amelia's owner would have the pleasure of seeing one of his prime pieces of property returned to him.

Abolitionists had been outraged with that infamous Supreme Court decision. Conservative judges had taken the view that escaped slaves were chattel and as such could be treated as stolen property. Canada had become the last refuge for these poor souls as they sought to escape slavery.

Adeline changed. She refused to return to college to finish her studies and chose to spend most of her time in her room staring blankly out her window. The events of that day played over and over in her mind. Why had she not helped? Guilt now became the force now driving her spirit. She began to loathe herself. All those noble words about freedom for slaves became that, just empty words trumpeted vacantly without backbone or action.

Played in brilliant color she could manipulate that fateful day coming upon the scene from different angles and watching her frozen form encased in fear. No word was too vile to describe what she had done that day. She was trapped within her conscience and it was not about to free her from her moment of inaction. Her values had been tested and she failed that test. The downward spiral of mind and spirit took her to very dark places. She imagined herself hanging from some gnarled, dead oak tree with the word 'coward' inscribed on a sign placed around her neck. Unwittingly she had become suicidal. One day she tried to make the dream come true but was found by her brother and sister before the rope could do its devilish deed.

Her first memory was awakening to the crying of her shocked mother and father. The doctor had been called, but his job was simply to state the obvious. No one really understood suicide in that day and age. Healing had to come within the mind of the person. She lay silently. She asked for no one or for food.

In desperation the Reverend Tolland was brought in to pray and listen to what Adeline might say. He was not a young man but had an understanding of the ravaged mind. He had seen so many. His gentle, peaceful smile brought an air of freshness to Adeline. He took her right hand and gently rubbed it. Its warmness penetrated her cold soul. He began.

"Adeline, I doubt there is much I can say to heal you. Your healing will come from your Maker and the inner strength that I know is within you. God has long forgiven what you must see as weakness. You have already given so much to this world, more than what most can do in a lifetime. Remember, you are alive because God has a purpose for you in life. It is up to you to find your personal redemption. It will come to you suddenly. You are a person of faith, have faith in yourself."

Wise words indeed, but would Adeline have the same confidence in herself as Rev. Toland? He closed by clasping both her hands and giving them a warm squeeze. After he left she continued to sob, but he had left her with a recipe for salvation. It was up to her to put it into action.

Life was to change quickly for Adeline. General J.P.T. Beauregard had ordered the bombing of Fort Sumter. War was now declared by President Lincoln and he ordered an army of 75,000 soldiers for a period of ninety days. That should take care of those Southern upstarts.

The war served as a distraction for Adeline. She studied these events carefully, concerned for her older brother who was eager to be the first soldier to go to war from Jenkins County. He was also afraid this war would be over before he could make his mark on history.

Then it happened; the unimaginable in the minds of Northerners! They had economic resources the South could not match. They had legal right on their side! And with superior officers and the bravery of these first volunteers it would end and the South would be brought back into the fold. How could a few wealthy landowners and a struggling middle class make their mark against the North? It was called First Bull Run (or Manassas if you were from the South). Why, the cream of Washington had come out that day to see the South put to rout. There was a rout but it was the Northern soldiers that flew from the battlefield all the way back to Washington.

Adeline's spirit began to revive. The Rebs were the reincarnation of the devil himself. This would be a test for her! This would be her redemption. Now the experience with Amelia and her personal beliefs were brought to the foreground.

So with her spirit revived Adeline began to conjure up a plan. First she looked in the full length mirror that ran the length of her closet door. Her eyes took on those of a recruiting officer. Her body type was not unlike that of a gangly country boy. She pictured herself in the uniform of most Northerner soldiers, double blue. She pictured her hair cut short with horsetail hair used to secure a moustache over her upper lip. She would use a slouch hat to cover her feminine eyelashes. She would make a point of looking male by adding grit to her face giving her a weathered appearance. She would sew extra cloth in areas where males would tend to be muscled, on the arms and legs. She practiced walking from side to side, with a bit of a slouch to finish off the changes. To toughen herself she took long walks in the woods to firm up her legs while at the same time carrying an axe over her head to firm up her arms. The next step was more difficult. She was from a farm area and it would be natural for her to use a flintlock or shotgun. She had watched her brothers hunt and unconsciously memorized the steps in operating a flintlock. On the days when she going deep into the woods she would take powder and lead balls with her to practice with on the neighboring trees. Adeline tempered this dream with the realization that she had to go about this carefully. She could not afford to be discovered when enlisting. She would rely on her instincts to let her know when she was 'ready to enlist'. To make her voice more masculine she had her accomplice brother buy some cigars which she hoped would add a rasp to her voice. Smoking would be her way of showing her newfound masculine identity. What a picture she made. Wearing men's pants and carrying a flintlock rifle and axe she would shuffle off in her new stride to practice her conversion in becoming a man. When firing the flintlock she made sure the men were away in the furthest fields before beginning target practice. More than once she managed to make the ramrod airborne, but she approached these as challenges to conquer, not defeats.

The war was expanding and with it Adeline's skill and proficiency in acting 'soldierly'. Her plan was to wait for the next call-up of men and she would sneak off. It would be pointless to debate this with her parents so she wrote them a lengthy letter outlining her objectives and the training she had been doing. It would shock them but at least they would know that their daughter had come back to them, just in an altered form.

****

Ben was an average boy. He had not excelled at school and was therefore pressed into service on the family farm. But Ben was a dreamer and his dream had been to join the army. From an early age he had played with toy soldiers bought by his father. His father could see the passion in his eyes when he brought home books about famous battles that he found in the school library. To Ben and his father, serving one's country was an honorable profession, one that bred discipline into a man. It was a profession where close bonds were established between other men, men who shared the same vision for this growing country. As well there were those unspoken bonds that formed between soldiers when faced with battle, knowledge of something horrible yet beautiful, friendships forged by facing a common enemy.

Ben had started his military career at the age of sixteen. He had made the decision to join the army and without his parents' permission, had snuck off to join. All he had on him were the clothes he wore and a new pair of boots. His failing was in forgetting to break in his boots before beginning his march to glory. Hours of walking brought him to a halt and so he sat on a log and removed the dusty new boots. Undoing his laces carefully he managed to avoid the sorest part of his feet, his heels. Peeling off his socks, he found a bloody patch of torn skin on each of the heels. A bubbling creek ran nearby so he soaked his feet while trying to clean his brand new socks. What was clear was that these slavish minions of travel desperately needed a rest! Leaning back against a stout oak tree he maintained this comforting posture while he took the time to rest the remaining parts of his body. He estimated that he had covered about ten miles but that still left ten miles from the nearest railroad station. He still had twenty miles to travel. Mr. Cowan's hay cart jostled his way another twelve miles to town where the two departed ways. Now he had to travel the remaining eight miles over roads he had never traveled before. He gulped when faced with the unknown. And so he set out hoping to reach the station by dark.

He could hear the familiar chirps from birds that comforted his spirit. There were chickadees with their 'dee-dee-dee' song as they hunted for seeds. Further above, a cackling crow announced his recent conquest of some small bird's nest. At his feet a bold chipmunk, with raised tail, shot across in front of him daring capture by this human.

As he continued on, his heels began to ache again. This time he could not afford to halt his journey. To overcome this pain he let his mind wander into the past history of his young homeland. What reading he had done told of famous characters and their revolution for freedom; the glorious ride of Paul Revere; the surprise attacks at Lexington and Concord; the rout of the Hessians at Concord; the cunning of the 'swamp fox' and of course their famous general and first President, George Washington.

War looks glamorous from a distance. Ben would not be the last to turn historical facts into signposts for action. All of this was followed by the noblest of constitutions. What achievements! Ben's mind was kept in a continual vortex of glory.

He heard it, first low, then unmistakable. The sound of a pair of light horses pulling a buggy. He looked back and around the corner appeared his father driving their family buggy at a fast pace. His father's countenance showed no emotion and the only words he spoke were firm.

"Get in Ben!"

Ben's escape to a nobler cause had been reigned in by his father. His cause would have to wait for another day.

But his dream never faded. The Mexican War had provided Ben with a healthy collection of written and illustrated heroes. He imagined the clashes that he read about and wished that he had been old enough to take part in the American victory.

His favorite battle stood out from the others. It was not even American! It was the famous Battle of Thermopylae in which King Menelaus and his three hundred Spartans had stood their ground against the forces of the Persian Empire. The illustration showed eighteen Spartans remaining. He had actually counted the figures, their rippled muscles standing out in firm defiance, knowing their fate but accepting it as any true warrior would. At their feet lay countless dead Persians who had felt the sting of the Spartan sword.

His sisters thought him foolish for thinking that death in this form or any other brought honor and glory to its recipient. They teased him mercilessly and he dauntlessly withstood it, accepting their barbs with the stoicism of an ancient Spartan.

Left, right, left, right …the three would mock his military bearing as he moved about their farmhouse. It was not that these girls were students of history but rather they acted as a group of silly sisters ganging up on their only brother who, if truth be known, they actually admired and respected.

But in the middle of this 'comedy' a more serious event was taking place. Ben's father, a mountain of a man but gentle as a mare with her young foal, had taken Ben out to the barn and over to his workbench. There lay a horse blanket that had seen better days. It served to wrap a hidden prize. His ham-like hands unfurled the blanket. There lay a modern, new Enfield rifle. He gestured towards the gun indicating that Ben was to be its new owner. It was a far cry from his well-used flintlock that had seen better days.

"This is yours, Ben." His father was a man of few words but when he spoke you knew he meant business. No other words needed to be spoken. It was one of those times when two people know exactly what was in the mind of the other, when the ghosts and joys of the past align themselves and point a new direction for the future. Ben's father knew that someday his son would be a soldier. He had accepted that fact and felt his role was to help his son hone his skills even though it might lead to his death in the distant future. Ben was now free to join the army. Father and son had reached a consensus on Ben's future.

"Now son we can hunt and bring your skills with a rifle to a higher level." His father had also purchased the lead and moulds necessary for Ben to make his own Minnie balls. This gun had a much greater range than his old flintlock.

So now the two could be found, after chores were done of course, heading to their private practice range out in the woods. The women looked on with interest but said nothing, for this deed was done with as far as they were concerned . When the two were returning from a hunt or practice session the girls would watch, with a touch of jealousy, while that huge ham of a hand was placed gently on the shoulder of his son. They knew that this was a 'right of passage' they would never have the pleasure of experiencing.

So it was that in the spring of 1857 that Ben, after seeding was finished, left that safe enclave of love and entered a world, which he could never imagine, to join the regular army of these United States. When his first letter arrived it became the first of many the family would collect over the next few years. Some would be instructive, some personal, and some terrifying…but that was yet to happen.

Dear Parents and Sisters, September 10, 1857.

I hope this letter finds you all in good health. I apologize for taking so long to write but I had to work on my writing skills. I regret now not having taken greater care in school to learn the proper way to write.

I am a trooper and our countless journeys into the western plains have made me a respectable rider. Good news! I have already been promoted to the rank of corporal and am in charge of twelve cavalrymen.

I am stationed in the Arizona territory. Our task is to keep the Indians in this area under control. This is no easy task. Their braves are excellent horsemen and can outdistance us even when we do find them. Daily we go out on patrols to search for them but rarely do we find any. Pa, thanks for the training you gave me with that Enfield, you should see how bad some of the city boys are as marksmen. The sergeant has picked me out to help train new recruits who desperately need practice. I think it was my skills with the gun that helped get me promoted. The sergeant says no, he believes it is my ability to work with other men and to give them praise. He claims I bring an 'excitement' to the job that rubs off on the other troopers. He says I was born to lead men. It feels strange to be spoken to this way but I did notice that the other men nodded when the sergeant said this. I have to make sure all of this does not go to my head.

Some of the Indians live outside the fort and trade with us. They are fine fellows, for the most part. Many of the soldiers treat them harshly and laugh at their ways but I believe they are wrong. One Indian in particular has tried to show me how to use a bow and arrow. He laughs. It takes hours of practice to use this weapon. They can outride us, out walk us, go without food longer, and find water where we would fail to look. They speak to animal spirits like they are both friends and gods. Their gods are based on nature and act as their guides for living.

Their children acquire their education both from the elderly and the parents. Practical things come from the elders while hunting, and yes, fighting skills, come from the fathers. They are not always on good terms with other tribes so their education is in fact making soldiers out of them.

Army life can be boring and unpleasant. The food is terrible. Sand gets into everything and we are constantly cleaning everything we own. When we aren't cleaning we are constantly drilling. Some drills help us to become better soldiers, but I fail to see how marching helps a trooper. Every morning the flag is raised and I feel then that I have made the right decision in joining the army. You have taught me well.

We have a number of Southern officers and troopers with us. They are mostly country boys like me and they come to the army well-versed in using a gun and caring for the horses. We all get along until someone mentions political issues and a commotion starts. Our views on the colored folk are certainly different. I have to get back to my English lessons so I can write you better letters. One of the educated officers is helping me work with both my reading and writing. Good- bye for now.

Your son,

Ben

Dear Parents and Sisters, December 15, 1857

Thank you so much for the vittles and warm socks. I shared the jam and other preserves with my men. They appreciate it. I apologize for not writing, but much has happened. We had our first skirmish with a band of renegade Indians and I killed my first man. I do not feel good about this. Despite his lifestyle he was still a man; a man with a family, a wife and children judging by his age. He probably had to care for his aged parents as well.

I take no pleasure in killing a human and I don't think I ever will. This part of the job I can do without. There is no glory in this but I am bound by my country to keep order and fight when necessary.

The sergeant is encouraging me to study hard for a promotion to sergeant. One of our sergeants retired and another caught dysentery and died. My reading is getting better but I have to lose my awkward style of writing. It keeps me from expressing what I think and feel.

We closely follow the political life of the country and hope we continue to find ways to compromise with the Southerners.

I had some fun at the regimental competition the other day. I came away with first prize in target shooting. Pa, I have you to thank for this. In the squadron drill we came in second which is good, as we had some new recruits added to our company. Tell the girls I actually miss their teasing. Yes, sometimes I do get homesick and hope I have made the right choice of careers. I will write soon. Ha.

Your loving son,

Ben

February 6, 1858
Dear Parents and Sisters

I am afraid I have some bad news. It casts shame and dishonor on our regiment. We finally left for an extended winter campaign. Colonel VanDorn led six companies on a long, seemingly pointless venture. We stuck to the rivers and creeks looking for fresh pony tracks in the new-fallen snow. Both we and the Indians needed a source of water for drinking. Good luck led us to the discovery of an Indian boy who had wandered from his camp and been thrown by his pony.

The colonel had no patience or care for the boy. He took out his revolver and put it to the boy's head. The boy did not twitch. Van Dorn fired a shot right by the boy's ear, deafening him. The boy pointed to the north. The Colonel felt that their camp must be nearby. To hasten our exploration the wagons were left behind and each trooper was put on three days rations of hardtack and salted pork. Reaching the crest of a hill we spotted a band of Comanches. My company was sent to chase them but they were traveling light, probably a hunting party. Reaching the top of another hill we could see their camp near the bend in a river. The officers conferred to decide what to do next. A trooper was sent back to inform VanDorn of our discovery. The officers were hesitant to go further until our command was brought up to full strength. During the wait we could see the braves of the tribe forming along the cover of woods which was between the camp and ourselves.

Finally VanDorn arrived with the rest of the command. The Colonel put one company on each flank and left them mounted. The rest of us were to march the half mile and face the Indians on open land. This action would be a good test for our new Spencers. We approached along a ridge of high grass which had held despite the winter snow. The Indians did not move. Suddenly the whoosh of an arrow tore through my uniform, grazing my skin. There was little pain, just a trickle of blood. We had been spotted earlier. They were just waiting for us to get in range. Suddenly the whoosh of one arrow became like a nest of angry bees. Troopers to the right and left of me fell. I could not tell how badly they were hurt. We all headed for a long rise that offered some protection from the barrage that had laid us low.

I now had my first real sensation of battle. In battle everyone resorts to surviving in their own small world, only with time does a soldier become more skilled at broadening his field of vision and understanding his role in the larger scale of things. I had to break this narrow vision quickly and take command of my men. I remember yelling at them to head for that low crest. It would offer us some protection. They had to be told to take their time and wait until they had a sure target. It was not enough. Some began shooting wildly, the Spencers setting off a cacophony of noise with their rapid firing ability. But my world was still too limited to take in the movements of the rest of the command which had leant us some support and extended our lines. The Indians still had the advantage of wooded cover. One by one they picked off troopers who then slumped to the ground, their light blue winter coats covering them like shrouds.

Suddenly the battle ended as fast as it had started and the bugler sounded 'cease fire'. We made our way to the fallen rather than pursue the Comanches any further.

It was then that it hit me. I began to shake and tremble, trying at the same time to hide my reactions from my men. The Indians had disappeared and we had but a few men struck with arrows. They were lifted from the field and the doctor was soon engaged in the art of arrow removal which simply meant pulling it out and stemming the flow of blood.

Such was my first real taste of battle and I feel it won't be my last. I was no better or worse a human for this activity. I will have to see what the future brings in this area. I hope that my writing will continue to improve.

Your loving son,

Ben

The newspapers from home made it a reality. Lincoln had been elected President. No Southern states had voted for him. It was a Northern victory. Then Democratic Party was in shambles with supporters in the North and South but failing to agree with each other. Ben sat as an observer appearing cool on the outside but torn apart inside fearing for the future of the nation. The dialogue among the soldiers did little to make him feel any better about the situation. Four men dominated the discussion.

"Damned if I will fight a war for 'niggers'" , exclaimed Sergeant Henry.

"I can see the need to keep the states together. If we fail to do that, any time a state feels like it they will withdraw and form their own little nation."

"Then what will you do when the federal government decides to trample on our rights? My father is a small farmer in Tennessee.

The question of slavery doesn't have any effect on him, but damned if he will let the Federals say the South doesn't have the right to have slavery." piped up Oswald who drawled his way through his views.

"Don't you people even understand Lincoln's position? He is not opposed to slavery in the South, just to its extension to other territories." Barrett tried to act as the voice of reconciliation.

Once again Oswald chimed in, "And what will be the result then, both the House and the Senate dominated by Northerners opposed to slavery."

"What you fail to see is the economic situation. Both Southerners and Northerners gain from the cotton trade. The industrial North favors anything that will keep their factories productive. The only mistake we Southerners made was to fail to build mills as well. My father is a plantation owner. His slaves are well-treated and content to work for him." added Clancy. "Do you honestly think that Northern workers would be glad to see a horde of darkies invade the North and challenge the whites for their jobs?"

"Lincoln is not about to invade the South. There would have to be a war begun by the South to start any hostilities." Barrett again tried to mollify the extremes. Ben found enough pause in the dialogue to air his views.

"What I fear most is that in this national debate the presence of cool compromisers has disappeared. There are no more Henry Clay's to try and barter a peaceful settlement. Now it is the voice of the Hawks and extremists who hold the floor in both Houses."

Dear Parents and Sisters, January 10, 1861

I must apologize for taking so long to write. This fort has not been a pleasant place these dreadful days. What has been feared has come to be. The officers and men have left the post to join their brothers in the South. It was not easy for them. We have been a unit since I joined and personal bonds made their decision more difficult then Southerners will ever know. Men openly and shamelessly wept. About one third of them have left. They came from all ranks and social classes. Their loyalty to their home state was a greater bond than any bond to this great Union. Those of us remaining await orders. Will we be left here, under strength, or will we too be called home to become building blocks for Lincoln's great army? Only time will tell.

Thank you for all the festive goods that you sent. Once again I shared them with my fellow soldiers. Until the next letter I remain your loving son.


Ben

****

He hunched over his beer, taking no notice of those around him. His red eyes had developed a glazed look. His name was Hallard, but his friends called him 'Big Hal'. At six foot three inches he was a monster of a man with hands like hams. Despite years of drinking beer he had not turned to fat, his work on the docks had seen to that.

He was a moody man, prone to brawling. He was indeed a mean drunk. It had been enough to drive away his wife of three years. With her went his only offspring, a son. He was doomed never to lay eyes on them again. Oh he searched for them…but after a while he found other ways to satiate a man's needs. Between the bar and the bawdy house Hal lived in a perpetual state of poverty, living in one room with a mattress and stove as friends.

To Hal cooking meant restricting himself to large steaks and scallions when he could afford them. A cast iron frying pan served as his only cooking utensil. A single plate, chipped and unwashed, served as his table. The knife strapped to his leg, was his only piece of cutlery. The pieces he cut grew smaller in size as the number of his teeth decreased. Clothes were not high on his list of needs and he wore much of his wardrobe on his back. When replacements were necessary he visited the local Catholic nuns who would give him used clothes they had collected. Thus Hal made a somewhat comical presence, dressed in what had been formal clothes and living a far from formal life. At first the nuns had checked to see that Hal was still going to Mass every Sunday but eventually they gave up after resigning themselves to the fact that at least they were doing God's work. With cap in hand he offered the identical response.

"Of course Reverend Mother, I attend Mass regularly, just ask Father Michaels, he will verify my story."

The nuns did not ask. What was the point of embarrassing Hal by catching him in a boldface lie? And so Hal fulfilled the legend his father had left him, a legend of drunkenness and friendlessness. His own father's abuse had prepared Hal as a street warrior. He had practiced on smaller boys, gradually moving up as his fighting skills improved. First there were harder kicks, attacks from behind, broken hands, and finally the use of a knife, not to kill, but enough to gather in a wallet here and there when funds disappeared.

If living was tough, so was the ability to try and escape from such a life. He might resent his life of squalor and periods of sobriety might prevail, but his past provided a dark model when all else failed. Any thoughts of personal goals escaped his thinking and a world of standards and true friends were beyond his ken. When instant satisfaction and numbness ruled they served as the only passwords to a soul that carried more scars than the surface of his body.

So Hal lived from moment to moment, letting his dark devils scratch away at his inner self. Hal was by no means a stupid man. He saw who and what he was. His empty thoughts were easily broken by the meetings of drinking buddies.

"Hi Hal, you drunken bastard, how are you doing this fine day?" blared the raucous voice of Eddy Ballou and his band of friends.

"Get over here you old sot and drink with us so you won't have to worry about the money you're carrying!" With that last cynical comment a round of guffaws belched out from the group.

"Watch what comes out of your pie holes you drunken slobs. Besides I can whip any one of your arse's." With that the comments stopped and the group, along with Hal, got down to serious drinking.

These were hardly friends in any emotional or other helpful way. They were more like scorpions, waiting for that moment when they could turn on one of their group members. The three things they had in common were, a common upbringing, a hatred for blacks and other immigrant groups, and an inability to rise above their present social status. For some of that, society had to bear the burden, but to a man they knew no way to, or showed any interest in bettering themselves.

Their topic of discourse for the evening would be the one that had continued to rear its head in the past year. The continual flow of blacks to the cities and their pursuit of hard labor, for they showed a propensity to this type of activity. The docks were the perfect place for such labor. Hal began the discussion as he was in the foulest of moods.

"Those damn niggers are a menace to us hard working men. We ought to start kicking them around and drive them out. They are willing to work for less, stink from years of living with hogs, and don't even dress like the rest of us." Heads bobbed in robust agreement.

"Their basic nature inclines them to work naturally in the fields," added Ballou, "and those Southern gentlemen know how to deal with them."

On and on went the diatribe filled with the invective of hate until he reached the epitome of his eloquence by referring to them as 'bastard spawn of the devil himself'. Again all heads bobbed in accord. This was a man, who despite a dismal life had given good service to his employer and was skilled at heaving heavy crates around like rag dolls. If only he had known that his whole crew was about to be replaced by the greedy owners of the shipping companies who placed a dollar before the consideration of their actions. Blacks were indeed about to take the white workers' places on the docks of New York.

He woke the next morning on the well-worn mattress. He had no memory of leaving the bar and going home, but that was no shock for Hal. It was Sunday and like he promised the good nun, he would be at Mass. Fat chance, he mused to himself, picturing himself like some pious old goat, praying to a God he doubted even existed. His goal this day would be simple. Lie still and recover. Take a couple of swigs of whiskey and go back to bed. By early evening he would feel hungry enough to eat and his main and only course, steak. This evening he decided to 'dine out'. In his parlance this meant sitting on the front step of his tenement and watching people as he savored his steak.

Tonight was no different from any other. The same faces, the dull colors of the street, the same vivid curses coming from the windows. Life for Hal was predictable and he liked that.

But tonight took on a new glow. Below his feet and initially unnoticed by him, was the presence of a small white dog with a splattering of black over his left eye. Suddenly a serious yap was vented, but only one. Hal looked down and in amusement surveyed the newcomer. Now if Hal had a weakness it was his liking for dogs. And there was a reason for this. As a ten-year-old boy his father began kicking him in the ribs as he played in the park. His father did not need a reason; it was his idea of play. The adults present simply stood by. For many this was part of their culture as well. Suddenly, from nowhere, a large mixed breed dog lunged at his father's throat. Now his father was occupied with survival. Hal had a chance to scamper off to a hiding place, hoping his father would forget about him. His father did forget about continuing the beating. When his father arrived home that night Hal noticed the torn shirt and puncture marks on his arms. His face bore long bloodied scratch marks. Nothing was said between the two but an unseen upturn of Hal's mouth told the story. After that day Hal would befriend any stray dog. He could not take them home but would share any scrap of food he was carrying at the time. They were to become Hal's first friends.

"Well little fellow, you are a polite son of a bitch!" Silence. After a minute or so the small dog raised himself up and sat squarely on his haunches. It was then that Hal noticed it. The dog with the eye patch had no right foreleg. A mere stump hung down two or three inches from the shoulder socket.

"Good God, what happened to you young fella?" queried Hal. Again silence. Hal cut a good sized chunk from his steak and tossed it to him. The small creature immediately sat, barked a 'thank you' and proceeded to pounce on the steak. For the dog this was Christmas come early. Hal continued street gazing. No one appeared to take possession of the little dog. Upon finishing his morsel the small canine raised himself up and turning around faced the street. He then plunked himself at Hal's feet. The two sat in silence, each reflecting on humanity as people marched in varied cadences up and down the street. Hal moved and began to walk up the stairs and his movement was followed by that same single 'bark'.

"Sorry fella but I can't afford the luxury of a food user." He continued up the stairs and a small whimper came from the small beast. Hal turned around and all he could see were two, dark, pleading eyes facing him.

"Alright, come on along, but just for tonight," Hal cautioned.

When Hal awoke the next morning, there staring him in his unfocused eyes were those two large, pleading orbs of brown. No word was spoken between man and dog. Hal just knew that he was about to begin his career as an animal caregiver. Hal's past had left a soft and spongy spot in his hardened heart.

"All right, all right, let's find out just how smart you are. We go off to work now. Let's see if you can survive nine hours of watching and waiting." And so the two trundled off to the docks, looking quite ludicrous due to the difference in their sizes. Hal looked down often to see how his new found friend was managing on his three legs. To his amazement the little dog was still frozen in his spot with the good front leg focused under the epicenter of his little body. At break time Hal went to visit him.

"Well, aren't you one tough little customer, little fella, just like me." Hal laughed to himself. As the day progressed more and more blacks began to show up at the dock. The supervisor came out of his office to inform the workers that their jobs had been terminated. It didn't take much thought to figure out who was replacing them. Workers began throwing rocks and any other available object at these new workers. Suddenly from nowhere the city police appeared and pushed the whites away from the dock area. Hal demanded to know what was going on and surrounded by his friends they found that they had indeed been replaced by the black workers for five cents less a day. Hal led the fray and threw clenched fists at the blacks as they passed by. Unfortunately most of the blows landed on the New York Police who did not receive a beating passively. Hal's face turned beet red as these scavengers from the South took their place.

It never seemed to occur to them that it was the owner who was the real instigator of this situation. His desire for further profits was the force behind their rampant racism. As events unfolded more and more police appeared to thwart their protest. The blacks began unloading a ship and a smug face in a fine suit and smoking the best of cigars, snickered wryly from his third floor office window.

Within an hour the disgruntled whites ambled away in small groups. Turning back, they cursed as they left. They had chosen the wrong enemy and in doing so had condemned themselves to failure. Predictably they plodded off to their favorite pub and drank away the last of their money. Hal was in good form and spoke vile words of hate and condemnation while nods of agreement traveled around the table. But without a leader, a plan, or a real understanding of who the enemy was, they became empty words spoken through a glass of beer. Hal had also failed to notice that his new found friend had found a safe place under the table. The little dog was shaking with fear at the sound coming from his master's voice.

At the table was a chap by the name of Nielsen who was the only one with an education and therefore capable of reading. Tiring of Hal he had picked up a newspaper and began thumbing through it. A certain ad caught his attention.

"Good God, look what these rich people are willing to pay to get out of doing military service. As much as $500.00 to any man willing to serve in his place!" he exclaimed.

The disaster of First Bull Run had just taken place and these people sensed the writing on the wall. This was going to be a long war. They also knew from their military friends that the Union Generals were not strong leaders. They knew that some method of forced call up of men would be mandated on the Union once volunteering lost its appeal.

"Why would I fight for some rich man and die while he lives? Let them die too!" barked Hal, as a 'hambone' of an arm was swiped across his stubbled face removing spit and beer foam at the same time. After an hour of endless pros and cons the volume of the debate continued to rise.

"Enough!" squawked Hal. "I've heard enough!"

With that last comment Hal rose and steadied himself and staggered to the exit. Faithful friend and master began the long trip home. On their way home they encountered three men of color. Hal's eyes bore down on them like a hungry wolf.

"Get out of my way you job-robbing niggers!" The three men saw no point in encouraging Hal, so they moved out of his way. Unfortunately for the smallest of the three he stumbled over the curb and fell against Hal. Needing little provocation, and believing that he was under attack, Hal responded in the only way he knew how. He reached for his leg and brought the knife up quickly and shoved its sharp point into the man's ribs. Instantly the nameless man fell to the ground and blood flowed like the branches of a river amid the spaces of the brick lining the sidewalk below. Hal had hit an artery and the poor man was paying the price for it.

"Good God dis white man dun kill Amos!" screeched one of the remaining two men.

Hal feared the arrival of a policeman so he and Patches made a hurried exit. Ducking down a dark alley Hal stopped to think about his next step. His heart was racing in dire panic. He had an idea. He raced quickly back to the bar. All his mates were gone, but what he wanted lay on a chair like a piece of lifeless litter. In Hal's mind this would be his savior. He made a dash for the paper followed by his nimble three legged friend. Hal could not read but he managed to recognize the page that he sought. As he exited the pub, a well-dressed gentleman was walking quickly in his direction.

"Pardon me sir but I have left my glasses at home and need some help reading one of the ads. I wonder if you could help me." The man was obviously agitated by the intrusion of this man who stunk of alcohol.

"Yes, yes let's just see it. It says the address is Twenty-three Coltbridge Court. Is that what you need? I must be on my way."

"Thank you so much, sir." Little did Hal realize he had encountered Inspector James Mason of the Boston Police Department. Some days our star shines and we don't even know it. Such is life.

Hal scurried, if that's possible for a giant, to the address given him. He approached the door carefully. He was not used to the environs of the upper class. Hal gathered up his courage and knocked on the huge door. The door was opened by an obvious 'gentleman' decked out in an elegant dinner jacket the likes of which Hal had never seen before. Hal was instructed to wait outside. The 'gentleman' had offered Hal a cigar to keep him occupied. His name was Purdy and he was ready for the transaction. The man returned to the door and held a sheet of paper that Hal realized must be the legal document that would release this man from military service.

"Sign here please," asked the man with an air of deference.

"I am sorry I can't write," was Hal's pitiful response.

"Just make your mark. That will be just as good. Now here is an envelope for you to carry this document. Present it to the officer who is signing you up for service. Once you have done so you will have papers showing your willingness to serve. Bring the papers back to me and I will pay you. Oh, don't even think about skipping out on the army when you get your money. The army thinks dimly of that kind of behavior and it could put you at the working end of the hangman's noose."

"Not to worry mister I plan to join the regular army so I can serve my country longer." Hal was trying hard to give Mr. Purdy the impression that he was an honorable man. Purdy had no interest in what area he would serve, only that Hal would serve in his place.

"Good luck, Mr. Hallard," came the meaningless response. Purdy just wanted Hal on his way.

**** 

He stood proudly in the ranks of the graduating cadets. How could he have guessed that the superintendent giving the address to the graduates, Robert E. Lee, would be fighting for the Confederacy in the war which was still three years away? Now he was satisfied with his commission as a second lieutenant of cavalry. It sounded good to his ears and his ego. His name was called.

"Second Lieutenant Robert Macy!"

Rob walked confidently to the podium and shook the hand of Colonel Lee. Little did either man know what lay in store for them in the upcoming war. Rob wheeled on his heels and returned to his seat amid the quiet applause of his family.

Since he had finished in the middle of his class Rob had not stood out as an academic scholar. With the exception of Military History and Horsemanship his grades were in the bottom third of his class. He was intrigued less with the history of famous battles and leaders, than he was with 'military intelligence', the gathering of information from any sources that could add an advantage to one's ability to destroy an enemy. In fact his essay, "Wellington's Use of Intelligence at the battle of Waterloo" had become somewhat famous and his professor had asked for a copy of this work. Rob had excelled in 'Cavalry Tactics in Modern War'. It was no surprise that his first appointment as a junior officer would be in the west taming fractious Indians.

Like many students he had had an influence, in this case his father who was on a first names basis with the governor who had nominated him for admission to the academy.

However, he had another side to his character, one that had almost cost him his placement. He liked money. At first he had tried gambling, but lost miserably. It was his good fortune that he was gifted with a straight face that allowed him to lie without showing it to another. He had had to explain his continual requests for funds to his father.

"I am afraid I have made enemies and I am certain it is these cadets who broke into my room and stole my money." His father accepted this explanation and allowed Robert to walk away, smiling inside.

To make up for these losses Rob had gained access to the records of the Ordnance Department and realized that their records were woefully out of date. Many cases of cartridges used on the practice range could not be accounted for. Given this state of affairs no officer was going to complain if a case of cartridges disappeared. These cartridges, as Rob learned, had a ready market in the local general stores. And so began Rob's career as a trafficker in ordnance.

Bold and brash, Rob made a point of appearing cocky and confident. Who would suspect a loudmouth from keeping secrets? His secret side also extended itself to the world of young women. He was able to handle multiple romances at the same time, convincing each that she was his one and only love. He was full of good looks, and had a solid family background. What more could he add to the attractiveness of a man in uniform? He carried both of these relationships to the point where carefully made plans made for many sexual adventures. But unlike many a young man who would brag about his conquests Rob had the sense to keep all of this to himself.

He had made no bones about his loyalty to the Union, to the point where fisticuffs had taken place between him and Southern sympathizers. While these fights were considered contrary to the values of the academy, they created the image of a dedicated soldier who could be counted on to defend his country. Yes, he was a calculating young man, yet it was the events occurring around him that brought out a particular part of his personality.

Rob had no control over his placement to the western posts, but it was he who would make the best of a hard situation. He sought out someone who could best serve him. Like a fussy vulture, he picked over the Indian scouts, bribing them with alcohol, but making sure they provided him with solid information. He then made a point of releasing this information to the officer who would best help his career.

This ability worked best in his dealings with a native by the name of Screaming Crow. Screaming Crow had been dressed down in front of his peers over some trivial incident. Rob could see the resentment boiling up within him.

Rob knew how to get the Indian on his side. He first shared a bottle of bourbon with him and explained how he could save face with the other Indian scouts. The army was searching far and wide for five renegades but they had disappeared like phantoms into the endless desert. Indian scouts did not always give up information and such was the case with Screaming Crow. Rob assured him that his knowledge of their whereabouts would bring back the favor of the Commandant. Screaming Crow liked the plan so it was he who suggested that Rob lead the expedition. They would have to track the renegades.

In the end the five were apprehended easily and without a fight. The commandant was impressed with both men. Now all

Rob had to do was get this 'police action' into his personal file. Rob patiently waited until a rainy day allowed him to approach Colonel Hawkes. It was then that Rob described in detail how he had befriended the scout, easily winning his confidence. At the conclusion of his story Colonel Hawkes decided that this account should be written up in detail and placed in Rob's file. The Colonel went further and informed Rob that this event would be mentioned in his reports to Washington. Feigning great humility, Rob again smiled to himself. As war approached, tensions grew among the various officers. Rob made a point of staying out of the debates.

One morning Rob made his usual trip to the officer's mess. There he noticed a newspaper lying on a table. Officers, like the rest of the men, he relied on newspapers sent from home to keep abreast of the events taking place there. The headlines grabbed his attention: "THANK GOD - JOHN BROWN FINALLY HUNG." He noted the date, December 1859, *almost three weeks ago*, he thought to himself. The paper was from Georgia so Rob picked it up to see what Southerners would have to say about the events at Harpers Ferry. He began reading.

"Our readers will be only too pleased that the court sentence of this traitor has finally been carried out. This was a man headed to damnation from birth. His father was a well-know abolitionist and the son inherited his disposition to these extreme and violent ideas. It was bad enough that he gave land to known slaves but his participation in the North instigated troubles in Kansas. He was nothing more than a murderer who wanted death for every slaveholder. He was a guerilla fighter who led the slaughter of countless innocents in Lawrence, Kansas. But still the Federals did nothing. It took the infamous raid on Harper's Ferry for them to see the light. The plan originated in an unbalanced mind. It is difficult to think how abolitionists could see him as a hero. But what will this do to other slaves? Will they see that they have the power to rebel? Will those hideous abolitionists aid their cause?

Perhaps, as many people are suggesting, secession from this poisoned North will be the only path to our security."

Rob threw the paper to the floor. *How can people get so worked up over nothing*, he mused to himself. *Now I am sure there is going to be a war. The North can't accept secession. On the other hand, it will give me opportunities to raise my rank and at the same time make more money. This war is one I must put to my advantage.*

****

He did not know who to curse, Southerners or Northerners. Now that war had come, he had to make some decisions, but intelligent ones. Alexander Braithewaite was not your ordinary Southern planter. He walked among the rows of maturing cotton. It was a good time for reverie, for field after field of white laying before him gave him the feeling of walking on a cloud, a man-made cloud to be sure, but the image gave him relief during these serious times. On the other hand, the stalks of waving corn produced images of soldiers in defined discipline. This image always brought him back to reality.

Alexander was a logical thinker, a man, in some ways, ahead of his time, particularly compared to his fellow planters. He was a man with a deep-seated collection of beliefs. His self-confidence stemmed from his actions and their resulting economic success and the expansion of his agricultural empire. Alexander could attest to the fact that he was a man of cool logic who had managed to avoid the emotional whirlwind that swirled around the heads of so many of his fellow planters. He had tried, he believed, to give slavery a human and humane dimension. He also knew that most planters saw him as an eccentric, out of step with mainstream plantation management. What Alexander liked about the South was its ability to let each owner generate his own economic model where each could stand independently as its own fiefdom. It had given him the freedom to experiment with 2,000 acres of prime Georgia farmland and at the same time co-exist in a non-competitive way with his fellow planters.

Like most Louisiana plantation owners, he had the option to focus on sugar or cotton as his cash crop. After the instability of the 1830's, the 1850's turned into a banner decade with prices and crop yields expanding threefold. While this trend to greater profits was typical of the 1850's, his profit-making was spectacular, and for this Alexander could claim the credit.

As a young boy he had far too often witnessed the failings of slavery: the whipped slaves at auction with their defeated and humiliated demeanor. But he knew well that there was another side to the blacks and constantly reminded himself of the failed slave revolt of 1811.

To Alexander, the squalor of slave habitation was unnecessary. It ruined their health and simply made them a burden to the system. The sexual adventures of certain male owners had become infamous and showed up at auctions with the presence of mulattos. At the same time, many a good owner, particularly of the smaller plantations, worked as long and hard as the slaves. Unlike Alexander, who put his profits back into his plantation, other plantation owners used their profits unwisely purchasing homes in New Orleans or sending their children off to Northern colleges. How could a Northern education benefit a planter? At slave auctions he heard the stories of slaves running away, sabotaging crops, equipment, and livestock, even the occasional attack on whites, in frustration of their treatment. Alexander had learned from all this and developed what he termed 'The Pride of Slave Freedom'. These terms sounded contradictory but they made for sound economic logic.

In his system slaves could win points toward their freedom. On average it kept a slave at work for five hard years. Alexander changed the points, not at his whim but in the face of changing economic times. When the slave earned the required points, he had the option to stay or leave as a free man. Alexander made a point of telling his slaves about the restrictive laws created to control the free blacks in the south. They were made by whites to control the lives of the free blacks and drive them north because they were no longer of value to the slaveholder.

He offered them an alternative, to stay on as a paid worker. He made sure that the free slaves would use up some of their income at his well-run store. This system was aided by the fact that freedom was only given to the individual slave. The freed slave would have to buy the freedom of the rest of his family, but at reasonable prices.

He also sought to subtly keep the slaves within the values of a white society. He did this in a number of ways. He did not destroy black culture, but replaced it. This led him to run schools for slave children from age six to eleven. A slave learning to read was outlawed by Louisiana law, but he placated those who objected by focusing on a curriculum which emphasized the rule of law and all its social and political implications. Religion was Episcopalian in doctrine, with the use of non-controversial hymns and songs. To entice the ex-slave further, he granted each male slave ten acres of land which would be deeded to him when freedom was granted.

The free land was usually not the quality of Alexander's but could be brought up to much higher quality with work. Still it was something an ex-slave could call his own. He could begin working to improve this land while still working off his five years of slavery. The one stipulation of this was that Alexander controlled the types of crops grown. He did this to develop a variety of crops which developed independence for the plantation. Excess crops could be sold at market for profit.

Also, slave houses had to be built from cleared land. The house had to roughly follow a plan intended to create a healthier lifestyle. Windows that could be opened, wood floors, separate rooms, and fireplaces, all attempted to reach this goal. To emphasize the need for a healthy domain he gave the slaves simple plans of the ideal home. To help the free slave build his home there were skilled workers on the plantation. To validate this way of life Alexander would purchase a slave at auction. Usually he would look for one who had been abused. This guaranteed that his slaves knew of the horrors outside their plantation while the slave now learned that there were humane plantations.

To expand the free blacks' view of their good fortune, Alexander personally taught classes that emphasized his philosophy: 'Treat men like men and they will respond with hard work that is mutually to the benefit of all'.

Technically, Alexander did not oppose slavery. He did believe in their right to earn their freedom. It worked for him. He was both admired and castigated by other plantation owners, but no one could argue with his success so he was left alone and accepted visits from more liberal owners who came to see what they could learn from his system.

Now all of this was put in jeopardy by a war which Alexander knew the South could not win. They could not manufacture enough goods and would run out of needed resources. They did not have the rail lines to bring troops and material to battle sites. And importantly, they did not have enough manpower to fight. Their only hope was for a quick victory.

What had happened to the compromises worked out in the Missouri Compromise of 1820 and the Great Compromise of 1850? Weren't they formed by those who believed in political compromise because they saw the implications of their failure? Weren't they formed by men of common sense, men who accepted choices in lifestyles and after all wasn't this the molding fabric of America, that men had the right to live as they saw fit? But these men of compromise were no longer in charge. Extremism on both sides had taken hold and threatened what they had put together. Let Southerners live as they had. Let the Senate be equal in numbers who supported or opposed slavery. Let the House be ruled by the North.

*What else had gone wrong*, he mused? The rise of the abolition movement drove Southern landholders into a frenzy. They saw this political voice increasing, and knew that it would someday be an accepted political position. Could they not see that this group would always be a minority? As their radicalism spread, so did the opposition of a large number of Northerners. The ordinary Northerner only saw slaves as a threat to their jobs. Then he considered the bad political decisions that were being made. The Kansas-Nebraska Act of 1854 let popular opinion decide if a state should be a slave state or not. It only attracted radicals from both sides to lay claim to the territories. He had predicted violence back then and unfortunately he was right. The result had been 'Bloody Kansas', followed by the inane actions of that buffoon, John Brown and his taking of the armory at Harpers Ferry. Despite its failure, it generated importance in the minds of the extremists.

How foolish to think it would be only a thirty day war! The North would take longer to bring its economic strength to its full potential but in the end they would have the last say. The South's agricultural power would become a noose around its neck as thousands of bundles of cotton would lay idle at the depots. The Anaconda plan had managed to stem the possible trade with Europe. England needed this cotton but was not willing to go to war with the North. To get it would also make them appear to be supporting slavery, and that was not going to happen.

Paradoxically the South needed thousands of men to deal with the North but refused to put guns in the hands of the blacks. Alexander feared for his empire, not this year or the next, but a prolonged war would devastate his plantation.

Alexander snapped out of his train of thought, probably because he knew where the train ended. He had arrived back at the magnificent porch that wrapped around his twenty room mansion. It was a tribute to the fine craftsmanship of his black slaves. He realized that he owed a debt to these men who had been able to read complicated architectural drawings.

Quietly another idea was beginning to take shape in his mind. He did not see himself as a part of the hordes that would form around the stars and bars. Yes, it would cost him money, but he had cash reserves and could sell some of his bottom land before prices dropped out of the land market. If only, if only...

\*\*\*\*

He knelt at the end of their graves holding the lone, red rose tightly in his hand. He had failed to notice the blood that trickled from his hand, the product of a mind deep in memories, memories that never left his tortured soul. It was their anniversary, if one can truly use such a word to describe tragedy. In five days he would leave this spot, perhaps never to return.

It was just one year since they had been taken from him. His expectant wife was only twenty four years old. She was plump and ripe, ready for the skilled hands of the midwife who was waiting for the glorious moment. His unborn baby lay within the womb, ready to emerge into this rural world where Homer Ames had built a very successful horse breeding farm. Customers came from afar to buy one of Homer's well-bred horses. He imagined his unborn child as a skilled horseman like himself. Oh, what a grand future!

But then it all went wrong. The emerging infant had a larger than normal-sized head and his wife screamed in ruthless agony as only a delivering mother can scream. To make matters worse the midwife found the umbilical cord wrapped around the child's neck. This made strangulation a real possibility. Both Homer and the mid-wife began to panic. If only she had called for the doctor before contractions began.

After much twisting and turning the baby's head appeared. But it was too late. Strangulation had occurred, enough to stop the flow of oxygen to the unborn child. She cleared the fluid from the mouth and whacked its back, but all to no avail. The mother could not contain herself as she tried to watch the blessed event unfold. The baby was stillborn.

Now, to trouble the tragic events further, the mother had a seizure, partially from the pain of delivery and the copious amounts of blood staining the sheets. Her body writhed in pain, white foam dribbling down the right side of the pillow, taking its own perverted toll on the health of the mother. Now her eyes began to roll back and forth as a white frost began to fog over the sky blue eyes. Then silence. There was one last gasp and she was dead, the shock to her heart too traumatic for this kindly soul to bear.

Homer had stayed quiet, trying to assist the midwife when he could. The eyes of the midwife met his deep brown gaze and he knew it was all over. He was numbed by the sheer tragedy of the reality before him…he went silent. He knew what he had to do.

All night until dawn, on a grassy knoll overlooking the farm, he began to dig with the frantic madness of someone searching for peace and unable to find it. An unnatural form of catharsis, perhaps, but not unknown among males, and as the digging proceeded the energy with which he dug heightened. His heart pounded furiously until he finished, then like some ancient ancestor he let out a scream that no one but he and the surrounding wildlife could hear. Only the horses below heard the scream and those asleep woke from their reverie, snorting as if they were being faced by a phantom predator.

The solicitudes and tears of dear friends and relatives waned over time as it always does, each returning to their enchantment or misery but leaving Homer to work out his personal grief. Like many men Homer drove his hate, loss, and pain into his private cave where even he would not enter.

Work consumed his existence. He had hired a local woman to do the chores and cook for him but after she left for the day and the horses were bedded down an exhausted Homer retreated to the grim solace of a bottle of liquor. His nights were composed of long binges of drinking. He stopped at dawn and barely made it through the day. Still, no one else knew. He even took the trouble to chew sprigs of mint to hide his addiction.

He still attended the local horse shows as a diversion from pain, displaying a phony smile for those he met.

"Look how well Homer copes with his loss!" They would exclaim.

"His faith in God must be keeping his life together!" They rationalized.

"When the time is right I am sure he will search out a new wife. He is too young and would make a good catch." They hoped.

If only they knew the real Homer, was dead inside and unconsciously looking forward to his own demise. As a result Homer had little interest in the outbreak of hostilities. He would mask his inner despair and seek out a place on the field of war. After all, he had served at the academy and fought as a young second lieutenant in the Mexican War as a cavalry officer known for his coolness under fire, fair to his men, and a talented horseman. A war was a perfect place for him, and so volunteering his services was also a perfect place for him, or so he thought. He chose a regular army infantry regiment. As a colonel of infantry he was entitled to a horse so he left home with his prized stallion, 'The Grey Ghost'. Homer considered the horse his closest friend. He had raised him himself. Only this animal heard the tears that were shed at night away from human contact. Like the phoenix rising from the ashes, Homer would find himself on the field of battle.

# CHAPTER TWO:
# THE FORMING OF THE TWENTIETH U.S.

They came from almost every state still in the Union. There were men there from Maine, New York, Michigan, etc., and the regular army itself. But why did they do this? Most other men chose friends, neighbors, and relatives, state loyalty.

These men had chosen because of obscurity. Perhaps they had not been popular in the community. Perhaps they were petty criminals who wanted to escape their reputation. Some were transfers who wanted to escape their military heritage. Some came because they knew they would have the benefit of regular officers. For others it was the loneliness they desired. Bereft of relationships they did not want to experience the loss of friends. They came with no built in sense of elan, for them it would have to be earned on the field of battle. So it was that this amorphous group of men met for the first time at a training base in northern Illinois.

There were a number of officers in well-worn uniforms. Like Ben, they must have been serving in the west. The mustering of his company was being handled by one of his lieutenants, notably Second Lieutenant Jeremy Hostings. Like many a new officer, he had been released from attending the fourth year at the Academy. The Union needed officers and this would have to do.

At least, Jeremy thought to himself, this put him well ahead of some of the 'elected' officers who knew nothing.

While only age nineteen Hostings seemed full of confidence and ready to work. Hostings approached Ben.

"All present and accounted for Captain." Hostings had formed them into two ranks of fifty in preparation for this first meeting between Ben and his men.

*What a variety*, Ben mused. Some chins were held high, ready for service, while others drooped like so many beaten dogs. Some already had a uniform and Ben noted that they often displayed a brown stain in a variety of locations, testament to some previous encounter. He wondered about their personal histories. Would these men mold easily to military life, or would it be a struggle to accept discipline? Some were barely five-foot two, others dwarfed them by comparison. Men like Hal looked like a giant in this group. Some were city boys. They exhibited more of a swagger, while the country boys were experiencing their first journey away from home.

"Stand easy, men." Ben ordered. "Gentlemen, I am glad you have volunteered to join a regular army regiment rather then a state volunteer regiment. Your reasons for joining probably vary greatly, but makes no difference, for the only matter of great importance is that all of you develop the courage to uphold your honor. From this moment on you must see yourselves as defenders of this great Union. The battle at Bull Run should clear your minds of the notion that this will be a quick war. The Confederates are more familiar with guns, and their horsemanship is ahead of ours. Listen to your officers and sergeants. Drill will become increasingly important if we are to develop our tactics well." He glanced to his first sergeant, "First Sergeant they are all yours to train." Both men saluted each other to make the transition official.

First Sergeant Emile Lacroix was one of those southern 'anomalies'. After fighting with distinction during the Mexican War he had returned to his native Louisiana. He worked forty acres of good land, increasing the volume of its output over the years. He did not believe in slavery and had hired two free slaves to help him work the fields. Over the years he married a local girl and had produced five fine children, all of whom had survived infancy, a rare occurrence in this time period. All were boys, so Emile eventually had his own work force. Uneducated Emile could not read or write so he had dedicated himself to the belief that all his children would become literate. He insisted that they learn proper French not the Creole of Louisiana and had hired a young French girl to make this happen. Nor did Emile have time for the local Catholic Church. He viewed the parish as a social club rather than a place of worship. So he took it upon himself to spend his time teaching his children his own personal moral code. Emile was not tall, but what he lacked in height he made up for in a stocky, muscled body. Yet he was a man who could be moved to tears by the sight of a wounded domestic or wild animal. He saw them as a part of God's world, for in his mind his family, slaves, and nature itself was a part of one unity. It was no surprise that his eldest son chose to go North with his father. For their trip north he had given his son the *Manual of Arms* for light reading.

Emile had often had to show his strength of character and had been willing to stand the remarks, and even threats, of his Southern neighbors who openly taunted him for his views on slavery. Knowing Emile's background had given Ben a great sense of confidence in his First Sergeant.

The men were dismissed to receive their uniforms and other accoutrement. Ben took the time to observe his surroundings. Each of the eight companies had their places in a line of open-ended rectangles placed neatly in a row. The officers and command tent stood at the front of the open ends. Ben was to share a walled tent with another captain.

Up to this point Ben had little chance of meeting the regiment's commanding officer. That situation was about to change for coming across the field at full gallop was Colonel Homer Ames mounted on a magnificent grey steed. Colonel Ames was another veteran of the Mexican War and had served as a cavalryman during that conflict. By nature and training he was a born rider.

Colonel Ames was not a man of large stature. That explained the rumor going around that his career in regular times was that of a jockey. Rumor also had it that he had had a serious riding accident and had broken his leg in four places, thus bringing an end to his riding career. One could not tell by watching the man ride. He held his head steady, his seat was firmly set in the saddle, and his legs locked against this thundering steed. Colonel Ames and the horse came to a skidding halt, throwing earth on those standing nearby. Foam dripped from the stallion's mouth.

A wide grin of pure joy crossed his face as it does when one is immersed in something one enjoys with a passion. As he stood there it was apparent that rider and mount were meant for each other. Colonel Ames leapt from the horse only to land squarely on two feet. Before introductions the Colonel made sure that his orderly walked out the horse for at least twenty minutes. After that he was to have a tepid bath followed by a grooming, ...then off to the blacksmith to have his shoes checked.

Ben's career had taken place in the saddle so he too could appreciate the quality of this fine animal. The light dappling shone against the grey tones of his body. It was clear the bond between man and animal had already been sealed. His name, 'The Grey Ghost' was an apt one for this beast filled with both of those qualities. Despite Colonel Ames' obvious love of horses, when it came to men it was a different matter. No one could ever get close to this man. He was firm when necessary and could talk with any man, he was hardly shy.

Again rumor said that he had married in his twenties to a woman of great beauty but no sense of faithfulness. She left him childless and had taken up with a gambler to pursue a more active life. These rumors had gotten back to Homer and he was quite willing to leave them intact. His real past was too painful to recount.

As the men began to gather about in small groups they were getting the first chance to try on their new uniforms. Chuckles from the groups told the story. The limited number of sizes benefited those who got there first. The tendency was to make the uniforms larger rather than smaller. With some elementary sewing men could refashion pants into a sack coat. The smarter soldiers hoarded excess material to use to cover rips and tears they knew were coming. This war was to test all men on their abilities to cope with any difficult situation.

Ben excused himself from the colonel and strode over to help the first sergeant with the men and show them what to put where. Where did the canteen fit? The same applied to the leather cartridge and cap pouch. Oil skin, knapsack, and bed rolls all had a proper place in this jungle of attachments. The laughing continued as these men tried to look like military look-alikes. Ben had enjoyed this, but it was time to look for the colonel's command post. A flapping American flag stood guard and as Ben noted all the states were represented. A rebellion was no reason to change the flag. After all, that was what they were fighting for. As the war dragged on, Ben was to ask himself whether the price paid to retain the Union was in fact worthwhile, but that would come much later.

A nattily dressed major was conversing with Colonel Ames.

"Join us if you can Captain, I have someone for you to meet." Ben could tell by his dark blue uniform that this major was a staff officer.

"Captain, meet the illustrious Major Macey," The colonel announced.

Both men saluted. While noticing his clean and tailored uniform, Ben could tell he had the air of an academy graduate. Ben had met them in the west, but in Macey's case Ben suspected he was not here to serve as a line officer.

"The colonel has been describing the officer's with military backgrounds. You certainly stand out from the rest, Captain," articulated the well-spoken Major. "There aren't many of you who have worked their way up through the ranks in western command. You must have been one hell of an Indian fighter."

"I like to think it was my leadership skills, Major." remarked Ben in a half-humoress tone.

"You will be seeing Major Macey from time to time as our regiment progresses, Captain," added the colonel. That comment attracted Ben's attention and he began to wonder if this regiment had been created for some reason other than just fighting.

"You will excuse me gentlemen, I must get back to observing my first sergeant and his training methods." Ben pardoned himself as gracefully as possible.

Ben's focus was on the training of the soldiers standing in front of Emile. He was starting to get impressed. They even began to look like soldiers.

"Do I have permission to begin drill with firearms?" requested Emile.

"Most certainly, First Sergeant, but I need to speak with them for one moment." Emile gave the center of the field over to Ben.

"Men, you are probably aware that we need to promote six more sergeants and twelve more corporals by the end of training. Listen well to all the instructions you are given and perform them with enthusiasm, if you wish promotion." Ben hoped this might motivate the men to perform with excellence.

Both men would have to learn the nuances of these new rifles, particularly its ability to fire up to 1,000 yards.

The men had been issued the two man tent made from oilskin. This would increase their agility in the field. They would no longer have to wait for the transport of the awkward Sibley tents which served eight men. With this new tent however, one would have to try and find a short pole to support the ends. They would also have to become used to an open ended tent. They could use their rubberized groundsheets to keep moisture out from beneath.

The men were dismissed and he could hear them grumbling as Emile informed them that drill would be practiced four times a day and more if the desired level of perfection was not achieved. The appointed cooks, or victims if you chose, picked out a place in the center of the company street and then proceeded to the commissary to obtain ingredients for the evening's meal.

As time went on the inefficiency of this task and the poor quality of meals led the men to cook in pairs or fours, then they would have no one person to blame. The remainder of the men had been given alternate tasks, from digging latrines, to gathering wood for fires, to guard duty.

"Emile, how did you get such willing cooks?"

"It was easy, sir. I simply asked the city boys if they had cooked in restaurants, and as luck would have it these two lifting the pot had worked together at the same restaurant in Chicago. Sometimes men don't know when to not volunteer!" Both men chuckled over this comment, knowing that what they had to work with was certainly a step down from a Chicago eatery.

At this point dinner was cooked in two large pots of different sizes. This was done for purposes of simplifying the travel. Every space was needed. The cooks had chosen stew for their first meal, and just about every other meal. No one could guess the age of this evening's victim so the stewing process was lengthened. A healthy addition of potatoes was added. What wasn't mentioned was the use of dried out desiccated vegetables. God only knew what they were originally. A hefty addition of salt finished the recipe. It was one they would see again and again. But this day, to hungry men, it was a feast. Fresh bread was added to the meal for sopping up the remains and to wash the dishes.

All of this was washed down with mugs of coffee, the staple drink for all Union soldiers. As war progressed Confederates were forced to use chicory in the place of coffee. Sudden truces between men on picket duty provided times for exchanging Dixie tobacco for Union coffee. Soldiers did not let war interfere with their necessities. The men who could make these deals were often all the richer for their ability to barter. For men with no place to spend their pay, barter often replaced currency as a means of running a 'soldiers' economy.

Men sat about after dinner smoking, talking, bragging, or just resting. Adeline found her secret hard to live with. While she acted the male role well, she continued some simple incident would reveal her identity. She had to protect her identity. Unless her presence was needed in camp she made a point of taking extended walks. This was not the time to be making friends. When signing up for the rigors of warfare, she had searched out a doctor who was very lax in performing his inspection and the backlog of volunteers made a detailed examination impossible.

To keep her mind nimble she found other men who were readers and bought books from them, exchanging them when possible.

Addy, however, found herself a popular writer of letters for the illiterate which was about 50 per cent of the regiment. In this way she came to find out about the men she served with. Quietly she built closer relations with select soldiers, admiring in them their open display of emotions and their fear of warfare. She learned about the large families and the horrendous death rates among their children when hit with a disease; about the shiftless fathers who, most commonly in the cities, were known for abandoning their wives and children, very often forcing the mothers to sell their bodies to save themselves from the poorhouse. Oh, there were happier stories, memories of holidays and birthdays. Many families had at least one member who could play an instrument or sing well. Too often she heard the stories of restless spirits who could not find peace in religion and had to live life by trial and error rather than a guiding light. Sometimes Addy would offer a tid-bit of advice to worried souls. In the end she was able to put a human face on the men she served with.

Ben was totally absorbed with the military dimension of his life. It was his guiding light. But to grow as a man he would have to face many failures and successes as well. In the meantime, he focused his thoughts on one problem he had noted while stationed in the west, and that was the inability of the many soldiers to shoot straight, particularly those from the cities. He decided that he would wait no longer, but instead, approach the colonel about the need for target practice. As he approached the colonel's tent he received a crisp salute from the guard.

"May I have permission to speak with the colonel in private?" he asked

"I am sorry, but Colonel Ames is busy with Major Macey at the moment and has asked not to be disturbed."

"Do you have any idea how long they will be?" questioned Ben

"Major Macey did say they would just be but a few minutes," offered the private.

Just as the private finished his sentence the Major exited the tent.

"Ah! The professional from the west. Good evening Captain Halliday." As usual the brief hello was accompanied by the wide grin.

Ben had a strange feeling concerning the Major. It had something to do with his 'military circles' as well as his social background, so different from Ben's. He was a man who had a much larger scope of what was going on in this war and played a different role than Ben. Little did Ben know how close their roles would become over time. Ben saluted appropriately and wished the major a good night's sleep. Then he was promptly ushered into the colonel's tent.

The colonel was an orderly man. His uniform was impeccable and except for a pair of slippers the colonel remained in full uniform. Strange the small things we observe. Ben also glanced at the chain of a watch fob, the watch itself tucked tenderly into the right hand pocket of his vest. The chain glistened, even in the dim light. This was not just a timepiece but a part of the man's life, another small, if not tiny part of the puzzle to ponder about this man who would be his commander in battle.

"Yes, Captain, what can I do for you?" The Colonel queried. Ben had prepared his speech well.

"Colonel what I am going to ask is somewhat irregular as a training procedure, but based on my experience the west taught me a valuable lesson."

"And what would that lesson be, Captain?"

"Well sir, if I may be so blunt, most infantrymen are terrible marksmen, particularly those from the city. I should add sir, that I do recognize the tremendous need for ammunition." Ben paused, and the colonel waited.

"Look at the problem another way, sir. With these new Springfield rifles our men should be able to accurately shoot the rifle at three times the distance, breaking the enemy's spirit before he can even return fire. The result for us should be lower casualty rates. Sir, it is no secret that the Rebs are still confined to the use of smoothbores with a maximum effectiveness of one hundred yards. These new rifles could alter cavalry tactics as well. What Cavalry commander would want to make a frontal charge against this greater distance?" Ben paused to catch his breath.

"Captain Halliday, you do not have to convince me of these sound arguments. I am aware of the deficiencies in this area, but consider the response at the divisional level. They will argue that the demand for ammunition will exceed the supply available. In addition, we already have 'sharpshooter' companies assigned to each regiment. What will you do with those men that simply don't have the eye for accuracy at these distances, or what we don't know yet, how accurate our soldiers will be under fire? How can I select your company, or the whole regiment for that matter? I can see all the captains in the regiment marching into my tent looking for specialized training, and so they should if they were conscientious. Ben, I have to look at a larger picture here." The colonel awaited Ben's reply and clasped his hands behind his back as if he enjoyed out-arguing the logic of one his officers.

"Sir, I understand about the sharpshooter company in each regiment, but what I am suggesting is a major change in battlefield tactics. One that will require a major re-thinking of frontal infantry assaults." Ben's eyes brightened as a new idea crossed his mind. "Sir I have an idea. Is not one of the problems inherently found in the making of cartridges?"

"Of course, Captain. But if you are going to ask the Union to take a step back in military preparation" the colonel was interrupted by his junior officer.

"Sir, just give me this chance. Allow me to requisition gun powder, Minnie balls, and paper and my men will do the job themselves." Silence reigned as the Colonel put his hands together forming a steeple and rested his chin lightly on his fingertips, deep in military thought.

"Captain, you are obviously a man of ideas …and a convincing debater as well." Silence again. "The general is a good friend of mine and I do want to see the effectiveness of these Springfields at a distance. Very well Captain, but you must be prepared to do two things. First, squeeze this practice into a regular day so that there is no complaining of favoritism. Secondly, and perhaps the hardest, you must be willing to part with those soldiers that show no promise."

"I agree completely, Colonel." Ben was not sure how his men would react to this compromise but it would be his job to sell them on the idea.

"Goodnight, Captain, and I will have an answer for you in five days."

"Very well, Colonel," came the response. Ben was left with some concern about how well this compromise would work.

Training continued at a rapid pace and Ben had Emile drill the men over and over on moving from columns of fours to ranks of two. It was a necessary and important skill if his men suddenly had to deploy for firing. Wheeling on the flag in straight lines was the second essential skill his men drilled. They would have to do this under fire and it was imperative. They would have to become automatons if they wished to limit casualties and disorder. The last skill was retreating in order. The ghost of Bull Run stuck in the throats of many a Union line officer when it came to the debacle that had taken place that day. The line of battle had to be disciplined and men had to overcome their tendency to flee. Ben stood back from his men and let Emile handle much of the training. A regimental sergeant was critical to the overall command of the regiment. Emile was constantly handing out sage advice to these men.

"Remember, always, always remove your ramrods otherwise we will be fighting Indian style!" That remark brought a chuckle from the soldiers.

"When you have fired follow the ball out of your rifle. In the din of battle it is easy to have an undetected misfire and you will continue to reload and misfire. Now if you do this you could easily cause an explosion that will take your head off. Unfortunately, I remember a soldier standing beside me at the Battle of Chapultapec doing just that and the side of head was splattered with his brains. These lessons you never forget"

Then Emile carefully reviewed the fourteen steps needed to load one of the new Springfields. Not much had changed in the firing sequence since the Mexican war.

A corporal from the colonel's command post headed Ben's way. Saluting he announced, "Sir the colonel would like to meet with you."

"Very well corporal tell him I will be there in a minute."

Ben listened to rest of Emile's speech then strode quickly to meet with the colonel. He hoped for good news.

"Good morning Colonel, I see that you have returned from division sooner than you expected."

"The Grey Ghost and I had a good workout so that sped things along."The Colonel rubbed his buttocks as a reminder of their trip. "Well, Captain it appears my relationship with the upper echelons is better than I thought. But a bottle of whiskey never hurts in these situations." He added the last comment with a twinkle in his eyes. He continued. "It seems the general's military experiences have taught him the same lessons. However, he would like some first-hand observation of your training and its effectiveness, so he will send Major Macey along as an observer. It appears the Major has a lull in his formal duties at present. The needed supplies will be here in two days. Your willingness to make your own cartridges tipped the scales in your favor. Good luck, Captain."

\*\*\*\*

It was a hazy and gloomy day, the kind that makes a man feel lethargic, but it did not stop Hal from waxing eloquently on one of his favorite topics: what he saw as the 'black' problem. He paused only to stuff a hearty mouthful of barely cooked beef into his mouth. Then he started on again about the problem of jobs being lost to freed slaves. Addy sat on her favorite log, sipping a hot cup of coffee and warming her hands at the same time. But she couldn't stand it any longer. Her gentle placement of the cup on the ground hid the churning in her stomach. Jumping up, she began to hurl a chain of invectives at Hal that flowed like waves in a frothing foam hauling itself against the shore.

"Hal, you don't have the foggiest idea of how stupid you sound. What drove those poor black people to take those jobs? Starvation and poverty, that's what. They experienced the first chance to earn real money that they desperately needed! You have no idea of the trials they endured on the plantations! Women raped! Children taken from them and placed in a barbaric auction! Working a sixteen hour day in the heat of summer! Then returning to some insect-ridden shack to care for their children if they had the energy. Before you open your foul mouth do some reading about the problems in the south." Hal did not take umbrage about the problems of the blacks, but he did resent being reminded of his inability to read. He approached her, coming within a foot of her face.

"Well, you do speak after all, and with a pile of trash for a message. Why don't you go back to your silent cell and remain there like a good little nigger lover!" And with that a huge fist, already clenched, landed squarely in Adeline's face knocking her three feet backwards and into an unconscious state. Blood streamed from the corner's of her mouth.

Ben could hear Hal's voice from his officer's tent. He exited quickly to discover the cause of this apparent turmoil. On his arrival he found a soldier pouring a bucket of water over Addy's face. That was enough to stir her and return her to her feet, ready for round two. Hal still stood his ground, his face red and fists clenched. Ben had heard Hal's cursing of the blacks before and had ignored it, knowing full well a number of the company would agree with him. Obviously, this had been a mistake, for now he must take action. What had taken him a back this time was the discovery of Addy's bleeding mouth. He had wanted to promote this soldier to corporal, unknown to Addy."

"Who started this ruckus?" Silence.

"I did sir," mumbled Addy, her mouth full of blood. "Hal was just expressing his views on blacks and I took exception to what he was saying."

"There is no room in this company for fighting! Save it for the Secech. If you can't listen to another man's views then remove yourself. In the morning I want the two of you, under supervision of course, to fill in the old latrine and dig a new one. The first sergeant will appoint an acting sergeant to supervise. Is that clear?"

Ben's voice was still elevated and no sound came from anyone. This was the first time that they had heard him angered. Ben turned away and marched off to his tent as if he had just finished disciplining two children. He knew that this would not be the end of the discussion, and that he needed to make a strong impact the first time.

His thoughts returned to the equipment necessary for target practice. Suddenly he rose, left the tent, and headed for his second lieutenant's tent. He had been relying too much on Emile for all of the training. It was time to break up the tasks.

"Jeremy, could I speak with you for a moment?"

"Certainly," was the eager response. Ben filled him in on his ideas and the additional materials he would need for target practice.

"Lieutenant, I want you to find some company scroungers and make forms roughly two feet by four feet at a height of about six feet. Anchor them in the ground in an even row, preferably in an area away from the regiment. Oh, and make one for every man in the company. Is that clear?"

"Yes, sir!"

"Start this right after breakfast and try to work as quickly as possible."

"Yes, sir," came the compliant response.

Grumbling could be heard all the way to the colonel's tent.

"Make our own cartridges! The hell I will!" Expectedly, Hal objected to doing what he viewed as a job that should be performed in a factory back east. Ben was still eyeing him for one of his sergeants, despite his negative views on blacks. He had also watched him from a distance playing in a company baseball game. He encouraged others, gave instructions when necessary, and thrived on competition. Ben hoped Hal could bring these skills to the battlefield. There were many ways to find your leaders, not all had to be found on the drill field.

The training now included extensive marches. The men and their brogans had to work together if their feet were to survive. They needed to be hard and calloused for the future.

For the instructions on cartridge making, Ben let Jeremy get more experience at leadership.

"Remember men, that the cartridges you are making will be the ones you use in practice so do a fine job. Fortunately the papers were precut. This will save you time. Wrap the paper around the wood dowel. Leave half an inch at the bottom. This can be twisted so that the powder will be held intact. Now dip it into the container of powder and use the loader to measure the correct amount. Insert the Minnie ball into the opening and twist firmly. The more you do this the faster you will make the cartridges." Hoskin's voice was firm and clear. Ben sighed, reflecting that every small step in command was a good thing.

Target practice was an after dinner exercise. As time passed and guidance was given, the rates of contact at 100 yards began to improve. At this point the targets were moved back to 200 yards. Curses could be heard as the men had to learn to adjust their sights and elevate the rifles. If they were successful at this range they would thrash the Confederates who could not hit them at 200 yards. So far the exercises worked well and even those less accurate were able to raise their rates of personal success. This was the best that could be expected. The real test was yet to come, but that was about to change.

# CHAPTER THREE:
# THE TWENTIETH MOVES OUT

They were to move out immediately, board trains in Illinois, and travel as quickly as possible to Tennessee. That was all the regiment knew. Within three days they were encamped in Northern Tennessee. By this date, late September, 1861, no significant action had taken place in this, the Western Theater of war.

Tennessee had torn loyalties and had produced regiments for both sides. Camp rumor had it that there were numerous bands of Confederate partisans in the area. To the Union supporters these were like bands of salivating wolves that ventured out to plunder what they could find. They struck quickly and hauled away their trophies of war like so many vultures picking at the carcasses, be they civilian or military. They were viewed as killers rather than soldiers and were motivated more by greed than patriotism, or so the stories went!

Hal sat in his tent muttering to Patches, who by now had thoroughly endeared himself to the company. Hal pondered what he viewed as an injustice. Why hadn't he been promoted? They knew he could fire accurately. His loud voice was an asset when giving commands. His personal survival in the city spoke volumes about his strength as a survivor. It was all because of that damn Addy. He had made him lose his temper. He vowed to take revenge against him someday. Patches remained the sole audience of his mutterings. This was his best friend who neither judged him nor asked for much, just a morsel of meat and he was happy. The only satisfaction that Hal got was the knowledge that Addy had not been promoted either. Little did he know that Addy had turned down the chance to make sergeant. Adeline wanted anonymity, not a place in the sun or a chance to command. She had to guard her secret carefully and she had made one mistake already.

The regiment was assembled and ready to march. Colonel Ames leaned over and whispered in the horse's ear and he settled down. The colonel was one of those men who could speak to the animals. He spoke to all assembled: "Men we have been given our marching orders and I want to deliver them to you personally. We are to march south five miles and meet up with a column of supply wagons. It will be a long train and we will be spread out. To assist us we will have two squadrons of cavalry from the newly formed Tenth U.S. Regular Cavalry. It is better to meet the face of war gradually and hopefully this will be a quiet escort duty. You too will have a chance at the real thing. Good luck to you all!" In a burst of exuberance he galloped The Grey Ghost from one end of the column to the other. Waving his cap exuberantly brought out a large cheer from the men. Well, thought Ben this man is full of little surprises.

So began the active duty of the Twentieth U.S. Regulars. It was a quiet beginning, but a good way to get the men into marching condition. The soldiers were relaxed, even jovial. The air of manhood swelled in their untested hearts and minds. All that was to follow would set them apart from family and friends forever. War does that to men.

They had indeed benefited from the presence of experienced officers and this paid off immediately in the quality of their marching. They had managed ten miles in columns of fours without a single straggler. They had been conditioned well to marching and had managed to break in their brogans. Skirmishers had been sent out to gain experience in this skill and to guard against raiders suddenly coming upon them, but all they came upon were stands of tall trees and fields of tall corn standing like soldiers mimicking the soldiers as they marched. Fifes and drums added some spirit to the marchers as familiar pieces were used to keep the men in cadence.

The grass was still holding its greenery as warm weather and rain delayed the onslaught of fall's changes to the scenery. The trees had started to change and provided a canopy of colors for the marchers. The country boys' memories of their rural upbringing were rekindled. For the city boys this was like a new adventure where nature dominated the landscape rather than brick or wooden tenements.

The colonel was leading the column with his new lieutenant-colonel, Angus Beasley. Few words were exchanged between the two. No one knew much about him. He had been formally introduced to the regiment and his short speech certainly did not inspire the men to attach themselves to him. All they could see of him on this march was the sway of his large buttocks in the saddle. He certainly did not come with the natural horsemanship qualities of a seasoned officer. Rumors circulated in the camp, and according to the source of those rumors he had friends in politics and had earned a fast promotion up the military ranks. Eventually Beasley would play out his role in the history of the Twentieth.

As Colonel Ames topped the crest of a rolling hill common to this part of Tennessee, he raised his right arm to halt the column. In the small valley below was a supply wagon park. One hundred wagons lined up in columns of ten. With them already were the two squadrons from the Tenth Cavalry. Colonel Ames took off at a gallop, the only speed he truly seemed to appreciate. Following him were the flags and swaying buttocks of Colonel Beasley. Colonel Ames was oblivious to Beasley's lack of riding skills and the smothered chuckles that permeated the regiment. Trotting out to meet them were two majors.

"Good afternoon Colonel, we are glad to have you with us. I am Major Hicks and I am the commander of these two Troops for the Tenth U.S. Regulars. I hope your march was without misadventure."

"Just a good walk on a beautiful day. I believe you are familiar with Major Macey, and this is my second in command Colonel Beasley."

"Very much so, we have met Major Macey a number of times. It is good to see you once again Major." The major nodded.

"I had spotted your skirmishers in the distance Major, anything to report?"

"All is quiet so far Colonel, but raiders can be a problem at any time. I doubt we will run into any military formations."

"If we do major, we are ready. These men have trained well but have yet to 'meet the elephant' and need to do so to advance their studies". The Colonel's analogy to education brought a mild chuckle from the group of officers.

"I have eight companies with me, Major. You know how it is to fill out regular army regiments when states can offer bonuses for signing up." A hint of resentment rose in Homer's voice before it trailed off.

"Not a problem. Quality always wins out over quantity," added the major encouragingly.

"Well major, let me get my regiment into a camp setting and at the same time post guards against raiders."

The company streets quickly took shape as the men looked forward to whatever food came their way. Soon fires were started as one of the accompanying cattle met his fate of acting as human fuel. Those who finished their work wandered off to pick berries from fall's abundance. A few, with foot problems were sent off to Lieutenant O'Malley, the regimental surgeon.

O'Malley was quite young to be a doctor but unlike less qualified men, he had graduated from a prestigious New York City medical school. The men appreciated his quiet yet efficient manner. Those with foot problems were sitting around a large tub of cool water extracted from a stream that ran through the base of the small valley that would be crossed in the morning.

In the twilight they could clearly see each other. Addy could see Patches faithfully sitting beside his master receiving handouts of beef from those huge hands. She wondered how such an intelligent little animal could put its loyalty in Hal's hands. Perhaps he knew something no one else knew.

Hal looked up and saw Addy staring at him. Slowly he drew his hand across his neck and laughed. Addy needed no translation. It was at times like this that she had doubts about joining the military, but in her soul this was the only way to seek redemption.

Ben had no problems identifying his company. In the center of their street a huge bonfire burned brightly while a fiddler had encouraged the company to break into song:...

"Mine eyes have seen the glory of the coming of the Lord:

He is trampling out the vintage where the grapes of
wrath
Are stored.........."
So the music continued. The fiddler was getting ready to
wrap up and had decided on a song all would know...
"The years creep by, Lorena, the snow is on the grass
again;
The sun's low down the sky, Lorena, the frost gleams
where the
Flow'rs have been.........."
This pre-war song was well-known to all these men and
Ben could see heads droop to avoid others seeing the tears
that came to many a man, particularly those with a wife or
sweetheart.

Suddenly the mood was broken by the pounding of a
horse's hoofs. Someone was taking a risk in this dimming
light. It was one of Major Hick's more distant pickets.

"Major Hicks, Major Hicks!" screamed a voice whose
owner had totally abandoned military protocol. The rider
brought his horse to a violent halt as a vexed Colonel Beasley
emerged from his tent wondering what could cause such
turmoil this time of night. After a few words with the rider,
Hicks approached the guard standing in front of his tent.

"Soldier, locate Colonel Ames immediately and bring
him to me at once!" Hicks' apparent calm caused many of
the onlookers to drift off into the night even after Colonel
Ames appeared in quick order.

"What is the problem Major Hicks?" Colonel Ames
queried.

"Sir, one of the more remote pickets has reported seeing a
brigade of Confederates heading right toward our position."
Ames kept his calm.

"How do you know it was a brigade soldier?"

"Sir, I had a clear view between some trees and the setting sun shone on their backs so I got a good look at them. There were three large regimental flags and each of those regiments looked at full strength." The trooper gasped for air after that mouthful. Ames wanted an accurate as possible assessment of their size so he could make an informed decision. He continued. "How can you be sure of each group's size?" Ames challenged.

"They were marching in columns of fours and each large group was separated into smaller groups of about one hundred men." The trooper's voice began to rise so Colonel Ames gestured to the trooper to lower his voice. He did not want a panic among his fresh troops at this time of night.

"Is there more, trooper?"

"Yes, sir." He frantically nodded, trying to keep his emotions in check.

"Go on, trooper."

"There was a full regiment of cavalry in front of them. No need to worry, sir I watched carefully for cavalry scouts, but there weren't any, just some skirmishers riding around the column. But there is more, sir. I was on a hill and they were on a flat piece of farmland. Sir at the end of this brigade of infantry there was a battery of Napoleons."

"How far away are they, trooper?"

Wrinkles formed on the trooper's brow. "I would guess about five miles from this spot, Colonel."

"Well, that's the good news then, trooper!" Amos tried to make light of the trooper's last statement to keep the situation calm. Ames reached out with a gloved hand and placed it firmly on the trooper's shoulder.

"Son, you have done a thorough job of scouting. Congratulations, but at this point keep the information to yourself until we decide what will be done." He turned to Major Hicks.

"Major I want this man well fed, rested, and if possible be prepared to ride on your fastest horse. Major Hicks, I want to meet with you immediately. Please come to my tent."

"Yes, sir colonel." Assembling at the colonel's tent, Ames continued to talk.

"Gentlemen, we have but a few options here, but I will assume the following: that they are aware of our position and that they will take their time getting here. What is the name of that fine trooper, Hicks?"

"O'Mara sir, one of my finest riders."

"I am going to want to use him again so have a re-mount ready for him."

"Yes, colonel."

"Assuming I am correct about having been detected I will also assume that they want these wagons intact. We do have the option to destroy them if it is apparent they will capture them. Even if we broke camp at night they would eventually catch up with us. They can afford to take the swiftest route. We are bound to stay to the roads. They can pick us apart if we are caught on open ground but we will not abandon these wagons. General Grant needs them desperately. Given their strength over us we will not be able to engage them for a lengthy period of time. We presently have one advantage over them and that is 'good ground'. I have ridden this perimeter in preparation for the night and so I believe we can work this ground to our advantage. Gentlemen, we shall march down this hill, cross the creek at the bottom, and come up the hill on the other side. Both sides of the open plateau we shall encounter are protected on each side by two solid stands of forest. Each of those stands has cut outs in them as if some farmer had used them for building. We can park about half of our most valued wagons in these open areas while using ten or so to block our rear at the crest of the hill. The small area in front of our positions beyond the plateau becomes swales and gullies in a downward pattern, flattening out at the end of its descent. Gentlemen, this land between the forest, the rise at the top, and the gradual descent make for good ground. I'm prepared for us to make a stand in this position and inflict enough casualties to make this defense worthwhile. Major Hicks, your troopers will fight as dismounted cavalry so you will have to find a good location for the placement of your horses. Your Spencer rifles will be worth ten muskets in the line."

"Trooper O'Mara is here," announced the sentry.

"Send him in…oh, and have the bugler call Officer's Assembly, double quick,""Yes, sir." And the sentry set out to locate the bugler. Meanwhile Colonel Ames set out to make a rough table for the maps he was carrying. After that he sat at his small desk to write a letter and proceeded to furiously compose it.

"O'Mara you must get this message to General Grant. I know this will be a night ride but these roads are generally safe. Good luck, and may God be with you."

"You can trust me, colonel!" O'Mara's head nodded furiously as he answered the colonel.

"O'Mara is there any chance you were a steeplechase rider back in Ireland?" Queried the colonel, half-jokingly.

"Indeed I was sir, and the best. How could you tell Colonel?"

"Experience son, experience."

With that O'Mara mounted a fresh horse and began his trip to find the general.

# CHAPTER FOUR:
## THE PLANTER GOES TO WAR

Lieutenant Braithwaite relaxed in his saddle as the hundred or so troopers and their mounts ambled in casual fashion, heading north on a path up the Shenandoah Valley but hidden by a canopy of aged trees. The column, was for the most part, silent, no doubt reflecting on their last mission where their presence was detected by their carefree and communicative manner. Alexander had joined an 'irregular' formation headed by a fellow planter, Colonel Ambrose Fielding. Fielding and Alexander were not on close terms. Communication was minimal and Fielding had insulted him by making him a second lieutenant.

Alexander was here to gain a military education and his stay would only be for two or three months. These two would have made unlikely friends had he stayed any longer. Fielding's views on plantation life were at the opposite pole of Alexander's. Alexander made decisions and engrossed himself in the improvement of the plantation's operation. Fielding left his plantation to the supervision of an overseer, and not a very good one at that.

He spent most of his time at his house in Atlanta seeking out the next party he could attend. His officers and men knew that Fielding was not the epitome of the southern gentleman. What wealth he did have came from an inheritance left to him by his father. Ambrose had no other brothers and his father had been tempted to leave his fortune to his sister. The father had hoped that when faced with the burden of actually running the estate, and being forced to make decisions, Ambrose would take responsibility. But he failed to achieve his father's wishes. His slaves were abused and often sick and unable to work, leaving crops to rot in the fields. Fielding had turned the operation over to one his gambling friends and this friend could barely tell the difference between cotton and wool. On this trip he had brought with him his two favorite bounty hunters. One never knew when they might run into one of the numerous slaves that had tried to escape their abysmal existences. These two kept no records but it was rumored that they had probably brought back about eighty percent of the slaves they had been sent out to find. They enjoyed doling out punishment as well. Their favorite method was to tie the runaway to a wagon wheel and lash him until he passed out.

His request to President Davis to form an irregular formation was clearly accepted in deference to the family name, not to Ambrose. His men passed the time making jokes related to their belief that he had fathered more mixed blood children than any other planter in Georgia. The war had brought out the 'best' in him, at least as a raider. He had learned well the skill of hiding and attacking Union wagon columns that were not well protected. These were his standing orders and he was productive and proficient at this skill. Thus Alexander had been assigned to him for a reason.

Suddenly a rider galloped toward the column as if chased by the devil himself. His frothing mount skidded to a halt.

"Sir we are in luck. I spotted a wagon train on the road immediately to our west!" He stopped for a gulp from a bottle, and then continued. "Sir there must be at least fifty wagons in this train and they are traveling without cavalry support. They look to be supported by about five companies of regulars!"

The grin on Fielding's face resembled that of a hyena. "They probably feel safe because they are still traveling through Maryland and the worst they have to face are the insults of the civilians." Fielding raised himself in his saddle. He knew he would be outnumbered five to one, but he knew that one good cavalry company of irregulars could handle these Yanks. Surprise would give them the advantage. Wisely he had cached small volumes of ammunition on his favorite trails and right now they were only about five miles from one of those caches.

"Lieutenant Braithwaite!" His voice was always tinged with sarcasm when he referred to Alexander. "I want you to take the wagon and head for the Cripple Creek cache of ammunition. Bring back at least fifteen cases of cartridges, and do it quickly. Oh, do you remember where that cache location is Lieutenant?" He added with an even deeper bite of sarcasm,

"Of course I do, sir." Alexander would not let Fielding see his inner rage. This made Fielding work even harder at twisting his words to add more sarcasm. Alexander had the common sense to create a map with all the caches carefully located, including significant features of the site to help if needed.

"Sergeant Anderson!" Alexander always used a firm but fair voice when giving commands. The men had never said anything, but in his gut he knew they appreciated being treated as soldiers. "Empty the wagon of anything we won't use in the coming engagement, select twenty men, and let's move quickly and try to be back before nightfall."

With that command given, Alexander wheeled his small column and headed at a cantor to the hidden cache. Meanwhile, Colonel Fielding had searched for and found the perfect location for their upcoming raid. It was a muddy section of the road that stretched for about a hundred yards then turned to the right in a gradual arc. The wagons would get bogged down, but not stuck. The federal troops near the rear would hear the shooting, but in this muck it would take a few minutes to reach their comrades. He had no doubt of the ability of his troopers to destroy the enemy with the aid of their Spencers. It was perfect! Fielding reveled in the thought of killing men who were at a disadvantage. His sense of honor was non-existent when tactics were concerned. He preferred the sneak attack.

Fielding may have been a fool when it came to operating a plantation, but when it came to warfare he applied his ability to use minimum resources to their maximum effect. He could pick apart an enemy piece by piece and be ruthless in the attack. Just as he was congratulating himself on the plan he had devised, Alexander returned with a wagon of cartridges. Fielding then announced his plan.

"We will place twenty men in the scrub behind fallen logs on both sides of the road just in front of the end of the muddy section. Don't fire until they have just passed and force them to a halt. Twenty more men will place themselves on that small hill at an oblique angle to the Yanks. When these men engage, Sergeant Miller will send reinforcements from the hidden company to the front of their column to seal off any chance of moving forward. I want thirty men opposite the place where the federal third company should be, about two-thirds down the column. Take extra cartridges with you. The firing will be furious and I don't want men running out of cartridges. Any questions?" No one dared say a word. All it would accomplish would be to bring stinging comments from the mouth of Fielding. Such was the nature of the man. Now it was the job of the sergeants to place their men in the locations Fielding had demanded. Another trooper arrived from the north on the road the Union infantrymen would be following.

"They should be here in about half an hour, Colonel!"

"Good! Put your horse with the others down the road and take up a position with your company!"

Alexander detested the man but it was hard to find flaws in his military logic, even when handed a natural ambush location. He was to be in charge of the second group. As they moved into position his men were helped by the harder soil up the hill. His men's boots would not find the bog that filled the center of the road. It was early fall and the trees had not yet shed their leaves. Above them was a canopy of color. Soon this peaceful scene would be covered with the blood of Union soldiers.

It was not long before these raiders could hear the rolling squeak of wagon wheels mixed with a tromping sound of worn brogans. This first group was to pass by Alexander's position. He could feel his heart quicken so loudly that he feared the Union soldiers would hear it. The air was silent and nature had taken a rest to let this part of history play out its ugly scenario.

Alexander spotted the lead company. A major rode leisurely at the front of the column. This was an excellent location for an ambush and the major had not even bothered to send out a scout. All held their breath as the lead company passed the Reb position. The second company arrived, led by a young lieutenant, his bearing reflecting that of a new officer trying to impress no one in particular. Now the wagons approached and slowed as they entered the watery muck.

Typically there was one company to defend ten wagons. Now Alexander's target came forward, a paunchy greybeard dragging himself along on his worn boots.

The first shot was from Fielding's pistol. All of the men pulled the wrapped cloth from their barrels and fired at will. Alexander could feel the adrenalin rush to all parts of his body as he took aim at the old officer. His first shot hit its mark and the man dropped like a stone. Smoke filled the still air, but the screams of fallen Union soldiers ripped the mist apart. Given the cramped quarters, the federals tripped over each other and did not fire a shot. Sergeants' and officers' voices added to the confusion as they tried to give commands to their men. The Spencer rifles were taking their toll. Some Union men had panicked and began running to the back of the column only to add more confusion for those who were trying to fire.

From the rear two columns of troops tried to rush forward to give aid to their comrades. Suddenly a huge explosion accompanied by a ball of fire rent the air and tore into these two columns, incinerating them immediately. The wool uniforms worn by the men in blue were turned into human candles and they began that scream that is particular to men being burnt alive. They ran about in the confined space accidentally igniting their fellow soldiers. Some of the Rebs aimed purposefully at these men to put them out of their misery. The horses thrashed about and their primeval instincts told them to flee but they could not, as their reins held firm. Those that did break free trampled more soldiers.

In the meantime, the Union fourth and fifth companies left their wagons, raced forward, but could do little given the chaos. They were given little choice and climbed frantically up the hill to try and reach the sound of battle. Alexander held one of the oblique rows of men and could now fire directly into these climbers. Upon seeing this movement Fielding sent twenty more men to come to Alexander's aid.

The raiders were still outnumbered but that number was decreasing as terrified Union men took off and headed for the rear of the column to escape the carnage taking place. The firing was being reduced as the federals started to throw down their rifles in panic and ran about in helpless circles. Some of Fielding's men deliberately targeted these helpless ones. After another five minutes only an occasional 'pop' came from the area around the wagons. These Union men had been thoroughly decimated and Alexander found himself turning away from this valley where hundreds had been decimated. Now the smell of battle crept up the valley walls and the odor of burnt flesh mixed with the burning of wooden wagons to attack the senses in a most nauseating manner.

There were also the sounds of wounded soldiers challenging the eardrums of those near-by. Cries of "Mother, mother!"

"God please shoot me and free me from pain!" were common in this scene from hell.

"Help me, please," wailed some, while others could barely find enough strength to whisper any sound. Those who had surrendered were rounded up. They were the unfortunate ones who could not make it to the rear and escape northward. A sergeant and five other men guarded this group of ragged survivors. The sergeant had already been given his orders and he and his fellow soldiers took out their revolvers. Those who had surrendered were told to kneel. The Union men started to realize their fate and four tried to run as fast as they could up the hill. Fielding calmly aimed his revolver at these four and put them to death within seconds.

"Sergeant, will you speed up this action so we can attend to the wagons?"Alexander could see that the sergeant was hesitant to performing his duty.

"Yes, sir." came the reticent reply.

Suddenly a Union soldier jumped up from the kneeling position and grabbed the nearest Confederate he could find, pulled his knife and grabbed him by the neck. The Secesh dropped his revolver and tried to release the claws about his neck. Finally, three other Rebs standing behind him managed to subdue him.

"Bring that man here!" Fielding howled. "So you want to be a killer of good soldiers, do you? Hell is too good for you!" He continued to rant at the poor man. He took out his revolver, opened the barrel and removed two cartridges.

"If my revolver clicks innocently, then you are free to go. If not, well, you know the consequences."

Without delay Fielding raised his pistol to the man's temple but not before the poor man spat in Fielding's face. Fielding said nothing but Alexander gave a silent hurrah to this soldier facing death. Barely had the hammer clicked when blood and brains shot out the other side of the man's head. He crumpled to the ground like a rag doll. Those standing near wiped grey matter from their arms and chests. With that event over Alexander made up his mind what he was going to do.

The remaining, kneeling men were paralyzed with fear. They had just seen their own fates played out before their own eyes.

"Kill them, damn it!" Barked Fielding, and shots rang out until a pile of Union dead, numbering in the twenties lay in mud and dirt. The Colonel then had his assassins kill off any wounded that had survived the attack.

From the perspective of the raiders the attack had been highly successful. Forty of the wagons had been 'liberated' intact from the enemy and were now being prepared for the trip south. Fielding was smart enough to get away from this southern part of Maryland and head to Richmond. After a march of three hours Fielding called a halt to his column and made camp about forty miles from Richmond.

While his men prepared for an evening of celebration Fielding set up his writing table and filled out his report. He drastically altered it to make it sound not only like a victory, but one in which most of the enemy had left the field early in the engagement, thus explaining the absence of prisoners.

Alexander had no appetite. He sat by himself thinking about the wisdom of signing up for the position of 'raider'. Out of the corner of his eye he could see Sergeant Anderson coming toward him.

"Sir, may I have permission to speak freely with you?"

"Of course sergeant, what can I do for you?"

"Sir, some of the men, me included, know right well that you disagree with all of this. Raiding is one thing but killing prisoners is another. We want out of this regiment but don't know how to do it. We know Fielding has his favorite killers and would use them on us as quickly as he would a Yankee if we asked to leave."

Alexander sat thoughtfully sitting on his stump, staring ahead and wondering what advice he could give. He had known that this might happen some day and had thought about it before.

"Sergeant, I have always known you to be an honorable man and that is borne out by the very fact that you have come to me tell me that these are not your rules of warfare. We all joined with the aim of helping the South but the colonel has turned our goals into something evil and macabre. I will assume that you still want to help the South in her time of need. Northern newspapers will report this as another act of treachery that must be avenged. Thus anything Fielding does only encourages action from Northerners. Fortunately, I have friends in Richmond who know about his style of raiding. It has been my intent to bring honor back to the 'art' of raiding. God knows the South needs every bit of equipment it can get its hands on. I am, once again, going to write a friend and see if I can get my own regiment. If I get approval I will find a way to locate your regiment and you men can transfer to my regiment. I will need good men for the start up so I will put in a special request for you and your friends."

"Thank you Sir! You are a good man, God save the South!" With this Anderson ambled off, clearly carrying a lesser weight on his shoulders. Finally, Alexander had been given the final push to fulfill his dream. At least he had learned the skills to be an effective and fair raider and so he began to pen a letter.

October 21, 1861
Mr. Thomas Filton
Southern Cross Plantation
Tidewater, Louisiana

Dear Thomas,

I hope you are doing well in these hard times. We must hold to the cause or all is lost. I am fortunate that you and I kept up our correspondence after our meeting in Baton

Rouge in 1854. We are of a common mind about many of the issues and problems facing the South. I believe if our life is to continue, changes and sacrifices must be made.

I have made mine by taking up arms and joining 'Fielding's Raiders' but my experiences have taught me some harsh lessons. I am afraid what the Northerners write in their newspapers is too often true. If the other raiders' actions are similar to Fielding's then their actions are indeed abhorrent. Unfortunately, I have seen first-hand the work of this man.

I know you are a good friend of President Davis and I desperately need your support in presenting my ideas to him. He will listen to you because you are a man highly regarded in many circles. If you put in the request for a particular assignment for me then it will appear to Fielding that I was not the initiator. Fielding is a violent, spiteful man who would use his influence to damn my plan if he knew that I had started the process, but he can hardly challenge the President of the Confederacy. Fielding merely tolerates me now because he knows that I have won the favor of many soldiers in his command. I will lay out for you the particulars of my plan so that if you decide to support me you will have some idea of its essence. I trust that anything I describe to you will be kept in confidence.

I wish to create a regiment of cavalry raiders who will be trained by me at my own expense. Civilians and soldiers alike will be treated fairly and not harmed when practicable. My focus will move from the burning of towns and supply columns to the robbing of known Northern banks with gold on hand. Raids will also include breaking the means of Northern communication. This will include telegraph and train rails. We will use Southern intelligence to gain information on legitimate targets.

The positive results of my raids will weaken the infrastructure that is so necessary to the North on the fields of battle. Raiding for gold will lead us deep into Northern territory and will necessitate the use of disguising ourselves as Union troops. But the rewards will be beneficial. With the gold we can buy needed items on the world market, particularly those we can't manufacture. As a result of these raids Union troops will have to be taken from the fields of battle and so weaken their fighting capabilities.

I hope both you and the president will see the advantages of enacting this plan. If it is successful it will help bring the North to the negotiating table. We must act quickly, however. I don't know how much longer we can sustain such a war.

Yours in God,

Lt. Alexander Braithwaite

December 18, 1861
C/o Fielding's Rangers
Lieutenant A. Braithwaite,

It was good to receive your letter and find you well. I have discovered that word of Fielding's actions have reached high places in the Confederacy. The president had to read Northern newspapers to find out what transpired, as Fielding leaves out any hint of malfeasance. International observers are not impressed with our cause when they hear of such activities. The limited results of such raids do little to aid our cause.

I must admit that at first your presentation sounded fanciful, if not impossible. But I know that you will have given these goals considerable thought so I assumed you have more details that you left out of your letter. Too often we are influenced by impetuous glory seekers or men of questionable character. After giving your ideas some thought I arranged a meeting with President Davis.

I was as persuasive as I could be and at first the president was skeptical, but fortunately he too had heard of you and the successes that you have made in the area of plantation development. He agrees with your aims as necessary if we are to fight a prolonged war. He too agrees that while we are doing well now, the North can outlast us in a prolonged war. It was with this in mind that he granted permission to begin the organization and training of such a force and he wishes you well in your plans. He suggested that you keep out of harm's way. He will write a letter directly to Fielding requesting your transfer to a 'special command'. That should keep Fielding from hindering you in any way. Good luck, Alexander.

May God Go With You,

Thomas Filton

When Alexander received this letter he was elated. Now he just had to wait for the letter from the president to reach Fielding. Within a period of days the letter arrived and Fielding called him to his tent.

"You must have friends in high places Braithwaite, read this!" Fielding snarled as he spoke and tossed the letter at Alexander. Alexander read it and a smile came over his expression.

"Do I have your permission to leave at once, colonel?" Alexander fought hard to keep from smiling.

"You don't need my permission. Just get the hell out of here!" Fielding wanted to add more but did not want additional negative information reaching the ears of President Davis.

"Oh, sir do I have your permission to take some of your men with me? I will need key men in starting up my own command . Alexander knew he was pushing his luck on this issue.

"I don't give a damn who you take. If they want to be with you it will only strengthen my own command to get rid of them. If they want to be with you there must be something wrong with them!" At least, thought Fielding, I get to use some sarcasm and insults on this uppity bastard.

The next day Alexander, Sergeant Anderson, and five other men left the camp and all breathed a sigh of relief to depart from such a man. But now the real work would begin.

# CHAPTER FIVE:
# THE TWENTIETH GOES TO WAR

Quickly the orders went out, passed from officer to officer, sergeant to corporals, and so on down the chain of command, until each soldier knew his place in the preparations for battle. With only a few lamps lit the men stumbled over each other in the moonless night, partially from fear and partially from waiting until their eyes adjusted to night conditions. Fortunately the wagoners knew the location of buck saws and shovels. In the meantime, the soldiers moved across the creek and up the hill through the woods to what would be the frontline of this action. Furtive bats dove near their heads offering insults to the men who had disturbed their nighttime feeding.

Across the gently rolling hills Ben could see the dinner fires of the Confederates. They had marched a long distance this day and needed a good meal and rest. Colonel Ames was busy preparing the much needed plan to deal with the enemy. Trenches were to be dug to a depth of four feet and two feet wide and extend from the beginning of the wooded area on the left to the wooded area on the right. The line would create a single row for firing so that this entrance to the woods could be covered. The soil was relatively easy to dig and formed a small berm at the front of the trench about two feet in height.

The crews that had the hardest job were those cutting trees. The location of tall trees was a guess and more than one tree got hung up on another. It was fortunate that this column of wagons was carrying a good supply of saws so that the cutting moved along well. Another group removed the trees from the back of the woods where the cutting took place, to the front lines and were placed on top of the small berm for added defense. The walk was exhausting and many a man fell over some nighttime obstacle. Grunts and expletives filled the air as these men shuffled to the front.

The trench was actually constructed in circular form, making up about one-quarter of the circumference. The ends of this circle would be the weak points along the line as the enemy would try to flank the defensive wall. Troops were to be placed in greater density at these two locations and others were to take cover in the woods. Meanwhile, the cavalrymen cut down more trees to allow more space and offer protection to the wagons. Those carrying weapons and ordnance were given first preference as the openings came available. Suspicious of a cavalry attack from the rear, Amos created two rows of wagons at the opening of the forest in the rear. These wagons contained food and tents, items that could absorb shock. They also were to be located at the top of the rise, making it difficult for an enemy to move against the defenders of this rearguard. The horses for all the wagons were moved away from the forest in the rear. If a shell burst was used, as Homer expected it would, the horses would not add to the chaos of the engagement.

The diggers, meanwhile, continued, and even in this cool evening air managed to raise a sweat. Curses could be heard from the diggers if the person next to them struck a part of their body. Some had even stripped to their skin to try and keep dry and cool. Steam from their bodies only added to the ground fog that had formed on this October night. Pickets had been sent out to cover their work and occasionally the crack of a musket told all that they were facing Confederate pickets.

Ben, always in an experimental mode, tried an idea. Larger rocks were found and painted on one side then placed on the anticipated battlefield at distances of 100 and 200 yards. The white side would tell the riflemen their range and hopefully improve their accuracy.

Men would take staggered breaks from digging or sawing to have a drink of water and torture their teeth with hardtack. At least at night soldiers could not see if any weevils lived in their particular cracker. Staggered breaks were given to allow the men a chance to catch some sleep, at best two to three hours. Few could sleep, despite their exhaustion. Minds wandered to the following morning and their initiation with battle, and all knew that while it was only intended to be a skirmish, it was one in which they were outnumbered.

To their right shades of pink started to appear in the eastern sky. A sailor's sign of bad weather, the men feared balls coming down on them more than any rain. The Confederates were having a good rest and the night sky lifted before they started to make breakfast. They did not hurry. They too knew that the Union troops were about to make a stand. They just wanted to ensure that they reached the wagons before the Union men put them to flames. The Confederates also knew that if the Yanks were going to go to so much trouble to preserve their supplies they must be valuable resources. From the center of the defenses came a loud voice,

"Look artillery!" All eyes stared at the four Napoleons facing them.

"Not there, look to the rear!" What the informant forgot was the fact that trees blocked most men's views. He just happened to have a view directly along the pathway through the trees. If they could have seen what he viewed, they would have seen O'Mara leading six pieces of artillery, three-inch ordnance rifles. These smooth, cigar shaped pieces of ordnance were under the command of Captain Williams and being pulled by horse artillery so that every man in the gun crew had his own mount. This had certainly sped up their trip to rescue the twentieth and its wagon train. Colonel Ames had heard the news and had already decided where he would place these weapons that helped equalize their underdog position.

The colonel stood with his hands on his hips smiling, as a kepi waving O'Mara rode across the creek and up the hill to the open half-circle between the trenches and the forest. The next to arrive was the commander of the horse artillery, Captain Williams. As the gun carriages and limbers arrived Ames could tell this had been a grueling ride. The horses were sweating and their mouths oozed white foam which was due to the pull and loosening of their bits.

"Sir, I did it!" puffed a breathless O'Mara.

"How did you get here so quickly, O'Mara?" queried the Colonel.

"It was a miracle, sir. I was galloping along the trail in the dark when I saw the nighttime fires of these artillerymen. I can tell you sir it didn't take much to get Captain Williams to offer to help us. His men are untested and anxious to fire their guns." O'Mara was still huffing and puffing. Finally, Captain Williams got a word in.

"Colonel Ames where would you like me to place my guns?"

"Spread them evenly along the front of the trench, but give us a few minutes to dig the locations deeper and cut away some of the trees so that you can drop your barrels into a protected area."

At that point Ames stopped talking to the captain and directed Colonel Beasley to carry out the necessary details that he had just described.

Returning to Captain Williams he continued. "Captain, it is going to get crowded but try to place your limbers at the edge of the forest. This should give you about sixty yards from your guns but I know you want to protect your powder. As for your horses, wait until we move the supply wagon horses and we will add yours to the wagon park."

"Very well, colonel. We will make the best of what little space still remains." Ames turned to his orderly and instructed him to tell Beasley to get shovels for his men so that they could make the area around the artillery denser, and he hoped, safer. As an afterthought, he also commanded that more logs be cut and placed around the guns to increase their protection.

"Captain, have your men have not seen any action, is that true?"

"I'm afraid not colonel, but they have been well-trained and can fire two rounds a minute without any problems."

"Excellent, captain. Now let's take care of these Rebs."

Both men went off to check on the work that needed doing before the Confederates decided it was time to start lobbing shells over at them.

This war had few things to admire, but one of them was watching a good artillery battery prepare and fire in battle. The men of the Twentieth had not seen this frequently practiced drill and many a head turned to watch and listen to sergeants bark out orders to their men.

Those who had been watching earlier could not help but notice the similarity in size of the horses pulling the artillery. All had to pull equally or a gun carriage would wind up in a ditch. The dappled spots on their sweaty coats shone through, indicating fine grooming and feeding. These animals consumed twelve pounds of oats a day when they were working. It bothered many a soldier when a horse was cut to ribbons by artillery or infantry. They had not volunteered to fight this war. Men had done that for them. All was ready now.

Captain Williams raised his sword and as he did, the three lieutenants barked out at once,

"Commence firing!"

The gunner who also stood at the back right of the gun would yell,

"Load!"

At once an artilleryman would load a bag of powder in the muzzle. The soldier at front right of the cannon would sponge the tube with water. Another artilleryman across to the left of the muzzle took a shell from a man placed at the back and to the left of the cannon. This shell would be pushed to the back of the tube with a ramrod held by the man at the front. Meanwhile another artilleryman located at the back of the right wheel would hold a finger over the vent hole located on the top of the barrel near the rear. As he did so, the gunner, usually the sergeant, would sight the barrel. The man at the back right would move the tail of the gun carriage as directed by the gunner. The gunner then gave the command, "Ready!"

At that command the men at the front of the barrel moved out of the way to the right and left. The artilleryman who had his finger over the vent punctured the cartridge bag with a vent prick. Now the man at the left of the vent attached a lanyard to the friction primer and inserted the primer in the vent. When the gunner saw that all was ready, he would yell "Fire!"

Now the men at the back of the carriage moved away and the man at the left of the carriage pulled the lanyard attached to the friction primer. The gun jumped and shot back as the shell started its brief journey to the target, which in this case was the enemy's artillery. Within three seconds the second gun fired and so on until all six had fired. While the artillerymen were not affected by the firing, the infantrymen all plugged their ears. Cheers went up from the trenches as the first cannonade landed near the Confederate artillery and men standing around the enemy cannon could be seen falling to the ground.

At the same time, a return volley landed just in front of the trenches and a rainfall of dirt and rocks landed on the entrenched infantrymen. Screams could be heard as jagged rocks tore chunks of flesh from its victims.

The first ten minutes was consumed with an artillery duel. The Rebs wanted to silence as many of the ordnance rifles as they could and soften the enemy for their impending infantry attack. The captain went to a lieutenant and a slight elevation was added to guns one and two. They wanted to target the enemy's caissons.

A Reb shell scored the first hit and gun six disappeared in a cloud of white smoke. Splinters of wood from the gun carriage struck men at guns five and six. Piteous screams tore through the air as malformed arrows of the splintered wood pierced unprotected soldiers. Infantrymen hugged the floors of the trenches, now wishing that they had dug it deeper.

Addy found herself wishing she could hide beneath an invisible blanket of steel. The infantrymen felt helpless as the artillery of both sides continued to hammer each other. The Confederates changed targets. Two of their Napoleons were fused to explode among the trees, knowing that falling limbs would create havoc in the Union rear.

The Confederates were the first to cease fire. The Union followed suit. Without supply wagons both sides knew that they had to conserve their shells. As the smoke cleared, both sides examined the damage. The Confederates still had three guns able to fire. One of the Napoleons had been blown apart when a direct hit crippled it forever. Each side had lost artillerists but the men were trained to handle more than one job. The Union artillery had suffered as well. Two guns were damaged beyond repair, leaving their crews to help the other crews or deal with their wounded.

Ben turned his head from his place at the top of a trench. Directly behind him lay an artillerist's head with the kepi still in correct position. Blood oozed from the neck and the sparkling blue eyes looked heavenward, calm and at rest. Men crawled or limped to the woods, hoping stretcher bearers would take them to the medical tent. As a result of this artillery duel some infantry had been killed. With little room to move, their bodies had to be lifted out of the trenches and lay on the grass behind the trenches. Huge holes in the earthen defenses mocked the efforts of the men to create a safe haven for all. Some sergeants had taken to screaming at some soldiers who had been frozen by this first chaotic burst of destruction. They would forever hold a healthy respect for these weapons of war. Ben now boosted himself from the trench and walked along the back of it, calming and encouraging those who had taken to ground. He noticed the smell of urine and could tell that some men had soiled themselves during the brief chaos.

As if curtains had been drawn across a stage, the second part of the battle unfolded. Two Reb regiments emerged from one of the knolls in the rolling landscape. Officers and sergeants could be heard yelling at their men trying to get them into proper lines. Soldiers' shoulders were squeezed together and only eighteen inches separated the rows of soldiers. Flag bearers with their guards, drummer boys, and an officer appeared on a magnificent bay and trotted up and down the ranks that had formed from the two regiments. The bobbing of his head indicated he was exhorting his men in their march across the open swales. The distance was about a thousand yards, but for the Confederates much of it would be uphill with the exception of a few choice gullies to offer them a modicum of protection. As the wind blew in the faces of the Union men they could hear a band playing a rendition of Dixie that drew cheers from the ranks of Rebs. Two colonels led their regiments on foot, preferring to avoid the use of their horses which would only make them better targets.

Colonel Ames sat on The Grey Ghost and a surge of tingling trickled down his back. There was something magnificent about this parade, but alas it would soon reap blood and violence. He was content, for this battle was clear to his view. Tactical decisions would come easily. From his vantage point he could see the sergeants and officers carrying their swords parallel to the ground as they marched behind their men.

"Captain, renew your shelling and target the rows of soldiers!"

"Yes, sir!" yelled the captain.

"Time your fuses for three seconds!"

Homer could see this command being passed down to the men responsible for the cutting of the fuses to their proper length.

"Commence firing!" issued from the mouths of the lieutenants.

As the enemy approached Amos could see nothing but grey uniforms. Fresh regiments, Amos thought to himself, we have caught a break. The chances of them breaking grew as fire became greater. The Confederate artillery remained silent. Now Union shells began to fall among Secesh ranks. Their targeting had been precise. Swaths of bodies were swept away as direct hits took their toll. The ranks closed to fill the gaps made by the artillery. One poor Southerner threw down his musket and tried to head for the rear. A Southern officer re-aimed his pistol and fired at the fleeting form. His shot pierced the back of the poor soldier. The soldier fell and lay silent. The soldier commanding these troops wanted to make an example less others be so unwise and follow suit.

Another Union cannon volley was equally accurate and deadly. Like rag dolls groups and parts of men were tossed in the air and landed with graceless abandon. Amos could see grey forms crawling to the rear.

Now acting as a counter battery, the Confederate artillery broke loose, once again clearly targeting the Union artillery. Within two volleys they had managed to silence one of the ordnance rifles. The Union artillerists now stepped up their rate of fire so that they could return to an artillery duel. The Confederate infantry had been given the 'double quick' order to hasten their chance to enter the fray. In response, Amos rode to Ben's position in the trenches.

"Try your distance shooting, captain!" Amos had to yell at the top of his voice as a Union volley spat fire from the ends of their tubes. Ben jumped in front of the trench and raised his sword to prepare his men for a volley shot. Major Macey moved into the sheltered area Ben had just left. Ben dropped his sword and yelled, "Fire!"

Now it was their turn to disappear in a cloud of white smoke. The first volley took its toll on both rows of advancing infantry. Confederate bodies blew backwards or simply slumped to the ground. Meanwhile, the colonel leaned across his horse and told Captain Williams to switch to targeting Rebel artillery. William's still had four guns firing and he wanted the chance to attack the Confederate artillery which stood in the open. Within three volleys the ordnance rifles had silenced all but one of the Napoleons.

Ames now brought all of his infantry to target the advancing grey forms. The results were immediate as soldiers fell among the Confederate ranks. The Union lines now switched to firing by individual. The noise of the muskets and artillery made the giving of commands next to impossible.

Major Macey had been given the job of counting bodies to measure the effectiveness of Ben's distance firing. He had to do this so that walking wounded could be included in the count. Macey was now forced into harm's way as he tried to elevate himself for a more accurate count. The Confederates entered into one of the swales, which took their bodies out of view of the Union infantrymen.

Hal stared out into the space before him as he searched for more targets. His adrenalin had his spirits up. Harming another man caused him no feelings of regret. His past had become the grim reaper of his conscience. He had turned his head to something more frightening, victory. To conquer an enemy would bring fame to his beleaguered spirit. The adrenalin that flowed through his body gave him the fuel to seek out courage.

"Let's give them hell, boys!" Hal's booming voice could be heard over the thunder of cannons and crack of rifles and muskets.

"We just whipped them once, we can do it again. We ain't been trained to be beaten!" Eyes turned in his direction with these sounds of victory. They were stunned. What had taken hold of this gruff troublemaker? Whatever it was, it had a positive impact on his men. Gone was the gloomy countenance and words of hate. He was now imbued with words of optimism and a twisted form of patriotism. But it took away the fear of more than one soldier. Ben stood at the back of the trench listening to this outburst and put it to work for him.

"Listen to this soldier, men. Turn his words to victory."

"Huzzah, huzzah, huzzah!" rippled its way among other companies.

Suddenly there was a palpable silence. No artillery. No musket fire. Both sides knew their limitations of ammunition. The Confederates had stopped shelling in fear of hitting their own infantry. The Union, on the other hand, was preparing to switch to canister shot and was in the middle of depressing their muzzles.

The first signs of renewed warfare took the form of the appearance of the Confederate stars and bars elevating itself above the depression in which the Secesh had taken temporary relief. Already the fresh new flags showed signs of battle. Rips and tears appeared, but still waved in the breeze like some wounded bird flapping its wings. Soon the soldiers appeared and the first ranks of both Confederate regiments went to the kneeling position.

"First rank, prepare for volley fire!" echoed the voice of some Rebel leader. The wind blew this command to the Union trenches and acted as an alarm.

Soon this order was rescinded as another in command noticed they were still not close enough for their smooth-bore muskets to have any effect. Now a new command was issued.

"First rank stand!"

"At the double-quick, march!"

Whoever possessed the voice for this command was on a par with Hal for volume. Now the grey mass rose higher, reaching the top of a knoll much like some giant sea snake rising from the depths.

But the Union put their rifled Springfields to advantage.

"Fire!" became the common command from all sections of the trench.

"Reload, independent fire!"

As the first volley hit the lines of grey, a groan went up from those stricken by Minnie balls. Again men fell, never to move again. Others writhed in anguish, having been slashed by the soft lead smashing against flesh and bone. Again the Rebs closed ranks. Another Union rain of fire hurled Confederates in all directions and a new set of shrieks added to the first.

Now it was time for the Confederates to return a wall of death.

A sheet of flame shot out from hundreds of muzzles.

"First rank, reload. Second rank, aim, fire!"

It was the Union troops, turn to feel the impact of volley fire. Ben could hear the sound of bees buzzing by him. He had survived this first volley. Others had not been so lucky. The injuries were confined to heads and shoulders. The trench system offered solid protection to lower extremities. Addy saw the soldier beside her hurtling to the back of the trench. His face had virtually disappeared and what was left was a sea of blood and flesh.

In a frenzy, the swords of sergeants and officers beckoned their men to hurl more devastation at the enemy. More thumping sounds could be heard as those hit traveled that short distance to the back of the trench. Some crawled over the back of the trench in search of medical aid. Some were innocently trampled by their comrades as they prepared to fire.

With the command to go to 'independent fire' each soldier entered into his own private war. It was a space no larger than himself and directly in front of him. Few soldiers could see the larger picture that was being painted across the line of trenches. If he did look sideways all he would see was smoke from the battle. The dismounted cavalry beside company E were wreaking slaughter on the poor Rebs in front of them. Their ability to fire rapidly and their position shoulder to shoulder gave them a rate of fire three times that of the returning fire. Soon many of them had to stop firing as their muzzles heated up with such rapid fire. These cavalrymen switched to their revolvers when this happened and thus kept up the withering fire coming from the trenches.

What seemed a lifetime, in fact, lasted a mere twenty minutes. Now a new order issued forth from the ranks of the Confederates.

"Fall back to the gully, fall back to the gully!"

To their credit, the Rebs did this in good order, each rank covering for the others as they ran to new positions. By this time the reserve regiment had been thrown into the fray. The Rebs wanted those wagons. Colonel Ames gave runners new commands to pass down the line. It was an order the enemy would not be expecting. Homer sent out runners to each company commander for his next command.

"When officers and other ranks see me raise my sword, make sure all rifles are loaded and bayonets are fixed. When I drop my sword climb from your trenches and be prepared to charge the enemy."

The Colonel mounted The Grey Ghost and took out his sword. After the clanging ceased he raised it as far as he could, checked to see that eyes were fixed on him, and then dropped his sword. Some men leapt in one motion, others clamored over the top of their relatively safe trench. Without practice all yelled 'Huzzah' as one and two ranks of double blue formed on the plateau.

"Charge!" The word echoed up and down the lines. The regiment had but one hope and that was to terrorize the enemy with shock before an organized effort could be brought against them and tear them to shreds. They had made about twenty yards before a shot was heard from the Rebs. Individual companies were told to fire at will but only so many could use the brim of the shallow gulley at one time. Many Confederates simply could not get their footing.

"Stand and prepare to receive bayonets!" Became the panicked yell of many a Reb officer and sergeant. Despite encouragement, many Confederates started to back away from contact and were literally frozen in time and space. Individual Union men were taking hits, being so close the Rebs could not miss and many a Reb still had the good sense to fire and reload and more seemed to re-enter the fray. But in a fit of panic two Confederate officers chose, without thinking, to turn and bolt to the rear. This was enough for the besieged Rebs and many unwittingly followed these officers like young cubs following a mother bear.

Officers in the Twentieth started to realize that momentum had shifted to their side and in reckless abandon followed after the fleeing Confederates.

"Ready! Aim! Fire!" could be heard from the ranks of the federals as small groups tried to bring volley fire to bear. Many a Reb took a Minnie ball in the back, an ignoble way to die, and not the actions of an honorable soldier.

Each Union soldier managed to get off three to four rounds before 'cease fire' was hollered up and down the ranks.

Colonel Ames now showed his ability as a cool man under fire. He had pulled the dismounted cavalry squadron from its position on the line and hid them under the canvas on the wagons that were protecting the entrance to the woods. There were about ten men to a wagon. The Confederate commander, believing one regiment would be enough, had dismounted his cavalrymen and sent them around the woods to attack from the rear. He mistakenly chose to start from the depression at the bottom of the hill near the creek. The Colonel led them, assuming all Union soldiers were at the front. They advanced on foot carrying anything, pistol, saber, and shotgun at the ready. When they reached the deepest part of the little valley, a Union officer fired a signal shot. Down came the canvas covers exposing the cavalrymen with their Spencer's. The shock of this action froze the Rebs and Spencer rifles fired in rapid sequence, bringing many a Reb to a stop when faced with this wall of fire. A retreat was bugled and many more met their fates shot in the back. That was the last to be heard from these troopers on this day as they scurried back through he woods.

Back at the main Union attack line there was no loud cheering. The exhaustion that comes from intense battle had gotten hold of them. Now all that was left were the horrors that come with violent clashes that leave the living walking among the dead and dying. The only sounds were the usual plaintiff calls coming from the wounded men.

"Am I dying? I can't feel anything."

"Where is my arm? I can't feel it." "Please send this letter to my wife!"

"Water, please give some water!"

"Why me? I have children at home."

Some of the wounded said nothing, but sat upright against the gully wall, their eyes wide open. Others could be seen trying to shove their intestines back into their abdomens. Only shock kept them from going mad. Some skulls had been cracked open like eggs and the infamous grey matter oozed from brainless bodies.

With the encouragement of senior officers, the living revived from their stupor and sought out friends or wounded trying to give them succor. Some tried to apply tourniquets to fountains of blood draining the life force from its victim. The more fortunate were being aided by the doctor's assistants who placed them on stretchers and took these shattered forms back to the medical tent. Lieutenant O'Malley, the regimental surgeon, brought his tent right to the plateau to help friend and foe. Now new sounds were raised as friends found dead friends and even relatives. Curses and tears were shrieked with abandon and gave a resonance to every dead form that was found. This only added to the cacophony of sounds that made the Grim Reaper see harmony in what he heard.

At this point both Union and Confederate were left where they fell. Some were being held by friends who could not part with them. Now survivors had to be comforted. Dusk was beginning to form in the October sky and the survivors had to assume their regular chores. Fires were started and pickets were sent out in extra strength to secure their positions. Like the night before, the Rebs started their dinner fires.

The injured, both Union and Confederate had been unofficially sorted by Dr. O'Malley's assistants. Gut and chest wounds were set aside. Their fate would be a death of suffering. Thankfully some were unconscious. The limb wounds were the most common and their fate would be amputation, with or without anesthetic. Those with flesh wounds were trusted to their own care or that of a friend. The surgeon was simply too busy.

As the sun rose, the grim job of collecting weapons and burying the dead began. One thing that is common to all wars is the humane and macabre events which take place on this field of dubious honor. Some chose to remain in camp, assuming all was over. Others chose to wander the corpse littered field strewn with the dead, mainly Confederates.

The first to arrive had come at the slightest of hints of the cessation of hostilities. There weren't many of them, but they plied their trade carefully, avoiding the detection of their identity and even avoiding the glance of their fellow mates. In their semi- crouched stance, they tried to act as casual as possible. They looked quickly at the ring fingers of fallen men, hoping to be rewarded with some golden trophy. If the finger had swollen, a rapid slice with a sharp knife solved their problem and relieved the dead of the reminder of relationships that no longer existed.

Trophy hunters arrived, also ignoring their mates. They had different trophies in mind. For them an officer's red sash, pistol or saber or even a belt buckle would give them a form of currency to use in the future. They stood more upright than the first ghouls. To them this was but souvenir collecting, something to take and remind relatives and friends that they had risked their lives to preserve the Union.

Then, without meaning to be curious, the curious appeared,those who had an attraction to death itself. They left the corpses alone but did not see them as quite human. Rather they were effigies of the previous day's events, reminders of a glorious day's work and no harm was intended since the souls of these men were already in heaven.

Lastly, and they were in the minority came friends and philosophers. They wanted to put meaning to all that had transpired. They wanted to know why man insists on dying for noble causes. Most could find no answer to their questions. They could only see the tragedy particularly if the face were young or the dead man had children and a wife back home. Some were vexed with their God for allowing man to do such dastardly things. Only the idea of free will satiated their Christian beliefs.

When Addy arrived, she chose to walk among the Confederate dead. They were the same as her in form. Why couldn't they see that their goals were so wrong? They fought for evil. She expected to see the devils that had ravaged Amelia and given her the idea that Rebs were dirty, drooling men without morals or convictions of any kind. Would their silent forms help her to find the redemption that she so craved? She would not find it this day.

Far above, vultures arrived on the scene and flew lazily waiting for the living to depart. They sensed their time was near. They sought out a morsel here or there: hazy eyes, ruptured intestines. What a different scene was presented to the devourers of carrion. But they saw it all. Rag dolls in parts or whole, the sweet smell of blood honing their senses. Intermingled with them was a range of humanity doing exactly what they wished. They were being deprived of their existence.

****

The battle was not yet settled. The Confederates were still encamped and still held superiority in numbers of soldiers, although their ranks had been severely depleted. All of this was about to change.

In the distance could be heard the unforgettable whistling of the fife. Union soldiers ran through the woods, down the hill, and up the other side to catch a glance of what was happening in the rear. Their view was hampered by clouds of dust rising from the roads. An officer, with his staff, was approaching bearing the federal colors and a regimental flag.

"Where is your Colonel?" queried an infantry captain. Upon obtaining directions, he turned in his saddle and a colonel with his flag bearers approached. Colonel Ames walked briskly to meet them.

"Good morning, Colonel Ames. It appears that you are still in command of General Grant's supply wagons."

"I see that General Grant still has confidence, and knew I could hold out for one day. Welcome captain, and what have you brought with you?"

Homer noticed that the captain's uniform was flecked with dust and blood.

"Two of our finest regiments, colonel, General Grant believed they would even the odds out somewhat," replied the captain as he dismounted. Both officers shook hands. Colonel Ames led them to his tent. Turning away from the captain he addressed his orderly.

"Would you find Colonel Beasley and have him report to me as soon as possible?"

"Yes, sir."

"Captain General Grant must be closer to us than I thought."

"His main force is still a considerable distance, what you have been running into is one of his divisions which is about twenty-five miles from your position."

As he spoke Colonel Beasley came huffing and puffing into the command tent.

"Ah, Colonel Beasley, I would like you to take charge of replacing our men with these new troops. You will have more than you need so send out pickets in quantity and extend the ends of our line another one-hundred feet."

"Yes sir," was the agitated response. Colonel Ames took note of this and decided to find out its cause later.

****

Hal sat on a stump behind his tent. There was an open space and he was able to play fetch with Patches who he had tied to a tree during the battle. Hal felt the thrill of victory still coursing through his veins. A bird noisily exited a tree which caused him to look up. A beam of light shone through its branches and ended near his feet. Hal would be the first to admit that he was not a philosopher. Upon reflection he knew that he was a simple and uneducated man who lived by his emotions rather than through his critical analysis of the human condition. His strengths were physical and oral. Yet even Hal could not ignore this golden metaphor that lay upon the ground in front of him. Its shining rays warmed both his body and soul on this day of victory. It was as if this ray of light was a giant spotlight that shone upon him, bringing with it honors and glory for his actions. He moved the stump into the center of the ray and basked in the light that shone upon him. For Hal this was his first time in the limelight and he found it easy to bask in the compliments and slaps on the back that came his way from admiring soldiers.

"Hal, you took away my fears with your courage. I felt protected by it!" exclaimed one soldier.

"Hal you were a fearless giant on the battlefield throwing yourself in harm's way to protect others!" cheered another.

Why, even the Captain had seen fit to comment on his bravery.

"Hal, I want you to know that your bravery today led others to follow in your steps," Ben said.

What could this mean for a man who had become used to taking barbs all his life? What does it mean when a completely new aspect of one's being is laid bare for all to see? Hal saw that he had a chance to be someone else. Hal, for the first time, reflected on the meaning of what he had done and what others had said. He thought some more and came to realize that he had never really paid attention to who he was and what he did. Now he did, and it felt good. He started to think more about what others said and how he should react to their words. Hal now saw that this would be his chance to forge ahead and make something more of his life, perhaps he could become a sergeant, even an officer. There were no limits to where this new Hal could go. His train of thought was broken by the yipping of Patches demanding attention.

Hal let out a deep sigh that ended with, "Come on Patches!"

And like many before him off they went to examine the carnage of yesterday. Like many of those before, he did not really understand the attraction of this place of death.

General Grant had just assumed that a battle had taken place and there would be casualties, so he sent along a small detachment of blacks who would be responsible for the grave digging. These were freed slaves who could not fight for the Union but felt it was their place to help out in some way, and so it was that Joshua found himself on this field of battle. He had grabbed a shovel from the wagon and made his way to the group forming around an officer who was directing his fellow gravediggers on how they should bury the dead. Joshua moved along. He wanted to get the job done before the midday sun started to raise a stench from these poor boys. Joshua looked like a scarecrow! His gaunt form was made ghoulish by the tattered clothes he wore. Ripped pant legs and torn sleeves had been faded by the summer sun. The soles on his brogans flapped to their own cadence and attracted the gazes from those around him.

"Boy, why don't you get yourself some new shoes from these dead boys!" spoke one of his fellow gravediggers.

"No suh, it just ain't right to take from these boys. They died for us and I'm not in the mood to take from them." The other black man just shook his head and mumbled something in Joshua's direction. Ben had been allotted the task of cleaning the battlefield and stood at the front of the trenches watching. He casually noted that Hal had also come onto the battlefield. Then it happened.

"Don't you dare touch that soldier you shiftless nigger!" bellowed Hal. All those standing within earshot froze. His words were directed at Joshua.

"Massa, I jus do'in bes job I can for this poor boy," came the humble response from a man who was well-used to being yelled at.

"Whether dead or alive you haven't earned the right to touch your betters!" Hal added to his tirade.

"But massa dis my job. I love dees dead white boys. I know dey fight'in and dy'in for our freedom. If I could, why I'd pick dis gun here and go fight with youse boys, but massa Lincoln ain't said so yet." With that comment Joshua returned to his digging. Feeling reproached by Joshua, Hal stormed in leaps and bounds to where Joshua was digging and like a black thunderhead stood menacingly over the ex-slave. He reached out and laid one of his huge paws on Joshua and dragged him to the ground like a rag doll. Suddenly two hands dropped on Hal's broad shoulders, stopped him and grabbed his face and beard, twirling him around. Addie, her adrenalin pumping, was not going to lose twice to this redneck in blue.

She brought the full force of a rock to the side of Hal's head. He dropped like a sack of potatoes.

Men came from all over the field, followed closely by Ben. Two soldiers grabbed Addy, whose face was livid with rage, while two others stooped to help Hal who was already starting to revive. Most men would have been knocked unconscious by the rock, but not Hal. He shook his head as the men tied a clean cloth around his bloodied skull. Now it was time for Ben to intervene.

"You two men see that Hallard is taken to the hospital tent and is cared for properly."

As Hal rose, that snarl, common to him when angered, could he heard. He looked straight into Addy's eyes.

"You're dead, soldier! Maybe not today, but you always better be looking over your shoulder!"

Ben's stomach did a flip at the hissing threat issuing from Hal's mouth.

"I want you two men to get your rifles and put Hallard under guard while he is being treated. Wait there until I show up."

"Why me? I'm the victim here!" Ben gave no response. Now he turned to Addy.

"You other men, I want this private secured to a tree, and stand guard until I have you relieved." Ben once again used his calm voice, but inside his stomach continued to churn. This was the second time these two had clashed and Ben wanted to make sure that there wouldn't be a third. Ben felt it was time to speak with the colonel. He searched until he found him.

"Private, may I speak with the colonel?"

Even though the private knew the colonel was busy writing a report, he could see by the set of Ben's jaw and tightened lips that this must be an urgent matter.

"Ben, what can I do for you?" queried the colonel who also could tell that Ben was not in the best of moods.

"Sir, we are going to have to do something with Private Brown and Hal." Ben's voice was quivering by this time, but he remained as professional as he could while recounting the events that had taken place. The colonel stood up, walked over to his trunk, opened it, and pulled out a bottle of bourbon.

"I think you need a good shot of this Captain."

Ben did not realize that he looked so tense. The colonel began filling the cup with the liquor.

"Just a finger's worth will do, colonel."

The aged liquor burned warmly as Ben took a good mouthful.

"Yes, it does sound like there is a problem between those two soldiers. Ben I would like to hear more about those soldiers before I offer an opinion." A more controlled Ben answered the colonel's inquiry.

"Both are of entirely different personalities. Addy Brown is quiet and reserved, while Hal is loud and outspoken and can be obnoxious. Both have entirely different views on blacks and hold dearly to their convictions. Both make excellent soldiers and are relentless in battle, putting themselves in dangerous situations to help others."

The colonel was silent for a few moments, deep in thought.

"Ben, neither of us can afford to lose two excellent soldiers. We must find ways to keep them apart. They must also be punished. My personal suggestion is that we continue to confine them and do the same on the march. They must realize this is a serious situation. I also recommend that they be transferred out of their companies and placed at opposite ends of the street organization. And lastly, I suggest that both be brought to me and I will review what I have just told you with them. Their knowledge that we believe that they are good soldiers might help to keep them in line. Do you have any further suggestions, Ben?"

"No sir, that is just fine." I will have them sent to you tomorrow morning if that is convenient for you."

"Absolutely, Ben, and good luck with this project." Both parted ways and continued with their routines.

\*\*\*\*

"Confederates approaching sir, and under a flag of truce. Should I assemble the senior officers sir?"

"Not at this time, Ben," was the instant response. Colonel Ames had his orderly straighten his uniform and remove as much dust as possible. The two officers cantered in an almost casual manner toward the Union lines. The officer in charge wanted the Union camp to absorb their appearance and prevent some crackpot from taking shots at them. Many of those not on duty flocked to see their first close up views of Confederate officers. It was apparent that one was a staff officer with the rank of major. He was riding an impressive chestnut that must have stood a full seventeen hands high. Of the remaining men he was of lower rank and had been given the job of flag bearer. All three avoided the work that was still going on where the battle had been fought, and chose to ride along a ridge near the woods. Both came to a halt when they reached the opening to the woods.

"Could I speak with your commanding officer please?"asked the Confederate major.

"That would be me," answered Colonel Ames with a slight air of reserve.

"Sir my name is Major Mellanby and I am an aide to General Tuppett. I wonder if I could speak with you privately."

"Most certainly, major, and I will see that your horses are cared for while you are here." Homer had taken on the airs of a diplomat, courteous and calm. He led the major to just outside his tent where he promptly lit a cigar and rested feet on a box of cartridges. The Confederate major was somewhat startled by his manner, but tried not to show it.

Homer treated the major with all the courtesy possible. The difference in how the two sides treated each other from the day before was glaring. Homer rose from his position outside and entered his tent, offering the major a chair.

Major Mellanby began, his Southern drawl suggesting he was from the Deep South.

"Colonel, we find ourselves in a bit of a predicament. We are cut off from our division and the wagon carrying our chloroform broke down during this expedition. The same wagon was carrying our shovels as well. As you can imagine, our surgeons are in desperate need of the chloroform and we wonder if your surgeon has any extra. Oh, and colonel I see that you are using the battlefield as your burial site. Would you object if we laid our dead to rest beside yours? It appears to be the best land for such a necessity."

Homer put his hands in their steeple position indicating that he was deep in thought. *How clever*, Homer thought. The general *has let me know in a round-about way that he has no further intention of waging any further attacks against us and that he is a man of compassion thinking of his wounded and dead.* Homer spoke.

"Most assuredly, major we can accommodate you on both requests, but I do have a request of my own. Will you promise not to wage any further attacks against our supply column?" The major made the decision without even consulting his general.

"Yes, I suppose we can make that promise. We have strayed a distance from our division and need to march in another direction," was the major's carefully phrased response.

Homer knew that a major could not make such a decision. His general had probably instructed him to agree if the issue was raised. It was the politics of warfare, but a gentleman's way to wage war. Homer continued. "Excellent, major. I will assume your general's acceptance of my request. We will begin gathering the necessities you need and will see that they are in your camp as soon as possible."

"Very good, colonel and thank you for your co-operation."

****

Meanwhile, Major Macey was hunched over his writing table writing his report to his direct commander, one Colonel Abraham Winston.

October 16, 1861
Colonel Abraham Winston
Special Requisitions Officer,
The War Department,
Washington, D.C.

Dear Colonel Winston,

Thank you again for your help in providing supplies and granting approval for the firearms range experiment conducted by the Twentieth U. S. Regulars. We had occasion to use the plan we discussed when we met. A random company was used to see if regulars could effectively fire from a distance of two hundred yards using both volley and independent firing. I inspected the battlefield afterwards and found twenty Confederate dead. Injuries numbered ten, and an unknown number could have crawled back to their lines. The company used in the experiment had a full complement of one hundred soldiers. I consider this an excellent result considering it produced a hit ratio of approximately seventy to one. This compares favorably with the standard one hundred yard ratio of approximately one hundred to one.

We can certainly outshoot the Confederates as long as they continue to rely on smoothbore muskets.

In conclusion, I fully endorse the continuation of this program as long as it is practicable.

Respectfully yours,

Colonel H. Ames   Major R. Macey   Captain B. Halliday

Rob leaned back in his chair quite proud of himself. He knew that this report was accurate and by including the signatures of the colonel and captain it would keep them content. Now he took out a second sheet of paper and began a second letter. It was intended to never be seen by Ben and Homer.

October 16, 1861
Colonel Abraham Winston
Special Requisitions Department,
The War Department,
Washington, D.C.

Dear Colonel Winston,

It is with some regret that I write this report. Good intentions do not always bring the desired results. We had the opportunity to engage hostile forces from a defensive position. Three volleys were fired by the company using the two hundred yard technique. Upon examination of the battlefield I could find but ten dead and two wounded Confederates.

Given the training this company received, I don't consider the time consumed warrants a continuation of such practices. While it works in practice, it falters badly in battle. Given the standard hit ratio of one to one hundred at one hundred yards, it would be impractical to consume such time and resources as are necessary. It appears that the stress of battle ruins the results gained in training.

It is my recommendation not to repeat this tactical exercise which will allow for a more reasonable use of our resources.

Respectively yours,

Colonel H. AmesMajor R. Macey Captain B. Holliday

Rob kept copies of this material to send on to his Confederate contacts, it would fetch a good dollar in his collection of Union documentation. Macey secretively hid this last letter. He now took his first draft and proceeded to the colonel's tent feeling a smug sense of satisfaction. The flap to Homer's tent was open and Rob could also see the back of Ben's body. There was no guard present so he invited himself into the tent.

"Colonel Ames and Captain Halliday, could I speak with you privately?"

Ben wondered why there was a need for such formality. It piqued his curiosity.

"Certainly, major," piped up Colonel Ames. The three men took up chairs around Homer's desk.

"First," Rob started, I would like each of you to read this letter and see if you are satisfied with it." Rob knew they would be content with this letter, but he had to gain their trust. Each in turn read the letter and nodded their heads in agreement. Neither could do much to object to this letter. Not only did it favor their program, but each had been too busy making war to notice much else. They had left Rob to do the evaluation.

"Could you please sign your names in the proper location?" queried Rob. Each took the quill and signed approvingly. Rob felt like the fisherman who carefully sets his bait well. "Colonel, I would like to get this letter to Washington as soon as possible. Could I use that young trooper O'Mara? He has a natural affinity for traveling quickly." Ben listened carefully. He found this exuberance odd. Major Macey had never made any effort to see these men being trained. Ben stored this thought in that part of the brain that holds our natural curiosity.

"I have forgotten to bring an envelope with me. I will go to my tent and get one and return."

Upon his return to his tent Rob took out the second letter and signed it. Then he laid the first letter over the second and copied Colonel Ames' and Ben's signatures. The second letter was the one he placed in the envelope when he went back to the colonel's tent. When he arrived he found O'Mara listening intently to the colonel's orders.

"Trooper, when you get the letter, secure it in your saddle bags and travel to General Grant's camp where it will be forwarded to Washington." O'Mara nodded his head furiously.

"When you arrive at General Grant's camp tell him to telegraph the contents immediately and then forward the letter to Washington."

"Yes, sir," came the eager response.

O'Mara left immediately. His horse had been readied for him.

After O'Mara left Ben put his doubts out of his mind. He asked to take leave of the two men so he could return to his tent and perform the difficult and heart wrenching task of writing the parents of one of his dead soldiers. He sat at his writing table, took out paper, ink, and quill and began.

October 16, 1861
141 Wales Ave.
New York City, New York

Dear Mr. and Mrs. Langford,

It is with a heavy heart that I write to you this day. Your son Moses was killed in battle. The master sergeant of his company was standing next to him when he was hit by gunfire. The sergeant informed me that he fought with the courage and dedication that comes from one who believes in the cause for which he fights. He died instantly and did not suffer. He will be remembered as a model soldier by his fellow mates.

He has been buried properly on the battlefield upon which we fought. His soul has left his body to join his mates in the heavenly realm. I hope that this will provide you with some semblance of comfort and may God be with you in these difficult times.

Yours in God,

Captain Benjamin Halliday
Company Commander,
Twentieth U.S. Regulars

Ben heaved a sigh, folded the letter, and placed it in an envelope. He did so with mixed emotion. His company had incurred but a single death yet he knew there would be many more to follow.

****

The following morning saw the regiment preparing themselves to continue on with the duty of guarding the wagons and moving them to General Grant as quickly as possible. The trip took two days but good fortune shone on them and no further engagements with the enemy took place.

Addy marched mechanically beside an ammunition wagon. Her mind wandered back to the one day battle that had just taken place. She felt that she had performed well under fire and a sense of pride coursed through her veins. Her only regret was the needless encounter with that bigot, Hal. She felt in her bones that this was not the end of this conflict but she knew she had to work harder at keeping her identity secure. Such conflicts did nothing to maintain her secrecy. Her meditation was broken by the crack of wagoners keeping their animals on the move.

When they had started out she remembered seeing Colonel Ames and The Grey Ghost flash by her going in the opposite direction. Behind him were the captains of the companies. The group returned to the small cemetery that held the remains of thirty-nine soldiers belonging to the Twentieth. Captains walked around the graves of their men. Ben could hear the choking sobs coming from the mouths of some officers. If only these men knew what was to come. The treatment of the dead would become a natural occurrence and rarely would time allow for such formalities.

"Bugler, I would like you to play your best rendition of the Battle Hymn."

"Gentlemen, order arms!" The twelve officers snapped their hands to their foreheads. The colonel nodded to the bugler to begin. The strains of the Hymn carried to the end of the marching column and drifted over the graves of the fallen. The Confederates were still burying their numerous dead. They stopped digging when the hymn began and stood at attention, for in death there is camaraderie that all soldiers share. The music ceased and with that the officers returned to their places in the column.

And there the dead remained, buried in graves barely two feet deep, each covered with a mound of earth and a cross protruding from the mounds. What none of the living present would ever know is that by the following spring the earth would be strewn with the bones of these brave men. All flesh would be gone as some wandering animals feasted on their remains.

# CHAPTER SIX:
# WHAT MEN ARE WE?

With his usual brash swagger Robert Macey flung open the door of his parents' fifteen room mansion and shouted with his confident flair for all to hear.

"I am home for all to see and admire!" He did this deliberately, knowing it would gnaw at the first of his sisters to appear. Anna was a twenty-two year old beauty whose radiant smile could lift the spirits of the dourest of men.

"Rob, it's good to see you safe and sound. In fact it looks like army food has added to your fine figure." Anna's voice had a matter-of-fact- sound to it. Her brother was only two years older than her. As a teenager she had had to keep flocks of girls away from Rob. They swooned over this young Military Academy's student, particularly when he was in full dress uniform. How easily swayed these young women could be, simply because of clothes.

She was followed quickly by Martha, the academician of the family. She had gone on to study languages at college and had a job at the war department translating documents from the French Government for the Union General's staff.

Hobbling along with his cane in one hand was Steven Macey. He shuffled along quickly to greet his only son. Here stood a man of a mere fifty-five years of age but with the body of a seventy-five year old. Balding and vastly overweight, doubtless the result of too many dinner parties, he stood in stark contrast to his son. He was a businessman by nature and profession. If his body was decaying, his mind was not. One could almost see the gleam of the 'Great American Dream' in his sparkling eyes. His own father had come from the same mold and had done a fine job of passing it along to his son. Steven Macey had expanded his financial success in the steel industry and had diversified into other mid-sized industries, particularly the Winchester Gun Company. His guiding rules were few: trust no one, success is measured in dollars, say no more than is necessary, and know your enemies as well as your friends. In his life his first priority was to succeed in business, and his family came second. His wife Francis, made an appearance, giving her only son a generous hug. Francis tempered the rapacious Steven by participating in charitable foundations and encouraging her two daughters to be compassionate of the weak and unfortunate. Robert, however, was beyond her reach. Francis returned to the kitchen where she was supervising dinner preparations. Upon common agreement that Rob had not suffered from his war experiences, father and son retired to the library where both headed to the well-stocked bar.

The room echoed the wealth of these rising industrialists who had profited in the 1850's and now that the war was in full swing they had doubled and tripled their profits. Flowered wallpaper covered the walls showing Francis' influence and her love of flowers. Smaller, carved ornate tables were located here and there and were resting places for equally ornate vases or expensive copies of some famous sculptures. Heavy, velvety drapes hung like hunchbacked bears from the large bay window. The dominant piece of furniture was the heavy, dark-stained oak bar which took up one half of a wall. Sofas and loveseats complemented the resulting glamour in colors both dark and light.

Without saying a word, Steven held up a decanter of golden colored bourbon. It was Rob's favorite and he simply had to nod to earn a drink.

"Well Rob, how does the war go from your perspective?"

Oh, how often this question must have been the opening line of many eager citizens of Washington, both Union and Confederate. Rob chose to evade the question.

"What of your perspective father? You hear more than a poor soldier stationed in the backwash of America."

Rob wanted stay away from some of the ventures he was involved, like the letter he had just changed to aid the Confederate cause which he also served. Even though both men were involved in smuggling Rob did not really know his father's ties to the Union cause. Jockeying for understanding, his father continued.

"You know Rob, there is a lot of money to be made from this war. I know that must sound terribly callous of me but of course in doing so we aid the war effort, provide workers with more jobs, and put an end to the senseless racial bickering that exists now." Rob listened and realized that this was just another version of his father's desire for money. To Steven Macey the ability to make money was the measure of a man. Gaining it tested a man's ability to work with others, and promoted the 'hard work' ethic upon which this nation was founded, encouraged men to use the brains and brawn that God had given them to the utmost, and in so doing benefit all. Rob had heard this and similar versions time and time again and he wondered just how far his father would go to reach those ends.

Steven wanted to find out, as a military man, if Rob would see his vision of capitalism as 'callous'. He knew that Rob had a love for money too, but he also knew that war could change people, that it could make them feel a part of something much larger than themselves. Rob knew his father well enough to know that he had just been thrown a piece of bait and like a fisherman his father was trying to set the hook for something larger. Rob decided to reduce his father's pompous delivery and cut to the quick.

"Father, let's get to the heart of the matter. We both know that money can be made in this war. It is the how that is important."

"Very well, Rob." Steven Macey felt slighted by his son's response and wanted to re-establish his position as head not only of his financial empire but of his family as well. "Remember Rob, I am your father and what is said in this room must not be repeated. Agreed?"

There was silence. Rob indicated his agreement with a curt nod.

"Very well father, I will play by your rules but don't assume I will agree with any project that you have devised."

"Rob, I want you to listen to the whole proposal before you say anything. This evening we will be having a small dinner party as you know, in your honor of course."

A slight wisp of a smile grew from the corner of Rob's mouth. Steven lifted his glass as a mark of agreement between the two.

"At this dinner will be one Thaddeus Green, presently the senior plant manager at one of the major shops producing the Winchester rifled musket. My plan is to set Mr. Green up as the owner of a new plant producing nothing but Winchester rifled muskets. There will be a difference, however. It appears the government is fastidious about the numbering, packing, and shipping of these guns from the factories to the federal government or state governments. What they are not so good at is keeping a tight inventory of each individual part produced at the factory or elsewhere. Oh, they know the number of parts sent, but wastage, lack of security, and auditing accidents all occur and are next to impossible to trace." Rob bent his head and leaned closer to his father.

"My plan Rob, is to siphon off parts from all the factories using only one key employee to do the actual removal. These siphoned parts will turn up at Mr. Green's plant." Steven paused to take a healthy gulp of bourbon, thus allowing Rob a chance to interject.

"And what would be the destination of the final rifled muskets made at Mr. Green's factory?" Rob inquired naively, but already knowing their destination.

"I believe that you already know the answer Rob,…the Confederacy of course!" Steven raised his voice in anticipation of Rob's role in this plot.

"Why father you sound like a traitor to your country and you are addressing an officer whose job it is to defend that country." Rob's response was facetious and intended to get an emotional response from the senior Macey. Steven just ignored Rob's false air of loyalty and continued.

"Rob it is a guaranteed money maker. Our Confederate sources are already willing to pay twice the price that the war department is paying and not in useless Confederate currency but in gold or Union currency."

"So why have you given me all of this information father? I am but one soldier." The last part was intended to motivate his father to reveal his part in the plot as quickly as possible.

"I need army troopers to guard and transport these guns to the South. Their presence will add legitimacy to the delivery and I know that you move in high enough circles that a request for a company of troopers would not raise any eyebrows. And if we have to, we can offer a financial incentive to a superior. The only problem would be the actual transfer of these guns to the Confederates."

"And how do you plan to do that father?" Rob's curiosity was heightened by the fact that his father was moving into his area of expertise.

"Quite easily, actually. Your troopers would turn these guns over to another Union detachment. The difference here would be that the soldiers would actually be Confederates dressed as Union troopers. To avoid curiosity among the Union troopers the exchange of cash would take place at another time and place." Steven took another gulp. He could hear himself revealing the whole plan and it made his heart beat faster. Rob allowed the ensuing silence to act as a break to give him time to think. Finally, he spoke.

"And how much money is there in it for me, father?"

"Considering that you are putting yourself at some risk, how about fifteen per-cent of the total value of the shipment?" Steven made a fatal error. He raised that amount as a question. He had not taken a firm enough stand with his son.

"Twenty-five per-cent and not a dollar less," was the icy response.

"But Rob we have others to pay off. What you wish is an unrealistic amount." His father's voice started to crack ever so slightly. Here he was negotiating with his own son. It would be easier with anyone else.

"Father, twenty-five per-cent and nothing less." Steven was a student of negotiating monetary agreements and he knew he was at the end of the discussion.

"Very well, Rob you can have it for twenty-five per-cent. I see that I have taught you well, Rob." He tried to lighten the air by adding this last comment.

"Fair enough father, you have a new partner, but will your conscience stand the knowledge that these guns will be used to kill Union soldiers?" Again Rob added a factitious remark. He had no personal problem with that implication of the deal. He was simply toying with his own father.

"This is not a question of ethics Rob, but one of calculated risk and profit."

Rob smiled when he heard this answer. He knew his father well.

"Thousands of men are making questionable ethical decisions in this war, Rob. Cotton is still being sent north for the manufacture of clothes. Political decisions are raising men to positions of power in the military. In war ethics have no place. Our honor comes from our successes in acting wisely, not dying on some battlefield." Rob definitely felt he had gotten the best of his father, who had felt compelled to justify his actions. Rob smiled to himself.

"To preserve our distance from the actual production of the guns we will make Mr. Green the sole owner. The name Macey will not appear anywhere. Mr. Green is a tradesman who wants his share of the profits but he is not a political or legal mind," his father assured him.

At that point the game played by father and son was interrupted by the arrival of the Green family and a drink or two would be shared in the library before dinner. The family that entered the library was not quite at the social level of the Macey's. This fact was evident in the inferior quality of cloth used in the making of their clothes and the occasional grammatical error in their speech. Rob smiled and politely nodded to the parents and then his eyes fell on their daughter Rose. Tall and slender, with brilliant blue eyes, blond hair, and just the right amount of makeup to highlight her beauty, she made a striking appearance. Oh, Rob had met many a beautiful young lady before…but this one… she was delightfully different. Rose Green would be a very admirable quest. She gave Rob a curtsy and sent the flicker of a smile in his direction. But if Rob only knew that she was well-informed of his past adventures.

"It certainly is a pleasure to meet you, Major Macey. I have heard much about you from your sisters."

"Well, then I hope you will speak with me Miss Green. You see my sisters are my toughest critics and it is hard trying to reach the high standards they set for us poor males." Again Rose gave the slightest of smiles.

As they had arrived late it was decided to forego drinks in favor of dinner. As the Greens entered the long, brightly lit dining room they were captivated by the opulence of the presentation. A fine lace tablecloth adorned the heavy oak dining table. Imported bone china sat, in all its pretension, upon the table. The silverware shone like stars, bright and clean, awaiting their use. The adults, under Francis' direction, were placed at the head of the table. The younger ones sat next in line and prepared for the conversation that accompanied such fare. Rob made a point of placing himself next to Rose Green. Even the large roast of beef that sat awaiting the carving had its attractions. For Rob however, there was only one focus of attention, Rose in all her beauty. Decorum forced Rob away from viewing her ample cleavage that was enhanced by a set of stays. Rose chose the first topic among the young people.

"You know Rob, that Anna and I have seriously considered working in the hospitals here in Washington." Rose wasted no time in getting Rob's attention. She had judged him to be from the old school in this regard and expected a negative response. Instead Anna added her own version.

"Yes Rob, I am sure that you have heard of Dorothea Dix. She was appointed recently by the secretary of war, Mr. Cameron, to be the superintendent of Union Army nurses."

"Oh, you mean 'Dragon Dix.' She is well-known to all soldiers," (this was a deliberate lie of course,) "but I am sure you are also aware that she does not want her nurses to be comely. She wants them to be plain girls who will not prevent the wounded from concentrating on their healing process."

Rob added a chuckle with his comments fuelled by the fact that he actually knew something about this topic.

"They are more interested in someone like Martha." Rob had made a pastime of throwing barb's at his younger sister knowing full well it would sting her fragile self-image. Anna was incensed and her long fingers formed tightened fists that she kept on her lap. Quietly she added, "Why would you even raise Martha's name, Rob? You know that she is sensitive and beautiful at the same time."

In the developing discussion no one paid heed to the tears that dripped like drops of rain from Martha's eyes. Since her youth she had grown accustomed to absorbing these barbs from Rob's mouth and had never fought back, and with Rob that could be a fatal mistake. Rose Green had noticed the tears as well and to divert attention away from Rob went on with her own discourse.

"It might not be known by you Major Macey but she is highly respected at top levels of government. I had hoped that you would have thought more of Miss Dix than the thoughtless labels given by the ill-informed of Washington." Her own use of verbal barbs stung at Rob, gaining his instant respect and making Rose even more attractive.

"You see major, Miss Dix did not have her life handed to her on a platter. Her own mother suffered terribly from mental illness and her father was a brutish alcoholic. She was left to raise her own brothers in the absence of a competent parent, and instead of running away from that life, like others might, she embraced it and went on to help the mentally ill. She became a leading voice in the reform movement surrounding the institutionalized souls by visiting them and publically vocalizing the horrid conditions in which we keep these poor souls. So major, her actions were ironically experiences that would have left most in shambles. No major she is more. She is one of this country's true heroines. She overcame life's obstacles and took them as her own. Thus I find that it takes far more courage than the bravest of soldiers on the battlefield, for he needs but a few minutes to be elevated to the level of hero."

Rob was not ready for this dignified barrage from Rose. He blushed ever so slightly. She was easily the winner in this repartee. He also realized two things: one, was that much of what Rose had said was aimed directly at him, and secondly that he was facing an articulate young woman whose perceptions of people did not tolerate injustice at any level.

"Come Rose, you are a guest of the Macey's." Her father had interceded before Rose could continue.

"You are quite right father, how rude of me, but I thought I was a guest of Mr. and Mrs. Macey."

Rob continued to reflect to himself. What a controlled little wildcat this one could be. She even has the gall to keep her father in place. He was not used to such outspoken and clever women who would stand up to any male if she felt he deserved it. If he wished to gain any ground with her he would have to go out of character and be forthright with her.

"Miss Green is obviously upset with my treatment of Martha, so I apologize to you too, Martha. I am humbled in the presence of one who is so knowledgeable and can take a stand based upon her convictions. Am I forgiven Miss Green?" Rose felt trapped. She had not expected such coolness in his response. She knew it was probably false humility at any rate.

"Of course you are forgiven," She emphatically responded. Then she added in a deeper and steady voice. "I am sure you making jest on both counts."

Now Steven interjected.

"Come, let us return to this delicious meal prepared by my talented wife. This is a time of celebration, after all."

"And what is it that we are celebrating father?" queried Anna.

Steven realized he had just opened a door he wished had stayed closed. He would have to wiggle his way out of this one and with credibility.

"Mr. Green and I have just entered into a business agreement that should profit both families."

"Congratulations father, I wish you well," was Rose's genuine response.

A visible sigh of relief came from Mr. Green and his shoulders heaved their indication of that relief.

The rest of the meal proceeded according to the conventions of the day and those present mulled over such topics as, the war, life in Washington, Mr. Lincoln, and his position on slavery. There was an unspoken agreement to stay away from topics of personal contention.

The men then retired to the library for aperitifs while the women decided to help the maid in her attempt to clean up the aftereffects of the well-appointed dinner. The males grappled with the dynamics of the plan they would soon launch. All knew the dangers inherent in it. What Mr. Green failed to see was how the other players were positioning themselves from appearing deeply involved in the day to day operations. None of these men had been involved in acting as traitors to their nation, for that is where the whole plan was heading. For death would be the reward for those caught in their plans. In their minds they simply wanted to act like others in their position and take economic advantage of the war. If they were successful they could tour the world and live abroad, if it so required. Thus each had to have an emergency escape plan to use should it be necessary. To maintain secrecy the three agreed that only they would know the entire picture of their plot which was essentially gun running. Some attention was paid on the point of not putting any serial numbers on the Springfields, making it impossible to tell their place of origin. As the guns made their way into the war they could definitely be identified by their lack of identification numbers. This would be their saving move as long as their southern friends were careful their gun sources to themselves.

Thieves are supposed to have a bond of loyalty among themselves; a fraternity so that there was a veneer of trust and caring among the members of the brotherhood. This trio lacked that ideal criminal bond due to their innate self-interest and greed. It would take time for this weakness to become apparent. Rob laughed to himself. If they only knew that this was but a minor part of his escapades with the enemy. Steven was feeling slightly guilty for turning his son into a treasonous American, but then Rob could always have said 'no' to the whole idea. Thaddeus Green was the closest to having an actual conscience. He worried about the men in double blue who would die on the fields of battle because of their actions, but, he rationalized that if they didn't do it someone else would. He would be watchful of Steven. He knew how capitalists acted. Now it was his turn to reap the harvest of their greed.

The details were put in place and Rob was to take the first shipment of guns in forty days. Rob was already planning how he would arrange his military orders so he could obtain this first shipment and deliver it quickly. Little did his father know that once he had made the first shipment he would turn the gun running operation over to another officer. Yes, one had to be prepared for all eventualities, he thought to himself.

By ten o'clock all members of the party met in the opulent entrance to say their goodbyes. Rob made a point of making eye contact with Rose and expressing his sense of regret for having insulted her. Yet he put on his most attractive smile. Rose, alert as ever, detected his overtures and punished him by failing to respond to any of his feeble attempts at socialization. She acted stiff and oblivious to what he was trying to do. This was something Rob was not used to. The members of the Macey clan were exhausted, all for different reasons of course. Goodnights were extended and promises of future contact hinted at.

For Rob sleep had been replaced by a rehashing of the exchanges between Rose and himself. Yes, he thought, she would definitely be a challenge and he expected setbacks in his attempts to woo her, but in the end he would succeed. Rob had tendencies of a sociopath who has little concern for the other person and dwells on his ability to conquer and subdue her. Sometime during his development his social conscience had taken a tumble into unconsciousness. It was left to the angels to see if there was a better Rob that they could take hold of and turn him into a loving human. Already Rob was beginning to formulate plans that would provide him with opportunities of chance encounters with Rose.

****

The following morning found Anna and Martha in apparent luxury and comfort reclining on Anna's bed with decorative, opulent blankets piled on.

They were hiding beneath the handsome four poster bed that filled an appropriate proportion of the room. The apparent comfort was broken by Martha's opening question.

"My God, Anna, what are we going to do about Rob's attraction to Rose? You saw his enjoyment talking with her and those furtive glances were seen by all. He won't stop until he has made another conquest."

"Stop Martha!" Anna interjected.

"I am quite able to see what went on. Rose is no fool. All she needs is a little more information from us and that will allow her to put Rob in his place."

"But Anna…!" Anna snapped her body to attention as she sat on the bed.

"I am quite able to make judgments about my brother. Martha, after what he has done to you I stopped having any feelings about him. My sisterly role is simply to see that he does not ruin any other lives."

This comment brought tears streaming from Martha's eyes. She was the gentle one, the vulnerable one who forgave all their transgressions.

"Why did you have to bring up his treatment of me? I spend my time trying to put it out of my mind. You are the only person who knows about it and that is the way I want it to stay."

"Martha admit to yourself that you are a kind and gentle person and what he did is even more of a transgression against one so pure of heart. You know that you can't confide in mother. God knows what she would do…probably take Rob's side or worse. Or do nothing in an inglorious attempt to keep this family together. Father and Rob are two of a kind. Their personal goals keep them from being caring human beings."

The tears continued to flow and Anna saw that Martha needed a good hug. Silence reigned as the two sisters clung to each other. They rocked back and forth as if Anna was a mother giving solace to her young daughter. After a couple of minutes the crying ceased. Anna moved Martha away from her so that the two could make eye contact.

"Martha, that no good brother of yours raped you. Nothing will change that fact. The only remaining question will always be the same. How do we handle Rob?"

The determination in Anna's delivery, the firm set of her jaws, and the furrowed brow told Martha that Anna would take care of her, and seek justice against Rob in some form or another.

"Martha, I have not told you everything. I think it is time you heard the larger story about Rob. When Rob was at the Military Academy he got one of the girls pregnant. It happened to be one of the town girls whose family could not take any steps against Rob. To silence them permanently father bought their silence for $100.00. Even mother does not know about this. I found out by pure accident."

"But Anna…"

"There are no buts…the poor girl found out what happened and realized she had been sold out by her own parents. Martha, the distraught girl took her own life while she was still pregnant. That event was masked in silence as well. Her family did not want public shame to come to them."

Martha's face was frozen in disbelief. The scenario was like a miniature pyramid with Rob at the top and supported by layers of conspirators.

"Anna, if Macey money can reach its tentacles into any situation, then what hope does Rose have in even thinking of toying with Rob? She will be putting herself at risk."

"You are partly correct, but two things are very different in Rose's case. In the first place she will not be impressed in any way by Rob's amorous advances. Secondly, the girl who took her life was one of Rose's best friends from college. It was a finishing school for 'young ladies' appropriately built near the Military Academy. Her parents, although they weren't rich, worked hard to try and climb socially. This is not about revenge Martha, it is about justice, a justice not always recognized by a society that sees the blame for these misadventures solely as the fault of the girl. Rose is a bright woman. I have full confidence in her and I am ready to play any part she might need to bring about justice. I hope we can count on you for your support, Martha. God knows you also deserve justice!"

"But what will justice be in this case Anna?"

"Whatever is necessary to stop Rob once and for all time." Anna's face took on that determined look again.

"But how far are you willing to go Anna?" Martha asked with a worried tone in her voice. Silence was Anna's only answer, a silence that opened the two young minds of the women who had replaced love with justice.

# CHAPTER SEVEN:
# THE TWENTIETH GROWS

Upon return to Illinois the Twentieth took on a new look. It was to join three other regiments and form a brigade. But they would be the only veterans. As they approached the camp upon their return, sentries saluted them. The colonel and The Gray Ghost stopped abruptly. Horse and rider wheeled and took off on one of their patented, arms steady, nose snorting, dirt raising gallops for which horse and human had been, and would continue to be famous. Homer never said a word, but his actions created a thunderous yell from his men. It was their form of welcome.

Meanwhile, each company's captain 'dressed' his men to look like soldiers. They had 'seen the elephant' for the first time and survived in successful fashion. So in this column of 575 healthy soldiers, a shimmer of pride could be seen in the way they carried, not just their equipment, but their heads as well. In their hearts were the memories of the 39 dead men they had left on 'the plateau'. Little did they know what was in front of them in the near future.

Joining them were the 52 Iowa Volunteers, The 151 Indiana Volunteers, and their sister regiment The 152 Indiana Volunteers. Each was a newly formed well-equipped regiment full of untested military bravado. The Twentieth knew fast that bravado could ebb and flow. Each new regiment carried more than 1,000 officers and other ranks. The new regiments quickly observed how diminished in size the Twentieth was already, granted the wounded were following behind in wagons and would help renew the size of the Twentieth. Colonel Beasley raised his sword and the men continued to finish these last few steps of their march.

Their hobnailed boots joined as one, creating a cadenced thunder. The new men responded with shouts of welcome and whoops of 'Huzzah' for good news traveled quickly in this war even without the telegraph.

"You sure gave Johnny Reb hell Twentieth. I hope you saved some for us!"

"Show us how to fight Twentieth!"

"Sure is good to hear western boys can fight. Might have to send you boys east and teach that army how to fight…"

Chimes of laughter followed that last comment. These men were only too aware of the problems of the Army of the Potomac. The ice had been broken and a bond was beginning to form that would last to the trenches of Petersburg.

Much to his surprise, Colonel Ames was met by General Grant himself.

"We needed a thorough victory and you certainly gave us one, colonel." Grant waited until Homer had taken care of The Gray Ghost. The troops were dismissed to set up their camp once again.

The two officers walked about, slowly casting their eyes on this much greatly expanded body of soldiers. General Grant broke the ice.

"This brings this group up to brigade strength Homer and it will need a brigadier, General Ames." Grant smiled as he raised Homer in rank and power. His offhand announcement caught Homer off guard and the colonel stopped in his tracks.

"Are you sure you want to do this general?"

"By all means. There is no man better suited to do the job."

As General Grant finished, Homer noticed that three colonels were approaching.

"I would like you to meet your regiment commanders, Homer. You know John Emmerson, another Mexican War veteran; Emmett McDermott, an Academy man who had served under General McClelland; and Thaddeus Braxton, a 'reformed intellectual' who saw the light, put down his books, and put his sharp mind to work in his desire to aid the Union."

This was General Grant's way of getting around the fact that Braxton had no military experience and would have to be nurtured by Homer on the tools of command. Fortunately, all three colonels saw this as humorous and laughter broke out among them.

Grant continued, "Gentlemen, I would like you to meet the newest brigadier general in the Army of the Tennessee, General Homer Ames. You will learn much from this man. If his recent encounter with the enemy is any example, his decisive use of defensive tactics saved the day for his small force against a much larger enemy force. I first heard of his success from Major Robert Macey of the Intelligence Corps."

Ben had just happened to be walking near this conversation when he heard Rob Macey's official role in this war.

"General Ames, I am sure you are tired from your recent march and have business to attend to as commander of this new brigade."

General Grant's aide brought his horse into range.

"Good luck, Homer. You deserve a chance at higher command." With that comment the meeting was officially over and Grant mounted his horse and walked away waving his gauntlet in Homer's direction.

Homer was left with his mouth uncharacteristically agape. He had not sought promotion, nor considered himself worthy of higher command.

In this war men of courage and ability would be awarded quickly, for often both qualities were hard to find. Amos had to make a decision he would often regret, but such are the politics of war. Someone had to replace him as colonel of the Twentieth. Reality told him that it was logical to promote Colonel Beasley, but in his mind and heart he knew the regiment would be poorly served by such an appointment. Beasley had yet to make a major error but eventually time would catch up with him. Homer offered the position and he accepted. Homer had hoped that Beasley had some self-awareness. But if he did it did not stop him from making a dreadful mistake. The men themselves kept their silence, but there was no cheering.

****

"This is another insane Washington decision, damn pencil pushers!"

Ben kept silent. He had never heard General Ames lose his temper before. But like the fox outwitting the hounds, he had faith that Homer could find his way around any decision that defied logic. Major Macey had made a point of being with the general when he opened his mail. He believed that he understood both Ben and Homer well enough to know that neither man would take this decision well.

"I know how to get around this, Ben. I am going to write General Grant and get his permission to go ahead with your training. To hell with Washington." Even with this decision in place, Homer paced up and down in his new command tent, hands folded behind his back. Now, to protect himself in this deception he had instigated, Major Macey spoke up.

"General I am as dumbfounded as you are but may I offer a word of advice?"

"Certainly Robert, you know I respect your analysis of these decisions."

"General Grant will probably agree with you. This is not a high matter for those in Washington or, General Grant, for that matter. I know for a fact that spring campaign planning is already taking place. Secondly, this colonel in Washington is an influential man with many ties among the politicians of Washington. By challenging him you might ruffle the feathers of someone whose influence you might need in the future."

Homer stalked quietly about his tent like a caged animal, his lips pursed tightly and his jaw bones flexing in and out as he ground his teeth.

"No Robert, there are times to take stand on things that are obvious. This tactic was proven on the field of battle and God only knows how many Union lives we could save with it. I am writing General Grant and will send the letter out tomorrow with our jockey O'Mara." Once Homer had made up his mind he was not one to change it quickly.

Rob now faced a conundrum. He did not want the possibility of Grant sending the contents of this letter on to Winston. On the other hand, to continue to disagree with Homer would look strange in light of the fact that he had actually signed his approval. He could tell Ben's eyes and ears were standing at full attention to everything being said. He did not want another watchdog on his tail. If he could distract the General for awhile and the message never reached Grant, Homer would go ahead and act on his own. He knew what he must do.

At eight in the morning O'Mara was ready to go. His steed would not be The Gray Ghost, but no matter his own steed would do. She was known for her sure footedness rather than speed and O'Mara was going to travel over hilly, primitive roads.

"Bring her back at leisure O'Mara. We will certainly need her again!"

"Yes, general you don't have to worry about us!" The rider was more excited than the horse. The general loved his horses and cared for them as if they were family. In war this was bound to bring great sadness to a person who loved horses so much. Like a cautious father, Homer watched the two disappear up a sloping hill, the start of a race to General Grant's camp.

After an hour of slow cantering up and down hills O'Mara paused at the top of a narrow wooded ridge. In the distance, about a quarter of a mile away, he spotted a horse and rider poised in the middle of the narrow road. He approached cautiously and soon recognized the form of a Union soldier. Another one hundred yards told him it was a Union officer and it soon became apparent, judging by the uniform and mount that it was Major Macey. O'Mara touched the reins and the soft mouthed mare slowed to a walk.

Major Macey put his finger to his mouth, indicating that O'Mara should approach quietly. Then Robert turned his mount facing the steep ravine beyond. These actions were intended to distract O'Mara as Robert removed his Colt Revolver from its holster. O'Mara cautiously brought his mount up beside Major Macey. In one rapid motion Macey elevated his right hand and arm which were hidden from O'Mara. He fired a single shot through the forehead of the innocent and unprepared rider. At the same time he grabbed the reins of O'Mara's horse so that it would not bolt.

Blood oozed from the fatal wound and with eyes wide open, as if in disbelief, O'Mara slipped silently and slowly from his saddle to the road below. There was no movement from the young courier. Major Macey, like a brigand on the highway, jumped to the ground, tied his own horse to a tree and led the paint horse to the edge of the ravine. Instinctively the horse resisted this threat to its life and so another shot rang out, this time going into the brain of the faithful steed. Tumbling onto its side it did exactly what Robert hoped. It began its slide, slowly picking up momentum as it continued its downward journey. The four legs flew akimbo like some rag doll discarded by its owner. After what seemed an endless period of time the dead animal came to rest against a rotten log. The major had spotted the courier pouch attached to O'Mara's body. He walked quickly to the remains of the dead form below him, opened the pouch and examined all the contents until he found what he was searching for.

Major Macey had to prove to his Confederate contact that he was indeed a loyal spy and worthy of collecting the $10,000 fee that he had extracted from him. He would have to prove how this plan to raise the distance of infantry formations would indeed be a threat to the Confederates. Now he dragged the body of the rider to the same spot where the horse had fallen, and lifting the body up gave it an inglorious burial by using his foot to send it hurling downwards to join rider and horse.

Macey's grin extended from ear to ear, absurd as it was in this deadly isolation. This was the first man that Major Robert Macey had killed and he did it with the conscience of a torturer during the Inquisition. And while this was far from the end of his exploits, it marked a watershed that removed him further and further from the humanity of those around him. He had proven John Donne wrong: a man could indeed be an island unto himself.

Robert trotted slowly back to camp and pondered over what he had just done. He examined his feelings and could only find elation for once again his deception had been successful. No one would question his absence. He was accountable only to himself. He also knew that O'Mara's failure could be explained in many ways and no one would ever find the remains. Yes, he was quite pleased with himself. Caution and planning had satiated his need to be successful. If only he could tell his father the stories of the world in which Rob found himself. Or was his goal purely economic? What if money was his only goal? Robert gave a mental shrug of his shoulders, satisfied with what he had just done. Occasionally thoughts of Rose crossed his mind and like a juggler he played with new combinations of actions that could win her heart and ultimately her body.

Humans are not given the ability to see themselves as they truly are, but reflecting on the past is always a common way to uncover who we are and what we want to be. But in Rob this was missing. There were no moral standards that he could use as a tool to guide him. For him the journey of conscience was an unknown experience and with this absence he condemned himself to never experience the true journey of the soul. Life was but an accumulation of experiences and for him the measure of a man was in the success or failure of his experiences. In this way he placed himself in the category of Devil's Disciple. For him words like love, altruism, caring, heartbreak, pain, and sharing, were just that…words, to use when seducing those around him.

He could hear the sounds of camp life, the sounds of orders being blared at robotic-like creatures. Rob viewed himself as a man of independence, not a part of this mindless rabble. He entered camp from the woods that came right up to the path. His entrance was unheralded, and for that matter even noticed.

****

It was the end of active campaigning for this regiment in 1861. The Twentieth Regulars had three tasks ahead of them. The first, given the luxury of time, was to make preparations for the winter and all that was entailed in doing so. The second was to act as big brothers to the three new regiments, and the third, and perhaps greatest challenge, was to stay healthy.

There was an air of giddiness among the men. Their first experience in war had been very brief and sharp but most of all it had been relatively bloodless and most successful. They had yet to experience the boredom of winter camp. Sometimes the unknown brings with it an air of exuberance that breeds a comforting naivety.

****

Once again the variety of the men's backgrounds in the Twentieth came to its rescue. How was a regiment to build a satisfactory winter camp without the advice of those who had experienced one? Captain Bedard came to the rescue. He was an engineer by profession and an organizer by personality. A refugee from the French military, he had overseen the building of unfortified winter camps. He sought out his regimental commander. The problem was that there wasn't one. General Ames was still the leader of the Twentieth. Bedard went to Beasley and offered his background and experience to the regiment rather than let every company design its own camp. Beasley quickly concurred with Bedard and so Bedard retreated to his officer's desk to diagram the 'perfect human domicile' for winter use. Bedard would be the first to admit that what he created would hardly be called engineering. He realized that the individual skills of the men would result in the success or failure of the final product. To the good fortune of the whole brigade they were on 'virgin' ground. The forest had not been stripped away from this part of Illinois.

Wagons of all kinds were commandeered and sent out to the local forested areas like bands of termites. Their task was to find straight softwood when possible, between four to five inches in diameter. Axes and saws were in ample supply. Even some badly needed buck saws were available. These were given to those strong of frame. They could fell a tree in a matter of minutes. Rations in the form of a variety of stews were consumed during half-hour breaks.

Another company was given the task of finding roofing. The roofing materials would be in the form of bark carefully skinned from the larger trees that were being felled for firewood. Still another company was given the task of finding, or making, an area of mud which could be hauled to camp and used as a plaster to fill the cracks between poles. As the mud dried more would be added to prevent whistling winter winds from chilling the dwellers within. Morale was high… for the most part.

November 18, 1861

Dear Mother and Father,

I know this the first letter that I have written. There is no real excuse for my tardiness. You deserve much better. My desire to find redemption in this 'holy war' has not lifted the burden of cowardice from my shoulders. I have done my best as a soldier and against my will have been promoted to sergeant. I can thank our company commander Captain Ben Halliday for encouraging me to 'move forward' because of what he calls natural leadership qualities. If only he knew he was saying these words to a female.

Except for father I have never met a man, who possesses so many positive attributes. He was not formally educated. His education took place in the west trying to keep the Indians at peace. His officers saw something in him and they encouraged his formal education while in a fort. Occasionally he will sneak to my tent when the other men aren't around and like some admonished schoolboy has me read the letters he writes to his parents for spelling and grammar. His trust in his company is unshakable and his belief that any one man can make a difference bonds us to him. It is refreshing to find a man who has an almost naïve belief in the honesty and reliability of mankind. He also has a true belief in the Union and the need to maintain it intact.

I have given him some of the tracts of the transcendentalists to stimulate his mind and turn him into a reflective soul.

I am quite sure he has not a whiff of my true identity. I do want him to know someday, but he is not ready yet. A revelation of that kind at this time would cause him to lose faith in me because of my duplicity. I feel it would also end my military career.

I have little contact with most soldiers and keep to myself. This is not punishment. I enjoy the time to read the books you send. Besides that, I would just as soon avoid the vulgarity of some of the soldiers. It is strange because these same men can be brought to tears when one of the camp dogs must be destroyed due to illness. I hope for these men, that the war will be but a comma in their lives, but also one that will allow them to pause and reflect on the meaning of their lives.

I have killed the enemy. I am not proud of this. I view them as our brothers, even though they are misguided about the slave issue. I believe the collective consciousness of defending your country and your fellow soldiers deadens the normal sickening nature of killing a fellow man. It numbs the moral bonds that keep us in check and sane. I am rationalizing of course, but that is me!

I promise to write more often now that winter is soon upon us. Say hello to my brothers and sisters and please write me as soon as you receive this.

Love,

Addy

Then, like many times before, Addy filed the letter among the others that she had written but avoided mailing. She knew her parents would be worried but she also knew that they would tell the military and try to bring her home.

**** 

The men who had been sent out to collect firewood for the winter fires returned a different group. The bounce had left their step. Uniforms drooped like wet rags. Their soaking undergarments clung to their skin giving off a cloud of vapor and an unbearable stench. Axes and saws dragged on the ground as if they were the weapons of a defeated army.

The only word spoken was 'water', and fortunately a prepared officer had a ready supply obtained from the fresh stream a mile from camp. Some bypassed the water and headed directly to the medical tent, no doubt to find a potion for ripped calluses and torn muscles.

The cooks had prepared an extra amount of beef stew, some even using their own money to obtain fresh fall vegetables like parsnips, turnips, and cabbages from the local farmers. Dinner was always silent on these kinds of work days, when soldiering was forgotten in the name of survival. They chose instead to sit back and watch the stars twinkling out personal messages to those who could read them. Embers from the fires rose to the sky and soon burned out falling to the ground like miniature comets.

When not on work details the men would be trained by Captain Bedard, using a model that he dragged around with him to show the simplicity of the typical winter quarters suitable for two men.

"Gentlemen here is a miniature model of the cabin I want you to build for this winter. Some changes might be necessary if the men are taller. Dig a level, rectangular pit, with a flat floor some two feet below the ground. Make the dimensions four-and one-half feet wide and eight-and one-half feet long. Cut the wall posts six-and-one half feet long and drive one end half a foot into the ground. The pitch of the roof is your decision, but a minimum of ninety degrees will keep the snow from causing it to collapse. The hard part comes in trying to build a leak proof roof. Use an adze and try to use larger logs we have brought in to form a flat side and secure these pieces to a frame of smaller logs laid two feet apart and stretching from peak to peak. Let the wood extend one foot beyond the wall to aid in spring run off. Failing this method, use home- made shingles from barrel staves or cedar trees. Now before you lay the roof, place your tent halves and oilskins on it to prevent leakage."

"Your fireplace requires the most creativity and skill. You can build an interior pit, making it deep enough so that you can also create a tunnel to the outside. Make sure the angle rises as you reach the surface. Empty barrels lined with mud or even tin, will help reduce fires in the chimney. Remember the taller the chimney the greater the draught. Find a rock about the same size as the pit and suspend it just above the pit and it will provide you with heat at night."

Bedard knew when his audiences had had enough. A loud "Huzzah" rose when he finished the talk. The men were on their own. The better the cabin, the easier the winter would be.

# CHAPTER EIGHT:
# TREACHERY IN BLUE

It had all happened so quickly. Robert was settling in for the night when a message arrived by courier form General Grant that he was needed in Washington on 'urgent matters'. What in God's name could be so urgent? Had something gone awry with his father's plan? Had they been discovered before they had even begun? Thus it became a long lonely ride back to Washington. To sedate his queasy stomach and mellow his mood he gulped down several shots of bourbon and eventually drifted off to sleep.

Passing soldiers and stewards took no notice of this snoring officer who had put himself to sleep with the aid of liquor. When he finally did disembark he looked like a rider who had been in the saddle for hours riding a steed with a bouncing, prancing gait; the kind that looked good but were 'hell' to ride. Every muscle ached from his calf to his neck. He also felt worse for the copious amount of bourbon he had consumed. Fortunately, he was met by his sister Anna.

"My goodness Rob you look terrible. Are you sick?" she seemed more concerned with her brother's health than the mission on which she had been sent. Rob stared at her coolly so she delivered her message.

"Robert I am to give you a message. Immediately upon your arrival you are to report to the office of the secretary of war." Rob could feel the excitement in his sister's voice. He tried to remain cool. If any of his double agent activities had been discovered he would deny everything. He was an officer serving in the west. How could they find out? My God, they had not even made their first delivery of guns. No, this must all be a mistake.

Upon his arrival he was escorted to an anteroom. In it was a staff colonel to the under secretary of war and another man he vaguely recognized, but could not put a name to him.

"Major Macey, we are glad to have you join us. I hope you had a good trip from Illinois." Robert smiled and began to relax. There certainly was no sign of hostility here. He did find it strange that it was Anna who had met him at the station.

Then it struck Rob like a hammer. This other man, waiting as well, was the famous Allan Pinkerton, ex-Chicago policeman and the man who had prevented an assassination attempt on President Lincoln. He was reported to be as tenacious as a hungry bear when it came to hunting down criminal activity, but he was definitely not an administrative man. He enjoyed the work so much he had traveled into the south to ferret out information. Robert remembered senior officers telling a story that while in a southern barber's chair the German-American barber identified him and Pinkerton had to make a hasty retreat to the nearest alleyway. But his tenacious and resourceful character was of little help in obtaining military information. He had few contacts in this area. Time was not as urgent to him as it was to military commanders who wanted their information quickly. Such was the nature of war. Pinkerton had a good friend in General McClellan and for the time this solidified his position in Washington. Pinkerton coughed, putting an end to the silence. He began his delivery in a fixed but firm voice.

"Major Macey we need a man of your caliber to begin the development of a long range plan to intercept Confederate telegraph messages, using the military forces of the Union to do so. The telegraph will undoubtedly become an important method in the delivery of coded messages. We need you to research the present capabilities of our telegraph system, and then determine the capabilities of the South's as well. Then we need you to select and train a battalion of top soldiers, volunteers of course, in the art of intercepting, code breaking, and transmitting information that was being transmitted by the Confederacy. Would you be interested?"

Rob was sure his jaw must have dropped to his chest, but he regained his composure and offered a calm intelligent reply. "Well, Mr. Pinkerton this could take some time to prepare if the job is to be done properly, and I am afraid I have no experience in the field of telegraphy." Rob deliberately voiced his answer in as humble a way as he could. Plus he needed time to absorb this feast that had just been placed at his feet.

"We completely understand the problem, but here is a word of advice. The higher levels want things done instantly. I have already prepared them for the reality that this will take time as far as you are concerned. Except when your western activity calls, you will be re-assigned to Washington to first train yourself and then prepare a training course for soldiers."

Pinkerton had been prepared for Rob's reply but he had no idea of the utter glee that danced in Rob's mind. This covert activity would turn him into the richest double agent in the war. Then he remembered his commitment to his father, albeit driven as well by money not blood. He had to cover his tracks carefully to retain both jobs and keep feeding the south with guns and information.

"There is one problem. I was just about to begin another project which is of the highest secrecy, I don't know if I am free to mention it. It will cause me to be away from Washington once a month. It has to do with smuggling quantities of Springfield rifles to small pockets of Southerners still loyal to the Union. It too has required time and is just about to start and because I helped organize it, to leave it at this time could negatively affect these southerners' morale."

Rob could not believe that he just released the family's plans to secretly smuggle Springfields to the south. In a technical way he was correct in what he had said. The guns were going to Southerners but on the other hand, who would tell the head of Washington's Secret Service his plan to help fill the coffers of the Macey family? Rob quietly patted himself on the back for coming up with this idea. If the guns were ever stopped by Union troops he had an alibi and a ranking witness.

"I see, major. Let me assure you that your father has already informed me of these plans. If you can work around your schedule you are twice the patriot we hoped you would be." Only Rob could appreciate the irony of what Pinkerton had just said.

"I am sure I can work out some arrangement with my operatives in the south and those producing the Springfields."

Rob was somewhat shocked that his father had been working with the war department, but upon reflection it made good sense to be open about a part of their plan. What if they wonder what officer he was working for? Perhaps that problem would be solved today. He was still waiting to meet with Colonel Winston. Little did he realize this scene had been organized by the colonel and Pinkerton. Pinkerton continued.

"Major, the first thing is to get you raised to the rank of colonel, and then provide you with a staff of experts in the field of telegraphy." Rob's magic smile crossed his face at this announcement.

"Why, thank you, Mr. Pinkerton." Rob sputtered in false humility.

"It is time for you to have your meeting with General Winston. I will leave you in his capable hands."

At this point Rob was shuffled into Winston's office.

"General, take good care of Major Macey and I will see you next week."

"Sit down, Major Macey. I understand we have a couple of topics for conversation."

"Yes, general. The first has to do with our operation to smuggle guns to the south. I will need a squadron of cavalry to escort the guns to the south. Do you have the power to make this happen?"

"Well, major I don't know much about your plan but is Mr. Pinkerton aware of it?"

"Yes, he is, general." Rob was walking on soft ground here. Rob had to convince as few men as possible about the smuggling and that each believed the other had given his permission.

"The other problem was apparently already discussed by you and Mr. Pinkerton. How do you plan to provide me with space and experts to get the telegraphy operation started?"

"Not to worry, major, I will find you when everything is ready. It could take some time to prepare everything. When we get to your stage you will be the one to select the men for training."

****

The drizzle of November continued to roll like miniature falls down the poncho soaking his sky blue coat. Now in the reality of Colonel Macey's plans, with everything secured, some of his exhilaration was lost. The pleasure would come in the monetary reward that came with the work.

"Excuse me, sir." Rob looked up and faced the cherubic face of a young lieutenant.

"I am Lt. Mallory," he continued apologetically.

"It's good to meet you, lieutenant. Let me explain what your first job will be. Take two troopers with you as scouts and the task will go faster. Your job is to find the easiest way to move a small column of carts from Baltimore to any location within thirty miles of the Virginia border. The road should be one we can use over and over and generally untraveled, particularly by military forces. You will be picking up the empty wagons in Baltimore. We will use mule teams to pull them. If any of your troopers or people on the road ask what you are shipping tell them you don't know. That way all will be able to tell the truth. There will be no markings on the crates."

"Shouldn't we have some response to calm the curiosity of all?"

Robert dwelled on this. It might be a good idea. It might even be better to leak out some information.

"I think you are correct lieutenant. Let's use the story that we are shipping guns to southern sympathizers, but that is only if it is necessary. The story has credibility because Virginia was the last state to secede and it is common knowledge there are sympathizers to the Union in northern Virginia."

The lieutenant went even further. "I think that it would be a good idea to use the same troops again and again. I will drill them to turn the wagons into closed tight circles in case of attack and also teach them how to ground their own horses if practicable. The company will be practiced in rapid skirmishing should that be the best tactic. As well they will be issued Sharps carbines which allow them to defend themselves better if attacked. Their rapid rate of fire will give them the chance to fire as long as they don't overheat the barrels."

Unknown to Rob this young, bright officer was the finest of professionals. He was disciplined and a hard worker. Rob, however, could not appreciate the dedication of others. His world of deception and greed was foremost in his thoughts.

He was annoyed with his wandering mind. He found his thoughts returning to the dinner his family had had with the Greens. Engraved in his mind with the detail of a goldsmith, was the vivid image of Rose Green. It wasn't just her unquestionable beauty that had captured his mind, but the strength he could feel in her character. He had felt it in their minor disagreement, but this had only strengthened a growing bond that was unknown to him. He did know that if there was any sign of interest on her part. His sisters would have warned her about his past relationships and told her about his notorious reputation. His honor and defense of the fair sex was not equal to his social and military position… and he knew it.

While in Washington he had even visited brothels, particularly those set up for the senior officers. With his charm and handsome presence he had pick of the litter. He had even made the decision to not visit the same girl twice. He wanted nothing that would come close to resembling a relationship. Washington was filled with brothels and business was booming in the face of death and war. He had made his decision and it only meant putting it to paper when they made camp for the evening.

Rob had his orderly pull out his writing table from a company wagon, secure in the knowledge that he knew what he was doing and why.


November 18, 1861
Miss Rose Green
Greenfield Manor
Baltimore, Maryland


Dear Miss Green,


War places any relationship in a precarious position. This evening I find myself in northern Virginia guarded by a company of infantry. I feel safe.

War cheapens the value of lives. This I have learned.

In my case, however, my life has been made so much richer by the single meeting we had a month ago. It has taken me some time to work up the courage to be so blunt with you. Such are the results of war. I find myself coming back again and again to the beauty in your fair appearance and the confident bearing you bring to conversation.

But I am not without an awareness of reality. I know full well that either through Anna or some other sources you will have been informed of the stories surrounding my trysts with fair maids while a student at the Military Academy. As I look back on this part of my life I now see the foolishness and selfishness of my actions. They were the actions of an immature and unmanly character. I regret them because they blinded me to the real beauty of the opposite sex. My military life has severely limited my time with the opposite sex and given me time to reflect more on who I am now. I am not the same man. The fear of losing one's life in battle has awakened me to the need for a real relationship with one of the opposite sex.

I am a new person. I wish to meet with you upon my return to Washington. I know this must almost sound very brash, for we have met but once, but war has changed how we treat time and hence how we make new relationships.

Whatever your decision, please write and share your thoughts about what I have written. I believe you will be pleased with the change that responsibility can bring to the human psyche. Until we meet again, as I know we must, I will keep your fair vision in my mind to cheer me wherever I am.

Yours in Hope,

Rob Macey

Pleased with his literary acumen, Rob re-read the letter he was prepared to send. He knew the admission of his past life would put him in the position of the redemptive soul. The personal politics of his life made this admission a necessity. He folded the letter and placed it in an envelope.

There was no one to challenge his thoughts about war. She would not know how he had made a point of staying away from combat whenever possible. To add drama to the situation, he dispatched a trooper with the letter in a military pouch. He had to play to this new part if he was to have any hope with Rose.

****

It had been a month since the first 'Southern Winchesters' had begun production. They were like any other gun with the exception of one key element: there were no registration numbers which could be used to find out what soldier the gun had been assigned. It would also prevent anyone from finding out what factory had produced the weapon. It was good protection that would prevent any investigation into the guns' sources.

The guns had already been packed in cases that had no markings on the outside. Soldiers would not even notice this, let alone question it. And so the first caravan of contraband began its journey into the south, following the clearly marked trails that had been carefully chosen and declared as 'safe' for such a mission.

Far to the south another group of men were also preparing for a trip, this time going north.

Starting out at night, dressed in Union uniforms, and displaying the necessary military accoutrement of Union troopers, they prepared to depart following another map that would lead them, in time, to join up with the troopers heading south. Their only restriction was the need for nighttime travel.

Thus, if one of the two arrived first at the point of union they would hide during the day. Since this was the first 'mission' no one knew who would be the first to arrive. Rob had told the Southerners that if they arrived first they should continue onwards to lessen the chance of being found idling in the middle of the route.

The leader of this Southern mission would be Colonel Alexander Braithwaite. Alexander needed some practice in clandestine operations so this adventure would serve as a training ground for him. His troopers were informed of the contents so they would be motivated to serve well. This band of men was to stay together as a group. Their morale had to remain high. He sat on his still horse awaiting orders. From behind he could hear the rapid movement of one of his troopers. The tall, black, stallion slid to a halt in front of him.

"Colonel, the troop is assembled and we are set to depart."

"Very well, major. Bring them forward and we will begin our adventure."

The major was one Anthony Kilbride. He had been picked for this job. He was used to clandestine, cavalry operations and had been lured to join this particular band of men with the promise of this new rank. Soon Kilbride appeared with the squadron of troopers.

"Now major lead this squadron with pride and the knowledge that this is the best group of men the South could assemble!" In double line they took their first steps northward. The only sound to be heard was the eerie hoots of owls who would be their soul company on this night. Snapping twigs brought silent reprimands from one of the sergeants.

Alexander knew this trip would be the shorter, and probably safer trip of the two. Their present mobility would be a necessary aid if they were discovered. None-the-less, Alexander sent out two troopers to act as a forward guard for those following. Eight hours and daylight still left them without contact with the 'real' Union troopers.

Finally one of his forward troopers returned at a trot.

"Colonel, we could hear the wagon wheels of supply wagons out on the trail. This could be our mule train."

"I hope you are correct trooper. Remember the verbal sign if you challenge them. Choose a straight piece of road so that they have a chance to see you. Their officer will know the counter sign. If it isn't given, get back here in a hurry."

"Yes, sir!" With that the trooper wheeled and disappeared up the road.

Meanwhile, Rob rode quietly, knowing that they were now well into Virginia. The trip had been uneventful and that was just the way he wanted it. He had made another decision. This would be his first and last trip. It was intended to be quiet…but to Rob it was boring and without the chance for conversation. He made a note that he would have to find a willing accomplice to take his place. His father did not have to know.

"Colonel Macey, see in the distance." Rob stopped his horse to get a better view of two Union troopers approaching on foot. After signaling a halt Rob trotted ahead of his small column. Colonel Braithwaite advanced until they were almost beside each other. Rob gave the first half of the signal.

"Red."

"Rose," was the response. Rob began the short conversation by raising his arm to bring up the wagons.

"How did your ride go, colonel?" Rob spoke softly.

"Without incident, colonel. The way we wanted it," responded Alexander

"And how was your journey with the wagons?"

"Without incident as well," concurred Rob.

"Colonel, one matter that we forgot to iron out," Rob said "Whoever comes on the next ride, could you ask him to bring along the empty wagons? I don't want to keep borrowing wagons from the wagon park."

"Certainly colonel, that way we will always be working with the same sets of wagons," Alexander added. He had done a good job of not showing any disdain for an officer who was a traitor to his country. Alexander's men rode up to the wagons, relieving the Union men of their burden.

"Have a safe trip south, colonel." Rob saw no point in making small talk so he had made it clear he was breaking off the conversation.

"You as well," Alexander responded. While the Union troops had to be on guard for Confederate patrols, the Confederate column went thirty miles and then changed into Confederate uniforms. Their safety was now secured.

When the Union soldiers were out of sight Alexander checked two of the cases to make sure the Confederacy had spent its money well, and it had. Alexander's thoughts wandered now. The tension was gone. He was still wondering about the colonel he had just met. What kind of man was he? Why had he abandoned his loyalty to his country? He had no problems in making eye contact. Curious, thought Alexander. Now his thoughts wandered off to other topics of interest to only him.

Rob had no such thoughts. He put the wagons, guns and the colonel out of his mind and drifted into his image of Rose Green. He chastised himself for continuing to dwell on her. For all he knew it was a lost cause. More satisfying for Rob was the money that he made on this inaugural trip. That was his real satisfaction.

# CHAPTER NINE:
## LIFE IN CAMP

For the most part, life in the Union camp was tedious and repetitious. Roll call was at 6:00 a.m., then breakfast, drill, and more drilling throughout the day. Few military exercises beyond the regimental level were held. Worse still, three of the regiments had no notion of combat. General Ames worried constantly about this. They, would have to wait to 'meet elephant' in the spring when war commenced again.

The rest of the time was spent reading or writing, fixing the shelter, sleeping, or playing cards and gambling. Officially, the gambling was not allowed but most officers looked the other way and let their men discover the dangers of such activities. Only time would tell if the harsh warnings of some parents would be listened to by their sons. Since the brigade had not been paid in three months, little actual currency could exchange hands.

From the Atlantic to the Pacific oceans, the winter of 1861 was being played out in this tedious manner. But for the Twentieth, nothing seemed to be just 'ordinary' and so a series of events began to unfold to add to their distinctive regimental history.

It began soon after Christmas with the arrival of Amos Drury. Amos was what many would call a 'legal war profiteer'. He was a suttler. In Ireland he would have been referred to as a 'tinker', for Amos was a traveling salesman,  flaunting his goods to an audience that was starving for both a change of activity and a chance to spend some of their money once their pay arrived. He packed the goods of a typical suttler. Extra and different food was high on the list of 'wants' and included such items as candy, tinned meats, pickles, fresh pies, and sausages. The type and quality varied from suttler to suttler. Winter was in the air so Amos carried favorites for his customers: woolen gloves, socks, comforters, and even camp stoves.

Every suttler carried tobacco for pipes and cigars of varied quality. The aforementioned only added to the rattling and rasping coughs one heard at night or roll call. Playing cards, brogans, tin ware, and all kinds of other extras for the soldiers were part and parcel of the suttler's inventory. The favorite, of course, was liquor and if the camp was isolated like theirs it held even greater appeal. It was rare for a soldier receive liquor in a package from home. The suttler had a rapt audience for the booze even though it was illegal. It remained up to vigilance and beliefs as to how far he would enforce the no liquor policy.

What seemed strange about the suttlers was that their services were granted as a monopoly by the military. It kept them from having to provide extra services or worse still, having soldiers wandering through towns looking for goods. However, only one suttler was given military permission to operate within that regiment or larger group if necessary.

Amos Drury had all of the above items, but he kept quiet about the liquor. In addition, he had two very valuable assets with him. They were kept in another wagon in the woods. He claimed they were part of his family, a wife ten years his junior and two daughters, ages eighteen and twenty. No one had seen them, but none doubted their presence.

At first the men were glad to see Amos,...until they saw that a number of his goods were five times what they would cost in a local store. While fathers and dutiful sons hurried their pay homewards, the city boys and those looking for some excitement knew a good old time could be had with certain of his 'goods'. Most had not seen a woman for months now and those that had 'seen the elephant' realized that their lives hung by a slim thread. It was time to live life to the fullest.

It took little time for the word to get around and all interested parties knew that word had to be kept from the officers. It always took some time for the first customer to appear but when he did he found that the cost would be three dollars a visit. But each would get a ten per-cent discount on any items purchased.

During the day Amos used his great baritone voice and a banjo to gain the men's attention. When he finished men would crowd around and make arrangements for the evening. At night he turned from Dr. Jekyll to Mr. Hyde. He would shut down his 'goods' wagon and take up a place outside his 'home'. There, for the mere price, as he liked to put it, he would rent out one of his daughters for a period of ten minutes. He could handle two men at a time by placing a partition between the front and back of his wagon. If only a light had shone on the wagon, for it would have looked like some small skiff being bounced about on the high seas. Among the soldiers' dwellings there was much tongue flapping if one had bought liquor or visited Amos' daughters. Non-participants kept to themselves or castigated the offenders for their immoral ways. The guilty just smiled to themselves or harangued the critics for not having the strength to take part in such activities. There was but one unspoken rule: never turn in someone to the officers.

The country boys were the most curious. It was most often the younger city boys who were willing to spend their money. They were familiar with this part of life. It was nothing new.

Perhaps the most comedic event occurred when Amos ran out of his goods. He displayed a suit of armor suited for an officer. Amos had had inquiries at other camps, but no purchasers. Then one cold winter day, thinking he was alone, Colonel Beasley tried on the metal armor. It was meant for a smaller man, so when it came time to take it off it would not budge. Just then two men who wanted some sausages walked near the wagon, only to witness Amos huffing and puffing trying to remove the armor. It took them little time to reach the camp and inform others of what they had seen. Soon about seventy soldiers were quietly watching this comedy unfold. Finally Amos pried it off. The men broke out in cheers and clapping. The colonel tried to regain his dignity but it was too late. The men now knew what kind of colonel they had as a leader and it did not make them feel better.

The story reached the ears of General Ames. Within two days Ben Halliday found himself promoted to the rank of major. The men settled down and waited for history to unfold.

Within ten days of Amos' arrival Dr. O'Malley found himself standing solemnly outside Major Halliday's tent. The orderly could see the serious demeanor on the lieutenant's face.

"Private, could I have a few moments of privacy with the major?"

"Certainly sir, let me inform him of your presence." Within moments Ben appeared at the front of his tent.

"Lieutenant O'Malley, we never have enough time to chat. I am glad you stopped by. Are our cases of dysentery improving?"

"Yes Ben, but I am afraid I am not here for that reason." Ben's eyebrows furrowed with concern.

What is it then?"

"Let me summarize the last three days for you. I have had three men from this regiment complaining of sore testicles. Upon examination they were clearly swollen. Five soldiers have reported very painful urination and the pain is not subsiding. Two men are complaining about green pus dripping from their penises."

"What are you telling me doctor?"

O'Malley leaned forward and broke the news to Ben. "I am trying to inform you that we have a major outbreak of gonorrhea on our hands."

"But how could that happen?"

"You innocent country boys are all the same." The doctor sat back enjoying the present situation and getting a chance to mock Ben at the same time. "Ben, are you telling me that you did not know your men were visiting that suttler's second wagon at night? And this is only the start. Some cases don't appear for thirty days. At this rate, half the regiment will be infected." The doctor had never seen Ben look so paralyzed. He prided himself on the men.

"But how...?" He was cut off by the frustrated doctor.

"Have you not noticed that suttler's second wagon?"

"Of course it is his family home, "Ben stammered weakly.

"Ben, it's a whorehouse on wheels!" The good doctor was back at the edge of his seat feeling much like a father educating his son about the facts of life."

"My God! I will have to inform Colonel Beasley!" Ben spoke with concern and trepidation.

"And just what do you think our brilliant colonel will decide to do?" The bitterness in the doctor's voice indicated how much respect he had for the colonel. Ben said nothing. He leaned forward, elbows on his knees, his hands forming a steep roof with fingers resting under his nose. Still nothing was said. The doctor could see Ben's problem. Beasley was neither decisive nor creative. He would fall back on 'the book' in any situation regardless of the effect it had on his men.

"Lieutenant, I do know the men are angry with that suttler's inflated prices but he has done well and is talking of bringing in another wagon to replenish his stock."

"Does that include more women Ben?"

"I don't know. But I do know the men are going to go mad when they find out that his whores were infected when he got here."

"If it will help I will go with you to see Beasley, and should he have some outrageous plan, I'll go see General Ames.... God, how I miss that man even though he is just one mile away!"

Within minutes the two officers were in front of Colonel Beasley.

"Well for one thing I should have been informed sooner about the whores and I could have stopped this debauchery before it began!" Beasley stormed, trying to put the blame on Ben's shoulders. "This is scandalous. This was supposed to be the model regiment for the other three. What will the general think of my ability to lead and control the soldiers?"

Ben had to bite his tongue. Although he had never discussed this topic with General Ames he had a good idea of what the general thought about Beasley's leadership qualities. But he was hamstrung by Washington to deal with this political appointee. As Ben listened to the colonel rant and rave, he thought that this incident would be a good test of his abilities. Life as a colonel had been too easy for him up to this point.

"What does the colonel want the doctor and I to do?" queried Ben.

Beasley fell back in his chair as if he had suffered a heart attack. In truth it was a state of emotional collapse. Beasley was silent. Finally he collected his thoughts and spoke. "Gentlemen, tomorrow the two of you will address the whole regiment, in formation, on this issue. Dr. O'Malley will present the nature of the problem to the men and how it is cured. Halliday, you will deal with the source of the problem and the moral degradation of this type of behavior and the shame it brings to the whole regiment and those who experienced God's revenge. God knows some of these could be married men."

"Sir, may I speak?" asked Ben calmly. Beasley nodded. "Sir, I don't believe that this event should sully the reputation of the regiment. Secondly, I think the quieter we keep this information the better it will be for the morale of the men. Call the first sergeants together and let the information about the disease and Amos and his women spread down through the ranks. Try to leave the men with some self-respect." The two officers waited as this approach to the problem filtered its way through Beasley's unpredictable thought processes.

"No major, this is clearly a serious health and moral problem. We must snip the dead branch from the tree immediately!" Ben almost choked with this lame attempt at moral imagery, "You will do what I have ordered Major

Halliday. Meanwhile I will draw up papers relieving Amos as our camp suttler."

"Sir, there is another possible approach." Ben was trying hard to prevent this from becoming a full-blown regimental matter.

"What is it man? I have heard enough!" By now Beasley was turning red.

"Sir, you are the military and moral leader of this regiment. Call all your officers together and apprise them of the situation. They know their men and probably know the culprits as well. Let them deal with the situation. Give them a range of options and when to use them…"

"Stop, stop Major!" Beasley whined. "That is too complex, and besides why should the officers absorb the guilt of their men? No, no you will do as I say."

Ben realized there was no point engaging in any further debate. The colonel wanted to distance himself from the matter and he had found a way to do it.

The two officers rose in silence and without dismissing themselves left the tent. Neither officer said a word. They retreated to Ben's tent whereupon Ben immediately pulled out a bottle of Amos' so called bourbon and poured two long drinks. Finally Ben spoke. "Perhaps we can turn this disaster around."

"How so Ben?"

"The ultimate decision must rest on the shoulders of the commanding officer, in this case Beasley. Perhaps this will provide more ammunition for the general to press the military to move Beasley." All was quiet but for the sipping from Ben's cup.

"Ben, I hope you are correct. Beasley has demonstrated his desire to escape from dealing directly with a problem, but you know the military better than me. You know that those at the top will have to give Beasely a chance to prove his ineptness on the field of battle. What did you call it, oh yes, 'military politics.'" Both men let short smiles creep from the corners of their mouths. Tomorrow would be an interesting day.

Suddenly Ben was thrown back into a state of shock. "Oh, my God, what if Father Martins gets wind of this?" As fate would have it, one Father Aloysius Martins had arrived in camp as the chaplain for this isolated brigade. He had been recruited all the way from Boston to serve God on the field of battle and keep Satan in check. In reality he was a theology professor at a Catholic seminary. Lofty thoughts about the 'Summa Theologica' and the deadly 'Reformation' were the playground for his mind, not the day to day concerns of uneducated soldiers. Nevertheless, good Catholic priest that he was, he had accepted the challenges of ministering to these men and dreamed of raising their simple minds and souls to a higher plane.

Ben had attended a Mass he offered, even though he himself was not a Catholic. He thought the priest would in some way calm the hearts and spirits of these poor men about to be thrown into a maelstrom, most of which they could not imagine. Instead the learned man spoke about 'grace', its role in their lives, and what the famous church fathers had to say about it. Almost all of what he said went over their heads. Most men knew little of the content the priest imparted to them. Ben was starting to think that winter camp, with the exception of drill, was not a time to rest and recollect their experiences, but rather just another challenge facing each and every man.

****

It was a chilly November day and Ben looked toward the trees. They were shaking their tops like the wagging finger of a school teacher scolding her children. A chill crept down his back. The men were also shaking. It was a cold day and most men were still dressed in their dark blue frock coats. Ben always liked this picture. There was elegance in the simplicity of those coats. Perfectly attired soldiers standing like ramrods were a part of the silent majesty of military life.

But today the weather, the shivering, the poorly formed rows and the topic had stamped out Ben's boyish view of military life. There was no place for the playground officer. Due to the noise of the wind the company commanders change the long rows into a 'U' formation so that all could hear what he and the doctor had to say.

"Men, this is the first time I have had to deal with a matter concerning the behavior of certain members of the regiment. It does not please me nor does it apply to all members of this regiment, but we have to stop the problem before it becomes an epidemic."

Those infected could be identified by the shuffling of their feet and the dropping of their heads. Ben continued.

"You know that I have the highest trust in you as men and as soldiers. You bring honor to your country…" As Ben went on praising them, it was then that the doctor realized that it was he who would have to carry the bad news to the men, but then Ben changed directions.

"Since the arrival of Amos Drury in camp there has been an increase in gambling, minor scuffles, and drunken behavior. We are too far from any town for the import of liquor. But more importantly, and much to my chagrin, women of ill-repute are accompanying him and men are throwing away the money that has been released by the paymaster in exchange for bodily pleasures." Ben's voice grew louder and angrier.

"This is a military camp. One of many throughout this great nation, built to prepare you men for the inevitable military campaigns that will soon begin in the spring of 1862. Winter is not a holiday but a time to sharpen our skills and maintain our health. These surely will help save lives and bring this war of brothers to a rapid conclusion." The doctor had never heard Ben wax so eloquently about the war, but he did think Ben was wandering off topic.

"Men, I want you to listen carefully to Lieutenant O'Malley and be silent until he has finished."

"Men, I want to advise you that the women with whom you have been having sexual contact are infected with gonorrhea. I know you have never heard of it before. It is a disease that if not taken care of immediately, can actually kill you. If you have had contact with them look for pus or other secretions leaking from your penises. You might also feel pain in your testicles or pain when you urinate. Take hope, there is a cure. We carry medicines with us for the cure of this disease. Also beware, sometimes this disease can take up to thirty days to appear, so if you have had contact with them be vigilant and see me as quickly as possible if any late symptoms appear." The doctor stepped back indicating that he was finished and Ben could conclude.

"I hope that you will now cease this behavior and take responsibility for your actions. Each captain will now take command of his company and prepare you for morning drill. Have a good day men."

Both officers stood back, waiting for the men to dismiss but instead they formed into small groups. Ben could hear the cursing and swearing. It suddenly occurred to him what he should have done. But it was too late. He turned to his orderly.

"Private, get my horse mounted as soon as possible and report back to me."

Ben knew the fifty-second Iowa carried a Provost company. He would prepare them to help in this situation. He decided to let them continue their discussions, as it was unclear what they were going to do.

There he was in the kind of situation he understood, angry men. Hal could wax eloquently when the situation demanded it.

"Men, it is clear that we have been deceived and betrayed by Amos Drury. He must have known those girls could make men sick. Even if you are against prostitution and did not use them we must stand united. Price gouging is one thing,… disease is another. Follow me."

As seventy-five soldiers stormed in anger toward Drury's wagons, no weapons could be seen. Ben glanced around at the furious crowd as they marched forward thinking of how the strength of their bond overcame personal differences; this was about justice. As they marched Ben's orderly returned with a note. It was from the Provost Commander, a Captain Williams, advising him that their intervention would be a good idea as they would appear more neutral. Should Ben enter the fray it might cost him the bond with his regiment. They would be there in twenty minutes, but was that quick enough? While Ben stood as a neutral observer at this point in time; his position could change in a minute if he was forced to intervene. Suddenly, Colonel Beasley appeared on the scene angry and red-faced as usual.

He chose to attack Ben. "Damn it Major, I told you to inform not to incite a riot! Get out there and stop them."

"It isn't necessary. The Provost Company is on its way."

"Are you refusing my command major?" Beasley's mouth was wide open, saliva forming at the corners of his mouth, his plump stomach heaving and rolling with the rise and fall of his chest.

"Sir this is best settled by the provost's men."

As the body of men strode defiantly to Drury's abode they could see him at his table under a tent flap and counting his money. Lounging on cots and warmed by a large fire were his 'daughters' and 'wife,' covered in soft warm covers. As this horde strode toward them they sat upright uncertain of the problem or what to do about it. Hal egged the men on with more accusations about this troupe of money mongers. Drury could have feigned ignorance. He could have blamed it on the women. He could have even offered to give the men back their money…anything but what he chose as a solution. He chose confrontation.

"How do I know it was not one of your men who spread this vile disease to my family? Why would a father treat his daughters so carelessly?" The good doctor strode to the front of the band of protesters ready to defend his men.

"Mr. Drury I would like to inform you that as medical officer I have borne witness to the fact that these men have not been near any women for forty days, the maximum incubation period of this disease."

Drury was not ready to offer a rebuttal to this fact.

"Perhaps your ability to diagnose disease bears some inquiry doctor!" This was the best Drury had to offer and it certainly wasn't enough. Dr. O'Malley was well-respected by the men. Attacking him was like spitting on the flag. Once again Hal took the lead.

"Sergeant Swinton, take the horses out of harm's way. Sergeant Watson take ten men and find all the firewood you can and place it under their wagons." As this was taking place the women began howling like banshees. One dug her nails into Hal's face and jumped on his huge back. The 'mother' joined in, spitting on Hal and hitting the back of his head with one of their frying pans. Now other men began joining in, ransacking the wagon filled with stores, and others began chasing Drury who had taken off into the woods, only to be tracked down like a wolf who had raided a chicken coop and been caught. Howls of glee announced the capture of Drury and he was laid out, his hands reaching into the sky. The man feared for his life. Despite Ben's intervention coals from the morning breakfast as well as the wood were heaved under the wagons and soon an inferno engulfed the dry wood and the canvas of the wagons. The more the women screamed, the more the soldiers hooted with delight.

Over a small rise Provost guards marched at the double-quick, Springfields held in the 'charge' position and bayonets fixed. The captain created a cordon around the blazing fire but there was no stopping it.

Another group of guards created a secure circle around the Drury family.

The rest of the guards stationed themselves around the cheering band of protesters who now felt justice had been done. The officers present had not been prepared by their training to handle this affair. Ben did not doubt some higher officer was paid off to grant Drury his right to peddle his wares. This could all come back on him and his inability to take command of the situation.

Ben had an idea and he put it into action. After all, he held the money

Drury had been counting.

"Would any soldier who has taken advantage of these women like to step forward and claim his money? No one stepped forward. Each was too ashamed to admit his actions. "Would any soldier who is unsatisfied with the goods he purchased step forward as well and claim his money? Again there were no takers.

"Mr. Drury, do you have a ledger showing the purchases these men made?"

"I have no such elaborate accounting system." Ben knew full well these suttlers kept poor accounting systems so that they would not have to pay off some officer after the goods were sold. "Since no man has stepped forward to claim monies than I assume that all parties are satisfied. Is that correct Mr. Drury?"

At this point Drury was glad to get away with his life, let alone his money. Oh yes, he had lost his wagons but misadventures do occur and this Union major had succeeded in quelling the situation and making a 'fair' deal for him. Ben knew that there would be an inquiry into what had taken place but he believed he had given his men a chance to reclaim their monies and Drury walked away with his money and his life. The soldiers began to drift away. They agreed that a form of justice had taken place, but they were still out their money and that did not sit well with them. As the Provost guards formed to depart Ben wheeled about and took his wrath out on Drury.

"Sir, you have caused an unfortunate incident among a group of fine soldiers who are about to sacrifice their lives for this great country. Can you say the same for your actions in the future? I doubt it. The decision I took was far more politic than just. If I had my way I would have confiscated all the money and distributed it to the families who have lost soldiers in my regiment. I am going to see that the powers that be never issue you another license to sell as a suttler. You can protest. But then do you really want the stories of your daughters to haunt your good family name? I think not sir!"

Ben could feel the blood boiling in his veins the more he spoke. Perhaps this would be a good time to cease his tirade. Amos' head drooped. At least Ben had won a personal victory. Ben now addressed Captain Williams.

"Captain, could you see that one of our unused wagons is fitted to Mr. Drury's horses and that once they have gathered their remains they are escorted out of camp?"

"Certainly, major."

For Ben the whole incident had become a metaphor for life. One has to guard carefully when evil is about, for ultimately all suffer in a greater or lesser degree.

****

Ben was furious with Colonel Beasley. He decided it was time for a confrontation. This time he did not ask the guard if the colonel was in, but strode self-righteously through the tent opening, hurling the flap to one side. His chin dropped but before he could say anything to the colonel, who had his back to him, he spied the molded form of body armor standing in the corner of the tent. There was a chest protector that reached from the neck to the private areas, and gauntlets which fit the arms and legs lay on the ground. Ben had heard rumors of such equipment being sold to officers in the Army of the Potomac. Obviously, they had made their way to the west.

In one sense Ben was not surprised. The equipment spoke volumes about the character of their leader. Would Beasley prefer the hoots of his men and live his soldier's life in shame or was it better to die in battle with some semblance of respect? Beasely rolled over and tried to stand, but it was apparent that he must have bought some whiskey as well.

"Well, Holiday have you resolved the problem?" The colonel asked in his semi-delirious drunken state.

"Yes, I did colonel, while you were resting of course!" Bens' lips were pursed. He had never thought of speaking to a superior officer in such a tone. "Colonel, you unnecessarily involved some men by making me address the whole regiment. As a result more men were willing to take up the anti-Drury cause. They managed to burn both carts before the Provost guard arrived. I am going to note all of this in my report to General Ames as well your dereliction of command!" Ben's voice carried outside and soldiers walking by heard the full force of the major's words.

"Major, I would be very careful what I said and what I wrote. My fingers reach much further than yours!"

"Yes, colonel, we all know that you have political connections in Washington, but it is a long way from rural Illinois to the capital, remember that!" Ben wheeled and left, leaving the colonel with his mouth open, preparing a comeback, but it was too late. Beasley sighed, took another swig of the whiskey and lay back on his bed to enjoy the sleep of the drunk.

The issue was temporarily settled for the colonel but not for Ben. He strode quickly to the medical tent, trying not to take his anger out on some innocent victim. Fortunately for its inmates it was probably the warmest quarters in camp. The winter walls had been assembled with thicker logs, holding in the heat emanating from the stone fireplace built by regimental volunteers. Its greater height produced an unusually high flame and thus more heat. Buckets of water were placed around the hospital to prevent the air from becoming too dry. Ben caught the doctor's eye. "How are our gonorrhea patients?"

"Well, I think we are lucky that those first men came in so early. Two more have appeared but it takes courage to work up the desire to visit me. They won't be the last."

"How do you treat this disease, doctor?"

"Believe it or not with ink."

"Ink!" Ben's shocked voice elevated more than O'Malley wished. Quietly he put a finger to his mouth requesting a lower volume. Both glanced around to see if they had any listeners. Apparently not; all the sick and wounded remained unmoved.

"I just tell them to take it with mouthfuls of water and there is little complaint," chuckled the doctor. We also have cases of dysentery, but I think most of this resulted from buying tainted pork pies from the suttler. They are cases of food poisoning rather than bad water. They should recover in two to three days. All were otherwise in good condition when they reached the hospital." Ben just shook his head. "This is what happens when the government focuses on the wrong issue. Rather than demanding, or even expanding the food selection they purchase, they spend their time collecting fees for licenses."

"Major Halliday, your distinct sarcasm might leave me aghast." Again a curl of a smile formed at the corners of the doctor's mouth.

"While you are here major I must commend you on keeping a clean camp and trying to supplement the men's diets with fresh vegetables. All of this has contributed to a low rate of diarrhea. I hear of major outbreaks in other regiments."

"Thank you doctor, and having a quality surgeon helps as well."

Ben yawned. "I think it is time to make my way to my tent and get a good night's sleep. Goodnight Lieutenant O'Malley." Ben decided it was time for peace and quiet after the events of the day. He also planned to write a short letter to his parents.

January 19, 1862

Dear Mother and Father;

I hope this letter finds you in good health. Thank you for the box of cookies that mother baked. You have no idea how much food from home boosts the spirit after months of camp food. Little has happened here. Everyone looks forward to the arrival of spring which is still a ways off. Battle plans are being formed as I write. Oh yes, Homer has been promoted to brigadier general and I have made it to the level of major of the regiment. I miss the closer relationship with the men from my company but such is life in the military.

The only real worry we have here is the inept colonel we have now. He is indecisive, and makes no attempt to make himself a model to the men. He has already lost the respect of the soldiers. I have thought of visiting General Ames to get some advice on how to handle this man.

Winter is hard on the men's health and unfortunately some have died from dysentery, God rest their souls! The other problem is the hacking men experience at night. Most of this is the result of leaky chimneys in our winter quarters.

I hope to hear from you soon.

Your Loving Son,

Ben

****

Needless to say this was not the end of the prostitutes. The reverend had heard the story about the whores from the 'saintly' men in the regiment. So he prepared himself for his weekly sermon.

Ben made a point of going to Sunday Mass to hear what the good father would have to say. After the gospel Father Martins motioned with his hands for those in attendance to sit on the cold winter ground. His concern for their health and comfort seemed minimal. He began.

"My sons, my fathers, my brothers in Christ, this is indeed a sad day. Sin, in its vilest form, has visited your camp in the form of Satan's sisters, prostitutes, selling their bodies to earn the wages of the devil that I am sure this day is rejoicing in the fires of Hell. You too, unless you seek repentance, will reside with him in that fiery place. This brings shame not only to you but to your families as well. What if they find out about your loose behavior? How would they react having tried to raise you in the ways of God? It is a weakness in the spirit. God has intended sex only for the married life and the bringing of new souls upon this earth.

"What has it brought you? Violence and disease! Are these diseases not a warning from God Himself? You have squandered your soldier's pay, money that was intended to help your kin through these terrible times.

"Think what you will say to them. How will you face them if they discover your wanton ways? What moral lesson have you older men set for these young soldiers whose lives could be taken in war at any time? They look up to you in silence remembering what they have seen.

"Remember you sons of good Catholic families, that if you have engaged in this foulest of acts you have committed a mortal sin. If you were to die in battle today your souls would be sent directly to hell. But it is not too late to repent! God forgave Mary Magdalene her sins so he will forgive your sins through the sacrament of penance. I have the power given to me by my position to grant you forgiveness. Come to confession so that your souls will once again be pure. Do so as soon as possible!"

"What am I to tell my bishop when I return to Boston? That the men I serve are the gravest of sinners? Think of the noble cause in which you are engaged. Don't diminish its nobility by this kind of behavior."

Father Martins paused to gauge his impact upon the men. He could see that the holy faithful were transfixed on him. But then he knew these were probably not the real sinners; those were the non-Catholics who had failed to seek the path of the Holy Mother and the Catholic Church. Now he lifted his head in indignation. "You men of other faiths, would your ministers say anything differently from what I have said? No! No! They too are men of God. You must look into your souls and decide if moments of pleasure are worth the fires of hell. Refrain you pagans from giving pleasure to Satan and beg forgiveness from our forgiving God so that this plague will be cleansed from your bodies."

As Father Martins continued to seek to put fear in the men's hearts,

Addy sat comfortably on a log. She agreed in principle with this man, as most people would, but she felt troubled in a manner not connected to religion but to the life into which the men had been thrown. When spring came many could be dead by shells or disease. Certain questions troubled her. Were these normal times and did God excuse men who fought in a righteous cause? Addy could only conclude that she was glad that she was not God. Acting as judge would be a job she would not want!

And so the mass continued. Few went to communion, fearing the cold lifeless stare of Fr. Martins. Soon it was over and the men quickly dispersed, leaving Fr. Martins to clear away his utensils. Strangely, from that day on little was said among the officers or men about all the events that had transpired in the past week. It was as if they had chosen an oath of silence for reasons not clear to them.

Hal had no time or interest in the morality of what had transpired in the Amos Drury affair. More importantly, he was not about to freeze himself on this wintry day. His goal was to stay warm and to this end he continued to re-patch his almost cozy winter home. All the men had agreed to leave Hal and Patches alone in Hal's own winter home. His large frame consumed a great deal of space and to live with Hal meant to live with the uncertainty of his unexpected outbursts of anger. Nor had Hal sought out anyone to live with. All was well left as it was.

Hal listened to the swirling wind as it swept around his house like a Banshee. Draughts were easily seen and fixed from the outside. Even the cement had suffered from the wearing winds of winter. To say Hal was deep in thought would have been incorrect. Hal had neither the vocabulary nor the inclination to take part in reflective thought. But Hal could feel, and his moods and feelings were reduced to good or bad. There was no gray. So it was that he 'contemplated' his condition in life and was satisfied. He had found a friend in Patches and for those who lack close connection with other humans, an animal takes the place necessary for the human spirit.

"Stop it you crazy mutt!" He scowled at Patches as he tried to lick Hal's stubby beard again and again. In rejection there was an air of acceptance and appreciation, for Hal this was an emotion closest to affection. While Hal could not find the words, he had found a place in military society and had experienced acceptance from his soldiers. He knew that everyone respected his bravery and leadership which had been displayed in their encounter with the enemy and although he might curse them all, they knew that Hal would give his life to save any of the twelve soldiers under his command what is more, Hal knew that he would do it if the situation called for it. This bond to the outside gave him a connection to the world of other men that he had not previously experienced in his life. This was all he needed. Hal let out a loud hack, a testament to years of cigar smoking.

Others, wrapped in winter greatcoats, trundled past his hut and heard the hacking. Some shook their heads. They saw him as the loneliest man on earth whose sole purpose was that of a soldier. Some walked by and deeply admired his blind courage, knowing it could save their own lives and end his. There was no one like Hal.

# CHAPTER TEN: WORRIED WOMEN

Anna and Rose were in a serious disagreement. The two sat teary eyed on Rose's bed, the letter from Rob sitting between them like some harbinger of bad news.

"Believe me Anna, I know what I am doing. Remember I am older than those children he had affairs with while at the Academy. I know the nature of the beast and how to handle him."

"If you see him as a beast why even think about responding to his letter?"

Anna was blind when it came to her brother nor did she have a low expectation of Rose's ability to handle Rob. She simply believed it was impossible that he could change.

"Rose, despite what you think, I find it impossible to believe that army life has changed him for the better. It is part of his character."

Anna's furrowed eyebrows demonstrated a distinct concern with Rose's decision to respond to Rob.

"Anna, it is only a letter. That's a far cry from having a relationship."

"Rose, you can believe that military life can give a person a new start on life but if you look at his behavior you will see that he has not changed.

Do you see him becoming a front line officer willing to put his life on the line for his country? No! All he cares about is getting promotion."

"You seem to forget Anna that working in the intelligence service has its own set of real dangers. What if he is captured on enemy ground? I think you give me too little credit. I am strong, older, and wiser in the ways of men, both good and bad and I give them the chance to act like a leopard and change their spots. Bear with me in this and for both of us it will be a test of Rob's honor and his ability to change. Anna, he knew you would tell me everything about his affairs. Why would he even take the chance to write if he believed there was no hope?"

"Rose, I believe that there is more than just his relationships with women at stake here. Father and Rob are as close as thieves about something. I don't think mother even knows." Anna was getting more and more frustrated with Rose.

"Yes Anna, and I believe that my own father is a part of their plans." Rose, unlike Anna, looked up to her father as an honest man. She believed that the war was not going to change that. Anna could see that whatever argument she came up with, Rose would counter it. Both had become silent, deep in her own thoughts.

"I have an idea Anna!" Rose prided herself on this one. "I will show you all the correspondence that occurs between the two of us. Will that help to settle your fears?

"Yes…yes, I suppose so," Anna's response was tentative. "But if you two meet you must promise me that you will have someone else present. Please promise me this Rose." Anna hammered her request home by taking Rose's two hands in hers and squeezing them emphatically.

"Fine, fine, fine," was Rose's response. She felt like she was being treated like a sixteen-year old rather than a twenty-two-year old. But Anna was one of her closest friends so she quietly accepted this ball and chain.

# CHAPTER ELEVEN:
# THE START OF THE STORM

Addy took her chances with this small adventure. She believed, and rightly so, that Ben still saw her as a good soldier and a leader of men. She decided to bypass the chain of command and seek Ben out personally. As she ventured her way to the headquarters' tent he just happened to be coming out. Her pace quickened. She saluted smartly.

"Excuse me, Major Halliday but could I have a word with you?" Ben returned the salute and came to a halt.

"Certainly Sergeant Brown, what can I do for you on this beautiful, sunny day?"

Ben was trying to be attentive with this soldier who had helped him with his letters. He respected both the intelligence and bravery the soldier exhibited.

"Sir, I know you will remember the exercises we undertook to improve our accuracy of firing from a distance. It was intended for all the companies." The memory of this brought the slightest crease to his brow and he raised his head. His memories, unlike hers, were clouded by some dimwit in Washington.

"Yes, of course, sergeant." Ben wondered what could be on the sergeant's mind.

"Well sir, I know that there are still supplies for those exercises left in the hands of the regimental quartermaster. I wonder if I could have permission to take the exercise one step further." Addy knew she was being very forward with Ben.

"What do you mean, sergeant?" With this statement Addy had hit a nerve in Ben's subconscious and he focused on her every word.

"Sir I would like to take the range of accurate fire up to three hundred yards. Think of the impact success at that distance would have on both sides." Ben was well aware of the implications. It could change the way this war was being fought and perhaps speed up its outcome.

"Of course sergeant, you have my permission. I will speak to your captain and you can take your men and set up a firing range. I wish you the best of luck. Please make sure that your captain writes me a report and gives it to me after you have finished your exercises." Ben brightened with the prospect that someone was willing to pick up his torch, but because of the letter from Washington it had to come from within the lower ranks. They had to have the initiative to make it a success.

"Thank you Ben…, I mean, Major Halliday."

Off she went, her gait quickened by her success. So it was on that following wintry day that Addie began her project. Men were sent in all directions. Requisitions had to be filled out, guns had to be cleaned, a shooting range with targets had to be built, and most of all Addy had to convince her winter worn comrades that this was worth their time. Within three days all was ready.

Ben had the political wherewithal to 'advise' the officers in her company lest they felt they were being left out of the chain of command and to avoid bad feelings between them and Ben or between the sergeant and the officers. Ben decided that he would casually appear at this exercise and handle Colonel Beasley in case he dared exit the warmth of his winter quarters to investigate the shooting. Addy spoke quietly to her men.

"We have permission to try and make ourselves even better riflemen. We will move the target range to three hundred yards and test for accuracy of fire at that distance. No Confederates would ever be ready to receive a volley at that distance. Success at this range could devastate their morale.

You made your own cartridges from the material left over from our first exercises, so you have no one to blame but yourself if they fail to work. Now remember that you must pay closer attention to the wind, if there is any, and the correction of your sights. Every gun might be different so don't be surprised if we are not on target right away. Your gun will have to be raised higher so remember to account for this with your sights. Are you ready to test this new range?" To her surprise a loud "Huzzah" greeted her last question.

"Any man, who fires a ramrod will collect firewood for three days!" With that order a chorus of cheers broke the still air and relaxed her men just enough to show more caution when aiming. Addy followed behind each soldier with the glass eye and tracked their shots. Her only comments were to give the location of the contact so that each soldier could readjust. Sometimes the readjustment was an over-correction. Sometimes the correction was dead on.

This sequence was repeated fifteen times and a pattern started to emerge. Only one soldier scored a hit in the first round. By the fifteenth-round their average was five, a direct result of repetition and correction. Not bad, Addy reflected to herself.

"Good shooting men. Remember your hits and tomorrow we will practice again. Dismissed" The soldiers talked among themselves as they ambled off. One private was taking a hard time for missing all fifteen shots!

Addy was so focused on her men that she did not see the crowd that had started to gather. Most significant of the crowd was Hal who was not to be outdone by this 'nigger loving upstart'. So the next day, after drill, as Addy and her men trudged their way to the firing range, what did they see but the large frame of Hal, hands on hips, barking out commands to his twelve men while Patches did his own barking as he chased sticks of wood thrown by his owner. Addy ignored these actions and repeated the drill from the previous day. Some minimal improvement occurred but she came to realize that this distance required more extensive practice. On the third day Addy and her men had to listen to the crackling of rifle fire to their left making it hard to hear and give corrections at the same time. Not about to have Hal simply copy her methods, she had her men halt as she arched her back and walked indignantly toward Hal. One of his men saw her coming, Hal prepared himself by facing her direction, puffing up his chest, and placing his hands on his hips in an air of defiance.

"Hal, you can practice all you want, but we have picked this time of day to fire. Can't you find someplace that is more appropriate and therefore not so distracting?"

"Well, mister sergeant man, who are you to give me orders?" His men nodded furiously in agreement, reinforcing Hal's bellicose stance. This day, Ben had followed Addy out to the firing range, and he recognized the need for stopping the problem before it developed.

"Sergeants, sergeants! Why is there a disagreement in such a worthy military cause? I have a suggestion. Why not have each sergeant fire ten rounds and the one with the most hits on the target gets to pick the time and place."

Both sergeants were taken off-guard. They had no choice but to accept what sounded like a reasonable idea. Two new targets were run out to the range. It was a chance to put the other one in his place, and so it began. Each took a turn aided by a potter. After eight rounds the score was tied at four apiece. Addy took her ninth shot.

"Hit!" The corporal barked. Now it was Hal's turn and suddenly he felt the pressure. His trigger hand started to sweat.

"Miss," barked the corporal. A slight smile appeared on Addy's mouth. She leveled her gun confidently.

"Hit!" shouted the corporal and with that a dozen kepis were thrown into the air. Hal didn't even finish taking his shots. He stormed from the field with Patches following in close pursuit. There was nothing he could say or do now. Ben began to wonder if this had been such a bright idea. These two did not need more animosity between them and he had embarrassed Hal in front of his men. He decided to have a talk with him.

****

Ben's talk with Hal never took place. Early one morning in the second week of April, his orderly roused him from sleep.

"Sir, General Ames wants you at a meeting at brigade headquarters at noon today."

Ben shook the cobwebs of sleep from his brain. "But Colonel Beasley should attend that meeting, not me."

"That is my second instruction sir. Colonel Beasley has a mild case of dysentery and has taken himself to the medical tent. The doctor said he was in no condition to travel and so the colonel instructed me to tell you that you were to take his place."

"Very well, private, thank you."

For this meeting Ben started by thinking of his appearance. A good grooming and wash up would be the first step. His uniform needed some minor repairs to the exhausted threads that held it together. He rose, went to the flap of his officer's cabin, and called the orderly who was trying to prepare some breakfast for Ben. Ben felt a twinge of guilt. He could hear the soldiers at morning drill. He knew that they hated it and there he was, the officer in temporary charge of the regiment barely awake. This was not like him. He must have needed some extra sleep, he rationalized to himself. He picked up his pace and moved quickly to perform his morning obligations.

Ben's mind wandered as he rode slowly to General Ames' headquarters about a mile distant. A small row of horses told Ben that he was late for the meeting. He dismounted quickly and holding his sword to his side, jogged to the general's tent. It was a mild April morning and Rob could see the three other colonels in the brigade in a relaxed position sitting around the general.

"I'm sorry to be late general but I just recently learned of Colonel Beasley's illness."

"No need to worry, major." Homer smiled. We will talk privately after this meeting.' With uncharacteristic gravity General Ames clutched his hands behind his back as he stood in front of his commanders, strode back and forth, collected his thoughts, and then began.

"Gentlemen, I am sure it will be no surprise to you that campaigning weather is upon us and I received orders from General Grant. First I will give you the very good news. General Grant has brought the Union some well needed victories that have opened the Tennessee River to us as a valuable route of communication. He has taken both Fort Henry and Fort Donelson. Neither was terribly costly, except to the Confederates.

"Let me remind you of the larger strategy of the Western Theater of operations. Our place in the Anaconda plan is simple. We are to capture Corinth, Mississippi and then close the Mississippi to Confederate military travel and those Southern planters and unscrupulous northerners who are still trading with each other. Personally, I believe the northerners are traitors and should be hung, but that is another topic. Secondly, by controlling the Mississippi we split the Confederacy almost in half, making their communications and operations even more hazardous. I am sure that this is not news to you. I repeat it because it will directly impact on this brigade."

That was the longest speech Ben had ever heard from Homer, but it was clear and to the point. Ben sat back and said little as the three colonels tried to gain knowledge and impress the general with their military acumen. Ben rationalized that this was the behavior of untested soldiers trying to posture their men and skills before they were even tested. The questions and rhetoric seemed endless, but finally the general cut it off and informed his colonels that he had another meeting to attend and that they should be ready to leave in three days.

General Ames waited until the officer congestion had settled down and then he sat, took out a cigar, lit it, stretched and crossed his legs. But there were furrows on his brow as he turned to Ben.

"Ben, just what the hell is going on down there? Is Beasley really ill or is it just another one of his drunken stupors?" Ben hesitated. He felt like a snitch despite the fact that he felt no real loyalty to his colonel. But if he had had his way this discussion would have been with Beasley *and* the general. He chose to answer, knowing that this was in the best interests of the regiment.

"Sir, it seems the regiment is without a leader. The colonel avoids decisions, spends most of his time drinking or is in the medical tent. What can we do?"

Homer flung his cigar away in complete frustration.

"I have sent more than one letter to General Grant but his solution is to let war take care of Colonel Beasley. He is too well-connected in Washington and Grant is not ready to throw away his own command on some self-destructive colonel." Homer paused and the furrows abated. Ben detected a wisp of a smile.

"I do have a plan. Ben I am going to promote you to lieutenant colonel as of this minute and I want you to tell me who should succeed you as major."

Ben was somewhat taken aback at this decision, but held it in.

"General, my choice would be Emile Lacroix. He is a natural soldier, experienced, a model for the men, and we both get along."

General Ames interrupted. "Say no more, Colonel Halliday. If you hadn't recommended him, I would have! Colonel, here are your silver oaks. Give your gold ones to Major Lacroix and offer him my congratulations. If Beasley protests, tell him to pay me a visit at my headquarters." Once again Homer paused and collected his thoughts. "Ben, you know your regiment is senior in this brigade, but remind the men that what action they saw was a mere introduction to the 'elephant'. Soon they will see large armies clash and that will be a serious attack on their make-up as men. God only knows where and when, but it will be soon. I never fear for myself Ben, I am not afraid of death. But I fear for those under me. I can't fight their personal wars. Somehow Ben, I know you will survive. Godspeed and I will be seeing you again." With that Ben changed his pins, saluted, and strode quickly to his horse.

April 2, 1862
Dear Father and Mother,

I hope this letter finds you healthy, and if possible, happy. The weather is warming up but the spring run off has flooded our camp. It is a good thing that we are preparing to move. I would guess that our trails will lead us to Tennessee. My soldiers are much excited and looking for action.

I don't think it was the inaction itself that has their blood up. Far too many of the men came down with the measles and other such diseases. They have come to associate prolonged stays with disease. In our brigade about seventy men died over the winter and the sight of a burial detail frequently passing one's tent became a far too common occurrence. The men can find no solace in this kind of death because they have not had a chance to test their manhood. It seems a death without honor. After all, isn't it one's honor that keeps one going? They even feel that they have not had a chance to prove their Christianity to God. They believe that courage on the battlefield is associated with pleasing God. It is better to die with a bullet to the head or with your body parts strewn about the battlefield. Then, according to my men, you have done God's work, for it is his will if you live or die.

At first I thought that these ideas were all hogwash, that they have not seen enough of war to have such ideas, but upon reading some of their letters from home I understand some of their thinking. It is not unusual to find reminders from wives and parents encouraging their boys to do their duty for God and the Union. This is even at the expense of their loved ones' lives. I guess my experience out west has caused me to think differently.

I hope that you are glad to see the signs of spring. The renewal of nature brings joy to my heart knowing that even in our nation's darkest moments God gives us the chance to nurture our good soil and live out our lives to the fullest. Until I hear from you stay well and pray for us all.

With all my love,

Ben

"So Colonel Halliday, the rumors are true!" The bitterness and cynicism in Beasley's voice spoke volumes. "When things don't go your way you run off to that damn friend of yours, Ames!"

Ben bit his lip, trying hard not to say anything he would regret.

"I warned you before Halliday, that my influence stretches a considerable distance, but you have chosen to ignore this. I will have a personal meeting with your good friend, the general, and we will discover who is in command. Believe me, I can make your life a misery. I think I will start immediately.

You will be my lackey, my errand boy." Beasely roared in laughter as he pictured a humbled lieutenant colonel standing before him. Ben had stopped listening to this foolishness and chose to watch his undulating layers of fat flapping like a poor beached whale.

"May I visit with Major Lacroix, Colonel Beasley?"

"Yes, yes, I think I will give you the honor of giving him your oaks." Ben saluted, wheeled, and then left, listening to the outrageous laughter emanating from the tent. Soldiers walking by either laughed or stared in disbelief.

Emile was relaxing outside his wet winter quarters, soaking in the bright spring sun.

"Hello, Major Lacroix, you look comfortable. It is difficult to imagine that we are in the middle of a civil war fighting for our survival."

"What, what do you mean?" Emile sputtered, jumping to his feet.

"You are the best we have, Emile. The general already had you in mind for a promotion."

"Thank you, Ben." Emile humbly accepted his gold oaks and Ben gave him a summation of the situation with the colonel.

"Emile, it will be our task to keep Beasley from ruining this regiment and at the same time preventing the men from killing him. That could be the harder task. At the same time we must assume that we will lead this regiment…"

Ben did not have time to finish. Beasley's orderly requested that he and Emile meet him immediately at General Ames' headquarters. Both officers looked at each other and knew that this meant confrontation.

They arrived, only to find four colonels and their staff members in a semi-circle around General Ames.

"Gentlemen, we have received our marching orders. We are to break camp immediately, march to the nearest railhead for transport to the Tennessee River and join with the Army of the Tennessee commanded by General Grant. It will be our first campaign as a brigade. Honor demands that we put forth our best effort and learn from our mistakes. Our objective is Corinth, Mississippi and when taken it will serve as a base of command for further operations. Be prepared to march by 9:00 a.m. and may God be with the righteous in this noble cause."

****

At times like these men react according to their own peculiar prescription. Laughter and bravado often hid a deep inner fear of the unknown. Others' words are likely to pull those with emotional uncertainty into this air of false comfort. Others could be heard praying, often rote prayers that they had learned as children on their mother's knee. The prayers were intended to calm their restless souls and find succor from God so that they would do their duty. Still others went about organizing their equipment with a quiet, reserved demeanor. These soldiers had a broader range of inner thoughts. Some were glad to be about their duties, others were in a stupor, shocked that the moment of sacrifice was finally upon them and staring them in their eyes.

One day later these same men found themselves standing about alone, or in groups, on the decks of a paddle wheeler heading up the Tennessee River. Addy leaned against the outer wall of a cabin vacantly admiring the arrival of spring to this river system. Fast flowing waters carried a variety of flotsam. The water level was elevated, covering flooded banks and giving greater breadth to the river. As they passed small towns, children waved, sometimes encouraging them to smite the rebels. In other towns the chorus echoed a Confederate flavor and the local band was present and playing its slaughtered version of Dixieland and the shouts of 'invading devils'. Tennessee was by no means a unified state on the issue of separation. Addy noted that the borders of this war could be found in the minds of men not on the actual landscape. For in this war, unlike most wars, land was not the goal. Addy sighed to herself after these thoughts. With the promotion of Emile, Lt. Hostings had become Captain Hostings. He spoke to Addy.

"Sergeant, take your men to the bales of straw on the upper deck. There are rumors that Tennessee rebs have created hazards for boats like ours. Remember, keep a sharp eye and cock your hammers. You will have little time to react as we are moving quickly." Addy grabbed just her basic equipment and hurried to her men who were sitting quietly, deep in thought.

"It is time. Assume your positions on the open deck above!" Up the narrow, metal stairs the dozen men marched, their hobbled brogans beating out a loud cadence on the stairways.

"Place two men to a bale. Watch for the bright reflection of gun barrels and puffs of smoke from the bluffs if we encounter any of the enemy."

Ben had given Emile the task of creating marksmen groups on each boat lest they be totally surprised if local militia groups loyal to the Confederacy harass the troops' movement. What followed was not foreseen.

Rounding a bend in the river, the Tennessee suddenly narrowed to a mere fifty yards and sped up as it was funneled furiously through a narrows. This would make a fine spot for an attack. To make matters worse, the gunboats assigned to protect them had not yet met them, they were coming downstream. Homer Ames, aboard the brigade's 'flagship', sensed the difficulty immediately. There was no choice. It was too late to turn around. He ordered the lead captain to proceed at full speed. Many of the soldiers sensed something was afoot and instinct drove them to the rails rather than look for cover.

It was too late. From well-hidden trenches two rows of Rebels appeared like a silent hawk waiting from above to pounce on its victim below. Their first row knelt and the second stood. Within seconds of entry into the narrows the hawks pounced. Following a signal shot, a volley of shots echoed from their commanding positions and disappeared in a cloud of smoke. Union soldiers on the first three boats fell from all locations on the boats. The main deck, the cabin deck, and the unprotected third deck, all took the hits. They were doomed by the location to move into this barrage of lead. It was as if some mechanical giant had spewed the contents of its irritated stomach to relieve itself. Four regiments of terrified soldiers clamored to find their guns and head for the inner cabins or prostate themselves on the decks to return fire. A second volley, in organized precision, aimed at the cabin houses to take care of those sailing these non-military craft.

For her part, Addy fought back furiously. They were at least prepared for battle and had a four shot head start on their fellow soldiers. They could see some of their shots creating holes in the Rebel ranks while taking few hits. She hoped that some of the fleet had done likewise to slow down the onslaught from above.

General Ames was in the first boat and ordered the engines at full speed to escape the attack. Ben was in the second boat and realized that the wooden shells of the vessels could not withstand close quarter gun fire even if it was from smoothbore muskets. Due to logistical problems he had wound up with a battalion of the Fifty Second Iowa Volunteers and for whatever reason, he seemed to be the ranking officer.

"Men, take all the tables and chairs you can find and line them against both sides." He found himself screaming at the men. "Any sergeants or officers try and organize volley fire as quickly as possible."

The Iowa men responded well to Ben's commands. Ben decided to run up the stairs to the third deck and found utter chaos and confusion. A major of the same regiment had seen fit to hide under a chair and issue orders from there. Ben took a hard look at this major's face and he would not forget it.

"Men, go to a kneeling position to lessen the target area. Load…" he waited, "Now ready, aim, fire." It was hard to tell if there had been any effect on the Rebs but at least there was some organization. Men were falling around him, the victims of poor preparation. The Rebs were firing 'buck and ball' and its result was devastating to the boat's frame. Men were now falling victim to arrows like splinters as the old wood gave in without any ability to resist. More than one man had arrow-shaped pieces of shrapnel pierce their eye sockets, leaving them in a bloodied mess and harrowing pain. Still, the remaining pointed guns at their enemy and rejoiced in seeing bodies fall from the cliffs into the swirling waters below. Ben jumped over the fallen bodies to reach the stern and view events from this vantage point.

"Oh, my God!" he blurted out to no one in particular. The boat behind them, carrying the rest of the Fifty-Second

Iowa had obviously lost its power and was trying to drift downriver but its paddle wheel embedded into the walls of the narrows. Casting his glance upwards Ben could see the Confederates, like a pack of wild dogs firing relentlessly into the cabin and third deck of this craft. Ben could hear their officers yelling at their men to 'pour it on'. Ben made a mental note to find out what group it was.

Ben had his first taste of grenades. Small groups of Confederates hurled them from above onto all the decks. Soon a conflagration had consumed most of the superstructure and human torches threw themselves into the boiling water rather than face a fiery death.

What had seemed like hours had been but fifteen minutes and the toll was deadly. The onslaught from above abated as they moved away from the narrows. Now it was time to deal with the carnage. Except for that one boat deaths and injuries were tolerable. After all, the period of contact had been brief,... but effective.

The boats carrying doctors ran up crosses and the most serious cases were transferred to these crafts as soon as they reached calm waters. Little else could be done at this point. The best they could do was to make haste to Pittsburgh Landing, Grant's camp.

# CHAPTER TWELVE:
# THE SOUTHERN WAY

The movements of General Grant's army did not go unnoticed by the Confederacy. They too recognized the potential danger posed by the splitting of the Confederacy. Corinth had to be defended. The Union had approximately 100,000 men between Missouri and Tennessee. The Confederates were forced to respond. It was then in the early months of 1862 that Jefferson Davis saw fit to re-act as quickly as possible. Concerned with this possible threat, Major-General Leonidas Polk marched his small army of 8,000 soldiers into Kentucky to thwart any Union advance.

August 30, 1861
To: Major-General Albert Sidney Johnston

I have long respected you as one of the Confederacy's most capable generals. It is because of this respect that I am sending you to the west in order to protect our integrity as a united nation. You are to take your own army with you (17,000) and build a much larger force to be known as the Army of the Mississippi. Draw from other commands and build a strong force. This must be done quickly and an attack can be made against whatever Union army first appears. We must defeat them before they bring all their forces to bear.

I wish you God's speed in this adventure and rely on your abilities as a leader to save the western Confederate states.

Jefferson Davis
President The Confederate States of America

March 12, 1862
To: President Jefferson Davis (C.S.A.)

Mr. President, after much effort and challenge I have assembled an army from our scarce resources. Soldiers have been drawn from as far away as the Gulf Coast to engage this army being assembled by General Grant. I have chosen Major-General J.P.T. Beaureguard as my second in command. I know you clash with this arrogant Creole but he does have successful battle experience as a leader (First Bull Run). Polk will assume command of the First Corps, Major-General Braxton Bragg (16,000 soldiers) the Second Corp, the Third Corps will be commanded by Major-General William Hardee (7,000) and believed to be a fine leader, as he is well-versed in the school of the military. Our Reserve Corps will be led by Major-General John Breckinridge (7,000). I will hold him back as he is a political appointee and has never seen command or battle.

I fear that our leaders are somewhat inexperienced at high levels of command and we can only hope that they quickly learn the realities of the battlefield and are able to work as one to smite the Yankees. As we now assemble at Corinth I expect our advance to begin in the first week of April.

Pray for our success on the battlefield and that with God's help we will stem the Yankee advance.

Yours in God,
Major-General A.S. Johnston C.S.A.

March 29, 1862

To: Major-General J.P.T. Beauregard (Adjutant, the Army of the Mississippi)

Dear General,

I hope this communique finds you in fine health and ready to fight. It is now imperative that we march against General Grant before he can join forces with Major-General Juan Carlos Buell. If that event occurs I fear we would be greatly outnumbered and unable to advance and defeat both Union Armies.

It is my plan to put our four corps in column and advance on the enemy. Such a structure would provide relief from the initial attack and keep these rear troops fresh. The terrain upon which we will fight is cut with ravines and forested areas and would make it difficult as we spread out into line. Our forces are untested in battle. Caution should be the key consideration of our plan.

However, in this situation I defer to your presence in the area and considerable knowledge of the fields upon which we must fight. I would appreciate your reflection upon my plan.

God save the Confederacy,
Major-General A.S. Johnston (Commanding the Army of the Mississippi)

April 1, 1862

To: Major General A.S. Johnston (Commanding the Army of the Mississippi)

Dear General,

You are quite correct General. We must move with all haste to meet the enemy, but I have another plan in mind. I would like to deploy each corps in line as follows: Hardee, Bragg, and Polk; and hold Breckinridge in close reserve. This plan will give us a three mile front as we move our forces between Lick Creek and Owl Creek and trap Grant in this narrowing funnel. Our flanks will envelop his flanks and he will be unable to escape. I strongly encourage you to adapt this new plan.

Yours in God,

Major-General J.P.T. Beaureguard (Adjutant, Army of the Mississippi)

April 2, 1862
To: Major General J.P.T. Beauregard (Adjutant, Army of the Mississippi)

Dear General,

It is with some hesitation that I accept your plan of action. Deployment by lines requires experienced soldiers. To move such large forces from marching in column to battle lines and to hold those lines connected, as we move forward, would be a challenge for veteran soldiers. The dispersal of artillery will endanger our forces. They will not have sufficient artillery support. As I understand the situation, General Bragg's army has not yet reached Corinth and I hazard this could delay our advance. However, I recognize your skill in operational planning and will enact your plan.

Pray for a Confederate victory,

Major-General A.S. Johnston (Commanding the Army of the Mississippi)

****

April 4, 1862

Dear Father and Mother,

I hope this letter finds you both in good health and that father has recovered from that kick by the bull. I had always stayed away from him and left his care to father. At this time we are only one day into a march from Corinth, Mississippi to engage the Unionists. The congregation of men, artillery, and supply carts, tells me this will be a grand campaign, although as a mere captain I am told little of the high strategy.

As I sit in my tent writing this letter I can reflect on the horrid day and evening spent by my company as we moved forward through woods, struggling up and down ravines of various sizes. At the bottom of each ravine there was an oozing quagmire of chilling mud and water, mixed with the accoutrements of soldiers who had shed or lost their equipment in these vile cesspools. Add to this the excrement of the straining beasts and one is offered up a blend of odors too horrendous to describe. The men were ordered to finish the job started by some poor brace of mules that were up to their bellies in some cases. Our men took hold of the sides to try and extricate beast and cart. The animals were barely able to extract their hooves from the sucking motion of these bogs which seem to come alive and reach up with sprays of mud and pull their intended victims even further into the dark abyss. Oaths and groans accompanied this activity as the mules brayed piteously. Sergeants hurled epithets at men who vocalized too loudly. They feared that the sound of struggle would be heard by Union pickets. Ironically, more noise was being made by foolish soldiers who clamored through the woods chasing deer. Some were so foolish as to test their muskets to make sure their powder was still dry. It was difficult to believe this cacophony of soldiery brought no response from the enemy.

Many of these men have already been ravaged by the scourge of dysentery and are in a weakened state. Our own company had to leave fifteen men behind, so desperate was their medical condition.

By the time you receive this letter we will have engaged the enemy and once again added more laurels to the Confederate cause. May God speed us to an early end to this war.

Your Loving Son,

Samuel

By the time Major-General Johnston arrived on the scene the problems had intensified. The delays due to impassable roads was compounded by the shear congestion of the large number of humans and material needed to fight a large scale battle. In addition the quirks of generals and the corps were beginning to show. Major-General Hardee refused to move his troops without written orders from his commanding general. Major-General Braggs had managed to lose a whole brigade, and the changing moods of Major-General

Beauregard had led him to suggest canceling the attack and returning to Corinth.

At this point Major-General Johnston took things in hand. He called his corps commanders together and ordered them in no uncertain terms to get on with the attack. Beauregard was concerned about soldiers fighting on empty stomachs but this was countered by Johnston who was adamant in proclaiming that his army could feast on the Federal camp when they captured it.

****

Unforgivable. Such were the afterthoughts of many a commander regarding Major-General Grant's decision to refuse to mount a defensive position for his soldiers as they encamped around Pittsburgh Landing between Owl and Lick Creeks. Until the actual start of the battle Grant believed that the Confederates were still encamped at Corinth. His division commanders were no wiser, sending out a few pickets to distances of no more than one or two hundred yards.

At the vanguard of his forward positions was the Fifty-third Ohio, a regiment greener than the spring grass and untrained even in basic drill. This was thanks to its old and nervous commander, Colonel Jesse Appler. However, Appler was not totally lacking concern like that of the Army commander. Some of his pickets had spotted the glint of brass cannons in the distance. This report caused Appler to send out a larger detachment to investigate. They were soon fired upon by Major-General Hardee's pickets and hastened a quick retreat to report that they indeed been attacked by a line of soldiers 'dressed in butternut', so they reported.

Appler promptly and correctly sent this information to his division commander, Major-General W.T. Sherman. The general insulted Appler with his lack of concern and as the message was being yelled to Colonel Appler, his men clearly heard Sherman's comments. Quickly they broke ranks and returned to harvesting delicacies from the environs.

However Major James Powell of the Twenty-fifth Missouri received reports from his pickets of a vast number of campfires in the distance. Powell reported this to his brigade commander, Colonel E. Peabody. The Twenty- fifth was a part of General Prentiss' division. He responded by ordering Powell to take out a reconnaissance force of three hundred men. Barely half a mile from camp they encountered Confederate infantry commanded by Major Aaron Hardcastle's Third Mississippi battalion. His skirmishers fired and fell back. The Federals returned a volley. Powell decided to stand his ground and fight. And so the first engagement struck the opening chorus of this grand symphony. Little did its participants expect what followed.

**\*\*\*\***

Having recovered from their harrowing experience on the Tennessee River, the men of General Ames' brigade was issued orders to join Major-General John Mclernand's first division. The rest of this division was already settling in to camp for the night. The heavy smells of frying beef and coffee mingled to leave a typical odor of a federal camp that was not directly engaged with the enemy. The still evening, combined with moist air, left the steam from dinners hanging like a vast hand of a spirit hovering above. For the men of Ames' brigade it was cause to salivate after sucking and chewing on hardtack all day.

The men of the Twentieth had snapped mental images of the other Union divisions near the landing and somehow felt diminished in significance in the presence of a full army that numbered more than 40,000 soldiers. For them it was humbling and strange, for they had landed on a very different landscape. Their small encounter with the enemy seemed to diminish as well.

Upon disembarking from the river transport they saw open land mingled with decaying stumps of ancient trees, but this quickly disappeared into dense woods and occasional open fields that reflected years of human toil. The navy had plundered the woods in the immediate area in search of wood to feed their hungry boilers. There was no need to do this job methodically, so the navy took what was best and easiest to reach. It was as if some insatiable beavers had their way with the landscape. Steep ravines, small banks, and muddy creeks lined the landscape on either side.

Last to arrive, General Ames' men were left whatever space they could find. What this meant was settling in along a line of trees and in the woods itself. The brigade of 2,000 men also made their impact on the land. They hacked away at the small trees developing near the fringe of the woods. As luck would have it many had to pitch tents on sloping ground which led to more precipitous ravines. Grumbling could be heard up and down the line as men fought to establish residence. Gone were the neat, u-shaped company camps that had been their homes for many months. The measure of their discomfort was prophetically aired by one soldier.

"I hope this battle starts soon so we can get out of this mess and settle into a proper camp." Little did he know how soon his wishes would come true.

Some things had definitely not changed. Colonel Beasley had continued to harass and even mock his troops on their camp making or chastise Ben for letting his men get away with such an awkward settlement. His treatment of Ben was just a continuation of his belief that Ben and General Ames were trying to undermine his authority. Beasley was one of those people who had no capacity to see himself in the context of the world around him, thus he fantasized about mythic plots.

Beasley had filed another report with General Ames complaining that he was constantly being undermined by his two staff officers. If anything, Ben and Emile had gone out of their way to prompt Beasley with situations where he could take direct command of the men. Every time Ames received one of these reports he filed them, planning to use them when the proper time arose. For now he had the luxury of an impending battle to explain away his disregard for these complaints. The Twentieth was the only regiment that had gone into battle. He assumed battle would be in line, but one look at the woods around him told him that the battle would unfold differently. During the winter he had carefully noted the apparent strengths of his regiment as he watched them move from column to line, a difficult command. But he had never put the four regiments together. Now he wondered if he had made a serious mistake. He had instead focused on working with regimental captains to identify candidates for the important role as sergeants. These men would be the backbone of the regiments and create elan in their men.

After observing the four regiments he decided to locate the two sister regiments to the right side of his line. The Twentieth would be center-left in position and firmly anchored to support the less developed Fifty-second Iowa. Homer hoped that the Twentieth would help hold this Iowa regiment together if things started to go badly. He felt that the only soldier to read through his battle formation would be Ben and that he could keep his eye on the Fifty-second.

He also hoped The Grey Ghost was up to his usual ability to flash from one regiment to another if it was necessary. His horse's ability as a morale raiser might keep them in the field longer.

The Twentieth ate their hurried dinners and were ordered to get as much rest as possible. Having gained the respect of their fellow regiments, soon the whole brigade was at rest. It was an order that came easily to these men after their harrowing experience on the Tennessee.

****

Major-General A.S. Johnston was a leader of men and a fighter by nature, but delays had taken a chunk out of the spirit of this brave officer. Johnston headed to the right wing of his army where he feared that his army was not strong enough to commence a sweep around the Union left. He wished he had listened to his own instincts about the strategy being employed.

****

Colonel Appler and his men were the first to make close contact with the Confederates. Each of the Union divisional commanders had no view of the future battlefields. Colonel Appler was the first to have that vision. A soldier from Powell's battalion staggered into Appler's camp with a screaming message: "They're coming, get into line!"

Looking at his untenable camp Appler wasted no time making his decision and began a retreat but stopped at a ridge covered with brush and placed his men in the prone position. Just as he did so, Major-General Sherman raced up on the first of four steeds he was to ride this day. Still not convinced that this was an attack in force, Sherman changed his mind when fire from the Confederates suggested an enveloping tactic by the Rebs. The ball that struck his right hand finished his decision-making process and he carefully jotted a note with his good hand.

To: Major-General Mclernand(Commanding First Division, Army of the Tennessee

The situation is developing quickly. My left flank is exposed and is weakly held by two regiments already in retreat. Send two brigades immediately. I stress the situation is urgent.

Major-General W.T. Sherman (Commanding Fifth Division, Army of the Tennessee)

****

Homer Ames could hear the gunfire intensifying and the reverberation from a number of batteries told him artillery was now involved. He did not wait for orders, sending riders out to each regimental commander. Then he took the time to send out a second written command.

To: Colonel Beasley (Commanding the Twentieth Regular Infantry)

Colonel Beasley, your men must be prepared to lead our brigade into battle. Thus you will assume lead regiment in our march to the front. Have your men prepared to move immediately.

Brig. General Homer Ames (Commanding Fourth Brigade, First Division,
Army of the Tennessee)

The waiting runner took the paper, spurred and wheeled his horse, and headed off in the direction of the Twentieth.

Homer missed nothing when it came to the abilities of horsemen. He stored that man's face in his memory and knew he would use him for important rides. It was at times like this that he missed O'Mara who they later learned had been shot from his horse delivering that message to General Grant.

Within a short period of time the aforementioned courier returned and skidded to a halt in front of General Ames.

"Sorry, sir!" He exclaimed.

"Never apologize for skill corporal. Oh, by the way I am adding you to my staff. Do you have any objections?"

"Absolutely not, general!" He almost shrieked out his response. General Ames could not fail to notice the broad smile that shone on the man's countenance. Ames believed that to subdue the horror of war one had to take joy in these small moments. If only there were more soldiers like him. His strong shoulders heaved a sigh as he thought of the many good soldiers like this man who would not see tomorrow's dawn. He had not finished this thought when another rider, moving like the wind, also came to an abrupt halt in front of him.

"General Ames?" He questioned.

"Yes, soldier."

"I bring an urgent message from General Mclernand. He requests that you march your brigade at the double-quick to reinforce General Sherman near Shiloh Church. General Raith will also be marching there and join forces with you!"

"I understand soldier, and we'll be ready to march in fifteen minutes!"

"Very good, general. I will relay your response to General Mclernand!"

The young officer from Mclernand's staff wheeled and threw clods of wet morning sod in the direction of the general. Homer first located Shiloh Church on his field map, then with a well-worn pencil traced a route of march on the map that did not look much more than a widened cart path. Runners were sent to the commanders of the regiments, identifying the route they would be marching. Upon receiving this information the drums of battle began to roll in each camp.

Ben had taken the orders for the Twentieth, started the drums rolling and quickly rode to Beasley's tent and burst into it despite the pleadings of the orderly.

"Sir, we must lead a march to Shiloh Church. We must prepare to leave at once!"

Beasley was stretched on his cot, his chubby legs crossed and in no particular hurry.

"Colonel Halliday, why wasn't I given these orders?" The colonel grumbled, using his casual manner to show his defiance of being treated irregularly. "I do not move on a drum roll, possibly meant for others. I need written orders man. Also, how is it that you know about leading the column? That information should have been sent."

Ben was in no mood to debate the orders. His face reddened at the deliberate slow and tedious manner of the colonel. He whirled and for the umpteenth time stormed from Beasley's tent. He spotted Emile mounting his horse and motioned for the major to join him.

"Major, have all captains form companies at the small clearing over there by that small path. No baggage, water only, and have them fix bayonets here. God knows what we will find."

Emile sensed the urgency in Ben's voice and dashed off to prepare each captain for the rapid march. As soon as Emile left, Beasley was out standing at the front of his tent in his underwear.

"Colonel I gave you no such instructions. I am the colonel of this regiment not you!" He blubbered.

"You are correct Colonel, you gave no such orders, but in this situation someone has to take charge and move the men." Ben could not be bothered to even look at this foolish man, granted he had slightly pushed his command.

"You have not heard the end of this, Colonel Halliday!" This time it was Beasley's turn to wheel on one foot and hurry back to his tent, a plan already forming in his corrupted mind.

As Ben stood there he could see The Grey Ghost appear in the distance, his skilled rider leaping over logs and skimming the edges of trees. His sudden stop through earth and grass tossed both onto a half-dozen soldiers. Sheepishly he apologized to the soldiers, who, due to their respect for the general, only laughed.

"Colonel Halliday where is Colonel Beasley?" The look on Ben's face told him it was time to begin fuming inside that some foolish excuse was bound to be the answer.

"In his tent, sir." Ben gulped.

"Doing what?" Ben could only cast his eyes in the direction of the colonel's tent.

General Ames wasted no time and rode directly to the open flap on the front of the tent. Homer got what he wanted and a huge plume of earth fell on and in the tent. Beasley was now in full uniform and fumed and stammered at this intrusion.

"Bailey where are you? I need to be cleaned, Beasley's pathetic voice cried out for his orderly.

Poor Bailey had to force himself not to laugh as he swept the colonel's uniform while Beasley stood there like a filthy scarecrow. Homer had dismounted and waited until he could gain Beasley's full attention. Then he approached him, lips pursed and eyes turned to slits. Homer tried to keep a civil voice.

"Colonel, you have clearly ignored the drums and my personal instructions. Sir, you are leading the finest regiment in this command and they expect the highest quality of leadership. Can you do that Colonel?"

Beasley was preparing a response but the General continued on.

"There is no possible response colonel, so I expect you to be on your horse and ready to lead this command in five minutes. I am giving that much time out of respect for the orderly who has the task of saddling and bridling your horse. I don't think you quite understand. The battle is on the verge of commencing and we have a ways to go, to take our place in the line. Furthermore Colonel, I will be up and down the line of march and if you make any more foolish decisions I will not fail to remove you from field command." Now it was Homer's turn to make the famous wheeled turn and leave the presence of this illegitimate leader.

****

Now at the march and doing so at the double-quick, the four regiments could only move in columns of two's. This meant the brigade was stretched out too far from one end to the other. Should they encounter Confederates they would be at a distinct disadvantage. The Twentieth drew ahead, not so much because they were in better condition but because they had churned up the ground with their hobnailed shoes. Ben recognized the futility of making a march at the double-quick in this muck. He asked Colonel Beasley if he could check the integrity of the column. Beasley answered by simply throwing up a hand. Ben interpreted this gesture as a 'yes'. Before he left, he leaned across to Major Lacroix and whispered to him to try and keep up the pace. Emile simply nodded. He turned his horse and cantered down the line which was starting to resemble a snake that had been stretched to its limit.

The men in the other regiments seemed to recognize him and tried to give him space to maneuver quickly. Occasionally a soldier would yell out

"We'll give 'em hell, don't you worry colonel!"

"Good luck colonel, we'll pray for you!" Three quarters down the column he found Homer uncharacteristically ranting and cursing at a captain from an Iowa regiment. He was certainly justified. The officer was taking all the good hard ground while his men wallowed in the ooze.

Both officers met and agreed that the path they were taking seemed to be taking them away from the sound of heavy fighting. Ben took advantage of the opening in the conversation.

"General, I am sure you have seen the difficulty of this march and that time is not our friend. Sir, if we try to use some scythes to mow down this long grass at the front of the column we can switch to columns of fours…"

Ben was cut off quickly by the General. "Ben I have ridden off into the woods and heard voices of panic. They were men in blue and one bore the flag of the Fifty-third Ohio." "Thank you for at least having a plan which is more than I can say for the generals of this command. I suggest we halt the march, send out pickets and when our other regiments have fully caught up we will leave this track if we have to and move in the direction of heaviest firing. But by all means we must keep brigade unity. We have about twenty seven hundred actives and that is a good size brigade by most standards. Oh…" Homer added in afterthought. "I have sent a runner to General Sherman requesting the immediate presence of artillery support."

****

Stories about the abilities of colonels and regiments travel quickly in an untested army. They look for men of honor and courage, for this what keeps them going. General Ames had acquired a respected position, probably from the lips of General Grant and from those below him in the chain of command. When Homer's runner finally found the general the name Ames tweaked a spot in his memory. He also knew any veteran regiment was worth a whole brigade on occasion. Sherman did not hesitate to act and found a battery of three inch ordnance rifles available for the colonel. Understanding the logic of Homer's plan he added two untested napoleons from a newly formed battery to join and aid the general. The ordnance rifles were mounted on horse artillery so they could move faster when the ground permitted. He knew that they would be somewhere near General Prentiss so he sent them off in that direction.

Meanwhile the Twentieth and their fellow regiments kept slogging through mud, over bushes and around trees, avoiding watery sloughs of mystery, and always moving closer to the sound of the guns. Suddenly they came upon a wider road. Wounded soldiers leaning against trees informed them that this was the Corinth Road, the main route to the very town of the same name. Ben requested that Colonel Beasley rest the men so that all the companies and regiments could tighten their marching formation. Meanwhile, Ben rode ahead with the sound of spent balls whizzing by him. Then he saw it, the unobtrusive, white, small Shiloh Church. Their goal was to find the Union troops fighting at this location. Unknown to Ben they had begun their strategic and necessary withdrawal to the protection of the 'sunken road'.

Ben rode to a knoll to find the location of the brigade. To avoid being trapped in the chaotic Union withdrawal he prayed that they were close by. To his relief his eyes quickly picked up the sight of a long column of blue moving like a river of men flowing to some lake or ocean. Ben spurred the little mare towards this welcome sight. Returning to the column he came upon General Ames in conversation with Colonel Beasley.

"You must move these men faster Beasley, the Rebs are close on our heels."

Ben could tell the general had been galloping, since The Grey Ghost was frothing at the mouth and heaving even under the saddle. Homer would not have pushed his horse unless the situation was becoming desperate. Without turning Beasley responded.

"Certainly, general."

Ben looked at Beasley and saw him roll his eyes in contempt of the general's order with the attitude that this was all a waste of time and energy. Ben noted, once again how little it took to bring out this man's weaknesses.

****

By 9:00 a.m., unknown to Ames' brigade, the battle or more correctly, battles, were developing and showing signs of a complete Confederate victory. But even in defeat the struggling Fifty-third had had an impact. The attack of the

Sixth Mississippi had been made at a tremendous cost. Over seventy percent of its troops had been lost and only sixty men stood in its ranks. The same regiment had earlier plundered Major-General Prentiss' forward positions and pillaged his camp looking for food. Many of these Confederates had not eaten for twenty-four hours. However, the greater acquisitions came in the form of artillery left behind by fleeing artillerists who had not bothered to spike their guns. Confederate artillerists simply had to turn the guns around and begin firing at the fleeing Union troops.

Ben left Emile to cope with Beasley. Now the Twentieth was marching admirably in columns of fours. He came upon Homer's adjutant directing soldiers up a path that spiraled up a vertical ascent of fifteen feet. The adjutant indicated that this was a short cut to what one might call the lines of battle. Ben tested his horse's agility and strength. He rarely had to spur this animal but this time it was necessity. The poor beast huffed and puffed with the aid of Ben's spurs. The artillery could never make this climb, but the adjutant pointed out a circuitous route that would eventually bring them to the same spot.

The scene before him was a kaleidoscope of chaos. On this field of about ten square acres Union soldiers were frantically retreating. They raced as if the angel of death itself was preparing to swarm down on them. Some were forced to side-step toppled tents which had also become the victims of haste. Some carried muskets, others had thrown away all their baggage. Some yelled wildly and warned of imminent calamity if they could not reach the Tennessee. It was as if they were giving impromptu speeches to a heard of galloping humans. The panic seized doubters by the collars and dragged them into the melee. All had one characteristic in common:

their eyes were popping out of their sockets and darting from one obstacle to another.

Dead and wounded soldiers intermingled with the escapees who trod upon them on their road to freedom. Strange how brotherhood flees when panic takes the field. Amid this scene and in spite of it were groups of staunch defenders heeding the commands of brave officers and disciplined sergeants. It was a stark contrast. Stopping to view the scene left Ben with a knot in his stomach. Would his men flee? What he didn't know was that this scene was taking place on other fields of the battlefield. In Ben's mind, these gallant few were men of honor. Not only did they have to fear the explosive effects of shell and ball, but the bayonet if they were caught from behind by a Confederate. Some threw their hands high in the air surrendering themselves to a conquering master. Ben felt no compassion for those that fled. Nor did he have any desire to join the melee and use his revolver to halt this desperate escape. Tomorrow these men would have to look into their souls to patch together the threads of honor that remained.

Ben absorbed all of this in seconds. He hurried a retreat to find General Ames. Soon he spotted Homer flying to and fro trying to keep each regiment to attempt a right wheel. It became clear what regiments had taken the time to learn this movement. What was also clear was the absence of the grand strategy of General Grant. Now their strategy was simply to get the brigade up to the short cut and onto the field and prepare a defensive arch in case a Confederate attack should catch them unawares.

Homer, in the meantime, had sent runners to General Grant to determine where they should position the brigade. The answer was not long in coming.

The Twentieth now found itself out of its proper marching order, but at that point it seemed unimportant. The brigade had to fit itself into the position where they were most needed on the field of battle.

****

Finally, Addy had a moment to examine her environment. Directly in front of her, ten feet away, lay a dead Union soldier still clutching his Springfield. He died with his sky blue eyes wide open. The pool of blood around his head formed a perfect circle. Flies were buzzing around him waiting to lay their eggs. He was only a boy, perhaps eighteen. Then her mind began to take on the persona of the dead boy. Why did I have to die today? Why did I have to die so young? What would my children have been like? How will my parents react to the loss of their only son? Who will take over the farm when father dies? Is my cousin still alive? She was broken from this peculiar mind game by the wet tongue of Patches who was making his way down the first rank, encouraging soldiers to move on.

"Get back here you crazy mutt and find your proper place!" Hal barked gruffly at the dog. It was only then that she realized how physically close she was to Hal. Without thinking she turned in his direction. Hal could feel her gaze with his gift of peripheral vision. He looked Addy's way and gave a barely perceptible nod. Addy snapped her head back. She was dumbfounded by Hal's behavior. No growl! No glare! No vile oath! But then the present situation demanded a degree of military propriety, a trait that had started to grow in Hal as he became more respected within the regiment.... still he did not have to nod. What did it mean? Her reverie was broken by the sound of galloping hoofs. Circling the right wing of the brigade the rider stopped beside General Ames.

The rider was speaking rapidly and pointing to the rear. His meaning faded into the next scene, a calliope of multicolored men approaching from the front and flank. It seemed like a hoard as the glimmering of reflected rays darted from so many shouldered muskets. The enemy was upon them! They strained up a slippery slope to try and gain an advantageous position. Now the sound of pounding hooves came from the rear, horses competing with the bouncing wheels of light artillery and their limbers. The advantage shifted as the blue uniforms with red striping drew up behind the brigade. A cheer rose uniformly from the ranks. The Union artillery came to a halt and rolled their guns just inside the tree line to give them some protection.

At the same time, Ben was searching for Colonel Beasley for orders. He was no-where to be found. He rode up to Emile and told him to start at one end of the regiment while he started at the other. Lines were to be straightened and tightened. General Ames took off to reach the furthest regiment. Ben could see him lean over to the colonel of that regiment and point at the approaching enemy. Shells started to land here and there. Tree shots were bringing limbs and leaves down on the brigade. Homer made his way down the line until he reached Ben.

"When I drop my sword, commence full volley fire. Repeat twice more. Give them hell, Ben." The Grey Ghost took off to the center of the brigade. The sword was raised....then it dropped and the full brigade unleashed a decimating fire on the advancing Rebs. Some Union men were falling but the Secesh had not unleashed a volley. The sword was raised again. Officers gazed at the sword. A continuous line of flame shot forth again. Now they could hear soldiers screaming in the distance. They prepared for the third volley. The sword went up again. It fell. The white smoke blurred everyone's vision of the field of battle. The horse artillery now joined Captain Hickenlooper and his Fifth Ohio battery of napoleans. They too hurled volley fire, but at the opposing artillery.

# CHAPTER THIRTEEN: THE HORNET'S NEST

The Confederates were still pushing the Union army back toward Pittsburgh Landing, but it was being done haphazardly. Corps commanders often lacked the knowledge of what was going on due to the elongated battle line and a patchwork of fields and woods. In fact, the battle line had broken down and, both large and small, engaged with the enemy wherever he appeared. The only constant in the battle was the movement of Union troops as they retreated to Pittsburgh Landing.

It would have to take one decisive and large scale Union decision to stop or at least seriously slow down the Confederate wind that was sweeping the battlefield. General Grant was beginning to make his appearance on the field of battle and he became the consummate student and observer, absorbing the ebb and flow of battle, identifying weaknesses in leadership and the position of troops. His apparent calm and bearing never failed to bring confidence to his subordinates. Most importantly, however, he encouraged the ordinary soldier. Cheering and chants of 'Sam, Sam' filled the air whenever he made an appearance at a new location on the battlefield. It was as if his men physically drew strength from Grant's calm presence.

When Grant reached Prentiss' beleaguered command, cigar still drooping from the corner of his mouth, he calmly leaned over and asked the general for a light. With his gauntleted right hand, already dark and greasy from his reins, he firmly held Prentiss' shoulder in his grasp, looked him in the eye and said,

"Today general, your ability to control this position, for it is good ground, will determine the day's outcome. You must defend this place and slow the Rebels so that we can build a staunch defense at Pittsburgh Landing. You must hold this position at all costs."

Guns booming, General Prentiss stared into Grant's eyes and simply nodded an understanding of his duty. General Prentiss men fought on a sunken road with fencing and scrub brush, backed by a dense wooded area. In front of them lay a huge open field over which the enemy would have to cross. The strategy was simple. Present a strong frontal defense taking caution to insure that flanking Confederate troops could not attack them at this vulnerable point.

Colonel Raith's brigade, with whom General Ames was supposed to meet, was pulled away to strengthen General Sherman's beleaguered left. General Ames was on his own defending the flank.

Meanwhile, Ames' brigade was still marching at the double-quick to a position at the right rear of General Prentiss. But at this moment Ben was sitting on his horse watching the retreat of the Iowa regiment. It was not a pleasant sight. These poor terrified men, many without muskets, were now being shot in the back and tumbling, like young trees in a storm, in all directions. Some rose to continue the fight, some crawled on all fours or were being helped by caring comrades, some lay still, never to move again. General Ames had spotted them and like a shield for the eyes of his own men raced up and down the column with The Grey Ghost, exhorting the men to move to their proper position.

The soldiers of the Twentieth wasted no time in seeking the imagined safety of the woven fence edging the border of the woods and the clearing. This was to be their protection and their dying ground. Instinctively they sought out the best positions and assumed the prone firing stance. Soldiers, amid the stinging of their eyes from the sweat rolling down their foreheads, felt the prickling punctures of winter stubble mixed with the fresh weeds and grasses of spring. Below them, their uniforms soaked up the cool moisture of the wet earth, enough to cause more than one man to shake from the chilly ground.

Two different Reb batteries opened up on their position. That run across the field had alerted the Secesh of a new target. Men watched in horror as the artillery crept its way across the field until it found its mark. Some could now feel the unwelcome warmth of urine as they uncontrollably soiled themselves. The bombardment was stripping away their personal sense of dignity and honor.

Addie, now the company sergeant, tried to keep her men calm in the midst of the thundering of artillery and eruption of shells. Such is the nature of war, promotion when the one above you falls. She also had to contend with her own hands shaking. The Confederates were firing solid shot as well and its effect was devastating. First the spheres of iron dipped into the sunken road, up the side of the rise, through the fence and soldiers alike. She glanced down her rows of men only to see heads ripped from their bodies and smashed like ripe watermelons. The bouncing solid shot continued into the woods and wreaked its hell upon nature as trees were toppled by the larger balls like a scythe of war.

Few could look around as the body parts of friends were skewered like pigs on pointed limbs. Bodies caved to the side, or back at unnatural angles with bones protruding as if yanked from their joints by some mighty carnivore. Dead hands still clung to their Springfields ready to commence a war they would never fight.

Now a new battery rained fire on them using contact fuses but in this soft earth they did not wreak the same damage as their predecessors. Still, if close enough, a soldier could be turned into shreds by the hail of steel splinters that ripped them apart. The accuracy was good enough that wounds could not be avoided. Jagged splinters ripped into fragile frames. Even one dart of steel was enough to create a fountain of blood and drain the body dry. Men struck in this manner turned shades of grey and white as their lives quickly ebbed away. The shells that landed in the woods started fires when they landed on dry patches of scrub or dead trees. Blue uniforms succumbed to the flames and crazed bodies dashed in utter confusion. When they finally fell their blackened bodies erased identities while contorted mouths spoke volumes of the intensity of their suffering.

In the midst of this carnage the untouched still lay prone waiting for the chance to bring their version of horror to the battlefield. Sergeants, lieutenants, and captains steadied their men as best they could, fearful of the panic that could also send them to the rear. But the Twentieth held. If one had the ability to rise above all this, like some bird of war, he would have seen the sideways glances coming from their sister regiments, looking for some sort of direction. Their courage hinged on that of the Twentieth. All thoughts of shame and loss of honor gave way to the primeval urge to run in the face of fear. Yet all still held firm.

Ben sat on his young bay mare talking to her and keeping her as calm as possible in the carnage. He could feel her dancing hoofs transmitting the desire to run. He moved up and down the prone regiment giving courage to shattered souls. He had not paid attention to the other regiments. Thus when he made his turn back to the center of the line it was then that he saw General Ames joined by another general of shorter stature, perched on his mount and sucking on a cigar. General Grant had arrived at their place in line. He did not look like a soldier and wore the common uniform of a lesser rank. Ben moved toward Grant amid the cannonading that was occurring around them. Grant was absolutely intent on understanding the military actions taking place in this one location so he could better understand the overall field of war. He was quiet and expressionless, playing the role of an imaginary camera.

Pulling on his reins he trotted down the line encouraging all to hold this critical position. It would not be his only appearance of the day. The fragmented field forced Grant to move from site to site, trying to glean a total picture from his wanderings. This allowed him to move troops when necessary and possible. He wanted to keep a watchful eye on untested commanders. He left his good friend and capable commander Major-General W.T. Sherman to fight his own war. Such was Grant's respect for this personally erratic but gifted general.

It had seemed like they waited an eternity for the enemy, but now the shades of beige and brown appeared in rows rising up as if they were the devil himself making an earthly appearance. Up, up the slope they came, these devil's disciples. Ben could see soldiers looking to the rear but from the fence line a deep, voluminous voice vengefully promised death to any man who bolted. To emphasize his point Hal waved his pistol in the air as a warning to those who might give in to their fears. Such was Hal's method of leadership.

In contrast, Addy moved among her men encouraging, placing her now steadied had on shaking shoulders, mothering them in a soldierly way.

The gallop of The Grey Ghost was like the start of a race, instead it was General Ames preparing his men for the onslaught. Again and again officers and sergeants yelled for the first rank to stay at the prone position and prepare to fire. The second rank was to kneel. All hid behind their imaginary wall, the brush. Captains of companies turned to eye the sword of Captain Halliday who would give the signal for volley fire. The sword dropped as if decapitating some unwanted individual. That first volley stopped the men of the South as if the god of war had dropped an invisible wall in front of them. Union cannon had a clear sight on the oncoming soldiers. Butternut uniforms were hurled skyward while others simply stopped in their tracks, never to move again. As the smoke cleared one could see the soldiers tightening ranks to fill the gaping holes this first fury had unleashed. Dead and injured now formed their own neat row, casualties of the barrage they had just faced. Again, another brigade volley tore through Confederate ranks and this army of the dead lay on the ground awaiting future disposal.

The Confederates got within a hundred yards of the brush and unleashed a volley of their own. The brush gave up its dead and injured as its false security fell apart. Independent fire created a different scene as one could now pick out individual tragedies. One man put two hands to his face and fell to his knees, frozen in time and space. Others twirled around like a child's top, but they only twirled once and became still. Shoulders were crushed by Minnie balls and bone fragments shattered men's lives forever. The lucky ones' hearts were pierced, ensuring a rapid death. If one strained his eyes he could see the Horseman of the Apocalypse riding among the Rebs. The Confederates disappeared into a cloud of smoke and another Southern volley struck home crumpling Union bodies and the cries for mother began. Clinging to their false hope of defense, the brush gave way to many dead and injured. Those who had crouched behind a tree fared better. After what seemed like hours of battle the Confederates began to back away from this maelstrom. But time had passed quickly. Soldiers ran out of cartridges and were scrambling through the pouches of the dead and wounded for a fresh supply. The wounded Rebels cried out for help, but few came. Men sought safety first. Loud "Huzzahs" emanated from the ranks of Ames' brigade. They had experienced their first major test and passed. This was not the case at the front and center of the formation where General Prentiss and his men fought it out hand to hand with the enemy like two boxers refusing to give in to the other.

****

To All Brigade Commanders:

It is of the essence that you bring your soldiers into line and prepare for a final blow against this Federal position. To bypass these entrenched Union troops would leave our right flank exposed and thus dampen our chances of driving them right into the Tennessee River. This position must be taken by frontal assaults even if we face the possibility of taking many casualties.

God save the Confederacy

Major-General Braxton Bragg (Commanding second
Corps Army of the Mississippi)

\*\*\*\*

There was a lull in the fighting as the Rebs drew back to
lick their wounds, and they had been considerable. Ben could
hear attacks taking place at other points in this horseshoe-
shaped position. The strange shape of their lines made it next
to impossible for the Confederates to stage a single frontal
assault and for this he gave a sigh of relief.

Now it was the artillery's turn to once again pound the
enemy's artillery. When a direct hit did occur, a cannon was
no different then the soldiers themselves. Wooden wheels fell
to pieces, some hurled though the air while others lay prone.
Still others created their own spikes of horror and pierced
the unfortunate artillerymen like arrows. The gun carriage
was bad enough but when a shell hit the limber an explosion
ripped apart the limber hurling pieces of exploded shell in all
direction and maiming or killing those manning it.

Those who did survive could do little, except help their
wounded gunners and find medical help if it was available.
The infantrymen huddled like giant fetus' hoping their
smaller target would somehow save them from the continuing
onslaught of hurling metal shreds.

The Confederate artillery ceased and a new wave of
attackers was preparing to advance. The horse artillery and
the Third Ohio opened with canister, cutting swaths into
this new line of attacking rebs. The Union infantry again
took their positions which had become a standard movement
for the Twentieth and their fellow regiments. Again another
volley from the Union artillery blasted bodies which were
hurled backwards into their compatriots. But these Rebs
refused to stop. A particularly animated flag bearer and his

guard seemed to be pulling his fellow soldiers forward. They drew up to within twenty yards of the brigade's position.

Ben watched in amazement as one of the men in his old company ran out to put an end to the charge of the crazed flag bearer. Such was the inoculation of pride in one's flag that men performed maniacal movements. Soon both men were engaged in a death struggle over a wooden pole and a piece of cloth. Shouts went up from both sides as they turned their focus to this singular engagement. Ben felt helpless, unable to help his heroic soldier. Finally, a Confederate ball pierced his leg, shattering the bone to splinters and forcing the soldier to the ground. When the man fell it was Hal's turn to attempt this heroic struggle. Using his musket as a club he smashed the head of the flag bearer and the poor man's head flew apart like a dropped pumpkin. At the same time he grabbed the flag while he used his pistol to put balls into the guards who now tried to reclaim it. Not satisfied with the flag alone, he picked up the wounded Union soldier with his massive arm and beat a hasty retreat to the Union lines. In the meantime Confederate men who were infuriated with Hal's actions chased after the thief who had taken their flag. Unnoticed by all, Addy had crawled forward from her position, taken her revolver and put shots in the heads of these brazen attackers. The men stopped in their tracks and fell dead. Hal heard the shots and turned over his shoulder to see the silenced forms behind him. Stunned by Addy's actions, Ben could see Hal give a nod in her direction. Addy just tipped her kepi and Hal scampered over the brush to the safety of the Union line, none the worse for his heroic action.

Curious how singular acts could enflame the actions of others. The Union rate of fire now intensified and the Rebs went to ground in the presence of this vigorous musket fire. Ben was glad that he had borne witness to this set of actions. For his part he continued to ride up and down the regimental lines, encouraging the defenders and at the same time trying to avoid the injured and dead. Fortunately most of the injured had been dragged back and placed behind the trees while the walking wounded moved slowly to O'Malley's forward aid station.

The next surge of nut-colored Confederates seemed even louder than the last but their speed of advance was slower as they faced the hell fire of the Union men. Ben rode to the center of the Iowa regiment to make a last visit with General Ames who was deliberately keeping an eye on this group of men. Silently, if that was possible, Ben asked how the regiment was holding out.

"They'll be just fine, Ben. Your men set a good example for them. Have you found Colonel Beasley yet?"

"No sir," the quick reply came.

"Ben, I am officially making you commander of the Twentieth. I think we will find him somewhere back at Pittsburg Landing but we can't worry about him in the middle of this melee!" Without further comment Homer dashed off to gauge the performance of the 'sister' regiments. Ben could see the Rebs trying to form for another charge at his position.

So on came the next wave, once again leaning into the torrent of Minnie balls that came over them, beside them, and splattered in front of them. The return volleys from these Rebs buzzed about the blue uniforms throwing men into grotesque shapes as lead balls hit heads and other vital organs. Again the wail of ravaged bodies rose like plaintiff cries from the netherworld. Ben's new role as colonel taught him to stand back as an observer and lead when his captains faltered. He wondered how much longer they could remain steady in the face of charge after charge. He wondered what would happen if a wave of Confederate devils refused to stop. But once again they pulled back getting as close as twenty yards of the fence and brush. Hickenlooper's powerful Napoleons had been a Godsend with their superior ability to spew out cannister from their barrels. It was always a sight one did not want to see again. Like a shotgun shell, they created a backward thrust on those unfortunate enough to receive their wrath.

Again the Union soldiers called out for more cartridges and again they were forced to scrounge the pouches of the newly fallen in order to keep up their fire. Ben sent Emile to plead with the general for more supplies of cartridges.

No man in the 'hornet's nest' was prepared for what followed. Twelve more waves of Rebels sallied forth and twelve times were driven back. The dead had to be pulled back from the fence to allow more space for the living. The gap between individual soldiers started to widen as their ranks withered. This battle surged back and forth for four hours. Canteens were emptied. Faces were totally blackened while ripping their cartridges open with their teeth.

In the distance Ben could see that General Grant had made another appearance on their battlefield and was calmly doing his battle analysis. He knew their situation was tenuous. Pats on the shoulders of his brigade commanders were the only signs of any emotional display. But his appearance gave hope and inspiration to those who saw him.

****

To: Major-General J.P.T. Beauregard(Commanding the Army of the Mississippi)

From: Brig. General Daniel Ruggles (Commanding first division, second Corp)

I send my regrets. I have just been made aware of the death of Major-General A.S. Johnston. No braver man has carried our flag into battle. I feel it necessary to inform you of the fruitless carnage and destruction of Major-General Braxton Braggs' forces in this place they call the 'hornet's nest'. If we cannot defeat them with repeated frontal assault nor move them from this position we must consider another tactic. We are unable, given the nature of the land, to make full-scale assaults against these stubborn Union soldiers. Nor is it possible, as Major-General Braggs has stated, to bypass these Federals and leave them to mount an attack on our right flank. I offer this suggestion. We pull in all our field artillery from brigade deployment and create an arc of death surrounding the enemy. In doing so we must ensure sufficient ordnance to offer a sustained bombardment. I estimate a concentration of about sixty artillery pieces. If we do not break these Federals physically we can at least break their spirits.

Brigadier General Daniel Ruggles

To: Brigadier-General Daniel Ruggles(Commanding first division, second Corp)

Move ahead quickly with your plan and call upon all ordnance reserves if necessary. I will deal with Major-General Braggs. May God's fortunes be upon us.

Major-General J.P.T. Beauregard (Commanding the Army of the Mississippi)

****

The various units in General Prentiss' horseshoe defense would never likely discover that they were about to face the largest concentration of artillery up to this point in the war. Fifty-three pieces, along with accoutrement of war were formed a mere five hundred yards from the defenders of the 'hornet's nest'.

Suddenly, the temporary lull ended with an explosion of every form of field artillery. They threw solid shot, canister, fused shells, and contact shells and like a thunderstorm these harbingers of death fell upon the defenders. The best they could do was hug the ground, hoping, in vain, to make themselves invisible. Some grasped their ears to try to shut out these sounds, others pulled wooden logs and branches over their bodies and this at least offered a token of resistance to the hell that surrounded them.

The Twentieth was no exception. Fortunately their position on the right wing of the horseshoe did not take the battering General Prentiss' men did at the very front of the horseshoe. With this came brigades of Confederates who marched double-quick to take advantage of the barrage and the silenced Union guns. But eventually the barrage lifted and Union soldiers still found the strength to repel two rebel charges.

Ben and the regiment had stood their ground, but by raising himself up in his saddle he could see companies and even regiments starting to flee from the battlefield toward Pittsburgh Landing. He could see officers using drawn pistols to try and discourage a haphazard retreat but to no avail. Emile and the remaining captains kept their men occupied and focused, and they held, but it became apparent to all present that the enemy artillery barrage, and the repeated assaults had given the Twentieth and its fellow regiments three choices, surrender, die, or try an organized retreat.

The Grey Ghost thundered down the line to where Ben was standing.

"Colonel Halliday, it appears our men have been saturated with war. That last bombardment has taken the fight out of many of these men. I want your regiment to model a correct retreat for the rest of the brigade and hopefully they will follow your example." Ben could tell that even the general was starting to realize that his men had had enough for one day. With that, The Grey Ghost wheeled and shot back up the line with the general making stops where men were starting to pull out.

First Ben sought out his bugler then he pulled ten reliable men from the ranks. He gathered them in a tight circle and spoke carefully and calmly, masking the raging rumbles of fear in his own stomach. And so he began.

"Men, I want each of you to tell the senior officers still remaining to number their soldiers, one, two, one, two until he has given each man a number. Then when they hear the bugler sound retreat the 'ones' are to rise up and begin a gradual withdrawal to a distance of about twenty feet. They are to stop and prepare to fire at the command of a corporal or sergeant. As soon as they fire, the 'twos' will retreat to where the 'ones' are and prepare to fire. Keep repeating this withdrawal and try to keep lines straight." To emphasize his command he used an area of sand to show them how to explain it to the officers.

"I will give you all fifteen minutes before I signal the retreat. Good luck!" Ben started to have second thoughts about his plan. The men had already learned retreat. He hoped this would not confuse them. The artillery barrage had lifted but now he could see another line of butternut coming his way.

The bugler finally sounded the retreat and half of the men rose up and began a double quick to the rear. The crunching and crackling of branches told him the 'ones' were making their way, without panic, through the woods. Then the noise stopped. It was time for the twos to move. As they did he could see the first line preparing to fire. As the twos reached them they let out a volley. That signaled their departure further to the rear. Now the twos prepared to fire a volley. Ben moved with the 'ones' encouraging them to keep straight lines. They came out in an open area and formed lines more readily. Ben signaled the bugler and the retreat continued, the two covering the ones while they retreated. Now the regiment could be identified.

As Ben reached the left side of the line he could see a group of soldiers frozen in place, oblivious of the war. All were standing on the far side of a large oak tree. Ben rode quickly to the spot so that he could get these men back into retreat formation.

When he arrived, there, propped against the large oak tree was the slumped body of Colonel Beasley. Blood was oozing from his right temple, trickling down his right arm, and dripping onto the leaves of the oak tree. Oddly the left eye was wide open as if this had all been a mistake. Prophetically both eyes had turned hazy, mirroring the way he had lived his life as a soldier. Pieces of grey brain matter had oozed out through the exit wound on the left side of his skull. His Army Colt revolver was still gripped firmly in his hand. Oddly Ben mused that this was not an unusual way for this man to die.

He had lived his army life alone and without honor, so he had ended it.

There was no grieving, comments, or concern, as if this man's passing had no meaning to those around him. Their reaction seemed fitting. Ben dismounted, closed both of his eyes, put the revolver back in his holster, and ordered the men to double-quick their pace back to the retreating troops. Ben never heard the troops talk about the man again.

And so the Twentieth continued its leap-frog retreat. The Confederates were having trouble seeing the men in blue. The faster they re-loaded, the faster their volley fire came. The Confederates were not clear on the volume of defenders they were attacking. Ben now had a complete view of his command and suddenly realized that its size had significantly dwindled. Others were limping or showed wrappings where some ball had pierced their body. Some were without kepis, some had no water, and few had anything to say. They had been beaten into silence. Ben pulled out his watch and chain. It was now 3:30 in the afternoon.

In the distance to his right Ben could see the form of an officer galloping toward them at full speed. Following him vainly were five other riders, presumably staff members and one trooper carrying the guidons. It had to be Homer, but....he was riding a large chestnut. The sliding stop was still present when he arrived, but not like The Grey Ghost's.

"General, where is The Grey Ghost?" Ben's voice was becoming raspy from overuse.

"Dead!" And that was all Homer said. Battlefield losses of horses were to be expected. Ben froze. He shifted his eyes directly to those of the General. The brevity and outwardly emotionless answer left both men with nothing to say. But in his heart Ben knew that this was a cover for a wounded soul.

A solitary rider approached from the area where the Hornet's Nest had been.

"General Ames?"

"Yes, lieutenant."

"Sir my last order from the hornet's nest was to reach as many senior officers as I could and inform them that Major-General Prentiss was compelled, along with about 1,000 of his men, to surrender to the enemy."

"Thank you for the information lieutenant." The officer scurried off as quickly as he had arrived. Homer felt some words were in order

"General Prentiss did more than most men on this day. He not only obeyed his commander but probably saved General Grant's army from destruction. What else could one ask from a dedicated and brave officer?"

Ben watched Homer with admiration. He had honored a man who gave honor and that was the best any man could ask for today. Ben found time, as the retreat progressed, to inform Homer of Colonel Beasely's demise. Homer looked off for a minute and then gave his directions.

"Ben you were the senior officer present. You should write a report of what you saw, but couch it in terms leaving room for the possible interpretation of a battlefield wound. There is no point in having an inquiry into this situation. I will hand deliver those reports and your promotion to General Grant myself."

With that said General Ames returned to military matters.

"Colonel Halliday I am going to try and find as many officers from our brigade as I can who still have mounts. I will send them in your direction for you to put some order into this retreat. I will need you and Emile to keep them moving quickly but straight. We have open field ahead of us and perhaps can even slow down the Confederate advance. Good luck Ben!"

Ben continued the regiment's controlled retreat. Soon remnants of the other three regiments hobbled and puffed in disarray to the open field. If seen from above they would have appeared like ants gone berserk. Ben rode to each small group as they joined the Twentieth. All were exhausted and many were bloodied. Those who were injured he sent immediately to the rear. Most had shed their baggage. Some of them were sobbing. It was not a happy sight!

Ben sent Emile to the center of his bedraggled pack, called for any officers or first sergeants, and had them draw their swords. Holding their swords parallel to the ground and waist high they used this familiar tactic to straighten this increasing herd of men into two straight lines linked to the end of the Twentieth's right flank. The largest Union flag that had been saved by its bearer was used as the dressing point and soon a respectable military ensemble formed. The new additions had observed the drill of the Twentieth and simply mimicked them. Like two huge logs rolling down a hill, the thin blue line continued its retreat. Galloping up and down the line, as Homer would do, Ben reckoned he was in command of about 1,000 men. Ben knew that he would eventually gain more of the brigade as Homer discovered them, acting like a shepherd bringing his wolf-ravaged flock back together again.

Within the period of an hour the line continued to grow and as they approached the top of a hill they could see the breastworks being built at Pittsburg Landing. General Grant had made the best of a bad situation, gathering retreating soldiers to work on the open, elevated land in front of the landing. He was even able to enlist the aid of those clinging to the sandy shoreline. Sometimes it was necessary to fire a pistol shot in the air to raise them up, but it worked. These breastworks would never be tested, for the Confederate forces were even more war weary than their Union counterparts. Confederate commanders could see that they would have to launch a major assault on the breastworks if they chose to attack, and they did not have the artillery support to bombard them.

Little did Ben know that the Confederates were also running low on ammunition and ammunition wagons were still far to the rear. All soldiers were glad the battle was over. The Confederates, despite their losses, were viewed as the winners. And so the first day at Shiloh came to an end. It was a day etched in the memories of all who had fought. And so ended this first major battle in the war of brothers.

****

April 6, 1862
Dear Father,

I send this letter to you as I greatly fear mother will not keep her sanity after reading it. I have just faced the nature of what this war is really like. It is madness. Father, so many wives, mothers, and children will weep and mourn after the reports in the newspapers are read and they find loved ones among the killed and wounded. The best they can hope for is a letter from a friend, or even a stranger, describing more about their loved ones.

After one has been in a battle like the one we just fought, any notions about the honor and nobility of war are swept away. It is merely a struggle for survival, a struggle that at its worst shows the savagery of man's nature. Killing loses any moral foundation. Survival is all we can understand. We fight in units but in reality we struggle only for our own primal need to stay alive and when courage flees from our hearts panic sends us hurling through an emotional void as we seek sanctuary wherever we can find it.

Undoubtedly you will read comments from generals about the heroic stands made by their men. They must say these things to maintain military support from the population and its political supporters. Reality will only come from the pens and mouths of those who have been here this day. Keep in mind we selectively remember those events that we see as grotesque or heroic. I had positioned our regiment at the center of the brigade and in contact with elements of another. I had reason to look to the left, although my men were to the right of me. There I saw two men cradling each other. I yelled at them as the enemy approached but they did not respond. Quickly I dropped to the ground and shook their shoulders, for their eyes were cast downwards and sobs caused their bodies to shake in unison. I slapped each one with my right hand and both heads snapped up. My God father, they were identical twins, no more than seventeen, and now, returned to the place they had shared for nine months, their mother's womb. How great the relief each must have brought the other. What at first appeared as an act of cowardice was in fact as natural an act of human bonding as one can imagine. The slapping had wakened them and four blue eyes, sitting in large sockets, stared into my eyes. Their mouths even gasped in unison. I was seeing double. I grabbed one and threw him against the scrub brush and immediately the other followed. Then a corporal from their company, having seen what happened, took over the situation. I returned to the regiment, the buzzing of balls flying overhead. The battle continued and I was absorbed with my own command. The volleys flew back and forth, but during one lull in the battle I remembered them and looked to my left again. There, lying with his eyes wide open lay one of the brothers. He stared in silent repose. The other brother had curled up next to him, as if in his mother's womb. Quietly he stroked his brother's dead hands trying to comfort him. He was grieving for himself as well as his twin brother who by now had reached out for the heavenly realm. Such a loss, no man should have to bear, for, in truth, I believe a part of the remaining brother had died.

Some men took to screaming. I was not quite sure what it meant. Could it have been a vain attempt to strike out the sounds of war? Often it took place when the men were closely engaged with the enemy. I believe for some it gave them a chance to vent the furies from their spirit as they become quite wild as well. One of my own men, Private Nelson, was one such man. His banshee yelps were endless, but it did not stop him from loading or firing. Then he launched his body into the air balling out, "I killed me a Secesh, I killed me a Sec..." and at that unprotected moment a ricocheting artillery ball cleaved right through his middle, hurling his body in two different directions. Thank God his end was swift and painless!

Then there was Private O'Day. He fought furiously and had managed to stop a wild Reb carrying his regiment's battle ensign with a well-placed shot. O'Day became absorbed with the flag, threw down his musket and wriggled like a mad snake across the space separating the two enemies. The Secesh could see his objective and spouts of earth fell about him. He grasped the end of the flag as if it were a lifeline and in a manner most inhuman reversed his reptilian wriggle and made his way back to out to the fence. Raising the Rebel flag high he planted the pole in the ground and dared the rebels to shoot their own flag. He now had the safest place on the battlefield!

But the strangest story of that day took place after the fighting had ceased. The 'popping' noises from nervous guards broke the evening silence. They feared a non-existent attack from the enemy. Since there was but a semblance of a camp, most men preferred to eat what they could find and in some secure spot near the trenches and breastworks. At the time I was resting but took time to glance over the gathered troops. The hoarse, but still load voice of Hal captured my attention. First he gathered some of the men from the Twentieth. He instructed them to find some digging tool of any kind, preferably a shovel. I would guess that he had about a group of twenty exhausted but willing souls accompanying him. Without seeking official permission, which they probably wouldn't have received, they secreted themselves down into one of the gullies that covered this landscape. My curiosity got the best of me and I followed at a safe distance taking my revolver in case this group ran into rebels. This curious group of men worked its way around the main camps and pickets with a definite direction in mind. After a time I noticed one of Hal's men pointing in an animated fashion to an open, smallish field that had been part of the day's battlefield. They began to dig furiously and had managed to find an area of fairly soft soil. Soon mounds of earth surrounded what seemed to be a hole about twelve feet in length and five feet wide. This silent pack of men then moved to an area close by, stopped, bent in unison, and then began dragging something out of the taller grass. As they did so I finally saw what it was and their purpose became clear. They were dragging a dead horse toward the hole. Even at night I was able to make out the form of The Grey Ghost. These men had taken up the task of giving this animal of war a burial. Tenderly they bent the legs and neck to fit in the hole. All stood for a few moments of silence, then they commenced to heap shovelfuls of soil gently on this noble steed. My curiosity was satisfied and I retreated back to the camp. I commenced to reflect on this most unusual event, for many a dead man did not receive the burial that this horse was given.

But why did this band of men do this? And if I was to enquire from them the reason I am not sure they would have anything more insightful to add. If I was to guess, I suspect part of the explanation exists in Hal's transition to a soldier. He became a killer but had a very large space in his heart for animals. His attachment to Patches, and vice versa, is evidence of this. In his code of military values courage and leadership stands high. The Grey Ghost was not just any horse but one whose bearing was one of beauty and majesty rolled into one. It was also a sign of an abiding respect for General Ames who led without much regard for his own life, much like Hal himself. I am sure he did not have to go far to find volunteers. Many of these farm boys form strong attachments in their hearts and have many memories of these 'good and faithful' servants who toiled without seeking a reward. How strange a being is man, a killer with a heart! My duties as colonel of the regiment are calling me but I want to finish.

The last story I will recount involves the brotherhood that I believe still lives in these embattled enemies. As you know a regiment keeps a regimental band which is used for marching, serving as litter bearers, and finally for entertainment. General

Ames, needing soldiers, had concentrated this assemblage at the brigade level. The air was still that night and sounds of music carried well. General Ames had probably prompted the band to play to help raise the spirits of the men. The first song they played had just been written in Chicago by a man named Root. Already it had reached the battlefield and was indeed a stirring piece called "The Battle Cry of Freedom". To accompany it, one of the soldiers in our regiment with a beautiful tenor voice sang the words while another man held a candle for him.

"Oh, we'll rally 'round the flag boys, we'll rally once again,

Shouting the battle cry of freedom.

We will rally from the hillside, we'll gather from the plain,

Shouting the battle cry of freedom.

Hurrah boys, hurrah! Down with the traitor, up with the star.

While we rally once again, shouting the battle cry of freedom."

Three more verses accompanied this memorable piece as men intently listened. Music after all, is a release for their emotions that know no other satisfying release. When they finished there was a pause, then some rebel band perched on a hill countered with another version of the same song.

"We are marching to the field, boys we're going to the fight.

Shouting the battle song of freedom.

And we bear the heavenly cross, for our cause is in the right.

Shouting the battle cry of freedom.

Our rights forever, hurrah! Hurrah, boys hurrah.

Down with the tyrants, raise the Southern star.

And we'll rally round the flag boys, we'll rally once again,

Shouting the battle cry of freedom."

Few words changed father, but the rallying sounds showed the expanding gulf between brotherly opponents. And so this chorus of music rolled back and forth, in tribute and in competition. The song I found most ironic was played furiously and often by Confederate bands, 'Dixie's Land', yet the song had been written by a northerner for northerner audiences and espoused the cause of slavery! We are a mixed up country! My eyes grow heavy under this glowing fire whose brilliant streams flow heavenward in the still night. Good night for now and be strong for me and pray for all.

Love to all,

Ben

**\*\*\*\***

Ben had joined Homer who had wanted to visit all regimental hospitals. They scuffled their exhausted feet from one to another. Some were in better order than others. Some had raised tents, some large, some small. They paused for a longer time at Doctor O'Malley's surgery. Outside the large tent lay blood soaked litters, holding in their flattened cradle, the victim of some major or minor calamity. Ben noticed that they seemed to be grouped. Those with flesh wounds or lower limb injuries sat together, some even spiritedly recounting some real or fictional story which helped to ease their pain. Closer to the tent lay those most in need. Limbs were missing or hanging on by sinews, shoulders were exposed, revealing bare and mangled bones. These men were often numbed by shock, begging for morphine, or moaning the word 'mother' over and over again. The last group seemed further apart from the others. They said little and revealed hideous wounds, faces torn away, intestines drooping from a gut, skulls cracked open revealing the grey matter of the brain. Often these men would find their rest in another world. Beside the open tent flap stood containers of various sizes. An aide would emerge from the tent and throw limbs into one of the containers with as little a thought as one would hurl garbage into a dump. What was tragic and inhuman were the grotesque positions these limbs made, like a stack of short branches, the victims of a terrible storm. All were human but in no way resembled a single human form.

From inside came the pleas and screams as men fought to keep what was a part of their very being. Few relented without protest. Often it took two or three aides to hold the stricken soldier as another patiently let chloroform drip onto a folded cloth, putting the poor man into a temporary stupor. Then the sawing began. It was a sound no one ever got used to.

"Homer, of all the sounds of war that I heard and will hear, I believe the rasping of that saw on a human bone will always be a lingering memory. I remember my father cutting up the bones of dead farm animals. That was bad enough. At least they were animals."

The air was fouled with the sweet smell of fresh blood. It was everywhere, but Dr. O'Malley's share of it had to be the worst. He would have to stand for hours in a white surgeon's gown caked in layers of blood. Blood from early in the day had dried and created a drip panel for the new blood that squirted on him. Fresh blood shone from the lanterns placed overhead, reflecting a lighter and brighter color as it wound its way down to a darker, dismal, damp, puddle on the dirt floor below. From the ground rivulets made their way to all corners of the tent. These rivers of blood were mixed with sweat and excrement from soldiers who had fouled themselves in their first contact with battle. The rank, putrid stench rising from these men who had not bathed in days or weeks had its own distinct fragrance. Uniforms no longer looked like uniforms, having been ripped, muddied, and often burnt on their poor owner.

"Damn it, he's dead! Get him out of here and bring me a fresh one. And make it one I have a chance to save. I can only take this futility so long!"

The bark of O'Malley's voice would leave one with the impression he was an uncaring doctor without compassion, but nothing could be further from the truth. But this war did change men in different ways. Hopefully it would not be permanent. Homer was another example. Ben could smell the wisps of stale liquor that the General used to keep his emotions intact. But Ben knew it was not his place to mention it. On the other hand, he knew he would think twice about offering him a drink. In Homer's case, despite the alcohol, he managed to keep his emotions and inner self to himself.

After watching O'Malley at work for ten minutes Ben queried.

"How is your work progressing?" He could feel an icy glare come from the exhausted eyes of General Ames who knew better than to interrupt the good doctor. Without lifting his head O'Malley hissed through his teeth.

"Some things are so obvious, colonel, why bother me with such a stupid question!"

Ben almost leapt back in shock. This was not the man he knew and respected. But then it began to sink in. Now that he had been interrupted the doctor went over and washed his hands in a bucket that was already red from previous visits. Ben watched as the doctor returned to his work station and swiftly cut through flesh and tendons to bare a white bone below. As he peeled back the flesh Ben could see that the knee cap of the victim was shattered into bits. The doctor spoke to his two assistants.

"Men, I want you to keep that leg perfectly still, this cut must be perfectly straight." His voice was a dull monotone. The grating of the saw on bone made Ben nauseated enough that he had to swallow a mouthful of vomit to retain his reputation as a solid officer. Now O'Malley began to speak.

"Now Ben you see first-hand the reality of war. How honorable does this seem to you?"

The voice was still a monotone but Ben could sense its mocking intent. He felt hurt by his friend's attitude. Ben would always be slightly naïve about realities. The doctor continued his attempt to raise Ben's reality level.

"Why don't you go outside and offer succor to those poor souls for whom I can do nothing? God willing they will expire tonight. This man I am working on might be lucky. Surgery at this point on the leg offers a fifty-fifty chance of recovery assuming he doesn't get gangrene. Nonetheless his life is altered forever. Just hope he worked in an occupation that did not lean heavily on the use of this leg. You know I could almost tolerate this job if it weren't for the abominable preparations made by the governments for this reality. What bothers me even more are the so-called doctors working in the other regiments. None of them have done this type of surgery before. All three of them have visited my tent at some point or other. Two of them vomited profusely. I discovered one was a political appointee who had a total of two months training and was handed a certificate by some nameless college disguising itself as a place of learning."

Now, at least, Ben had some understanding of the poor man's frustration. The end of O'Malley's brief speech also brought an end to the limb removal of this poor soul and the assistants quickly removed him to another table where another assistant quickly and deftly sutured the stump of the leg with the skin left over for this purpose. He knew his job. The stump was then tightly wrapped in white lengths of cloth. He was now removed from the surgery. O'Malley spoke to no one in particular as he continued.

"The best we can hope for is a slow recovery from the chloroform. The only heroes here are my assistants who have no training, but instead of fighting chose this noble profession. They never complain or hesitate to do their jobs. Soon their skills will be beyond that of some of the doctors. I should have known that this type of warfare would have resulted in such tragedy.

"I should have studied the Crimean War, but we learned nothing from that misadventure. Before this war there were one hundred doctors in the military. Their training might have adequately prepared them for pre-war conditions. Service in the west cut them off from new ideas. For this regiment I have but one field ambulance to bring in the serious cases or transport them to an actual hospital. Do you think that sounds like preparation? Pardon me if I sound bitter. I don't think any one could have foreseen the scale of destruction of which we were capable."

The doctor stopped abruptly. He had said what he felt and realized he had to focus on his newest patient. An assistant wiped the sweat from his brow.

The colonel and general were silent. How could they respond to what they knew was true? General Ames simply turned on his heels, his sword clanging inappropriately in this space. Ben followed suit and both men stopped outside the medical tent. The clear night sky stood in stark contrast to the moans of the wounded. The smell of burning wood from soldiers' fires drowned out the smell of blood. The only sounds of war were the occasional popping of sentries' muskets. Off to the side a small group of men lifted blankets from a long row of dead solemnly searching in vain for a relative or friend. Occasionally the words 'son' or 'brother' came from this group of body searchers. There was little either officer could do.

****

The following day seemed anti-climactic. General Buell had added his troops to those of General Grant and now had a distinct advantage. They were fresh, experienced in battle, and ready to engage the victorious Confederates. The problem, of course, was that the victor was diminished in numbers, poorly re-supplied and still exhausted from the previous day's battle. With a concentrated effort the Union forces drove the rebels off and they retreated all the way back to Corinth. Soon it would be abandoned and allow the Union forces reach closer to their goal, the Mississippi River.

This would not be the only meeting of these two combatants that would be costly and indecisive. A hard fought and relatively successful battle was wasted by the events of the following day. So many lives, so much suffering, so much effort, and while some land had been gained it was won without a decisive victory being established. This would not be a war where a single battle or campaign determined all. This was what the originators of this struggle had failed to see at the outset. Oh, the generals' reports would laud their victories, both large and small, but in the end there would be much time spent licking their wounds and waiting for another day.

# CHAPTER FOURTEEN:
## COLONEL MACEY COMES WEST

Rob grabbed the coach's railing and swung his body up and on to the small platform at the end of the car. This wait for a connecting train had been quite tedious. He hoped this connecting train would carry some military types who would be carrying information that he could siphon from them. A spy never knew when some trivial or significant information might spill from a not so cautious mouth. Rob was always intrigued by those who were willing, even anxious, to show off their real or imagined status by leaking information to what they thought was another comrade in arms. To his chagrin, the train was filled with replacement officers full of victories that they would win but lacking in the knowledge of anything significant. He understood why these men were traveling west. The loss of junior officers at Shiloh had been great and there were only so many vacancies that you could fill with your own men. Little did these men realize that their rank made them a target for the enemy. Both sides had claimed victory but Rob knew this was just the viewpoint of the newspapers covering each side of the battle and quoting generals who had to cover their mistakes. It was still early in the war. The day would come when the press would become the most outspoken voices of military blunders and campaigns waged by both sides. But Rob would always know different. He made a point of it. He had seen some of the casualty figures on Colonel Winston's desk and they told a different story, one that already could not have been imagined a year earlier. Rob might have been a womanizing traitor but he did possess some common sense. He agreed with General W.T. Sherman who had predicted a prolonged, bitter war that would change the face of this nation forever. After Shiloh, Rob envisaged armies of up to 100,000 soldiers. It would become a war of attrition and in such a war the South could not outlast the North. Rob was just thankful that he held a desk job of sorts, but one that let him into the field of combat just enough to keep him in touch with important generals. Bored by his own thoughts Rob leaned back in his seat, put his boots on the seat across from him, and tried to relax.

His mind wandered to his present pressing problem: Colonel Fielding. What Jeff Davis saw in this man he would never comprehend. Fielding was the epitome of one problem faced by the South. He came from old southern stock, but the good had been bred out of this family. Fielding's interests were women and war, not the management of a large and potentially profitable cotton plantation. He was the only child in his family so there was no one to offset his negative qualities. Worse still, he had left his plantation in the hands of an even more incompetent overseer; a man who abused his slaves and the land. Fielding was arrogant, temperamental, violent, and worst of all did not see any of his shortcomings. War held much fascination for him, but it had to be on his terms. That meant selling off half of his plantation and creating his own cavalry regiment. He then proceeded to tear about the countryside pillaging and mauling small towns and Union supply trains. Too foolish and uncaring to preserve some supply columns for Southern gain, he simply put them to the torch. Obsessed with public adulation, he craved to read about his exploits in southern newspapers, but many a southern newspaper was cool toward him. During his raids he had managed to kill a significant number of civilians and that was not the way the war was to be fought yet. President Davis was often blind to his exploits and tried to keep him in check by assigning him the task of picking up the Winchester rifles that Rob was sending south. When he came in contact with the Union guard delivering them he had even had his men try out the new muskets on members of the Union soldiers. Needless to say Rob was pulled into Colonel Winston's office and had to face an angry dressing down from both Colonel Winston and the secretary of war. It almost ruined his grand scheme. Rob wanted this operation to work quietly and on good terms with both governments. Fortunately, he was still able to keep the destination hidden from the powers in Washington.

Rob wanted the peace of mind that his operations were in good hands. He wanted to keep his hands out of the operation as much as possible. He had even gone so far as to hire an assassin to 'take care' of Fielding and that would take care of the problem once and for all. He had not heard the results of his efforts in this direction as yet. Tired of thinking of 'that fool Fielding' Rob chose to spend his time looking out the window of the swaying car as it trundled on its way through Pennsylvania. The tooting of the train's whistle awoke him from his reverie and he found time to walk about and stretch his arms and legs. Lemonade and sandwiches were for sale at a tiny stop. He admired the entrepreneur who had found a way to extort currency at high prices from a group of new officers who would never have thought to bring their own food with them. That would have been beneath their rank. During his moments of exercise, out of the corner of his right eye, Rob spotted a dapper little man, a civilian, probably about fifty years of age, furtively glancing in Rob's direction. Rob could not let this apparently intrusive behavior go without discovering its reason. As soon as the train blew its whistle and chugged its way out of the station, Rob found his chance. He grabbed his greatcoat and swung into the vacant seat directly opposite the man. Was this a Pinkerton agent? He wanted to find out.

"Good day sir, how are you?" Rob consciously put on his 'friendly' face to catch the little man off guard and put himself in a position to dominate him.

"I am quite fine, thank you for asking." Rob instantly knew this man would pose a challenge. He had reacted coolly and with decorum.

"You must feel out of place in a train car full of army types." Rob had softened his delivery and showed empathy for the man's situation.

"No, not at all, I feel quite comfortable among the military. I deal with them at all levels of power, from privates to generals." The man was again quite collected and showed no signs of being put out by this colonel.

"Your epaulets tell me you are a staff man. That's most impressive for one so young. It's just a question whether you are a field officer or a Washington type. You see Colonel Macey, I already know about you."

Rob gulped. He could feel his heart skip a beat. What exactly did this man know? Rob was in fact the person who had been put in an awkward position.

"I must admit sir, that you have me at a disadvantage, mister…"

Silence. Rob had shown the man through the use of his broad smile that he appeared not to be rattled.

"Hobart is the name colonel, Jason Hobart." He deftly reached into his inner coat pocket as if he had done this many times over like the fox entering its den. He handed Rob a business card. "I deal in the buying and selling of large volumes of commodities. I am freelance and therefore avoid the bother of having a boss. I am sure, colonel, you must find the chain of command a ponderous operation at times. I know that you like to operate on your own and get away from Washington sometimes."

Another gulp from Rob. Hobart must know something about his clandestine operations. The question was, which one? He would have to find out.

"And what specific commodities do you deal in Mr. Hobart?" Rob queried.

"Anything our vast farms in this great Union can produce, or even those commodities in the border states and further south."

Hobart knew he would get a reaction of some kind from Rob. He was as much as saying that he dealt with the enemy. It was a test of Rob's loyalty. Rob leaned closer to reduce the noise level of their conversation. Calmly and slowly he asked the leading question.

"Are you inferring that somehow the government of this Union would have an interest in trading with the enemy?"

Hobart had opened the door wide. His future depended on Rob's disloyalty to the Union and he would soon find out that future. Rob saw this as a potential trap. If this man were a Pinkerton agent and Rob showed any inclination to agree with him, he was in trouble.

"Mister Hobart I cannot believe that you would make such a statement to a complete stranger!" Rob put an emphasis on the words 'complete stranger' to indicate his horror at such a suggestion from an assumed Union loyalist.

Hobart was not taken in by Rob's feigned attempt at loyalty. He simply went on with his card dealing tactics. "You must first know two things before you make such judgments, Colonel Macey. The first is this; cotton is building up in the south due to the blockade and decreased purchases from the north. This will continue as the war progresses. Crop production isn't suddenly going to change because of this war. Secondly, and probably the most important, is the fact that you have experience in such matters!"

Rob feigned an insult and shot back, "What in heaven's sake could you mean? If you knew my actual job you would be shaking in your boots!" Rob acted as indignant as the situation merited. Now Hobart played his trump card. He did so with some trepidation, but his information came from a solid source.

"Why Colonel Macey, I find it difficult to believe that a Union intelligence officer would have such a fancy for Winchester rifles, or do you do a tremendous volume of hunting?" He had played the card and threw in a touch of sarcasm as well. Hobart swallowed hard for his mouth had turned dry. He made sure he kept his focus on Rob's eyes. Rob leaned back against his seat. He crossed his left leg over his right knee and folded his arms. It was a mild act of defiance against someone who knew far too much for Rob's own good. Hobart swallowed hard again.

"Hobart, do you realize that I could call for two of the guards on this train and have you arrested instantly?"

"Yes, I do colonel, but I have taken a chance and trusted my instincts."

"And what did your instincts tell you Mr. Hobart?"

"That like me, you too are a traitor to this great Union."

"If you were correct you would have to know far more than the two simple suppositions you have made. Anyone could say them!"

Rob had held his place and was going to bleed Hobart for more information.

"I know colonel that small columns, under Federal guard, are known to leave the factory of one Thaddeus Green's Winchester factory at night, for destinations southward and that these columns have been led by you and your subalterns." Now it was Rob's turn to gulp. Hobart had linked him directly to those southern bound wagon trains. How much more did he know? Did he have witnesses that could verify Hobart's information? Rob had to try and flush more information from him. Rob decided to find out exactly what Hobart had in mind. Rob knew that the man came with a plan of some kind.

"So tell me, Mr. Hobart why are you telling me this? You must have some proposition in mind?"

"I do have an idea, colonel. Why not make this a 'two way' trade?"

"What do you mean Hobart?" Rob was starting to feel frustrated with this man's tactics.

"Simply this: that as the Union column returns from its mission, it should bring back with it wagonloads of cotton brought up from the south."

Rob was not excited with this plan. He leaned closer to Hobart. "Mr. Hobart, cotton by its very nature is a bulky commodity, more suited to river travel. Delivering it north, it would stick out as out of place in Washington."

Hobart was prepared for his objections. "I have no intention of it appearing in Washington. The wagon train could lose its guard detail. Then it would turn east toward the coast and unload its cargo at a private wharf where it would be transferred to a vessel for transport to England." Hobart was becoming more animated as he spoke. Rob took note of this.

"Mister Hobart, you are assuming two things. First you are assuming that I am even interested in your scheme. Second that it has any viability whatsoever."

Hobart finally reacted. He wore a puzzled look that meant this was not the response he had wanted or expected. He suddenly realized that his knowledge of the gun running scheme had not led Rob to jump at the chance to make easy money with little or no effort on his part. The silence was now deafening. Neither man knew exactly what tack to take next. On his part, Rob realized that Hobart probably had no knowledge that he sold information to the south, or he would have used that as well. Hobart did not know that Rob was the master at taking command of a situation.

"Mister Hobart instead of finding a provost guard I am going to put your idea under advisement. I am going to the officer's bar to get a drink. However stay near-by and I will get back to you."

Hobart was left scratching his head. The colonel was trying to remain innocent and yet wanted to dwell on his plan further. He felt at sea. His stomach churned like never before. Meanwhile, Rob had collected his greatcoat and ambled off to the other car. Rob felt he was now in control of the situation. What he wanted to do now was take time to determine how he could take charge of the entire plan.

The bar car was hardly an appropriate place to be thinking up a plan. The hard drinkers among these new officers had obviously gotten themselves well into a bottle of whiskey and were becoming louder and louder. Rob felt that he could not move enough cotton to make this worthwhile. He would have to add wagons to the caravan by appropriating additional wagons coming up from the south. He also had a feeling that more people than Hobart knew of his activities. If he turned Hobart down he could be in deeper trouble than smuggling cotton. Rob waited an hour so that Hobart could boil in his own stew.

Finally he made his way back. He placed his coat carefully on the armrest of the outside seat and slid into the outside seat itself. He wasted no time with needless discussion.

"I believe we can come to an agreement but it must be one that rewards me satisfactorily. I say this because I will be the one taking the greatest risk. But there are ways around this. I want $100.00 for each wagon that is safely turned over to a ship waiting off the coast. If the wagons are stopped, the officer in charge must carry papers with him that indicate that it is government contraband cotton and it is being take to the coast for transport to England. But to make it credible the officer will have to give an actual port of departure."

"But, but colonel!" Hobart stammered. "I will be making almost no profit at your price."

"All you have to do is offer less for it from the southerners' and demand more from whomever you sell it to in the north. Hobart this is not a problem. Within a year the Mississippi river will be choked off as a means of transport north. The Anaconda Plan will see to that. After all, it is the grand strategy for this war. I have given you my first and only offer. You have the power to alter prices."

Hobart fell back in his seat like a rejected lover after a failed proposal of marriage. But it had been his marriage to make or break. "I fear this plan will be rejected by both my sellers and buyers."

Rob bent over him once again and hissed his next words like a snake. "Mr. Hobart, the only 'outrageous' element here is the fact that this poor nation has been torn apart by the forces of politics and greed. While the common man is dying, as we speak, in Tennessee and Mississippi, greedy entrepreneurs like you, are hatching schemes to bleed every cent they can from the people of this great country, both in the north and the south. Don't insult me over nickels and dimes. You will find a way to make this happen. After all, it is your area of expertise. In addition, Mr. Hobart, you are never to use my name to another person. If they wonder what Union soldiers are doing guarding wagon trains tell them they should consider themselves lucky. If you do use my name, by the way, you can consider yourself a dead man. Is that clear?"

Like a chastised child Hobart did not respond. Like a child with his hand caught in the cookie jar, he was busy wringing his hands. Did he have a choice, if he wanted to use Macey as a conduit? He wasn't ready to admit that he could pressure both ends of the operation to pay more. He lifted his head.

"Very well colonel, you leave me no option but to bring pressure to bear at both ends. It won't be my fault if they won't bend. But given their other options, I believe both parties will agree. Can you be in Washington in two weeks so that we can start up the movement of cotton?"

"I believe that I will be back by then. I am sure that you know how to reach me." Rob had not lost any of his cockiness. It was Hobart who had lost the war of wits. Rob simply nodded his agreement, picked up his coat, and went to sit with some of the young officers.

After some idle chatter about the progress of the Union and how it would smash the south, Rob excused himself and moved to another car altogether. Once comfortable he gloated over his victory. He had gambled that Hobart had options and it turned out that he was right.

They were nearing the next station. Rob thought it practical that he say 'good-bye' to his new partner and reassure him that all would go well. Hobart was still sitting in the same seat, staring aimlessly of the window.

"Hobart!" Rob greeted him like a long lost friend and quickly took up a seat next to him. "I want to meet you in Washington. Bring your cash with you when we first meet. It will be a measure of your 'honesty'. In return, at that time we will map out the best routes to use and also prepare the 'letter' and other documents we will need. Until then, I wish you good negotiating." Rob finished with one of his broad smiles. He had put someone else under his thumb, and that is where he liked to keep him.

****

Rob's thoughts now shifted to one of his favorite topics, Rose Green. A smile came over his countenance and his heart beat faster. He believed he was making headway. Without the interference of Anna he knew he could charm Rose over to his side. He had to do two things. The first was to show that he was a new man when it came to how he treated women. This meant his sisters as well. All of this was new for Rob and he was moving in a world that intruded on his life as a criminal. Could he live two entirely different lives? That was the second change. At the end of the war he would resume a just and moral life.

Rob snapped out of his romantic reveries and focused on the government's reasons for sending him to the west again. He was after all, an intelligence officer working under Colonel Winston and as such was concerned with communications. In this case the telegraph. He had made good contacts within the western department, all the way from General Grant down to the men of the Twentieth U.S. Regulars. This gave him access to men he knew and trusted for his assigned mission. He could not help himself. He kept tying to sweep away the picture of Rose burned into his retina by her manners and beauty.

It had started the first time he met her but had been encouraged by chance meetings. Now it was the winter of 1861. Traditionally Anna was driven by their coachman to Harewood Hospital and would stop and pick up Rose on the way. Rob discovered this and paid the coachman to beg off one day, claiming to have a stomach ache. Rob protested that Anna should stay home because of the blowing snow. Anna could see through his shallow attempts at chivalry. This drove her to want to go even more. Plus she knew that a number of nurses would be unable to go, which was all the more reason for her attendance. The discussion got louder and Rob volunteered to take the carriage and drive them to work. Anna's brow furrowed for she knew Rob had ulterior motives. The trip to the Green house took but five minutes and so the three of them took the fifteen minute ride to the hospital. Rob quickly opened the conversation.

"Ladies, I want to hear about your activities at the hospital. It must be rewarding work.""Oh Rob wonderful work is being done to improve hospital care. The time, that can be paid to each soldier is increasing. We write letters for them, even though they can be very sad letters. It helps to keep the soldiers' minds from dwelling on their injuries all the time."

"Tell me more, Rose." Rob was egging her on, but in a nice way. He truly enjoyed the sound of her voice. Rob was pushing his luck with Anna. Rose started in again and was not silent for the rest of the trip to the hospital.

"Well ladies we are here, colder but safe." Rose and Rob laughed together. Rose was thankful for the ride and even more so when he volunteered to pick them up.

"You know Rose it is good for me to learn more about life in the hospital.

It affords me the opportunity of telling soldiers who are making the trek back how well they will be cared for in the hospitals." Anna rolled her eyes.

Anna said nothing to Rose. Rose noticed her deliberate silence.

"Why were you so quiet in the carriage?" Rose queried.

"Rose, can't you see what Rob is trying to do?"

"What do you mean?" Rose responded.

"I know my brother. Ever since he met you at the dinner at our home he has been pestering me about you."

"About what Anna?"

"The things you like to do. If you were attached or seeing someone; whether you liked taking day trips, if you like to ride horses."

"Well what did you tell him?" At this point Rose was enjoying the conversation far more than Anna.

"Rose I finally told him to just forget you, that not now or ever, are you going to become one of his trollops."

"Anna don't you think you are being a little unfair?"

"About Rob?" Anna exclaimed.

"No Rose, about me!" Anna's neck snapped around and she stopped in her tracks. And so Rose began.

"Don't you think I am capable of making my own decisions regarding the men I am attracted to and with whom I will dine and visit?"

"Yes, of course Rose, but this is Rob we are talking about. Haven't Martha and I told you enough stories about him? Don't you realize that he is going to ruin our family's name? Anna paused and then she exclaimed. "Oh, my God! Now I see that you are attracted to him. And you probably want me to arrange a meeting with him when he is in Washington. Oh Rose! Let me go out and find you another man. You can do so much better."

Silence. Both could sense it. Their relationship was on the line. Finally Anna spoke. "Very well Rose but promise to tell me everything that happens."

"Fine, I will agree to that Anna. I don't want to lose you as a friend." The two women hugged. A seal was made. What would come next?

# CHAPTER FIFTEEN:
## CORINTH

Finally the train rolled into Corinth. Rob had placed himself in a position to be the first to exit. He expected to see an aide from the general waiting with a horse for him. Once again he grabbed the rail and swung down. He stopped in his tracks. He had not prepared himself for what he was facing. Before him, stretched on litters, were literally two to three hundred soldiers. They bombarded his senses. The odor was nauseating. It was enough to make Rob feel that he was about to wretch. It was a hard odor to describe because it was a combination of festering wounds, and pus emanating from wounds that would not heal correctly. The morass of the stench contained the sweet smell of fresh blood and the body odors of men who were urinating in their clothes if necessary or because they had lost control of their bladders. This was not an army but a slough of humanity. The visual impact was equally horrific. Red, not blue was the dominant color. Bandages had been displaced when these poor souls were put into ambulances for the trip to the train station. The trip from the large tent hospital outside Corinth had been accompanied by bumping and rocking which caused some healing wounds to disrupt. The parts of their uniforms that still appeared were a filthy brown from dust and war. Every conceivable part of the body had bandaging covering single or multiple wounds. The sound was a chorus of moans as if some conductor was leading these men in a post cacophony of misery. Rob felt out of place. This was not his war. This was a soldier who prided himself on the meticulous care he gave to his military appearance.

He did not belong in this place. He searched quickly for an aide. Quietly a tug at his sleeve gained his attention and he twirled around to see the form of a second lieutenant whose own uniform could use a good cleaning.

"Are you Colonel Macey sir?" The young voice queried.

"Yes, yes I am." The distraction gave Rob the chance to get down from the platform and move away from this 'slough of despondency'.

"I am here to take you to General Ames. Do you want to get started? I will carry your baggage over my horse."

Rob was given a horse that had seen far better days. Its head drooped as it spied some green grass. His bony ribs protruded like the section of a corduroy road,

"Is this the best horse you could find lieutenant?"

Blandly the officer responded. "Our good mounts are out on patrol and we are short of good steeds. We will find you a better mount when we get to camp."

Rob had been thoroughly spoiled by the army up to this point. The war was already taking its toll of niceties. The ride was completed in silence. Rob could not get the image of the station out of his mind. Soon the two riders arrived at a huge tent city. First were the standard company rows, but there must have been at least 1,500 men to a row. They contained the healthy survivors of General Grant's army. At the far end were much larger tents, too big for officers.

"What is this?" asked Rob. He had not seen this type of tent before.

"It is the camp hospital that was set up for the wounded after Shiloh, sir."

"In all of this you can find the general's headquarters?"

"Certainly, sir. I am one of his aides." The officer made a ninety degree turn past the hospital and looked off in the distance where sitting by itself sat the headquarters' tent surrounded by staff officers' tents. The reins from the young man's horse hung loosely. Rob was thinking that he must encourage Homer to look for better aides. The lieutenant's horse decided to defecate in front of Rob and the 'plop-plop' sounds fit in so well with the surrounding dwellings. After a few more twists and turns they arrived at the brigade's command tent. A huge flap was raised over the front of the tent. There was lots of sitting space for meetings with groups of officers. The general's orderly jumped to his feet and helped the colonel to dismount. The orderly took the 'bag of bones' away quietly.

"Is the general available?"

"Yes sir," snapped the orderly as if Rob's dapper presence brought some formality to the situation.

"Please inform him that Colonel Macey has arrived."

"Yes, sir."

Soon Homer Ames appeared and a broad smile covered his face. He spoke. "Lieutenant, could you please discover the whereabouts of Colonel Halliday and have him report here immediately"?

Silently the young officer saluted, wheeled, and jogged off, disappearing among the tents.

"Well Rob, are you impressed by the orderly way we go about our business here?" Homer could tell by Rob's expression that he wished he was any place else but here. "Just think Rob, this is what we have to face for God knows how long. I suppose we will all get so used to it we won't know how to tolerate living in a regular home. This too is a part of the war. At least you get to go back to civilization after this." For reasons unknown Homer found himself apologizing for the peaceful part of military life.

Homer seemed genuinely glad to see Rob. Homer judged men at face value. So Rob was a bit of a dandy. He was still cut out to be a soldier. All he had ever seen from Rob was a creative, helpful, and friendly man. He did not have any reason to suspect that he was a master traitor and liar. For his part Rob also admired the general. He just assumed that everyone had a dark side to their lives and that was that.

"Let's get a chair and sit under the tent flap. It is my favorite place of contemplation." He chucked to himself after that line. "May I get you a man's drink Rob?"

"You certainly may Homer, after what I experienced at the train station I need something with a powerful smell that is pleasing to the senses."

Homer went to retrieve his half-empty bottle of whiskey and called back as he did so. "Ah, I thought you would have something to say about that." The general smiled, but beneath it was a deep feeling of remorse.

Rob responded "What in God's name has happened to warfare? I thought I had seen enough at 'The Ridge'.

"War has changed Rob. It's gotten larger, and we are using tactics that suited Napoleon perfectly but have no place in this country. The rifled musket has replaced the smoothbore, which has been replaced by these Springfields. We have the capability of destroying an open attack with this weapon. We know that. The Parrott gun will eventually replace all smoothbore field guns. We are finding the capacity to kill from a distance but still choose to be on top of one another when we collide. We were at the 'hornet's nest' at Shiloh and once the Confederates got their artillery act together we were beaten. Those Confederates weren't that successful. We were just plain taken off guard. God knows I love that man, but Grant made too many mistakes early on. He was far too lax about the situation. His intelligence was non-existent. No roving cavalry, no breastworks. It was a debacle Rob. To me it seems that the first one to make a mistake was going to suffer."

"So the rumors in Washington are true?"

"Absolutely Rob. In spite of our success the second day, we took the beating of our lives the first day. The casualty figures are unimaginable. They make Bull Run look like a parlor game. I still admire the man. He did not panic. He would appear in one place then another and the men noticed it."

Rob could see that Homer's left hand was shaking. Homer continued. "Let me expand on the statement I made about changing warfare Rob. This is not Napoleonic times. The attacker is or should be at a much greater disadvantage. Stand up warfare in an open field is over. Our landscape is far different from Napoleon's open fields. Man-made and natural defenses have turned the war over to the defense. But I am going to guess the frontal attack will stay with us for the rest of this war. Our equipment mandates this type of warfare. Dismounted cavalry using Spencer breech loaders are only a transition to more kinds of rapid firing guns. What you saw at 'The Ridge' was a taste of what good defenses can do."

Rob sat quietly, listening, thanking himself for having a desk job. Just as Homer finished Ben arrived on the scene and handshakes and smiles were exchanged again. This time he could see the effects of battle. Ben was 'old school' trained and always had taken the concept of proper uniforms seriously. Today he looked disheveled. From his kepi to his boots, everything was covered in dust. Dark stains, probably blood, were visible on his frock coat. His eyes lacked some of the spark that he was known for. His lips were cracked and he had certainly lost weight. The uniform hung on his body as if he was a decaying corpse.

"I can guess what you are thinking, Rob. Homer remarks on it constantly and my orderly can't do anything with the uniform. I have also suffered a session of dysentery to make matters worse. It comes with the burden of command."

It was just then that Rob noticed eagles on his epaulets.

"Ben, it's your regiment, congratulations. What happened to your nemesis?"

Ben and Homer looked at each other.

"He killed himself Rob."

"Oh."

"So you see I won the job by default." Silence. Rob had grown weary of this depressing conversation. He moved on.

"While I have the two of you present, may I expand on one of the reasons I am here?"

"Certainly Rob, both of us have other duties, but we can stand you for awhile." All three had a good laugh at that comment. Homer was good at putting people at rest. Homer had already received an order from General Grant informing him of the nature of Rob's visit. If only he knew everything! And so Rob began.

"I am sure you remember Colonel Winston. He was that desk pusher who put to rest the experiment Ben was working on." Both soldiers nodded their heads in agreement. Rob continued.

"Well, now he has given me a proposal that came directly from President Lincoln." Rob now had their rapt attention and they drew themselves up in their chairs.

"It appears our president has a fascination with the telegraph. Daily he leaves the White House and walks across the street to the war office where the transmissions from different military centers are received. Even though we have broken the Confederate code, Lincoln believes that we are missing out on transmissions from Richmond to Petersburg. His theory really applies to all points south of Richmond. He is not a soldier but sometimes I swear he thinks like one. He has proposed sending small groups of soldiers into the south to employ them to tap deeper into the Southern telegraph lines. They would have to be trained as a group in the method of decoding messages so that they would make sense to the receiver.

Then a rider would be sent out with the message to the nearest Union center. Now before you ask me a thousand questions that challenges this scheme, I want you to remember this: The president and Colonel Winston have spent many an hour debating the mission itself, but who should carry it out?"

"Soldiers in blue uniforms would stick out like sore thumbs, unless they only traveled at night. At this time the president, has little use for Pinkerton. He claims he is slow and knows little about military intelligence gathering. As a result Pinkerton has been let go. He had tied his fortunes to General McClelland and significantly overestimated the number of Confederates in the Peninsula Campaign. Spies normally work alone but in this case it is going to take groups of five or six and soldiers that are trained to work as a group. Gentlemen, much to his chagrin, Lincoln has come to realize that this war could drag on for some time. Personally, on this point, I agree with him. He has left the total number of soldiers to be trained left in the hands of the soldiers. But he does want them trained in Washington at the war office. Colonel Winston approached me because I have had contact with experienced soldiers. He asked me if I knew a regiment that could handle such an adventure." Rob fixed his eyes on Ben. He did not even have to ask. Ben knew who he was addressing in this speech.

Ben adjusted his position in the chair and spoke up. "I assume that you are thinking of the Twentieth Rob?"

"Yes," came the emphatic response.

Homer relaxed knowing that the real content of the conversation would be between the two colonels. He chose the role of clarifier. Ben's eyes, in turn, drifted off into space. He collected his thoughts knowing that he would be sacrificing his men's lives. So Ben began. "What are the implications if I say no?"

"None!" Rob still stared into Ben's face.

Ben lifted his body and replied. "Fine. We will do it. First I have to find out if there are any soldiers willing to ride into hell. Why don't we start with my old company and that will be an indicator."

"Very well," added Homer, as if to reinforce Ben's plan.

The three officers walked briskly to the location of Company B, U.S. Regulars, or what was left of it. They continued to talk about selection strategy. Their conversation was often punctuated by the remarks of individuals or groups of soldiers. "Let's give them another whipping, general!"

"We are ready for the Secesh any time you are, colonel!"

"Good to see you, Colonel Macey!" Rob was taken aback that anyone remembered him.

"Nice to see you Colonel Halliday, come visit us some time!"

When they reached Emile's tent they found him sleeping in a chair with his kepi pulled down over his eyes. It was time for a little fun.

"Come to attention major!" Homer barked, totally out of character. The three got the desired effect. Emile fell off his chair, his eyes bulging in shock. Ben pulled him up from the ground and after a soft chuckle, reviewed the plan in a low voice. They weren't ready for Emile's quick response.

"I want to be your first volunteer!" Emile was assigned the task of assembling the men of Company B. Within twenty minutes he had assembled forty soldiers. Of the forty men, thirty-five volunteered without knowing the full details of the operation. The three officers were shocked. Ben then described the operation to his men and spelled out the potential dangers associated with such an adventure. The major one, of course, was the fact that despite the fact that they would be wearing Union uniforms they would still be shot as spies if detected. Most of their traveling would be at night and operation locations would be in situations as remote as possible.

Rob sent a letter to Colonel Winston informing him that they had no difficulty finding thirty-five without effort. He also requested that Colonel Winston find forty sound mounts, well-broken and quiet and preferably gelded. They didn't need mares that would season on them. Privacy and quiet were musts. They were to be kept in the Washington area and given supplies for extended travel.

Privately both Ben and Homer were slightly concerned with the complete loss of one company from the regiment. They decided to look for volunteers in some of the sister regiments of the brigade. With the selection process in place they started to plan some of the details of this 'invasion of the

South'. Their first priority was security. All the men selected, and even those who had declined, had to take an oath not to release any of the information to other soldiers, their families, or even among themselves. And so began this new adventure that would change Ben's life.

# CHAPTER SIXTEEN:
# THE BEST OF TIMES,
# THE WORST OF TIMES

Rob had been given an officer's tent near brigade headquarters so that communication would be simpler. He had a decision to make and was vexed at his inability to make it. His life as a double agent was getting more difficult. Informing the Confederates of these plans would certainly earn him some monetary reward, but he had his hands in too many pies. The Confederates would certainly request more information on the whereabouts of the listening centers they were planning to set up. They would all surely be taken. Union spy services would certainly wonder whether their plans had been leaked. He would certainly be looked at as one of the possible guilty parties as he was not going on the mission himself. No, he thought, better let this information stay with him. Let the Confederates find out for themselves. Plus he had already picked up a new project in the importing of cotton to the North. Enough was enough, he thought to himself.

****

July 16,1862

Miss Rose Green,

In writing you, I hope that you will not consider my behavior as forward. I know my sister Anna, well enough to suspect that she has communicated my weaknesses and drawbacks in relationships with females to you. I fully admit that, as a young man and cadet I had too high an opinion of myself and cared little for the feelings of others, but I have changed. What this terrible war has taught me is to treat those we love and respect with great care. I have seen enough tragedy to make me aware of the fact that we cling to this life by the thread of a spider's web. This might help you to understand my motives in writing to you. I found you most articulate and knowledgeable. It was unfortunate I did not have enough time to spend in conversation with you.

Even now, as I write to you, I am engaged in a variety of military affairs, but I will be returning to Washington in two weeks and would like to call on you for a visit. If possible we could go for a carriage ride.

I hope this letter finds you well so that we can commence visitations as soon as I return.

Yours in God,

Rob Macey

Rob sat back and re-read the letter and decided that is was formal enough yet spoke with honesty about his misadventures. He felt better, since he finally took hold of what was in his heart. There would be no tryst with Rose. She could be assured of that.

Now to the business at hand. Rob reached into his valise and withdrew an envelope. He removed its contents: a map outlining the features of this camp and all the outlets from it. In conversation with Homer he had managed to find out his troop strength, supply situation, anything else that would be of minutest interest to Confederate planners. A spy in the

Union ranks was to nail a bucket to a tree to direct him to the correct path that he should follow when delivering this information to his counterpart in the Confederate army. He gathered up, the stolen documents, the copies he had made, and the information he had learned and placed them in a courier's pouch ready for delivery. He double checked to see that nothing had been left behind. He was now prepared to meet with the Confederate courier at the pre-arranged time.

****

Addy arrived at her favorite rock in her present mood of elation. She had passed the riding test for the volunteers Rob was recruiting and was dreaming about this upcoming adventure. She no longer felt like an ant in an anthill. She would be an integral part of a rather small group of men who could have a great impact on this war. Oh she was such a dreamer. As she sat pondering her situation she could hear the footsteps of someone walking briskly along the path. The footsteps were firm and quick as if the person was in a hurry. Suddenly she heard a muffled bark. Out of the foliage appeared Patches followed by Hal. He stopped and looked to Addy.

"Addy I wonder if we could have a few words?" Of course, spoke the surprised Addy. Hal removed his kepi like a child facing someone who was about to reprimand him.

"I want to talk to you about the day at the 'hornet's nest'?"

"Go ahead Hal." She directed.

"You see, I know it was you that killed those two Rebs when I was trying to rescue that wounded soldier. You took a big risk exposing yourself. No one has ever risked anything for me before. I know you have reasons for disliking me.

Why did you do it?" Addy drew herself up as if she was about to make a speech.

"I like to think that I would have taken that risk for anyone. But your case was special and I have thought about it a number of times. What you were attempting Hal was an act of heroism. I now see you in a different light. You are fiercely loyal to your men and would do anything to protect them. You are a hero Hal and a man worth being respected. I guess I wonder if anyone has ever spoken to you this way?"

"I can tell you Addy no one has ever spoken such words. It makes me feel good about myself, something that I am not used to."

"In this war you have found a place among men, be proud of that."

Hal returned his kepi to his large head and once again dropped his head.

"I want to thank you for saving my life. I guess I never realized how much life means to me. You gave me that chance Addy."

Addy broke out into a large smile and spoke,

"You can stand the equal with any man Hal. I am so glad you had the courage to speak with me."

Hal turned back towards the path, followed by Patches, who nipped at his heels as he moved. Addy thought of what had just taken place. She was also proud of what she had said. It was so easy to make others feel good about themselves. Sitting upon her rock she now heard a new set of steps, firmer than Hal's had been. Addy was protected from being seen by the fact that a rock stood in front of her, so whoever would pass by would not notice her unless they knew she was there. In an instant the person was by her and predictably took no notice of her.

She was taken aback when she discovered that it was Colonel Macey. He appeared to be carrying a courier's pouch. Logical questions naturally rose to her mind. What was he doing walking on such an obscure path? What was in the pouch? Where was he headed? She concluded that all of this seemed slightly strange. At this time Addy returned to the sketchbook that she had brought with her and began to sketch Major Macey. She had portrayed him as the man she thought he was, manly, well-groomed; the impeccable staff officer who kept showing up at the camp. About fifteen minutes later she could hear the collected cadence coming back along the trail. Walking in this direction she would be in full view of the colonel.

"Hello, Colonel Macey, how are you this beautiful afternoon?" She called out so as not to shock him with her appearance.

"Oh hello, sergeant I did not see you when I came down this path earlier."

"No sir, it's almost impossible to see someone because of this large rock."

Rob had been thrown off-guard but the first rule of a spy is to be prepared for anything. As usual his too-charming smile made Addy think that he might be doing something unusual. Rob could not happen to notice that the sergeant was staring at the envelope he was carrying. He had traded the courier's pouch for the envelope.

"Well I must be off, business as usual." He chirped this last comment to convince the sergeant that nothing was amiss. Perhaps Addy would have felt that way if the courier's pouch had not been left behind and replaced by the envelope.

Well now she had her answer. He must have met with someone and made an exchange, but an exchange of what?

How strange, she thought. He hardly knew this sprawling camp. How did he know his way around? Her curiosity got the better of her and she traced his steps down the path to a small creek and it was evident from the wet ground that another pair of boots had stopped on the other side of the creek. In each case each individual had only gone so far, and then each had turned around and headed back up the valley. Having answered some of her questions, new one's cropped up in her mind. Why had this encounter taken place in such a secretive location? While she thought that all of this was none of her affair, her instincts told her that something wasn't right about this planned meeting. Perhaps she should mention this to Colonel Halliday.

Rob, for his part, had scurried back to the security of his tent, pulled off his muddied boots, hung his hat and frock coat on the rack, and lay on his cot. What should he do? Ben had told him that this sergeant was one of the brightest and most articulate of all the soldiers in the regiment. He was sure to arrive at the correct conclusion and perhaps tell Ben. Who would Ben believe? How could he account for the two parcels? Could he come up with a good excuse for being there? The logical conclusion to this dilemma was becoming clearer and clearer. He just had to find out where the soldier had his tent. He only had one choice.

Off he went to the hospital area. There lying outside were the mangled corpses ready for burial. They were off to the side and out of view. A number of uniforms had yet to be put back on the dead bodies. As quickly as possible he retrieved a pair of brogans, pants, shirt, and kepi. Some still had bandages on them. So he took the best of the worst. Ah the stench! As luck would have it he found a bag lying nearby and he stuffed his new wardrobe into it. Quickly he returned to his tent. His own hat would do fine to help hide his face. He just had to roll it in the earth outside. He took some of the wrapping he had also taken and wrapped it around his head. Now he was beginning to look like a victim of Shiloh. He remembered where he had been taken to meet with the Twentieth. Their tents had to be nearby. He walked to their quarters with a limp to make the act even more authentic. *God my feet hurt*, he thought, these *Brogan's are too small*. That damn Ben was working at his desk. He limped by unnoticed by the colonel. A group of soldiers were lying on the grass in one of the untrammeled areas. Rob stopped and prepared to make his voice sound like a farm boy.

"Does any of you boys know which is Sergeant Brown's tent?"

"Last one in that row," was the response.

"Much appreciated fellas."

Rob hobbled along in the direction he'd been given. Now he had a visual memory of Addy's tent. He turned around without disturbing the ground outside and headed for another group of men.

"Any o' you people know where big Hal's tent is?"

"Next street over, the last tent on the far side." The soldier hadn't even bothered to raise his head. Luck was with Rob that day. Patches was sleeping at the entrance and Rob had seen enough of him to know who owned the dog. There were no soldiers present. This sped up his plans. He shuffled his way to the corner tent, went around the back, lifted the center peg and squished his way into the tent. The dog did not stir. He found what he wanted, stuffed it in his pants, and left the way he had arrived. Immediately he returned to his own quarters.

Quickly he cleaned up his hat, removed the stinking uniform, stuffed it in the bag, and placed it under his bed. He would need this later tonight, but now he had to clean up and prepare himself for dinner with Ben and Homer. When he arrived for dinner Homer and Ben were already sipping a whiskey. The general looked like he had gotten a head start on both of them. Homer greeted him like a long lost relative. Part of it was the whiskey talking; the other was the general's comfort when Rob was around. He felt like he had found a good friend. Ben started the conversation.

"Wouldn't this have been a lot easier if you had just selected a cavalry regiment Rob?" Ben queried.

"To be honest, there aren't any that I am familiar with. I knew who I wanted. Aren't they coming along in their training?"

"For those who have ridden before, particularly the farm boys, this is just like being back home. But, there are some city boys who have never ridden before. I have an idea. It is awkward but I feel there are two distinct parts to this 'adventure'. First is the traveling and riding element, second is the interception of messages and deciphering them if we can. I would like my soldiers to come back from their training and use the ride through Virginia to acclimate them to night travel." Ben could see by their expressions that the other two officers were not in complete acceptance of this plan.

"Ben, that idea has some merit but it will consume valuable time and in crossing Virginia you could engage Secesh militia or worse still a cavalry unit."

"True Rob, but the same could be said about the trip from Washington." Rob countered with a part of the plan he had yet to explain. "Part of this is my fault for not telling you right away. I have already asked Colonel Winston to begin immediately searching for the type of horses best suited for the night time travel. If we use your plan we will have to ship the horses west and you know that train travel can be hard on them."

Finally Homer decided to intervene. He did not want to see these two friends head butting each other over this issue. The plan called for unity.

"Gentlemen why not compromise? Let's keep the men in Washington and ship both to a point where Virginia borders West Virginia. That way these valuable horses will have a new experience for a limited period of time. This way you will lose much less time. What do you think of this compromise? I find it more practical." Both colonels looked at each other wanting to solve the dilemma.

Ben broke the silence. "I can see the benefits of Homer's plan. How about you Rob?"

Rob held back his approval. This had become a political compromise. He decided to give in. "Very well, I understand the logic of your plan. Let's go with it."

Ben and Homer nodded their heads in approval. Homer was glad a solution had been found. Dissension was not needed in a plan such as this one. It was also agreed that these soldiers should be armed with Sharps carbines. This would give them some fire power advantage if it came to that. If all went well they would not have to draw their revolvers or carbines. Homer suggested another round of drinks before dinner. By the time dinner was finished Rob casually commented, "Well gentlemen, I don't know about the rest of you but I could use a good night's sleep." In reality his night was just beginning. He rose and bid good-night to his friends. Homer thought it unusual. Rob could always be counted on for a long night of drinking.

Rob returned to his tent, removed his formal attire, and lay on his bed until two o'clock in the morning. This guaranteed that the greatest volume of soldiers would be fast asleep. Quietly he took the bag from under his bed and began to put on this piecemeal set of a soldier's uniform. He wore this ghastly garb in case he encountered a sentry wandering the environs. The brogans would just not fit. His solution was to wear his cavalry boots with the pants pulled over them. He didn't bother to remove his spurs. He stepped from the tent into the night air. Immediately he felt the freshness of the cooler night air, probably because the soldiers wearing putrid smelling uniforms were now in their beds. He had marked the location of the sergeant's tent carefully on a map which he had to keep lighting with a match stick. He was aided by a bright night sky. The moon shone full and the sky was clear. Rob imagined it to be a giant eye looking down on his movements. In a matter of minutes he arrived at Addy's tent. He stopped to listen. He could hear him breathing heavily. He walked carefully, slinking around to the rear of the tent. Fortunately for him the back of the tent was also open, in order to maximize air circulation he surmised. Rob stopped walking to listen for footsteps. There were none. There he lay in mute silence. Rob crouched down and like a thief in the night put his left hand over his mouth, while the right hand drove Hal's bayonet deep into Addy's heart. His body lurched and then lay still. Suddenly he let out a breath of air that scared Rob. He thought that he had come back to life. Rob withdrew the bayonet which slid silently, lubricated with blood from his heart and arteries. He felt for a pulse on his neck. There wasn't one. He was dead. Now the midnight murderer stood and quickly moved away from the scene to a small wood nearby. There he cleaned Hal's weapon with a cloth, carefully left blood at the neck of the bayonet where one might miss it if cleaning in the night or in a hurry.

Now for the short trip back to Hal's tent. Damn it that bloody dog was sleeping at the front of the tent, thought Rob. What if he announced his arrival? Rob was lucky to be a patient man. He decided to take a chance and see if the 'murderer' would have to make a latrine visit. Rob waited an hour, and fortunately a night of beer drinking had caught up with Hal and he had to make a visit to the latrine. Even more fortunate, the dog decided to follow him. Hal crawled like a beached whale from his tent. Groggy with sleep and a hangover he ambled his way on a trip he had taken more than once. Swiftly Rob entered the tent and placed the bayonet carefully back in its scabbard, being careful to make sure the blood stayed on the throat of the bayonet. As he backed out of the tent his spur kicked a rock making an unwelcome sound which caused no reaction among the sleepers. Like the thief in the night, he stepped surely and silently back to his own tent. He needed a couple of gulps of the night air to calm his shaking hands. He had taken human life before. This situation was not unique. He just rationalized his actions to himself. He was only preserving his life as a spy. Why did the sergeant have to be on that path anyway? Crawling into his cot he fell asleep in minutes and slept, in good conscience, sleeping soundly.

****

Rob was not sure if he was dreaming or just half-awake. He could hear men swearing and yelling. They must have found Addy. He put on his colonel's uniform and walked quickly to the sounds. He was going to keep his distance. There was still one act to play in this drama.

The ruckus had begun at roll call. Sergeant Brown had not responded when his name was called. For the sergeant this was most unusual. He was always the first to appear ready for the new day. Emile asked Sergeant Flynn to check his tent. Flynn's yelp could be heard by the whole regiment. It carried tunes of shock and fear. Immediately Emile went to the tent to see for himself what was going on. He found Flynn holding his mouth as if he was about to vomit. When he got there Emile almost felt like screaming as well, but he knew he had to take control of the situation and keep the soldiers in their ranks.

"Danny! Come quickly." Danny was Emile's son. He had recently been promoted to sergeant.

"You are to go and retrieve the colonel from his tent and bring him to B Company's location."

"Flynn are you in control now son?"

"Yes, yes sir I am."

"I want you to find Lt. O'Malley and have him report here. Oh and have him bring two stretcher bearers with a sheet." Emile saw there was no need to rush. He could distinguish the face of death when he saw it, although in this case it left him in shock. Both officers arrived at the same time in various states of attire.

"Colonel will you and the doctor take over? I want to send my men to their tents and have them stay there until breakfast." Meanwhile the colonel and doctor looked in the tent. The first sight was the copious amounts of blood on his uniform and hazy, open eyes staring at the roof of the tent. O'Malley bent down, checked for a pulse muttering as he checked.

"Good God who would do such a thing?" When Ben heard this he knew he was dead.

"My God, O'Malley, he has been murdered!"

"I know," voiced the doctor in a cool, controlled voice.

"Who would want to murder Sergeant Brown?" Ben muttered to no one in particular.

"Sergeant Adams, come forward!" Barked General Ames, who had just appeared on the scene and was in the process of being informed of what had take place.

"Sergeant I want you to find the provost officer and tell him I will need twenty men as soon as possible."

"Yes sir," was the response.

Ben tried to get control of his emotions. Of the three ranking officers present, he had been the closest to Addy. He had been through worse. He wasn't sure why he had been so affected.

"Who could have done this? Everyone respected and got along with him…almost everyone." The thought raced through his mind. If he felt this way wouldn't others tend to think the same? Now he realized why the general had requested them.

"Doctor, I think we should move this soldier to the hospital as soon as possible." The general's voice was still very controlled.

"Yes, I see your point general." The doctor realized that this situation held potential trouble. He took the sergeant's blanket and pulled it up over his face. The stretcher bearers moved quickly to an empty tent beside the main tent. O'Malley used this tent for dying soldiers. O'Malley entered and did a closer examination from the cursory one he had done in the sergeant's tent.

Meanwhile confusion was starting to erupt among the soldiers of the regiment. They wanted know what had happened. Who was it? What was the soldier's condition?

Rumors flew wildly like a scared flight of bats. Ben was awakened from his shock by the increase in bedlam taking place. He was shocked into action. He sent Emile to find his company commanders and told them to assemble in the field behind their regimental streets.

Men gradually made their way to the field and Ben found an old ammunition crate from which he could address his men. Fortunately the provost guard had arrived. By now small scuffles were breaking out as men argued about all that had happened. He climbed up and could see soldiers pushing their way toward the platform. Ben withdrew his pistol and fired a shot in the air. This got their attention. Men were telling others to be quiet.

"What took place during the night is tragic! Many of you knew Sergeant Brown not for what he said in public but what he did privately. He led by example.

"From what I saw it appears he has been killed with a bayonet. It pierced his heart and he died instantly. At this point there is no indication of the perpetrator of this callous act. An inquiry will begin this very day but I have to consult with the provost officer first. I ask for your cooperation. And you will still form in regimental parade this morning. The roll will be called and anyone absent will be implicated in this nefarious act. We will find the killer." Ben could feel the sweat rolling down his face. Droplets entered his eye sockets and stung them. He then turned to the sergeant in charge of the provost guard.

"You men are to remain with this regiment and prevent any attempts these soldiers might make to enact their own sense of justice upon anyone." Without warning one of the stretcher bearers returned and placed a large hand on Ben's shoulder.

291

"Doctor O'Malley wants you to come with me to the hospital area." Ben glared at the man for interrupting him. But he knew he would not have done so unless it was important. When the two soldiers arrived the stretcher bearer led Ben to the tent where Addy's body was being kept. O'Malley looked up from the body and locked eyes with Ben. O'Malley asked all present to leave the tent.

"I have a surprise for you Ben." *My God what next*, Ben thought to himself.

"We found a note sown to the inside corner of the sergeant's shirt. In the note is a request to have the body embalmed and the address where the body should be sent if she should die."

"What do you mean, she?"

"It seems our sergeant somehow joined the army without taking the medical, which isn't hard. She posed as a male in order to serve her country. She is by nature tall, wide-shouldered and heavy-boned." Ben stood dumbfounded. Finally he spoke.

"But O'Malley I have never heard of such a thing happening. Why would a female join the military." Sometimes Ben could be a little naïve about women. Except for his mother and two sisters he did not have a female that he could call a friend.

"I think you need a bit of education on this subject, Ben. I have talked to other doctors and they too have found women in the ranks. There probably are others. We just don't know the numbers of them. As for your question 'why', I have to admit I am smiling inside a bit. Women have just as strong an attraction to protect this country as 'us'. Just because your mother did not approve of you going into the military does not mean she was opposed to saving the Union. Think man, what have we done to females over the years? We have relegated them to kitchen maids whose job is to run the household. In some ways we have even treated them like slaves. They don't even have the right to vote. Times are changing and this war will speed that up. Look at women like Clara Barton and Dorothea Dix and for that matter Harriet Beecher Stowe."

"Who are they?" Now it was the doctor's jaw that dropped. It then occurred to him that the two of them had been raised in very different ways. Ben was essentially a country boy without a formal education, while he himself had grown up in Boston. His mother had to become the breadwinner of the family when his father died. O'Malley was only too aware of both the physical and mental toughness that women could demonstrate.

"Ben we have greater problems than your lack of knowledge. Let's return to the matter at hand. Do you want your men to know that the sergeant was a 'she'?"

"I…I don't really know." Ben was still recovering from the first shock and had not given any though to this problem.

"May I give you some thoughts on this Ben?"

"By all means doctor!"

"Consider the fact that my stretcher bearers and medical assistant saw me at work and already know. Even if we committed them to silence, I don't expect they would keep this quiet, so assume that this will eventually become public knowledge. You could be viewed as dishonest or at best a commander who felt he could not trust his men with information about a soldier with whom they had fought and faced death. Remember that she was a first sergeant, in charge of a company, and that her bravery has been seriously tested in battle, and she came away victorious."

"How do you know this O'Malley?"

"From your own men! Good God Ben! We are at war and success makes for good stories. Also I saw a number of your men when they were ill. Talk can be a cure for some. Remember Beasley. He was the opposite and every soldier in the regiment knew it. She had already bonded herself to her own company and the regiment. The men are proud of her. I believe they will accept this well. Ultimately Ben, this is your decision." Ben sighed deeply.

"Very well I will tell them this afternoon."

"I don't think you will regret this decision, Ben." The conversation continued. O'Malley still dominated the discussion. "I am certain the weapon used was a bayonet. The opening to her chest is not wide and you can almost make out the exact width of a bayonet." O'Malley sounded quite confident in his delivery. Now it was Ben's turn to speak.

"After my speech this afternoon I will gather the officers and we will check to see that all men have their bayonets with them.

On his return to regiment headquarters Ben began to mull over in his mind exactly what he would say. As he approached, a large group of soldiers were swarming around in a circle formation like a human wagon wheel. Ben wanted to find out what was at the hub of this wheel.

This was a noisy wheel but when he heard a soldier speak he thought it time to act.

"Get a rope and let's hang the bastard!"

Again he found it necessary to fire his pistol. Now the mob began to close around him.

"Make way you men I want to see who it is you would like to hang!" As he approached the center he could see the provost guards protecting one man with their bayonets fixed. Soldiers rushed to tell him something.

"Colonel, we found the killer!" One finally acted as spokesman.

"Colonel it has to be him! Almost every man in the regiment knew that Hal and Sergeant Brown had been fighting. Most of the problem was because of Hal!"

As Ben drew closer he could see Emile with his pistol drawn standing beside Hal.

"Colonel, I want you to take the provost guard with you and proceed to brigade headquarters and remain with him until I arrive."

"You know me colonel, all bluster and bluff!"

A sweating Hal now looked terrified, his eyes were wide open and he was puffing for air.

"We shall find out Hal."

****

Ben finally made his way to brigade headquarters. As he approached he could see Emil talking to Homer in an animated fashion. Homer, for his part, stood tall, hands on hips and lips pursed.

"Colonel please come into my tent." Ben entered but felt terribly uncomfortable. It was a strange feeling for such a secure place. His emotions were truly starting to get the better of him.

"Is what Emile telling me correct?"

"If it is about Sergeant Brown's murder, yes and there is more. Dr. O'Malley has discovered that in fact the sergeant was a female."

"Do the men know this?

"No!" Ben responded emphatically. Both men sat at a small desk. Homer sat staring at the floor with his elbows on his knees with his hands in a praying position tucked under his chin.

"General, I could use you and your staff officers during the inspection of the bayonets. Dr. O'Malley has seen enough bayonet wounds and he is certain that is what was used to kill her.

"Certainly," was the laconic response. The general paused and then continued.

"I have heard of this female phenomenon before Ben. Privately, I admire them. My late wife probably would have been one of them. She was a free spirit who loved this country. It is sad that Sergeant Brown had to leave us in this manner."

*How unusual*, mused Ben, *for the General to add something of his private life at this particular time.* The general continued.

"I understand that many seem to think it was Hal. But you told me they were getting along much better Ben."

"What I saw on the battlefield was a subtle thing general. I am not sure that both even understood its meaning. General I am not sure I want to find the guilty party this afternoon. I would like the men to settle down first."

"If nothing else, Ben, it will appear that you are taking charge of the situation and trying to find out who is responsible." Ben nodded his head in agreement.

"I don't want to leave the regiment alone general. I think I should be getting back, until this afternoon." Ben leapt from the chair, saluting as he stood.

Ben decided he would make a personal inspection of the sergeant's tent and the surrounding area. He hoped he could find something incriminating.

Upon his arrival he found the tent to be guarded by some of the provost guards. They saluted him as he approached.

"Good afternoon men, I would like to survey the scene." They nodded keeping their best military bearing on their faces. First he walked around Hal's tent. There was nothing unusual within. Ben moved to the outside. At the rear of the tent he spotted a foreign object. He picked it up. It was familiar to him. A length of nickel plated rounded metal. Longer than it was wider, it would measure about one quarter of an inch wide and about an inch in length. From the wider jagged end it tapered back to a thinner end piece that had a small ball as its finishing point. What bothered Ben was the fact that it looked terribly familiar to him. He wondered why it had broken off and about a foot away lay a rock about the size of a grapefruit, but flat on the bottom as if some point in its history, had been broken in half. Across the top of the rock was a scratch mark as if a piece of metal had etched the mark into the rock. But what could have happened? It was as if someone walking behind the tent had accidently broken off this piece of metal. Ben made a point of putting the small piece in his coat pocket.

The time had come for the formal inspection of the bayonets and Ben felt he should appear in formal attire. His parents had sent him the money so that he could be the best dressed colonel in the division. He had only worn his dress uniform once and found that he had lost a few pounds in the meantime. Ben was pulling on his dress boots when he caught sight of his spurs. Suddenly he blurted out.

"The piece of metal!" Fortunately no one had heard him. He took the piece of metal from his other coat and matched it with his own spurs. It was almost a perfect match. But only an officer would be wearing such spurs. *Very unusual,* he thought to himself. He would have to take time to think about making a connection between the piece of spur and Sergeant Brown's death.

When he arrived at the open field some of the men were standing around in small groups. They too wanted to find out the cause of death. The officers who appeared had taken the same approach as Ben and brightened up their appearances. Ben took his place on the homely platform, and found himself nervously tapping the box with his boot, waiting for all the companies to form. In minutes, what had seemed like a few grew to a full regiment. He could tell by their expressions and silence that they were taking this very seriously. This time they were well-disciplined. He began.

"Men I have some news for you. The soldier we knew as Sergeant Brown was not a man but a female." Heads turned from side to side as men tried to absorb this information.

"Doctor O'Malley told me that this not an unusual occurrence. He has talked to other doctors who have found women in their regiments as well. You certainly can't blame them for their deception and they must be honored for their loyalty to the Union. Other than that there is nothing new. Her request was to have her body sent home to her parents. We will be doing this as soon as the arrangements can be made.As you have probably noticed there are a number of other officers present and they will help with the inspection of the bayonets."

Quickly, as many as eight officers chose a company and began to inspect the eight companies. The general had brought Hal with him. He had the right to be there while all the bayonets were examined. Two provost guards and an officer accompanied him directly to Hal's tent where a barking Patches rejoiced over his master's return. He jumped up into Hal's waiting arms. The officer with him went into the tent and returned with the sheath mounted on the belt. He removed the bayonet from the sheath. The shaft was clean, but when he went to the metal bend at the top of the bayonet there was a bright red color at the point of contact between the bayonet and the sheath. The officer immediately took Hal and the guards to Ben and Homer.

"I think you should look at Hal's bayonet hilt." The officer was quiet and purposeful. Ben could see the wet, red stain. He sniffed it and could smell the sweet smell of blood. It should have dried by now, but because the spot was where the top of the bayonet lay against the leather hilt it was delayed in drying. He let the general examine it as well. Ben tried to remain calm and his eyes met the general's. It was blood. There could be no doubt. Hal's bayonet contained fresh blood.

"Hal do you have any explanation for the presence of blood on your bayonet?"

"What? That's impossible. I didn't kill Sergeant Brown. Someone else took my bayonet to kill the sergeant and replaced it when he was finished!" No one could guess how accurate Hal's conclusion was. Unfortunately for him everyone else tended to believe the opposite. Hal was the murderer. Ben wanted this information kept quiet for the present.

Ben took his place, once again on the rickety platform and yelled.

"All men are dismissed. Your company captains will take you back to your tents."

"It's Hal, ain't it, colonel?"

"We have a right to know what you found!" Various men yelled out.

"For now just keep calm men and you will be informed. If Hal is charged he will have his day in court."

As the men left, Ben and the general joined Hal and the provost guards. Hal looked confused.

"Hal, how do you explain this blood on your bayonet?"

"I can't sir, except that somebody else put it there! I haven't used this thing since Shiloh! Anyways why would I kill Brown? He was my best friend, next to Patches."

"I am sorry Hal but there a number of witnesses that have seen you quarreling with the sergeant!" Ben's gut told him that Hal was right, but the facts were not in his favor.

"Guards, turn Hal over to the provost guard and place him in the brig until a trial can be held. Ben gestured for this to happen immediately. He turned to Homer.

"General, could we have a discussion at brigade headquarters?"

"Certainly, colonel." Both men wheeled and had to listen to Hal's protestations as the guards took him away. Neither spoke to the other.

The two men were mentally exhausted and slumped in the camp chairs outside of Homer's tent. Ben was particularly upset.

"My God, general, I just sent in a recommendation that Hal be awarded the new 'Medal of Honor'.

"I know Ben. I had to approve it as well." Homer pulled up his chair so that he could sit straight and think the same way.

"That medal is for exceptional valor. No greater honor can be given a soldier. What happened here today has nothing to with what took place on the battlefield." Ben carefully framed his reaction.

"But general I believe he is innocent, despite the blood on his bayonet. I saw their quiet interaction on the battlefield. I clearly see Hal's reaction to Addy saving his life. Nor was Hal the kind who crept around like a sneak, he was always direct to others."

"Ben, this is all very subjective and unfortunately will have little impact at a trial. We will have to do our best to prove his innocence. I will send a letter to Major-General Grant requesting the presence of three colonels to act as judges."

"General I want to defend Hal myself!" Ben pleaded.

"I don't think that is a good idea Ben. You'd be looked upon as favoring Hal and that could split the regiment. No, you will help Hal more by serving as a witness." Ben was disappointed but he knew the general was right. The two officers, soldiers and friends, parted ways. They both knew that at least Hal would have his day in court.

****

A soldier appeared at the front of Ben's tent.

"I wish to talk to the Colonel."

"One moment while I check to see if he is busy," was the calm response of Ben's orderly. Ben rose without the orderly even appearing.

What he saw distressed him further. A soldier in his old company named Jennings was carrying Patches, who was continuously whimpering. Jennings was a farm boy and his behavior was not unusual.

"Colonel, sir, do you want me to take this dog out back and shoot him?"Jennings was not ready for the response that followed.

"What man are you crazy? This is Hal's only comfort in life, his best friend. How dare you suggest such a thing!"

The soldier felt quite sheepish and held out the dog to his colonel as if it were now his problem. Ben took the dog and cradled him in his arms. He thought for a moment about what should be done. Then he realized the obvious. He called in the orderly.

"I want you to take this dog to the guards at the brig and inform them that I have ordered that Hal is allowed to have this dog with him. The dog is lost without him."

"Very well, colonel, I will do it right away." And off he went with this gesture of kindness on Ben's part.

# CHAPTER SEVENTEEN:
# A GENTLEMAN GOES TO WAR

Alexander had been busy of late. He refused to just go off on his own and start a personal war against the Union. He was no Quantrill. He decided it was time to be quiet and let the disaster die down. He knew that Colonel Fielding had a personal friendship with President Davis and this was keeping many officers from protesting over his tactics. Alexander felt it was time to write the president once more and request specific directions for raiding. He knew that the 'raiding cavalry regiments' were very different from the regular cavalry.

July 13,1862
TO: President Jefferson Davis
FROM: Colonel Alexander Braithwaite

Mr. President I hope this letter finds you in good health. I know that you are a busy man so I will keep my suggestion brief. My cavalry regiment has sat idle awaiting your instructions. We desperately need practice in raiding to prepare us for our great adventure in Chicago which will reverse the Confederacy's precarious financial circumstances. I await your instructions.

God save the Confederacy,

Colonel Alexander Braithwaite C.S.A.

July 20,1862
 TO: Colonel Alexander Braithwaite

FROM: President Jefferson Davis

It is indeed fortuitous that you have written me at this time. Colonel Bedford Forrest has a new brigade of cavalry under the overall command of Major-General Braxton Bragg whose mission is to attack Union forces, destroy bridges as they go, and capture any equipment possible. Take a route to Clifton, Tennessee. I understand that you were able to equip your men with Spencer repeating rifles. This is a miracle that I wish others would follow. You have to write me and explain how you achieved this coup of arms. This will also give raiders the chance to fight as dismounted cavalry when necessary. I ask you to break camp as soon as possible and join General Bragg.

May God save the Confederacy,

President Jefferson Davis C.S.A.

Alexander jumped at the chance. He knew General Forrest. He had once been a private in the Confederate army, but like himself, had chosen to put his money into the creation of his own regiment. He gave his men two days to prepare their baggage and artillery and be ready to travel.

The situation became clearer when Alexander met up with Colonel Forrest near Clifton, Tennessee. It was clearer to him why President Davis was so pleased with his use of the Spencers. Forrest explained that his troops were armed with a variety of guns, from shotguns to smoothbores, to Springfields and Enfields. Forrest had a large brigade of 3,500 men. As soon as Braithwaite reached Forrest the brigade became a small division. Their goal was to cross the Tennessee River and destroy communications between Louisville, Kentucky and Memphis, Tennessee. That task was not simple. Forrest had to ferry his men, artillery, and other baggage on a leaky old ferryboat while the horses were forced to swim the river. Drivers kept the horses in some semblance of order, all of this during a heavy rainfall. Forrest and his men were forced to fight in a small area bordered by the Tennessee and Mississippi Rivers and the Memphis and Charleston Railroad which was being defended by Union soldiers. During this campaign there were three heavy battles and Alexander's men were severely tested. In one of these battles Alexander and his men acted as the rearguard. He successfully acquired the tactic of fighting as infantry. One soldier would hold five horses while the rest, using their Spencers, held off two regiments of attacking infantry.

The Spencers did not have the range of a Springfield so his men were required to hold back their firing until the Union infantry approached one hundred yards. The rapid firing Spencers tore into the Union forces and like sheaves of wheat in a hailstorm the men in blue fell to the ground in bloodied waves. During a two week sojourn around the countryside this cavalry force managed to burn fifty bridges, thus making the railroad impossible to use. It also liberated 2,000 Confederate prisoners, captured 10,000 rifles and a million rounds of ammunition. They also captured a full battery of artillery plus the wagons to haul away the booty.

When the South took to serious raiding it meant the North was in fact supplying the South with the ability to wage war. The success of this raiding also meant that Alexander's name was appearing in more and more dispatches.

After fighting with Forrest for two months, Alexander's regiment was separated from the main body and assigned to run its own operations, particularly longer forays in preparation for the raid on Chicago. On one such raid his regiment had the chance to sack the camp of a brigade of Northern infantry. He chose to use his men again as dismounted cavalry. Skirmishers were sent out to silence any sentries who could alarm the Union troops. It was noon and most of the Union men were having their mid-day meal. When the Union guards were eliminated it meant the Southerners could virtually walk into the camp.

The camp backed up to a stand of young trees and Alexander had his men placed to take advantage of this deception. He had forgotten, however, to tell his men whether this was a prisoner-taking raid. The camp was noisy with the sounds of lunch time conversation so his men were able to reach the edge of the woods undetected. His 700 men were put into two lines and prepared for volley fire. First he had his horse artillery cut a swath through the tents to create clear targets. All was set. The battery of artillery used grapeshot to virtually destroy most of the tents. The Union soldiers acted like men who had their clothes stripped from them. The shock of the shelling caused chaos in the camp and then came the volley fire from the soldiers. The Union men were helpless. Most stood in shock and were cut down, unable to defend themselves. Their officers' commands could barely be heard above the Confederate artillery, and the Union artillery was unable to be used against the enemy. Soon some of Alexander's subalterns started to lose control and groups of soldiers took this as opportunity to pillage the camp. It took Alexander a few minutes to realize what was happening and when he did, he galloped into the fray trying to get his men to take prisoners.

He was horrified by the needless carnage. Union soldiers were trying to surrender but were being shot on the spot by the madness that overtook his men's minds. When order was restored Alexander's anger knew no limit. He had had to use his own pistol to discourage his men from turning into raging firebrands.

He found the Union officer in charge and simply told them to leave all their equipment and march to the nearest Union camp. The Union officer offered no resistance and was glad to get his men out of this melee.

After they left the argument started. He formed his men into their companies and stood facing what had become a tribe of wild men. He could see that the rage of battle still coursed through their veins. He began.

"You men are not supposed to act like savages! Our orders were to capture desperately needed equipment, not slay Union soldiers. In this action I saw far too many times with my own eyes nothing but cold-blooded murder! I never want to see this again. Do you understand?" Most nodded, but some disagreed and voiced their discontent.

"You had no right to just let those Yankees walk away like that! They are the enemy and we move quickly. We can't afford to take prisoners! We don't have time to look up in some book what our code of honor should be!" These voices of discontent also got nods of approval. Alexander's face turned red with fury.

"Any man who serves with me will always treat the defenseless enemy as an innocent victim of war and will be treated accordingly. If you disagree come forward now and be recognized so I can have you transferred to Colonel Fielding's regiment."

"Don't say nothing bad about the colonel. He's just a hard fighting man!"

Alexander repeated the offer but none stepped forward. He had made his point.

Alexander left his men to ponder the dressing down he had just given them. As they gathered up their spoils of war he had time to reflect on what had just happened. He realized that battle under these conditions created a heated moment in time and men are not always equipped to handle themselves as they would in other situations. He called it 'The Fury of War.' Honor was not something one could always call upon. It was part of the emotional being, not the rational man. Honor was something different. It developed over time and had to become an inherent part of a man's character and beliefs. It was possible that a man's actions in a time of great excitement could overcome his beliefs.

# CHAPTER EIGHTEEN:
# THE SEARCH FOR JUSTICE

Jul18, 1862
TO: Brigadier-General Homer Ames

FROM: Major-General U.S. Grant

Homer, I found your letter one of great sadness. The Twentieth U.S. Regulars are a well-known and respected regiment. I hope the events that took place will not tarnish their honorable reputation. To make justice possible I will send three of my own officers to act as the judges in this case. This will remove the possibility of objections based on bias. Find the best officer you can to defend the accused in these proceedings.

With the help of God,

Major-General U.S. Grant

Homer sighed with resignation. He had hoped Grant would send officers to serve as both prosecutors and defense. He would have to choose one of the colonels of the brigade to serve as prosecutor. He did decide that time would only cause this wound to fester. He wanted the trial to take place as soon as possible. As soon as Grant's officers arrived, the trial would begin. Within a week they arrived. Homer let out another sigh.

The prosecution was able to call a number of witnesses who had heard Hal say that he would 'get even' with the sergeant. There were those who had seen the fight at the 'The Ridge'. Trusting what he had seen at Shiloh, Ben took the stand to tell the story of how Addy saved Hal's life. He went on to describe what Addy had told him about Hal's recognition of her actions. But the defense challenged this as being Ben's interpretation of what was meant by Hal's gesture, the prosecution countered that one could hardly come to conclusions in the heat of battle. The prosecution called witness after witness.

"I remember Hal's anger at The Battle of The Ridge, when Sergeant Brown tried to stop Hal from harassing a black man." said one.

"I remember how angry Hal was when Sergeant Brown defeated him in the shooting demonstration." said another.

One soldier had heard them arguing about another soldier's behavior the day Addy was murdered. The evidence that fixed his guilt was the bayonet and scabbard with the blood on it. Hal had no explanation for them. Hal toyed with the idea of telling Ben about their encounter at the rock, but he realized it would just be seen as something he made up to make himself look better. Ben went on to describe Hal's excellent leadership and behavior as a leader. But he feared any positive comments about Hal's character were falling on deaf ears.

It took a mere ten minutes for the officers to reach their conclusion. Hal was responsible for Addy's death. Hal would be executed by firing squad within two days.

The execution was to take the form and style of most military executions. The whole brigade would form a U-shaped rectangle with an open end. Homer was against the newspapers covering this event and turning it into political fodder, but still it would satisfy the appetites of those who truly believed Hal was guilty. Once he heard the verdict General Grant also pushed for a rapid execution. He too did not want this event being dragged on and dwelt upon. It was early in the war and executions were still rare. Hopefully it would act as a deterrent for those who believed the military had no intention of severely punishing anyone.

And so the day arrived. The brigade was formed in the rectangular 'U' fashion. Now the soldiers were to find out how ghoulish such an event could be. At the open end sat a pine box which would serve as Hal's coffin. Immediately beside it was the hole in the ground where he would be put to rest. Within ten minutes the official parade appeared. Hal's hands and feet were shackled. The soldiers went deathly silent. Hal was led to the back of the coffin and made to sit down. He gave no sign or cries of anger.

He would simply fall into this dark abyss that would become his resting place. Out of the nearby woods Patches suddenly appeared and proceeded to bite the leg of one member of the firing squad. It was one of those occasions when one did not know whether to laugh or cry. The dog's behavior added a farcical effect to the whole proceedings. Emile was standing nearby and rushed out to grab the loyal beast. Hal refused the offer of a blindfold. He was uncharacteristically quiet.

Of the twelve men only eight had a Minnie ball inside the barrel of his Winchester. Thus the killers would never know whether they were the one who had put a hole in Hal's heart.

"Ready…aim…fire" The command came from the provost officer. Now Hal's execution took on even a more farcical dimension. One shot hit Hal's foot causing it to swing out and away from the other foot. One shot hit Hal in the stomach and he pitched forward in pain. The cries of pain could be heard by all. This time all in the firing squad were told to reload. In the meantime Hal was reset on his death perch. The hands of the firing squad were beginning to tremble. To them this was an omen of Hal's innocence.

"Ready…Aim…Fire". This time Hal appeased justice and fell back into the coffin. However legs were still thrashing as he fought off his death throes. This time the provost officer went up to him and put two pistol shots into his head. All were silent. Patches broke out into a wild yelping sound that pierced the ears of all present bearing witness to the injustice of what had just taken place. Immediately four soldiers appeared and squeezed Hal into the coffin. Hal was too large for the coffin and one soldier had to stand on Hal's shoulder to push him into place. The cover was nailed shut and lifted into the pre-dug hole. Their shovels filled the hole, leaving a mound of soil that would eventually settle on the grave or be blown away in a storm. Homer felt it was necessary to comment.

"Men you have just seen the execution of one of the most courageous men in our brigade. You should know that Hal was nominated for the Medal of Honor for his courage under fire. This honor we won't, nor should we, take away from this brave man. But no man is above the laws of this country. To forgive him would have been a greater injustice. Learn from it. We are a flawed race. His real judgment will come when he faces his maker. You are now in the hands of your officers to see that you return to your camps."

Homer stayed in place after his remarks and stayed until all had left. He walked to the grave and placed something beneath the soil. No one saw what it was.

Homer asked Rob and Ben to join him for a brief meeting after the dismissal. When all were present Rob launched into a presentation of some of the questions that needed to be considered for the Washington code training. Ben listened but he felt more like a bird trapped in a cage. His head was limp and being held up by his right fist. It had been so long since he had been home that people like Addy and Hal were a part of his family. He felt lost and empty. Homer had detected Ben's mood and interrupted Rob with a question.

"Sorry to stop you old boy, but I would like to get a stiff drink!" He had been standing while finishing his statement. Somewhere the question part of it had gotten lost. Ben could tell that Rob was irked at this. For him this was just another business day.

Homer led the two colonels to his tent. All were silent. Homer reflected on how different these two men were as humans. Ben let Homer get his drink and then spoke.

"Considering the day's events do you think we could hold this meeting at another time?"

"Sorry, Ben but we have to get things in order before we go and we can't be doing things at the last moment."

"Ben, I think that is an excellent idea. This can wait Rob." Homer looked directly and firmly into Rob's eyes. Rob got the message.

Ben felt he needed to do some soul searching. He also felt himself being pulled back to Hal's grave. As he approached he could see there was something sitting on the moist soil.

When he approached the grave the form moved....It was Patches.

"Hello, old boy what are you doing here?" he realized that he had just asked a senseless question. The dog was grieving for his master. Ben bent over and picked up the small creature that was shaking, possibly in fear, but more likely in terror. He had just lost his only friend. Ben sat down beside the grave and let the dog curl up once again. It seemed to calm him. He found himself babbling away to the dog and scratching his head. Patches nodded off to sleep. God knows he'd probably had little. At least his owner was at rest. For reasons he could not explain Ben felt better and decided to return to see if Homer and Rob were still available.

During his absence Rob asked Homer what was wrong with Ben. It was a question that told a thousand tales. From then on, Homer would always be slightly wary of Rob. Rob was not the social being he appeared to be, but rather a loner passing through a world he saw but did not feel.

Three decisions had been made as the riding training continued. First, they would double the complement of soldiers to sixty. Second, their training was not progressing as fast as the officers would like. As veteran cavalrymen Ben and Homer knew when a man looked comfortable in the saddle and was at one with the horse. Granted they weren't using the quality of horse they would receive. Some changes were made. New men were brought in. The third change was that Ben and Homer would take over the actual training.

Each day started with a review on equine care. Each 'trooper' would have to be the one in charge of those tender legs and feet. A horse without healthy feet and legs was of no use to them.

Rob decided that he would come out and give the two men a hand. After all, he was a cavalryman as well. He thought he could help bring Ben out of his shell. Rob waited until Ben finished teaching a drill and rode over to where Ben was observing. Ben dismounted to tighten his cinch. It was then he saw it. He was at eye level with Rob's boot. The end of Rob's spur was broken off. He was going to ask Rob about it but thought better of it. The piece missing from Rob's spur could be that piece of metal he'd found behind Hal's tent. He said nothing. He tried putting the piece of metal out of his mind. He could not. If that piece of metal he had in his pocket fit Rob's spur, what did it mean? Perhaps nothing? On the other hand, it could be used to implicate Rob in Addy's death! But that made no sense and it would look worse if he mentioned it even in passing. Why would he want her dead to start with? To say anything to Rob might jeopardize the trip to Washington. Plus all Rob had to do was deny everything. For the first time in his career Ben wished he was not in the army. In the end he decided he would speak to Homer about what he had found.

He found Homer in his usual spot, planted in his chair, smoking his pipe and talking to two colonels from the other regiments. As Ben approached he was glad he had decided on this course of action. The two colonels stopped their conversation, choosing to defer to Ben. Their discussion with Homer was at an end. Both stood, greeted Ben, and then withdrew.

"Our first order of business is an emotional one Ben. It is up to you how well you take it. In going through Addy's possessions I came upon a sketch book. She was quite an artist you know. Normally I would have sent this along to her family but when I opened the first page I changed my mind."

"Why is that sir?"

"Read the dedication Ben."

'To Captain Halliday, to whom I owe so much'.

"Now do you see why I saved it for you?"

"Yes, yes I do. Thank you, general." Ben was absolutely taken aback by this gift from the grave. He could not bring himself to look at it. So he planned to stow it in his personal effects trunk. Someday he would be ready to look at it.

"Sit Ben, I have been meaning to have a talk to you for awhile now about another issue…I think you deserve a furlough. You have been on duty since you joined the cavalry before the war. Why not go home and visit with your family. I am sure they wonder why you never come home. I have been informed that your special assignment has been deferred for a month. This would be an ideal time for a visit. This rest will clear the cobwebs from your mind. You need to be in top condition to handle this assignment."

Ben said nothing. Homer let this idea in Ben's mind. He wasn't surprised by Ben's slow reaction. He had seen this behavior develop in other good officers. They become so close to the military, all other significant parts of their lives were sent to the recesses of their minds.

"I think I will take you up on the offer general. It will be good to see my parents and perhaps those bratty sisters of mine have grown into real women. Emile and Rob can handle the horse training while I am gone."

Homer practically jumped from his chair. He had thought he'd have to battle with Ben to get him to take a leave.

"Good Ben!" he exclaimed. "I don't think you will regret your decision. Just don't become a deserter!" Both men laughed at the irony of this statement. If there was anyone incapable of desertion it was Ben.

As they were speaking a sergeant from Ben's regiment approached the two officers.

"Sergeant, I did not expect you to attend this meeting. What can I do for you?" The colonel said, still laughing from the previous comment.

"Colonel I think you should come with me. General you might be interested too." The sergeant looked somewhat crestfallen as if this was not going to be a pleasant encounter. Nor did he seem willing to go into any details. The three men traversed the camp and Ben and Homer soon found their destination. Hal's grave. It had already begun to show grass growing around its edges. There lying on the grave was Patches. Pieces of meat and other delicacies left by some soldiers surrounded the grieving dog. It looked as if none of it had been touched. Ben approached Patches and talked softly to the small dog. He gently picked him up. His body had become a skeleton. The animal had obviously not eaten a morsel of food since Hal's death.

"My God general what are we going to do for this poor beast?"

Homer knew exactly what to do. Despite Ben's being raised on a farm he had forgotten some of the lessons he had acquired.

Homer spoke softly yet firmly to Ben. "Ben we must put this animal out of its misery."

"But general we could force feed him until he gets some strength back. He will eventually forget Hal!" Ben sounded like he was thinking that the dog represented the last living connection to Hal.

"That is an order!" Homer still spoke softly but firmly. Ben's head snapped around and his eyes met the generals's.

"Sergeant I want you to take the colonel back to my headquarters. Get my orderly to pour him a stiff drink of whiskey. When you have done that go find the quartermaster and fetch me a shovel."

Ben knew what was coming but deep down his mind caught up with his emotions and told him that this was the right thing to do. About half-way back to the tent Ben heard the sharp report of a pistol. Tears ran down his face and he turned away from the sergeant. He knew it was time to go home.

# CHAPTER NINETEEN:
# GOING HOME

The train trip, like most train trips when traveling alone, was somewhat boring and uneventful. Occasionally wounded soldiers would embark or depart, continually reminding Ben of the horrors of this war. Two train changes later he disembarked from the train. It was a mere twenty mile trip to the family farm in northern Illinois.

Unexpectedly his family had traveled the distance by carriage just to greet him. He found himself speechless. Hugs were exchanged but little was said at this time. The letters from both parties had filled in much of the conversation. Ben could see the empathetic looks on their faces. How much Ben had changed in the ten years since he had left home. A boy of eighteen now looked like a man of forty. The war had quickened the pace of the changes.

Generally the trip home was good for Ben. He was amazed how his bratty sisters had turned into comely women. Each had married and brought their husbands with them. Ben barely recognized their husbands. They had been his friends while growing up. But they had still retained their boyish looks. The farm looked much the same, but a new generation of cattle filled the fields.

Ben was not aware his family had a hidden agenda with his return. His father revealed this agenda later on. One day, while branding calves his father spoke.

"Ben, you have served your country for ten years. Your letters have spoken of your growth as a man, a soldier, and the horrors you have experienced. You have given the equal of ten men. Ben, I am getting older and feel the aches and pains of farm work. Your sisters have moved away and the farm is a lonely place with only your mother and me. It is impossible to find men to help with the work. They have all gone to the war. Ben it is your place to fill the shoes as owner and operator of this farm."

At first Ben felt nothing. He was not a part of this farm anymore. He did wonder, why one of the brothers-in-law had not helped take over the farm. It was just as well that they hadn't. Their time would come in this war. The ugly issue of conscription was lurking somewhere in the future.

As time passed it became clear to Ben that he had another home with responsibilities and duties...his regiment. The remainder of his stay was relaxing. He made a point of riding every day. He would take their best horse and let him out at a full gallop. This he could do with his men. He visited his sisters, attended family picnics, and met with old friends but deep in his soul he felt that all of this had somehow been orchestrated for him to seduce him into taking over the farm. But his walks in the woods were the days that mattered most. Suddenly he had to get back to his regiment. The terrible Battle of Antietem Creek filled the newspapers. Both sides claimed victories.

But the real truth...the casualty figures... came within the week. They were enormous and a number of families had relatives who had lost kin. Fortunately Antietam had been fought by The Army of the Potomac and there were fewer western regiments serving in the east. The gods of war had cast their nets over these American brothers and caused destruction that made the first battles seem like skirmishes. The casualty lists spoke of tragedy not triumph. He grieved for his family. They could not see what was coming. It was his duty to make their lives a little easier by serving to protect this farmland.

They protested strongly about his decision to return to his regiment, but they also knew that once Ben made up his mind there was no changing it. Nor could he tell them about the clandestine operations that he and his men were to undertake. He left within a week after reading about the Battle at Antietam.

****

The return trip was an emotional contradiction for Ben. Now he knew his place, was on the battlefield. He knew only too well, and so did his family, that he might never return to his hearth and kin. This thought saddened him. His desire for honor had not been satiated, but in his heart he knew that it would be a cup never filled, until this horrendous war came to an end. Over and over his mind returned to Rob's broken spur and its potential link to Addy's tragic death. Perhaps there was a natural, logical reason for him to be in that location. He believed fate could play strange tricks on the mind and heart.

He knew that he and Rob were going to work together much more in the near future. He needed to know that Rob was a man he could trust. He hesitated to discuss the topic of the spur with Homer because his view of Rob might be biased. He knew that Homer had a deep and abiding respect for Rob, even if he was a 'staff' man and not a fighting man. Continually he returned to what motive Rob would have to kill Addy. It just made no sense. Ben had exhausted his attempt to rationalize the event. He would have to put it out of his mind.

By this time Ben was ready and eager to find a soldier's view of Antietam. The military train on which he was traveling was rife with conjecture about the significance of the battle. Lieutenant General Lee had been forced to leave Maryland and retreat to safety. Yet there was no attempt by the Union forces to follow up and pursue him.

By the time Ben reached Corinth Station he had heard every interpretation, from the failure to make good use of reserves to Union Major General A. Burnside's inability to make a timely capture of what became known as Burnside's Bridge. It was a part of military life. Everyone had an opinion and suddenly became experts. In assessing these kinds of debates Ben realized that no one man could be blamed for the successes or failures, since no one man had total control over the ebb and flow of battle. Nor could any leader have a complete view of the battlefield. Leave it to the historians to read and analyze the reports and try to make sense of them.

# CHAPTER TWENTY:
# THE ROAD TO WASHINGTON

Ben had to admit that he was tired of listening to the experts he met on the return trip. But that was one of the hazards of being a colonel. Rarely, but sometimes, a major battle would rise or fall on the successes or failures of one man who commanded five hundred to eight hundred soldiers. It was enough to be in charge of this number of men. How must it feel to be in charge of tens of thousands? How would it feel to give the command to begin an engagement and turn it over to all the sub-commanders? It made Ben think that he was quite happy being where he was and content with the superiors above him.

When he arrived he left his orderly with his baggage and went directly to General Ames to see how training had progressed. By sheer coincidence General Grant had been paying Homer a visit. Grant remembered Ben as a captain. It left Ben feeling that they had been fighting for years. Homer was just about to say good-bye to General Grant so Ben waited. Ben was offered a chair, drink, and a cigar. This must mean good news.

Ben opened the discussion eagerly. "Was the regiment able to get along without me general?"

"Get along? Why they are twice the regiment that you left a month ago."

Ben took this as a good sign. The time away had eroded some of the war weariness that Homer had correctly diagnosed in Ben. The banter continued for another ten minutes until Rob approached.

"Ah! The deserter has returned," quipped Rob. Homer had more social skills than Ben gave him credit for. Homer noticed signs of Ben's discomfort. He stiffened in his chair and rarely made eye-contact with Rob.

"Well, Ben are you ready to take that rag-tag bunch of excuses for soldiers off to Washington?" Homer was in good form today.

"Of course!" replied Ben enthusiastically.

"We will be leaving one week from today and I have the onerous task of introducing you to the capital of this Union. A country boy like you will get eaten up by the whirlwind of social life and the foul and feminine women of Washington." Ben managed a good belly laugh with Rob's opening salvo about Washington.

"Good," was Rob's simple response. "Well I must get to work. Some of us have to earn our colonels' pay." And so Rob departed.

"Ben I know you well enough to read when you are comfortable and uncomfortable and you, my boy, changed when Rob appeared. Why?"

Ben had to think quickly. Was it a good idea to put doubt about Rob in the general's mind? After all, the evidence was circumstantial. He decided not to say anything.

"I think Homer you should take this as a compliment. I am not guarded in front of you because we have been together much more often, thus I am relaxed. Rob, is still essentially a passer-by. He has no bonds of loyalty to this command the way you and I have." Homer accepted his response at face value but still believed something was not right.

"I want you to meet with Emile and he will give you a report of how individual soldiers are progressing." Ben would have done this anyway. Homer had another agenda and had tried to probe it once without success. For now Ben's thoughts about Rob would stay in the back of his mind.

The news was good. Not one man had fallen out because of their riding skills. Emile had made a point of having the men practice with Spencer rifles so that they would be used to operating them if necessary. Ben had borrowed a few from the cavalry unit camped near-by. They would receive their own in Washington. Ben and Emile talked at length about the nature of combat they might incur on this mission. It was decided that it should be avoided at all costs. They did not need any attention drawn to them. If faced with a small patrol they would engage in battle only if their chances of shooting all of the enemy soldiers were good.

One goal of their mission was secrecy. They would have to maintain this for a period of three weeks. Now they had the exact numbers to give the general. There would be twelve squads. Each would include one officer, two sergeants, four corporals, and eight privates. The time arrived to leave camp with their basic equipment and take 'the iron horse' to Washington.

Even their departure was kept secret. They swiftly assembled at the station and were given two rail cars which would be isolated from the other cars. General Ames wished them good fortune and desired to see them all on another day. Far in the background was Colonel Macey who was watching his plan take form and knew soon it would also take action.

Three train exchanges and three days later they arrived in Washington. The trip had been uneventful. Most of the men were country boys, so their wagon trip through the city was quite an eye-opener. The two buildings they all recognized were the Capitol building and The White House. Their formal education, what there was of it, had managed to inculcate a sense of history and romance attached to the President's home. The building they were headed for they had not seen. It was the home of the secretary of war and would be their training center. Their residence had been built from the back of the building. It was a wood frame building intending to serve as temporary sleeping quarters. It was just a few feet from the war office. They had arrived at 3:00 p.m. and were given three hours to tour the local area. Their training would start at 9:00 a.m. the next day.

# CHAPTER TWENTY ONE:
## THE TWENTIETH BECOME SPIES

"Gentlemen my name is Major Edwin Myer and I am head of the electrical division of the United States Signal Corps. If you have any questions about what you are going to learn, I want you to save them until the end of the day. I understand that you will also require time to upgrade your equestrian skills and you will also be getting more training on the Spencer. Those two topics are not my concern but are a necessary part of your training. For security reasons you will be in total isolation for three weeks. I have to warn you that divulging any of the information concerning your education here will be considered treason of which the penalty is hanging. During this session you will learn nothing about the Union's methods of espionage. The reason for this is quite clear. The less information you know, the less information the Confederates can beat out of you if you are captured. If captured we prefer you die honestly by pleading ignorance instead of having to lie." Myer's statement received some hearty guffaws from the men and helped break the tension.

"Here is a picture of your primary enemy and my counterpart in the C.S.A., Colonel William Norris. The Confederates have their own signals branch. Signaling is divided into two parts: methods of communication and ciphering. I will cover the topic of communication first.

"I must also remind you that everything, with the exception of the cipher decoder, must be put to memory. We have allotted free time so that you may use this room or your barracks for study purposes." He paused,

"Your first method of communication is 'wig-wag' signaling. Wig-wag can only be used during daylight hours and within visible range. It consists of only one flag tied to a staff constructed in four foot jointed sections. They vary in size from 2'x2' up to 6'x6' using the colors of white, red, and black."

"You need not memorize these flags as you will not be observing the enemy's flag messages.

"The second and probably the most unused method is the use of rockets. It is to be used at night for the main purpose mainly of communicating troop movements.

"The third is the use of spy-glasses which give the user a chance to more accurately assess enemy movement."

"The fourth, and most important for you, is the electric telegraph accompanied by a cipher system. It won't be necessary for you to learn the cipher codes. This will occur in Washington or other sites. What you will have to learn is the ability to translate the electric signal into letters which in most cases will be scrambled. We are not sure what the Confederates use south of Richmond. For all you know the message might be intact and not need translation. To transfer an unscrambled message all you will need to learn is Morse code. Remember Morse code can be scrambled or unscrambled."

"Let me show you what I mean." Myer paused and retrieved a chart from a nearby table that showed an example of a coded message: tflhodkrlhmvisditmblhl.

"Note that the letters are run together to make the job of de-ciphering it more difficult. But that will be our problem not yours. This message will be intercepted by fastening this metal clip to the transmission wire. The wire on your transmission clip is then attached to an ordinary receiving set placed in the woods or some other secret location near the clip-on point. When a message is received by you, you will send the message by courier to the nearest pick up point using one of your couriers. The rider will then make the trip back."

"We have already located the twelve monitoring stations each group will use and the trails and routes to be used for first, finding your center, and second, the routes for the couriers. We view the courier's trip as the most difficult part of the system. Depending on location, the courier should return within a given period. If the courier fails to return assume he has been captured and send another courier. You will stay at your listening station for three weeks, then return to Washington. We have been quite careful to find remote locations or wooded areas so that you will be free from Confederate militia. Your success will determine whether we need to change or do away with this system. Are there any questions?"

"Are there any times when it will be necessary to fight?" A sergeant asked.

"Good question. We have decided that if you are clearly discovered or about to be you may engage the enemy. The reason for this is that you are going to be shot as spies anyway." The room went totally silent.

Ben was absorbing this introduction into the world of spying when a voice from behind whispered.

"And make sure you don't sneeze when the enemy is close by!" Ben wheeled around and discovered that it was Rob. The colonel had snuck into the room and placed himself behind

Ben. The major was finished at this point so the two men engaged in conversation.

"Are you coming with us on this mission Rob?" Ben asked.

"Who me? I don't want to get caught and wind up being shot as a spy!" laughed Rob. Ben made a mental note of this. The man with the ideas doesn't want to die.

"Enough of this spy business, Ben. How would you like to come to dinner at my parent's house? They are having a dinner and I would like you to meet my family. There'll be lots of beautiful women and fat generals there."

"Oh, I would not fit in with that kind of crowd, Rob." Ben said, but Rob was not going to accept no for an answer.

"Nonsense Ben, you are as good as the rest of them at making conversation. And how long has it been since you had a fancy meal? I know. I will make sure that you are seated next to Anna, how's that?" Ben pretended he was thinking this over, but once Rob mentioned Anna, Ben's interest level rose.

"Oh very well, I guess I can put myself out for the Union." Both men chuckled at that response.

"Excellent Ben, I will pick you up at 5:00 p.m. in front of the war office. I'll have to use of one our carriages."

True to his word Rob appeared right on time and began the short trip to the Macey residence. Ben was commenting on the superb organization of their new adventure.

"The major has done an excellent job preparing the work that has been done. I assume he is responsible for the individual maps as well."

"I hope that is not a question Ben, because you know I can't answer. You are entering my world now." How ironic Rob should say that, thought Ben.

For Ben this was not something to fear but the start of a new adventure. Within minutes the carriage rolled up to the Macey Mansion

Ben was whisked into the Macey mansion to be met by Anna and Martha. Rob handled the introduction.

"Colonel Halliday, I would like you to meet my two sisters." Both curtsied politely to Ben who felt embarrassed in the midst of this upper class society.

"Anna, why don't you take Ben into the library and relax while I find two glasses and a good shot of whiskey to loosen up this country boy's tongue." Anna grabbed his arm and swung him ninety degrees toward the library. Anna chose two comfortable chairs near the piano. Martha sat at the piano and began to play a Mozart concerto very quietly. Anna moved her chair directly in front of Ben so she could absorb his good looks. Meanwhile Ben absorbed the beauty before him. Her soft features were framed by an oval face and large brown eyes.

"Colonel, tell me what life was like in the west with all those savages."

She said the sentence jokingly hoping she could get a smile out of Ben.

"I was expecting to hear the stories of 'wild savages' that some officers have told us." Anna was partly teasing him with this comment.

"Then those men are the type that has never looked beyond the violence between our two cultures. No, they are a respectful people who value all life, people, birds, buffalo, all animals have a place in the order of life. They kill only what they need and they see the dangers of white men who kill for pleasure." It was obvious that Ben's short speech caught Anna's attention. She hung onto his every word.

"How then is it that a country boy from northern Illinois sees so much that is good?" The wording of this question had a coquettish flair.

"Anna it is like this tragic civil war. We only see what is different, rather then those things that bond us as brothers."

"Colonel you are a well-spoken and thoughtful man, but your comments might not be popular in some circles."

"Well, when I was in the west I had the good fortune to be tutored by some West Point officers who brought their openness with them. In addition I felt I missed out by leaving school after elementary school. I felt there was much in this world I could learn from others who are better traveled and educated than myself."

"Please tell me more about the west Ben....Oh, may I use your first name colonel, I apologize."

"Feel free to do so!" Ben exclaimed. "Are we not among equals here?"

"My, you are a forward thinking man Ben."

"Remember I was raised with two older, educated sisters."

That comment brought giggles of laughter from the females present. For Anna however, it brought a greater understanding of a man who had a different vision of the place women could have in this country's society. Just then Rob appeared with drinks including white wine for his sisters. Anna then whispered something to Rob and he nodded in approval.

"Tell me what it is like leading men in battle, Ben." Anna eased herself even closer to Ben, hanging on his every word. Ben had given thought to this same question so once again he was prepared to answer it.

"I think any officer is like good glue. It starts first with the sergeants and grows in numbers until you have reached regimental level. The men come to trust that we will make correct decisions to keep them fighting yet watching over their lives like guardian angels. In addition, we must model honor and courage. If we fail in this, our lines wither away."

"Did you experience this at Shiloh?"

"Absolutely Anna."

Just then Rob appeared and called his sisters and guest to dinner. Now he knew what the whisper was about. Before entering the dining area Ben was introduced to Rob's parents. They commented on what a pleasure it was to meet Ben, Rob had spoken of him often. This took Ben somewhat aback.

Ben found himself surrounded by more brass then he had seen at any one meeting. Colonels, and generals with their wives, they were all there. Every woman had dressed herself in her best finery creating a collage of color and beauty. As the host Mr. Macey stood and greeted all the guests and pointed out Ben as a soldier back from the wars. He finished with a formal toast to The Union which brought cheers and hurrahs. Ben felt a strange façade to all this joviality and loyalty. They knew so little about the horrors of this war of brothers. He concluded that he must be surrounded by desk men who did their soldiering from a distance. Death by warfare was not a possibility for them. Anna was feeling somewhat jealous as these overweight, armchair officers plied Ben with questions about Shiloh. She was impressed that his answers were always thoughtful and to the point, and in responding this way brought a human face to the war.

First there was the presentation of dinner itself. The white tablecloth almost glistened. The silverware shone from a fresh polishing. Golden rimmed serving dishes paid tribute to the wealth amassed by Mr. Macey. The dishes were filled with foods Ben could not identify. At the ends of the table there stood two huge hams which were in the process of being carved by Mr. Macey. He seemed to revel in this task, probably because it gave him presence of position and demonstrated his place in the family. The next thing Ben noticed were the number of generals present at this dinner. Their uniforms shone and looked as if they were new. Ben felt embarrassed by the shabbiness of his own uniform.

He found it interesting that his place at the table was next to Anna. Was this an accident? He found himself unable to keep his eyes away from her beauty. So to maintain his gaze he had to find his own conversation topics. "Rob has informed me that you volunteer at one of Washington's large hospitals. What do you do Anna?" Fortunately for Ben, Anna, was not shy about talking, so she launched into a monologue about the hospital. "I spend most of my time reading to the injured boys or writing for them. God knows we need something to keep their minds occupied. Most are incapable of reading or writing because of some injury to their limbs or their faces. I have also discovered that these men have little or no education. The letters they ask me to write are pitiful Ben."

"Why Anna?" Ben asked this to keep the conversation flowing so that he could keep his eyes on her beautiful face. He noticed that her large eyelashes flickered like the wings of a hummingbird. When she wanted to make a point her eyes twinkled like stars. She continued.

"Many of these men are never going to survive. Either they contract dysentery or gangrene, and after weeks of fighting to survive, they wind up dying. The hardest word to hear them cry out is 'mother!' How natural for humans to seek that comfort given to them by the womb and maternal care."

Dinner sped by as Ben and Anna unwittingly forged a new relationship. After dinner, aperitifs added more time for conversation, and the evening ended with Ben agreeing to visit the hospital where Anna worked before his time in Washington ended Rob had to remind Ben that it was time for them to return to Ben's 'residence' at the war office. A bright smile of another anticipated meeting gave Ben the hope of meeting Anna another day.

During the trip back Ben was almost chatty as he recalled to Rob how his sister was most attractive and a superb conversationalist. Rob's retort only reinforced Ben's assessment of the budding relationship, "You didn't do too badly yourself, for a country boy."

****

Ben shuffled into the meeting room along with his officers and other men from different commands and departments. He had to admit that his focus today still lingered on the image he had in his mind of Anna. A mental slap focused his attention on an intelligence officer who was going to make this presentation.

# CHAPTER TWENTY TWO:
# WHEN STRANGERS MEET

Alexander was ecstatic. He finally received the orders to carry out what he believed would save the Confederacy. It would take a couple of weeks to prepare his men for the long march that would take them to Chicago. His first step was conditioning both men and horses for extended marching. This would take the form of several two day trips away from their camp in southern Virginia. The route they would be taking was both arduous and lengthy. After the initial phase of preparation he would single out those combinations of horse and rider that had the best chance of making the round trip.

The marching proved the undoing of some men whose hind quarters could not take nine hours in the saddle. At the same time some horses started to break down as well. Sore hooves, swollen pasterns, loss of weight all took their toll on some horses. Some cases were minor and others had developed serious tendon tears. This preparation did nothing positive for the morale of the men, but in the end they knew it was better to encounter these things before the long march.

From the regiment he was able to put together a good sized battalion of three full companies. The most difficult task was giving the men Union uniforms and having them give them something of a worn look. The danger they feared was being bushwhacked by a Confederate militia unit.

****

Ben watched as his hardworking soldiers practiced changing from single file, to columns of twos then to columns of fours. Better they learn all three. They would be riding on poor quality roads often thus necessitating the aforementioned training. They had already been working on spending time in the saddle to toughen up their horses and their behinds for the marching that lay ahead. He found the journey through Maryland unusual. They decided to stay on good roads for this part of the trip. It posed no risk. What he did note was that when passing through one town they would be cheered, while another town might hurl insults, and even apples, at them as they trotted along. He now saw firsthand why Maryland was classified as a 'border' state and why there were regiments from Maryland fighting for both sides in the war.

It had been agreed that they would travel through the south-eastern side of West Virginia. The state had supported the Union and explained why it had broken away from Virginia at the start of hostilities. Unfortunately the roads forced them into columns of twos. They trotted at a leisurely pace not wanting to disable men or horses. At this point it was still safe to travel during the day. Only when they entered Virginia would they switch to night travel.

****

Alexander had decided on a circuitous route, taking his men through the southern part of West Virginia. They would cut west along the northern border of Kentucky which would bring him into the southern part of Illinois. They too would be fairly safe in neutral Kentucky. Their night riding would begin in Southern Illinois which was divided in its loyalties, but supposed to be a Union state.

****

It was their eighth day of travel and Ben was congratulating himself on his choice of route. Up to this point the trip had been free of incident. In the distance he could see a column of smoke rising to lofty heights on this windless October day. He raised his arm bringing the column to a halt. Ben left Emile in command while he formed a small patrol to discover what lay ahead.

Within a mile he came upon a grizzly sight. Lying on the ground was a row of dead soldiers dressed only in their army underwear. They had been stripped completely of their clothes and equipment. As the tiny patrol moved ahead Ben ordered, "Sergeant, dismount with me and we will investigate further!" The two men approached with pistols drawn.

"Sergeant, pull that dead soldier out from the bushes." Ben drew his revolver and walked forward, shifting his eyes in all directions, concerned that they too would meet the same fate as these dead men. He walked over to the man the sergeant pulled from the bushes. Whoever had killed the others must have missed him because he was in full uniform. The poor soul turned out to be a Union cavalryman. His yellow epaulets identified him as a second lieutenant. He had bled to death from a wound to his chest but had managed to put a little distance between himself and the others. What other information did the remaining soldiers have to give? Ben and the sergeant walked to where they lay. Most lay with their faces down with a bullet to the back of their heads.

"My God sergeant these men were put to death at the hands of an executioner. Twenty good men murdered!" Ben could see a tear rolling down the cheek of his battle hardened sergeant and he could feel the anger welling up in his own cheeks.

"Whoever did this should be found and shot themselves, sir!" exclaimed the sergeant.

In the distance smoke continued to float skyward from an unknown source. Ben looked at the dirt road to see what secrets it could reveal. There were many horseshoe tracks in the soft soil. Given their positioning it appeared that they had been walking their horses at the time. Furthermore the dirt indicated that wagons had been present. Where were they?

In the distance the road took a bend to the right...but they heard a sound. Ben and the sergeant jumped into the bushes for cover. His first reaction was relief for before him lay a column of Union uniforms riding at the cantor. Ben and his sergeant stepped out, Ben could see the lead rider giving his men the halt command, but no one moved.

"Colonel there is only two of them. Let's just kill them." Alexander snapped his head around and looked at the major with a glare. "We are not murderers, major!" was the firm response. "What we have just encountered should teach you something about fighting a war honorably."

"Yes, sir," was the major's response.

The major had never heard such sharp tone from the mouth of Colonel Alexander Braithwaite.

"Major, come with me," dictated Alexander as he began a slow walk toward the two men. He stopped about five feet from the man who was also a colonel but bore the shoulder boards of an infantry officer, light blue.

"Good morning, colonel." Alexander spoke while saluting. Ben returned the salute." Ben maintained an air of friendly self-confidence. Alexander dismounted and walked over to Ben and at the same time eyed the dead soldiers behind Ben.

"What has happened here, colonel?" questioned Alexander. Ben then revealed what he thought had occurred. Alexander just nodded his head as he stared at the dead men.

"I can only surmise colonel, but it seems to me that this was a supply column judging by the wagons' tracks, and that supplies were what the attackers wanted. They must have been desperate to take uniforms as well." Alexander added his own observations. "What you see here colonel could be linked to what we found in the town we just passed through. When we came upon it the whole town had been burnt to the ground. Dead civilians lay in twos and three's. We could only find a boy of fourteen and his two younger siblings. It was a slaughter. But the young lad had been able to watch from the upstairs window of a store. His story is about all that we can draw on for information." Alexander paused. He felt again a swelling of hate rising in him.

"And what would that information be colonel?" questioned Ben.

"The lad claimed that a band of about thirty soldiers entered their town and emptied the general store of food supplies. Another group dashed to the blacksmith's shop, shot the blacksmith, and took wagons, horses, and supplies with them. They even hoisted his forge into one of the wagons. Their last stop was the saloon which they emptied of liquor, wrapping it carefully in blankets they had taken."

Ben interrupted. "What did he have to say about the soldiers?"

Alexander continued. "From what he could see they were a mix. They were wearing disheveled Union and Confederate uniforms and rode scrawny horses."

"Well colonel, you saw the disaster. What do you make of all this?"

"Speaking for myself I would say this was a band of deserters who have holed up in the security of the hills in a part of the world the war does not reach. I would also conclude that because of what they took that they were about to pack up their belongings, dress themselves as Union soldiers, and head west where neither side could touch them."

"I concur with you completely colonel." Ben responded.

Now it was Alexander's turn to do the asking.

"What do you think we should do about this situation?"

Ben responded. "What we should do and what we can do are two different things. My column is not a patrol column. It has another purpose."

"The same applies to my column colonel," answered Alexander.

"But on the other hand justice for these dead soldiers and those innocent citizens cries out like a banshee."

"I concur, colonel," answered Ben.

"But we do have some questions that I am sure our officers will raise. Can each of our columns afford the time this will take? What if we suffer many injuries to our own men? What will we do with them? How do we know that there aren't more of these deserters that did not take part in the raid?

Ben then spoke up. "I am going to take a look and see if they are close at hand. They wouldn't have to go too far away to hide. This is not a well-travelled road. Do you wish to come with us colonel?

"Certainly, colonel!"

"Let's turn back toward the town. I would like to see this carnage for myself." Both officers and their aides made their way down the side of Braithwaite's column. Ben could tell that his compatriot's column was larger than his. As they rode Alexander wondered what his men would think of stopping to trap a group of deserters. Would this cause them to slip and reveal their true identity? If only this Union colonel knew with whom he was riding. Ben slowed down as he reached the town.

"What did you do with the young boy colonel?"

"I sent him with his brothers and three of my men back the way we had come. Apparently he had an uncle who could care for them that lived about five miles down the road."

Both men paid close attention to the wagon tracks and after about a mile of riding they suddenly disappeared. Ben dismounted and walked to one side of the road. He kicked at the brush and discovered it moved freely. Pushing the scrub away he saw a narrow track that wove its way into the hills.

"Here is the way to their camp!" exclaimed Ben. The track was well-used and had been widened to allow the deserters to move the wagons.

"Colonel I believe we have found our deserters' nest. I suggest that we send a small patrol along this trail and find out how far it is to their camp and whether they have guards posted along the way."

"Fine colonel, your men or mine?"

"We could use your men colonel as they are closer to us. We can take four men from the end of your column." Alexander agreed with Ben. He appropriated four men and gave them very precise directions as to the nature of their mission and for the need to be as cautious as possible.

"While we are waiting for their return why don't we find a place to bury the citizens of the town and those soldiers I found?" suggested Alexander.

So both officers gave directions to their subalterns to find the local cemetery, if there was one, and create a mass grave for all the dead. Volunteers came forward rapidly, but Ben noticed a strange behavior. The other Union colonel's men hung back like neutral observers. Ben's men had no trouble attacking the resisting clay soil as if this was some cathartic action intended to express their feelings about this senseless slaughter. As soon as the burial was complete the four patrol riders reached Ben and Alexander.

"Sirs, the deserters have a camp in a valley about one mile in. We dismounted when we saw smoke rising from it. Fortunately they have no guards posted. All of them are busy packing supplies. It looks like they are getting ready to leave. I counted fifty-three men. It is a dead end valley. Perhaps you might want to seal the only exit while the rest sneak up to the top of the valley. We can pick them off from there." Ben liked this young soldier.

"Soldier is there a clearing where we can leave the horses?"

"That depends on how many men you want to bring with you. About two hundred yards from the start of the valley walls there is a clearing that would hold about 100 horses. Some could be left on the trail," added the soldier. Ben and Alexander agreed that soldiers should come from both columns and that they would try to use about one hundred men to do the job.

Soon the path was filled with horses while men moved as quietly as possible to the clearing. When they reached it a rope corral was quickly built and men mingled among the horses to keep them settled. Ben and Alexander began the climb, always looking for the less steep ground. The horses sensed the soldier's' anticipation and stomped their feet in an awkward chorus. The slopes of the hills were covered in evergreen trees so they did not have to worry as much about walking on fallen branches. About halfway up the group split into three separate groups. One went to the right under the command of Emile and Alexander took the other. Their goal was to cover as much of the top of this valley as they could so they could lay a cross-fire on the deserters. Ben had to wait until they reached the top. It would take the other groups more time to reach their objectives. This gave him a chance to view the valley below and its only exit. That young scout had done a good surveying job. The deserters were moving quickly and it looked like they would be ready to leave within the hour. Curses rose from below as the killers saw the possibility of a future battle. Ben waited fifteen minutes and hoped that all were in their places. He drew his revolver and as he did so the men around him raised their Spencers'.

The valley reverberated with the sound of carbines firing, a rapid cacophony expressing its moral outrage. The men below started to fall before they could get to their muskets. The only cover available to them was the wagons, thus making them less available as targets. The firing kept up for fifteen minutes and the soldiers had to slow down their rate of fire to keep the barrels of their Spencer's from overheating. Whenever a deserter moved to find a better vantage point, carbines drenched him in a sudden rainfall of bullets. Finally a white flag was raised from below. They had had enough and realized they were no match for the men above. Silence and smoke filled the air.

"Drop your muskets and stand in front of the wagons!" barked Ben in the loudest voice he could raise. He had to repeat his order several times until what was left of the deserters came forward. Ben was the first over the ridge and started his descent. When he did his men followed him over the ridge to the valley below. When all were assembled below

Ben searched out Alexander with a look of concern on his face.

"I think we have a problem, colonel. I have no time or much inclination to aid their wounded or take prisoners. How do you feel about this?"

"I have the same dilemma, colonel."

Both men looked away. These were men of conscience. Killing wounded soldiers and unarmed men was not something either looked forward to. Ben spoke.

"There is another way of looking at this colonel. It is one thing that they are deserters,…but they are thieves and murderers as well. Even if we returned them to the military their fates would be the same."

"I agree, but do we have the right to ask our men to take part in a firing squad?"

"Our men have seen what these men have done. Asking for volunteers would help," answered Ben.

"Hey colonel, what you going to do with us?" An appeal came from the apparent leader of these survivors. "We've got rights too and killing wounded soldiers would make you no better than us. At least we know what we are! Have you got the guts to finish us off?"

"I am afraid you lost most of your rights when you viciously killed those innocents," snapped Ben.

But still the question of acting as honorable men raised its ugly head. What to do? Ben thought some more. He spoke to the leader.

"It was your actions that have led you to this day, not us. Actions have consequences and I am sure you are aware of that."

"Fine colonel, it's your job to take the next step." Ben wished Homer was here. He would know what to do! He would know what was right. Then Ben thought again. The colonel's shoulder bars brought with them a terrible responsibility: men's lives, be they friend, foe, or deserter. Ben had made up his mind. He turned his back to face Colonel Braithwaite. "I will do what is right, colonel. You need not take part."

"Just a minute, colonel. We are of equal rank and therefore of equal responsibility. I will not hear of you doing this alone!" Alexander's response was firm and final. Both men drew their revolvers and replenished their barrels with cartridges.

"Remember colonels, you are going to have to live with this!" mocked the deserter who had spoken.

"Do you want blindfolds?"

"We ain't cowards. We're men just like you!" But Ben thought, that's just the thing, they aren't the same. Both colonels stood in front of each deserter and put a ball into their foreheads. They reloaded and went among the wounded repeating the procedure. Fortunately only three were still alive.

"The least we can do is bury these men, colonel," suggested Ben. His apparent calm hid a conscience resonating with regret. Emile could see the change in Ben. His shoulders were slouched in depression. Emile thought to himself. Is this what price good men pay for justice's sake or worse still? Has all the killing in war made it easier to kill in other circumstances?

As their soldiers dug a common grave for the dead the two colonels sought out casualties among their own men. Fortunately there were only a few minor wounds. The surprise had been so thorough the deserters had little time to load their muskets and return fire. Both colonels silently stood apart from the burial party. Each reflected on what they had just done. In their minds they knew that they had no other choice, but in their hearts, as honorable men they had trouble when faced with a decision that went against their idea of how war should be fought. They were also concerned with the effects this would have on their men. They would deal with that later.

With burial finished each colonel prepared to continue their journeys. The two officers shook hands, stared into each other's eyes and could see the sadness left by this action. Alexander's secret had been kept and he was glad to get away from this spot.

# CHAPTER TWENTY THREE:
## SPYING AND RAIDING

Ben turned his men back onto the road leading down to Virginia. He was quiet and reclusive in his own thoughts. He wondered how the other colonel was dealing with his conscience over what they had done. It was then that he suddenly realized that they had not even exchanged names. He interpreted this as the start of his 'spying' days.

It was a dark day for Ben and he was glad when they reached a small field where they camped for the evening. He had to snap himself out of these doldrums or he would be ineffective as a leader. The men were waiting for that moment as well. They knew the burden he was carrying. He raised his arm once again to bring them to a halt. Horses were cared for in the clearing and suddenly Ben chirped out,

"What's for dinner?"

The group nearest him responded with, "The same as always, sir."

Ben could feel the tension abate as the men heaved a silent sigh. Their colonel was back and focused. Ben rested among the trees and took stock of his environs. The carpet of leaves below him still held their fall colors but from his perspective they represented danger. They would be prone to making excessive noise as they traced a trail across Virginia. They had also lost an important source of camouflage. This would drive them deeper into wooded areas. It was essential that he find a telegraph position that came right to the edge of a wooded area. It was then his mind drifted back in time, all the way to his junior days as a trooper in the west. How naïve he had been. How little he had seen of his future. He reflected on Addy and Hal, realizing that he was probably the only one who knew that in fact there was a silent bond between the two; all the more reason to settle this leftover piece of unfulfilled injustice. And then there was Rob. Just who was this man that seemed to float in and out of his life and what did the spur remnant mean? Why had Rob chosen the Twentieth as the core of the spying activities? Did Rob have another motive for selecting his men? Then Ben thought of Anna. Beautiful, intelligent, cultured Anna, what role was she to play in his life? He felt a strong attraction and comfort in her presence. Life was more complicated now... and all of this amid what was shaping up as a tragic chapter in his nation's history

****

Alexander walked his horse amid the rustle of leaves. They had begun their journey across the remainder of West Virginia bound for southern Illinois. He could not pinpoint the reason for his dejection. He truly believed they had acted properly in the handling of the 'incident' as his officers called it. He still heard grumblings of how they should have wiped out Ben's small command. He had no trouble handling those foolish comments. Perhaps it was the deception itself. For only his men knew their true allegiance. But no...he had handled it honorably and at the same time handed out a measure of deserved justice...harsh as it was. But that was war. Certain circumstances forced good men to act under certain circumstances as 'gods' dealing out justice as they must.

The next part of their journey would take them through northern Kentucky. On occasion they would encounter small cavalry patrols. The exchanges were always friendly and sometimes his command would stop and exchange stories of war, fictional of course. This was a safe trip for a Union cavalry unit.

****

"Excuse me private, may I speak with the colonel?"

"Certainly, Captain Stairs."

Ben was blessed with an orderly steeped in protocol no matter what the situation. He disappeared into Ben's tent.

"Welcome, Captain Stairs, what can I do for you?"

Stairs was one of those who lived by protocol as well. To him it brought order to non-battle situations.

"Sir, may I speak freely with you?"

"Absolutely Miles," Ben's somewhat relaxed style was in stark contrast to the sub-altern in front of him.

"Well sir it involves that Union battalion we just encountered. I have had a number of my men come to me with an observation."

"And what would that be captain?"

"A number of my men overheard them talking quietly among themselves and they apparently did so with a 'deep southern' accent. I questioned these men and few had visited the south in their lives. But the few who had been south claimed that some of them spoke with accents heard in Louisiana and Mississippi." Ben sat silently trying to explain the natural occurrence of such a phenomenon.

"It would not be out of order. Southerners fight for the North and vice-versa."

"Very well colonel," Captain Stairs saluted, wheeled and left Ben's tent.

Ben entered his 'place of thought' by leaning forward, placing elbows on his knees and making the church steeple with his hands to support his chin. Ben had felt concern about these soldiers as well, but it had only existed in his gut and not surfaced until now. Could these have been Confederates up to mischief in the North? Or was this just another part of the face of this war? What had bothered him was the reversal of colors on their 'swallow tail' guidon. No self-respecting cavalry unit would make a mistake concerning the guidon. He also noticed the relative orderliness and cleanliness of their uniforms. They had seen neither hard campaigning nor fast riding. This was most unusual. What had bothered him still further was the apparent stand-offish demeanor of these men. Camaraderie was not in their minds.

So assuming the warning of his captain and his own thoughts were correct, what should he do in this situation? He could not afford a 'runner' and even if he did where would he tell anyone to go to find them? Whatever his misgivings, nothing could be done.

To-morrow would see the break-down of his command into the four, fifteen man groups and then all would part ways, if ever to meet again. That thought left Ben empty. Over half of these men were from his old company. They were like family.

****

Alexander could see the dust the two troopers were raising. They rose into the air like filmy clouds. Something must be wrong. Both were outriders checking the road ahead. Both riders timed their halt perfectly and the rears of both their mounts slid under their sweating bodies.

"What is the problem soldier?" the colonel asked quickly.

"Sir!" gasped the corporal. "There is a brigade strength wall of Confederate soldiers across the road, stretching half-a-mile each side of this road about two miles distant."

"How close did you get?"

"We dismounted, tied our horses, and crept through an outcrop of bushes and got to within a hundred yards or so." The soldier puffed out the answer creating a staccato effect.

"Did they see you?" asked the colonel.

"Absolutely not colonel!"

"They are perched just over a rise in the road. The rise continues on for a mile."

"Is there any sign of cavalry or artillery son?"

"No cavalry but a full battery of ten pound napoleans are perched on the next rise.""Sir this is intended as a trap!" barked the major.

"Yes, that is clear, but what is a brigade of Rebs doing so far north in Kentucky?" queried the colonel.

"Perhaps it is a strong militia unit. There certainly are enough Secesh in Kentucky."

"Possibly major, but what are they doing with a full battery of artillery?"

"Perhaps it is a combined unit. A regiment of regulars mixed with the militia."

"Possibly Major, but it does appear they are waiting for us."

"We must have been spotted yesterday colonel!" concluded the Major.

"I agree with you major. Unfortunately we are going to have to stop and wait for night time and sneak around their lines. But we are hardly a silent bunch so we shall have to make at least a ten mile southerly detour, resume our march, and then make a ten mile march north to meet this road again." The colonel, partially talking to himself as he formed this plan of action, was still silently dwelling on the question whether they had been discovered. It was pointless to try and explain to this force facing them that they were indeed Confederates dressed in Union attire.

"Major I want you and a company of cavalry to act as a screen to our right. Send a rider if they begin to move in our direction. Make sure you travel silently and leave your sabers in one of the wagons." The Major cantered off to carry out his assignment. Meanwhile Alexander raised his saber and directed the remainder of the men to turn in a southerly direction.

****

It was time to take up their twelve positions. These were good friends. The good-byes were said in earnest. All knew the perilous journey on which they had embarked. They were to meet at this location in three weeks, if able. Ben took his group on the furthest trail. Emile headed directly east, while the other officers headed in a south-westerly direction. The troopers in Ben's group were particularly silent. It would be another day till they reached their position directly south of Richmond.

Good fortune stayed with them and after one day nervously spent in a wooded area at the far end of a farmer's field, they were ready to march at night. It was a particularly dark night and the branches of the trees hung down on them like scraggly arms reaching out to trap them. Bats flew above even though their prey had ended their seasonal lives. Every broken branch seemed to echo like a cannon in the night. But then who was there to share the sound with them? The moon failed to break through and heavy, dark clouds above them foretold of rain.

After marching for two hours it began to shower. Ponchos were donned and the tiny column proceeded on its venture into the unknown. A dark, gray morning greeted the riders and now it was time to search for another wooded area. This time Ben chose a stand of conifers. They entered a path that showed no sign of human travel. Suddenly they came upon a small opening large enough for horses and men to move about. They decided breakfast would be hardtack and dried beef. This would satisfy their anxious stomachs. Then the men went about preparing to sleep. Two troopers were left awake to watch for unwelcome intruders. Restless sleep took the place of deep sleep. The men still had trouble adjusting to sleeping during the day.

****

Alexander could not resist the temptation to view his enemy. Leaving the column in the able hands of Major McCleod he took his first sergeant and followed the first path he could find that led north. The path yielded mainly scrub bush which made it easier to spot the Confederate blockade. It was about midnight so he hoped to see their campfires before he ran into any skirmishers. At the top of a gently graduated hill Alexander got his wish. There directly north of him lay a long line of waning fires. The brigade had obviously decided to camp right on the trail. He was glad to see that they had held this position. They obviously had no knowledge of his column. Silently they backtracked on the path, glad to have not made an adventure of this exercise. They reached the column in about an hour and resumed their places at the front. Showing a fatalist view of this exercise, he felt everything was going too well. To make up for lost time he continued the march into the rays of morning's fair light. Suddenly a rider appeared beside him.

"Colonel, Captain McNight has sent me to warn you that there are two riders coming fast from our rear."

"Tell Captain McNight to dismount four riders near the end of the column and instruct them to halt these two riders when they come abreast of them." Before the rider had finished saying "yes sir," he was gone. In about twenty minutes a young lieutenant and a sergeant appeared at the front of the column. The lieutenant, breathing heavily, stopped. They were dressed in Confederate uniforms.

"Colonel Braithwaite, I am Lieutenant Regan and I have two messages to give you." A pair of sweaty hands reached across with two envelopes.

To: Colonel A. Braithwaite

From: Major Moore (Aide to Pres. Davis)

Your destination in the city has changed to one bank only, the Federal Reserve of Chicago. Please use your troopers as you see fit.

The second letter was contained in a dog-eared envelope indicating it had taken a different journey to reach him. Alexander broke its seal quickly.

To: Colonel Alexander Braithwaite

From: Colonel Ambrose Jackman

Please be advised that our agents have found a leak in our security within our own agents in the field and reports of a cavalry column moving through northern Kentucky has reached the ears of the local militia. They will see you as the enemy. Suggest you increase the use of forward scouts. Avoid contact with this 'friendly' force.

Colonel A. Jackman C.S.A.

Alexander had a good laugh when he read this timely information. It was a little late in arriving, however. He could only take comfort in the knowledge that their field agents were doing their job.

The sun was rising rapidly and so it was time to quickly find a wooded area. His forward scouts should return soon to apprise him of new information. He decided to halt the column and wait. Soon the dust of riders appeared over the next hill. His men had returned and found a good open site in a wooded area about a mile ahead. The column resumed its march. The snaking, stretched form moved at a slow pace to keep dust to a minimum.

****

Ben had changed his route to create a wider birth between themselves and Richmond. The previous day they had experienced greater traffic on their humble path. They should only lose one day due to the change in plans. The horses had been given their portion of oats. Having to carry their own supply of feed for the horses had necessitated the use of three mules just for the horses. Eventually they would have to find a farm with hay still uncut. It was late in the season but a warm summer with adequate rainfall made another cut of hay possible.

The men were starting to show signs of exhaustion, even though they were riding. They could not sleep soundly during the day and it was starting to show as some troopers nodded off to sleep while they were marching at night. Their slow pace had allowed some men to become proficient at this mode of rest. Their spirits were good, knowing that they would reach their location the next day. They looked forward to eating something other than hardtack and salt pork.

****

Alexander and his men entered southern Illinois. The column switched to a main road to pick up the pace. They also had become aware that they needed to return friendly waves when the column passed small towns and Union travelers. Southern Illinois was the home to Confederate sympathizers but they were less likely to respond to a Yankee column. About thirty miles into the northern trek the column was to meet with one such Confederate sympathizer by the name of Marshall Dakin who was to be their guide for the rest of their journey. Furrows appeared on Colonel Braithwaite's brow. Unknown to his men, volunteers would be recruited to fight delaying actions when or if they encountered Union troops on their return trip. His sense of ethics fought his honorable nature for he would not be staying behind and he believed he should not give an order that he himself would not follow. He sighed. Such were the necessities of wartime. President Davis wanted him alive to be able to give a full report.

****

Ben's group had the least distance to travel before they would reach their first 'safe spot'. One night's march and a day of quiet brought them within a few hours of the spot. In fact the poles and wires appeared at two different points near their path, indicating the path of the Reb telegraph system. But the locations were always in open fields, unsuitable for their task. Suddenly they reached the corner of the woods where a post stood within two feet of a wooded area of mixed varieties of arbor. Ben had Sergeant Michaels light a lantern so he could read the map. Sure enough, this was the spot. According to the map the road took a dip down and to the right. Ben was satisfied this was the location. Light was coming up in the east and they wanted to find a spot in the woods which would become their new home for one week.

Michaels was sent off to see if there was any clearing in the woods sizeable and secretive enough for their needs. He seemed to be gone for an eternity as the sun was starting to finish its arc through the sky. When he finally appeared he was actually excited. "Colonel Halliday I have found an excellent spot that is near a stream which splits the woods and offers us space enough for our needs!"

"Lead away, sergeant we need to get out of this light."

The six soldiers walked their mounts deftly around trees and scrub until they reached the stream Michaels had found. The gurgling and bubbling of the stream acted as a companion as it coursed its way through the woods. Little could be done to establish their camp. Here and there rays of light peeked into the darkness but they needed more light to work. Finally as the sun befriended them the picture became clear. The stream was only two feet wide but over time had moved from side to side and etched an open area about one hundred feet long and forty feet at the widest, tapering to but a few feet at either end.

Tired from their travels, the men were glad to stop in almost any location. Dry wood was found and a fire was made to make some coffee. They had brought a hunting trap with them hoping that a bit of meat could be added to their monotonous diet. To deal with the feeding of men and horses a rotation was made for guard duty with two men on duty and four sleeping, if that was possible.

Ben found his mind racing with different scrambled thoughts and plans of how they would fare with their spy mission. Pine needles made a reasonably comfortable resting place, but the thoughts rolled like waves on a shore. Who had killed Addy? Was Hal really responsible? What had the broken end of the spur meant? Why were his thoughts leading back to the dinner with Anna?

When he could quell this uprising of thoughts Ben focused on his environs. The stillness thundered in his ears. The crack of a branch from some night hunter sent his right hand to his revolver. Looking up he could see the full moon more brightly then he had ever seen it before. It gave a ghostly appearance to his men huddled in varying shapes and positions. Occasionally a wisp of wind would scatter the fallen leaves resembling the footsteps of an army. This would be their only night of sleep and he was being torn from the cool abyss it offered. And so he waited, watching like a hunted animal who cursed their nightly foes. About three o'clock in the morning sleep finally swept over him like a comforting blanket. In the morning his men seemed to know of his restless night and moved about like children avoiding the admonitions of their parents. He awoke to the smells of coffee cured carefully to avoid detection.

The small band of soldiers set about putting their equipment together so that they could commence listening to what was transpiring between Richmond and Petersburg. The materials were quite simple and easily applied. At nightfall they would climb the ten foot pole and attach the tiny clamp to the telegraph wire, run it down the pole, along the ground to the receiver set which was different in that it only received messages. They had no need to transmit.

\*\*\*\*

As they approached Chicago, an enemy capitol, they paradoxically felt more secure. The uniforms were a guarantee of right of passage. The letters Alexander carried with him identified who they were and gave fictional orders to the unit. Alexander decided that they should camp outside the city and enter it early in the morning before the hustle and bustle of daily life encroached on their plans. Now the soldiers began to feel squeamish. Few ate their meals choosing instead to clean their firearms and check that their mounts were in good condition. It had been a long journey for these beasts of burden. The best they could do was rest. Few talked. Their minds were already picturing the events of the following day. At 4:00 a.m. Alexander had them check their gear and finally mount their horses. They had to travel another ten miles. Within eight miles they were at the outskirts of Chicago and began a slow trot into the city. The guide rode ahead so as not to appear to be a part of a military unit. That would appear unusual. Dakin took them through the lower class residential district. No need to stir the rich! Soon stores and tradesmen's facilities began to appear. The sun was making its first appearance in the form of a pinkish hue, hiding behind the horizon as if it were resisting its inevitable journey across the sky. At this quiet hour they could hear the neighing of horses, probably at some distant stable. Their own mounts raised their ears in quiet salutation.

Now Dakin made a right turn onto a brick road which created its own unwanted cacophony of jogging hooves. It was at this point that Alexander felt a nervous twinge in his mind and body for the narrow street gave little room for movement. This was not a common route for horses. Their columns of four ate up the width of the street. It was on this street that the Confederates would find their gold…if it existed.

****

The location they had chosen turned into an ideal recluse. The small bubbling stream wound its way around the tiny camp providing the five men and their mounts a fine source of drinking water. Though the leaves had fallen, the density of the trees provided a visual barrier from the path that wound around the telegraph pole. Now it was time to test their new found home. As the sun edged down below the western skyline the men moved quietly but quickly to their goal. It was a five minute walk around tall dark trees that stood like guards on their camp, while dense, young offspring added protection at the lower levels. Even in the last glows of twilight the pole stood out from the rest. Barton had been trained to use the hobnailed boots and belt to move himself up and down the pole. He strapped the belt around the tree and with the connection clamp and wire clenched in his mouth, made his ascent up the dried old oak. Deftly he made the contact with the telegraph wire and within seconds was back on the ground. The men attached this wire to the stake paced at the base of the pole. This was connected to the heavier communication wire that now wound back to the camp. The end was attached to the receiver and the reception of Confederate communications began.

Luck was on their side. The messages were all in standard Morse code. What's more it seemed that this was the government and military transmission line. Ben and Walton had both been trained to translate the dots and dashes into English. It soon became apparent the volume of transmissions would require one rider being sent out per week. Most of the messages were complaints or requests from higher grade generals. Some were politicians, particularly state governors, and others described troop movements. Ben paid little heed to most after the collection passed the hundred mark. But one piqued his interest, not so much because of what it said but who it might involve. The key phrase read: 'money sent to Macey as per normal route'. Ben rationalized that there could be many Maceys in this land. Besides if it was Rob they would have used a code name for a spy. It was probably a Confederate official. As hard as he could Ben tried to continue rationalizing the name 'Macey', but the thought that it was Rob kept returning to his mind. Then he realized he knew only one family of Macey's. He was letting his small personal life enter the vast dimension of this great struggle. He buried his thoughts in the back of his mind…there were far more important messages to worry about.

The first rider had been sent. Ben would have no way of knowing the success or failure of his journey. Only two weeks to go! Occasionally, regret at taking this task crept into his thoughts. It was not the danger that caused his regret. He missed his regiment and life in camp. He had no knowledge of their battle history. At times like this, thoughts of Addy and Hal were resurrected. He still believed Hal was innocent. He wanted to be alone with the real murderer for five minutes. When he found these thoughts taking over his thoughts Ben quickly turned them to more pleasant topics. He found himself thinking more and more about Anna, her fine features capped with a sharp mind and caring ways. He was torn with a desire to be with her and with his regiment.

It was during one of these moments of thought that he and his men heard it. It was faint but familiar. Ben put his ear to the ground. There was no doubt it was the sound of hooves. He could not tell the numbers but because the path near the post was so narrow it would have to be riders in single file. Ben put his finger to his lips indicating silence but he pointed to the men's revolvers as well. The four of them quickly drew pistols and pointed them at the sound which was becoming louder and more distinct. Now the sounds of men's voices could be heard. Suddenly one of the rider's horses whinnied. One of Ben's horses could not resist the temptation to respond. The sound of horses' hoofs came to a halt.

"Who goes there?" bellowed one of the riders.

"It is safe to come out," the voice was distinctly southern. "We are a small Confederate militia patrol." Ben took note of the irony in the soldier's introduction. All was silent. Neither group moved.

"We know there is someone there. Make yourselves known by answering!"

Ben could detect a quivering in the speaker's voice. Still, silence reigned. Then he heard the words that made Ben's mouth go dry.

"Dismount men, and Eagan you hold the reigns of our horses!"

When they had dismounted Ben could hear the cocking of their pistols. That put them one step ahead of Ben and his men. Now Ben knew there were about three to six riders and he had the element of surprise. He motioned to his men to crouch down further. It looked like they would have to do battle. The Confederate soldiers were not delicate about entering the woods. Branches snapped indicating their advance. Silence again.

"Advance men and keep a sharp eye!"

The bellowing had been reduced to a whisper, but Ben could still hear it.

Unknown to Ben he was facing five Confederate militia armed with smoothbores. Suddenly the sound of a musket pierced the silence. One of the Confederates had tripped over a root and discharged his firearm. A curse followed in quick order. But it was too late. A puff of white smoke wafted skywards through the dense brush. They were only about thirty feet away from Ben and his men.

"That was just a warning shot. The next sound will be a volley."

The soldier in charge tried to take advantage of their mistake. Ben raised his arm to indicate that his men should prepare to fire. He held his arm up, letting the Confederates come further forward and make better targets. No sound! Ben could wait no longer. He dropped his arm and the sound of four pistol shots rent the air.

"I'm hit," came the stunned response.

A volley of muskets followed. Fortunately none of Ben's men were hit. Now all hell broke loose although no one could clearly identify a target. In this situation the rapid firing of pistols gave Ben and his men the advantage. Silence again. Ben's men opened their spent pistols and replaced their barrels with a second barrel. These could not be seasoned soldiers for once again they stumbled forward against an enemy they had yet to see. Ben tried to predict their forward advance and waited until they had approached another ten feet or so. Again his arm pointed skyward and since the crackling helped identify the enemy's position Ben motioned about twenty degrees to the left. Pistols rang out again. Silence!

"Sergeant Hiller took a shot through his forehead. He's dead."

Ben put a finger to his lips commanding silence. He could hear moaning in the direction of their firing. Ben felt they were winning this mini-battle. Now it was his turn to speak.

"You Rebels are outmanned and outgunned. I want you to drop your muskets!"

Ben could hear the soldiers talking among themselves. Suddenly the sound of men rushing though the woods broke the silence. They were trying to flee!

Ben knew he could not allow them to escape. He ordered his men to follow suit. When they arrived at the path three remaining Secesh were trying to mount their horses. After they spotted the Union soldiers they once again aimed their muskets. Ben's soldiers instinctively leveled their pistols and fired repeatedly killing all three in a hail of balls. They checked the bodies of all three carefully and they were most certainly dead. Now they returned to look for the damage they had caused in the woods.

Carefully they stepped over branches just in case. There, twenty feet into the woods, lay two motionless bodies. Suddenly the retort from a pistol caught Ben and his men off guard. Ben felt the thud as a ball entered his leg midway down his calf. It was enough to crumple him to the ground.

"Damn!" was his only response. The pain surged up his leg as his brain's pain center let him know that he had been shot.

The three men rushed to side.

"Colonel where are you hit?"

"Don't worry about me. Find the source of that shot."

All three crept to where they thought the source of the shot was.

Ben gazed as if hypnotized at the flow of blood streaming down his leg. Nearby, the sound of multiple pistol shots told him the man who shot him had been found.

"We got him colonel. It must have been that wounded one we hit at the start."

Now all three began to fuss about Ben, concerned as they were about his wound. Ben had the good sense to wrap it with a piece cloth torn from his blouse just above the flow of the wound. Soon the flowing ebbed to a trickle.

"Get me back to camp men! Drag those bodies in here and bury them."

Ben had not lost his ability to give orders. "We still have to prepare for tonight."

The sergeant spoke up. "Sir I am afraid the mission is completed."

"I did not give up command yet sergeant!"

"Sorry sir but I was given clear instructions that if such an incident occurred I was to assume command."

# CHAPTER TWENTY FOUR: OUTCOMES

"But sergeant we still have two weeks to serve in the field and you know I can heal during the remaining time."

"Your wound could also fester colonel. That ball lodged in your leg! I am exercising my duty and you must know that the knowledge you gained will be necessary to make the mission complete."

Ben knew this was true but his desire to command was not something he was used to relinquishing.

"Sergeant let's agree to meet half-way. If I am in distress by tomorrow night I will agree to your wishes."

The sergeant was silent. "Very well colonel."

The other two soldiers heaved a collective sigh. They were not used to seeing their colonel in this situation. Ben ordered them to find the horses belonging to the dead Confederates and corral them with their own mounts.

With some help Ben was led back to the camp and placed, sitting on a few blankets against a tree. The Sergeant took command of tending to the wound and he observed Ben's white-faced countenance. This wound was not to be taken lightly. A clean shirt was torn apart so that it could be wrapped around the wound. Ben winced while the wrapping was taking place. Pain spread across his whole body. Some innocent nerve must have been victimized as well. The sergeant watched Ben's eyes for signs of greater problems. This made him furl his eyebrows and his experiences with wounded soldiers told him his colonel's physical problems were only going to worsen.

****

Even at night one could see this was a long street with the next intersecting street 200 yards away. Soon the sixty riders were held in the front a building. Men turned in their saddles as Alexander gave the order to switch to their Confederate uniforms. At least they would not be seen as spies, he hoped. A small squad of men raced to the front door and soon iron bars had turned the wooden structure into kindling. Entry was easier than anticipated but the vaults would present a more difficult obstacle. Dynamite, hidden in the wagon, was carefully carried to the two vaults with hope of turning the metal into bent shapes inviting the Confederates to their golden wealth. Two blasts in quick concession turned the steel to meaningless waste and more importantly it allowed Alexander's men to load eight bars of this valued metal into saddlebags. The hope of putting the remaining five hundred bars into the wagon however was soon dashed.

"Colonel come quickly!"

Dakin's voice held a nervous portent in its sound.

"Colonel, troops are forming at the end of each crossroad. We have nowhere to go. We're trapped!"

As Alexander mounted quickly to examine the scene his heart sank. At the end of each crossroad regular Union troops had formed in rows across each crossroad, each forming an arch to bring as many guns to bear as was possible. Alexander acted quickly. Eight riders were told to hand off their load to another. He then collected the remaining dynamite and cut the fuse to the length required.

"Volunteers!" his piercing yell could be heard by the Union troops as well. About ten men appeared and he gave them their assignment knowing full well none would survive. Quickly rows of four were formed up and four men placed in the wagon, while two rows of four riders led the way. They had chosen the southerly route. Quickly Alexander hoisted a white flag which he bore alone. The Union troops sent out a colonel as well. To the Union officer he quickly executed an exercise in bravado. He began,

"It seems our plan has been discovered, colonel. Do you wish to lay down your arms and let us pass?"

"The Union colonel was taken aback. "I believe you are confused about who is trapped today, colonel, but I admire your spirit."

Without waiting Alexander raised the front of his horse, into the air and wheeled in defiance. Union soldiers in earshot were taken aback by this Rebel leader.

"May God be with you sergeant!"

And with that the first four rows of soldiers, minus their gold, did their best to imitate the Rebel yell and thundered to their deaths. Close behind two men in the wagon crashed into the melee that had formed ahead of them. Suddenly the night became day and sticks of dynamite wrought havoc on both sides. The Union troops were crowded into packed rows. The first two were obliterated by the dynamite. Alexander now gave the command to charge and many soldiers were able to pick their way through the carnage of bodies that lay before them. The Confederates were the recipients of good luck as the Union cavalry had not yet arrived. Many a man would tell the story of Braithwaite's charge for after reasonable space had been put between both sides, the colonel called a halt. The frothing from the horses was so dense it formed a night time cloud. A count estimated that forty-five cavalrymen had made good their escape.

Was it simply luck or bravery that fuelled this tiny vanguard's escape from the clutches of the enemy? Many a trooper had wounds from the barrage of fire but they still stayed in their saddles. As Alexander surveyed his men he wondered from where the Union soldiers had come. It almost appeared that they had known they were coming and that they could take them in a trap they were off guard. Their guide decided to take them back through southern Illinois by a different route for he too was suspicious that their plans had been discovered. So began the arduous journey up and down isolated trails. He took them through streams and rivers, a convenience for men and mounts that were in desperate need of water. The clouds covered the presence of the moon making the trip harder but safer from peering eyes. As the lightening eastern skies gave view of their presence, a rider was sent out to find a clearing where they could rest during the day, eat a meal, and sleep off the night's wearing journey and events. It was time to part with Dakin. He had been of inestimable value and many a rider waved and spoke a few words of gratitude to this follower of the Southern cause. As men dismounted Alexander could see the toll this venture had taken. All were stiff from so many hours in the saddle and so stretches were a common sight. Some had taken balls in the leg and crumpled to the ground in agony. Splintered arms now could be looked after. Muffled cries of pain told the story. More than half of these men had sustained some kind of wound. The healthy cared for their brothers in arms, making silent comments to offset the curse borne by their fellows. While soldiers tried to eat the last remnants of their meager food and fill canteens, an outrider from point duty came to a halt and dismounted all in one action.

"Where is the colonel?" He spluttered the words as if he was speaking but one word. A sergeant casually pointed to the edge of the woods.

"Colonel!"

"Yes, Hobbs."

"Sir, there is a battalion or more of Union cavalry approaching from the west and the dust they are creating tells me they are heading in our direction in a hell of a hurry!"

"Very well, Hobbs. Mount up men we have to make a sudden departure."

He watched the healthy and injured climb into their saddles in one continual groan.

"Hobbs go back and see how much ground they have gained. You shall find me at the front of the column." The point guard took off the same way he had come. For the first time in the expedition Alexander felt a sagging feeling in his stomach. His men had no time to revive. He had expected pursuit but not this fast. The column reached the top of a hill only to gaze below on the forms of another blue battalion stretched out in two lines in an enveloping gesture. He considered letting the fastest left in the column try and penetrate the forces he faced. No, he thought, he knew that his men had given all they could in this gallant foray into enemy territory. He brought his horse to a halt, wrapped a white cloth around his saber and raised it high in the air. Behind he could hear sounds of disagreement with his decision, but it was his decision to make. A military slaughter would prove nothing. Strangely he felt no shame or loss of honor for this decision. The best had been given and the flag of surrender waved with a snap against a westerly wind.

Alexander was brought before the local commander, one Colonel Huckly.

"Personally I would have all of you shot but for reasons beyond my ken I have received instructions to send you and your men to a prison camp."

Alexander was somewhat taken aback by the decision. He tried to rationalize the Union decision. The best he could determine was that the Union intelligence service wanted to find out more about the events surrounding their failed raid. Alexander decided that their plans must have been known to the North. Or it could have been that their last minute change to Confederate uniforms had put them in the category of raiders and raiders who after all had done no little damage to land or limb. He and his men were forced to live outside in a field about five miles from the Reserve Bank. They were heavily guarded by militia units until their final fate was decided. After three days the Confederate prisoners were marched off to Camp Wiley, another three day march.

\*\*\*\*

January 3, 1863,

My Dearest Brother,

May this letter find you in good health and the plantation productive and placid. We have been in captivity now for three months and sometimes I wish I had made that fated charge I wrote about in my previous letter. No animal should be kept the way we have been. We arrived at Camp Wiley (Illinois) in late October and life has left my men sick and depressed. I curse all men who talk about honor in war.

The problem stems from our naivety about the course of this war. No one had foreseen the need for prisoner of war camps. We began this nightmare in order to parole captured soldiers. What a noble idea. Defeated men are returned to their homes with the promise not to take up arms until an equal number of Union men are exchanged with us. This system, I am told, worked reasonably well for the first two years. Honor in war has once again been thrown to the wolves.

The Union camps are poorly equipped to provide the necessities of life to Union prisoners. Union policy makers had come to realize that to weaken the Confederacy it was beneficial to hold back Confederate prisoners. It was the Confederacy that had limited access to men who could refurbish their losses. The Union was better equipped to acquire human resources to continue the war. Our lack of men explains why conscription and lengthy terms in the field became a fact of life in the Confederacy. Now to the camp itself. I suspect few are different from the others. The shacks constructed for inmates are overflowing. Men have had to build simple lean-tos to keep out the wind and snow. A small river separates the camp diagonally and men use it both as drinking water and for bathing. Is it any wonder that cases of dysentery have multiplied over the months? The lack of fresh vegetables and fruits has led to a dramatic rise in scurvy. But there is virtuously no medical treatment for these diseases so these men are huddled in one of the buildings furthest from the rest and are cared for by our own men. We have had to construct a cemetery outside the main gates and it is a daily occurrence to see a wheelbarrow taking out those who failed to survive the night.

Many of the veterans of this camp have wasted down to skin and bone and barely have the strength to make their way to the feeding station to receive our daily ratio: a slurry of animal bones mixed with potatoes. Surely the Union are in a better state to feed us. The guards are not regular troops but militia. Some of them are older and have lost sons and brothers in battle. They must see this duty as a way of getting back at the Confederacy. There is one particular guard who puts out our food. It is no coincidence that when he puts out our dinner that the pot accidentally tips over. I have watched him and I detect a small smile on his lips. Then there is the guard who taunts us for being cowards and not fighting like real soldiers who would have fought to the death. If they only knew.

The Union boys have a hospital. They built it outside the prison. The boys who are sent there rarely return. I had to help one of my own men to this place. Pus oozed from festering wounds and the bandaging had not been changed for some days. We do our best and beg for more care for them but our voices fall on deaf ears. Worse still one hears the wracking coughs from men who have contracted tuberculosis. It's insidious. When the so called 'nurses' do arrive to change bandages one can see the dried blood on the flimsy cloths. They have been passed down from some military hospital.

Even our own men have been responsible for Confederate deaths. Gangs, led by a small core of beasts have arisen. The groups, like the Four Horsemen of the Apocalypse, will wander the camp ferreting out men who have been able to receive packages through The Sanitary Commission. They usually give a good beating to anyone who resists. As a result, those who complain to the prison officials receive a further beating when the commandant investigates but can find nothing. But the Union boys are afraid of coming into the camp for fear of getting a beating themselves or catching a disease like smallpox. This knowledge just encourages the gangs to be more violent. I did manage to hide the package of tinned goods you sent me. I share some with my soldiers who do not receive packages. With all of this there is developing a mood of despair, men wishing for our defeat so that this horror can come to an end. I am not one of those. This is just another example that demonstrates how this war is changing and too often it is the darker side we see.

One bright light lies in the tunnels that the healthy men have been able to build. I was working with one group of such men and we were able to free twenty prisoners without the Union guards even noticing. We first collect wood from the buildings and from the trees in our open area. The wood is used to stabilize the walls and ceiling. The opening is only four feet by four feet so we have to work on our stomachs. A cart attached to rope retrieves the diggers and the earth they have managed to bring with them. All of this must take place at night in a dark tent we have placed over the mouth of the tunnel. The opening starts about twenty feet inside the prison walls and extends about thirty feet to the edge of the woods. We have tried to hide this work from the gangs, but I believe they are just sitting back until we have done the work and they will take the tunnel from us.

A committee has been formed to deal with this problem. We have recruited big men and armed them with whatever weapons we can: knives, clubs, and even pointed spears. It is not a great irony that the greatest blockade to our freedom comes from our own men. You can be sure there will be blood-shed when we decide to escape.

While I was writing this letter the decision was made to escape on the evening of March 3. It is a well-kept secret, and both the organizers and my own men want me to take part in the escape. If I am successful you will not receive any mail from me for awhile. Just pray for our success. Godspeed!

Your Loving Brother,

Alexander

**\*\*\*\***

As fate would have it Ben did develop a raging fever from his wound. His men decided staying in their camp site would not aid his medical condition. They came upon the idea of building a travois for Ben. One of the men had seen them while serving in the west. Two long two inch diameter logs were attached with strips of leather to the back of one of the men's saddle. The other end was allowed to drag on the ground. The inside of this 'stretcher' was covered by rows of short but strong logs. The inside of this cradle was lined with blankets and boughs to soften Ben's trip. It was decided to leave behind the telegraphic equipment and bury it in a wooded area and then cover it with boughs. Ben might not have agreed with them but it was the only way the three men could return to the north. This idea worked well on flat ground but not on the circuitous route they were compelled to use. After two days of the travois Ben tried riding his mount. If Ben moaned they would stop and apply cool cloths soaked in fresh water on both his head and the wound. The rest of the work was left to Ben's spirit. The men were from the Twentieth Regulars and would march through hell itself to return Ben to the North.

The three soldiers also decided that they could not afford the luxury of taking the same route. This time a straight line north would be the best for Ben. If captured they could claim to be a forward scouting detachment trying to find its way home. The absence of any telegraphic equipment would help add validity to their story. So on the evening of October 31 the small group set out to find their way back 'home'.

Two of the soldiers decided it was time to make a 'raid' on some isolated farm in order to feed themselves and provide some soup for Ben during his conscious moments. It was on the third night that they came upon an isolated farm that could only house a small family. It was agreed that all three would be needed to make the tiny farm secure. Ben would have to remain a few hundred yards back.

The three men dismounted and approached the farm as quietly as possible. They could not afford to gain the attention of some dog or horse which could act as an alarm. A single candle shone in a window allowing them the chance to see what they were facing. Fortune shone upon them this night and it appeared that the farmhouse was only occupied by a middle aged man and woman. Chase crept up to the window, without detection. He returned to report that a pot was boiling on the stove and the couple was eating their dinner. They waited some time to see if another family member might appear, but no one did. It was now decided that two of them would enter through the front door while the third would make his entrance through the small door out back. The doors were swung open rapidly. The woman screamed. The man's jaw dropped like he had seen a ghost. Chase took command.

"Place your hands on the table where we can see them and no harm will come to you!" Demanded Chase in a firm voice. "We mean you no harm. We have a wounded comrade who needs bed rest. A few vittles would be a great help!"

By now the shocked couple had regained their composure. The man spoke. "We are both Union sympathizers. It's not necessary to demand help we are only too glad to give it. Bring in your wounded friend. Mary get some warm water and clean sheets for the wounded soldier."

Now it was the three soldiers that were taken aback. It took a moment for Chase to respond.

"You two bring in the colonel."

Soon Mary was fussing about Ben and seemed to know exactly what to do.

"You are not the first Union soldiers we have aided, but we are always cautious that we are not aiding deserters. However, we are located a little too far south to encounter them. My name is Abraham and we have two sons serving in the Union cause. We just wish we knew more about their health and welfare."

This was the first time Ben had any real care given to his wound.

"I fear this wound is beginning to fester. Is he running a fever?" Mary answered her own question by placing her hand on Ben's brow. "Yes he is feverish."

"May I comment on my own health?" Ben was trying to add a touch of levity to the situation but he said nothing about the shots of pain that began at his leg and ended in his brain. Abraham had seen the men eying the ham that sat on their kitchen table.

"Let me get you men some vittles. We have some carrots and potatoes cooking on the stove."

The three soldiers needed no second invitation and placed their weary bodies on the inviting chairs surrounding the table.

Ben spoke up. "I suppose we are shocked to find Union sympathizers so far south."

"Don't be."

Abraham's pointed response was definitive in its delivery.

"There are more around the countryside. We just have to be careful. If our sympathies were known this farm would be burnt to the ground and our land confiscated and handed over to the nearest loyal Confederate. Make no mistake, the Virginia militia has a second role in this war and that is to flush out people like ourselves. This war was the result of greedy plantation owners who wanted to continue their agricultural system. My ancestors fought in the Revolutionary War for our rights and secession from the Union was not one of those rights."

It was obvious from the warmth of his delivery and that he had obviously repeated this position before. "If anyone's rights have been violated it's the small farmers like ourselves. We can be used as fodder for the Confederate military."

Chase felt he could ask for more assistance after such a positive pro-Union attitude was expressed. He spoke up.

"Abraham, would it be possible if we fed and watered our horses?"

"You go right ahead and take what you want. The barn is empty now since the Confederate cavalry bought our own horses with their worthless paper money."

Ben was starting to feel relaxed and revived after his rest and food. The other three soldiers were sound asleep on the floor with their blankets as pillows. He thought that it would be a good time to gain more information from these Union supporters.

"Abraham do you have any knowledge of the roads between here and Washington?"

"Most certainly!"

Abraham was willing to supply whatever help he could provide. "I've taken that trip many times so I can tell about the less traveled routes."

With that response the man rose and ambled about the house collecting paper and pencil. Ben noticed he was a large man, at least six feet taller or more.

His large arms and hands suggested a life spent working the land. He had spent many an hour driving a plough. He sat on a chair which was dwarfed by his frame. Ben could see Abraham drawing lines as the map unfolded, a gift to Ben and his men. As he drew he queried Ben about the war.

"Seen much action colonel?"

Ben responded knowing that he could make no comments about his current venture.

"I commanded a regiment at the Battle of Shiloh. I was fortunate to have a courageous and hard-fighting group of men who made the best of a difficult situation."

"Sounds like you take to the military life."

"The longer I serve the more it becomes my way of life, but this war has taken its toll."

"Why is that?"

"If I had any illusions about its glamour they were erased at Shiloh. To live a noble and honorable life is my dream but I am afraid war has worn away the nobility of my vision. Men become like creatures trying to survive in the direst circumstances. They become capable of any action that leads them to safety. Don't get me wrong, they also are capable of deeds of great courage and bravery but we don't need war to make a man honorable."

Abraham nodded in agreement with Ben as he bared his views on war.

"I have met the most intelligent and caring people in military service. It seems to me that what a man believes and whatever his nature is will be reflected in war."

Ben caught himself, suddenly realizing he was telling more than he wished.

Abraham spoke. "Well I have chores to do and you boys could use some more rest. Whenever you feel it is time for you to move on let me know."

Abraham put on his boots and coat and prepared to leave. He managed a courteous smile as he looked over his shoulder at his Union warriors. When he returned to the small farmhouse Ben and his men were ready to leave.

"Abraham, I need your help with the directions you promised. It is time for us to be on our way." Ben said.

"Certainly."

Abraham opened the drawer of a small desk, returned to the kitchen, and the four men huddled over the table bent on securing their passage northward. The map led them on a circuitous route, keeping away from well-traveled roads and using trails instead. Two of the soldiers moved quickly to the barn to saddle their mounts and prepare them for travel.

Soon Ben and the three soldiers were on their way. The night was dark and moonless, a light misting of rain dripping silently from the green canopy above. No man spoke. It was just assumed that their speed would be slower to minimize the impact on Ben's aching leg. Every once in awhile an unseen wince crossed his expressionless face, reminding them of his wound.

Ben welcomed the breaking dawn. It would be time to rest and be relatively free from the pain that made his horseback ride a time of stoic discomfort. Chase helped Ben down and the three pushed their way past rough scrub until an open space of land granted them a zone of rest. The men gingerly handled Ben and moved him to a spot which was first covered with an oilskin. Ben managed his own medical treatment and the old bandage was replaced with a clean wrap. Stinking pus reminded Ben of this badge of honor.

****

Alexander had played his part in this attempt at freedom. While the work was both nauseating and claustrophobic he managed to dig away at the earthen enemy facing him. Alexander fought the disturbing nature of this work and focused on the fact that every handful of the clammy soil was a step closer to freedom. During the day the miners would look at the location they imagined their endeavors would take them to. This work required two main daily tasks. First the earth they had removed had to be spread about to reduce suspicion of their toils. This they did by filling bags of earth small enough to fit inside what was left of their trousers. A length of string was loosely tied to the bag and held at the opposite end in the hands of the worker who in turn gently ambled as far as was practicable. When a desirable spot had been reached the soldier would look around for guards and then pull sharply on the string releasing the contents of the bag on the ground. This behavior had to be repeated countless times so little could be moved on any one excursion.

The mining had to be kept away from the prying eyes of other Confederate captives who would not be taken on the future journey. Knowledge of this tunnel could be used as bribery by selfish prisoners so that they could gain freedom without any labor…or worse a conniving Confederate man who would inform the guards in return for some favor. Hardship and captivity have a unique way of eating away at an otherwise honorable man and turning him into a self-centered creature.

The miners had been careful to guard the entrance by fabricating a large tent over it and in turn placing a pile of discarded boxes across the actual opening. No step to assure the secrecy of their work could be overlooked. The day came when the measuring string indicated that the tunnel reached twenty feet beyond the tall fence, just reaching to the edge of the woods.

Alexander felt some guilt doing this work for he knew that at least ten of his men had been left out of the plan. To overcome this guilt he had to remind himself that he had managed to get eighteen of his soldiers on to the work crew. Rank did have some privilege, even in a prisoner of war camp.

As March ended and April began the miners were becoming more impatient to exit the camp. The work was exhausting and the thin bodies grew thinner. No extra vittles were available to strengthen their battle with the soil. It was not unusual to run into a large rock and the whole night would be spent grappling with ropes to extricate it from its subterranean dwelling. By the end of April the string told them their goal had been reached. The thirty souls going on this adventure could barely hold in their excitement. They were ready to flee! The privilege of breaking through had been given to the chief organizer of the plot, one Angus Scot. The men had staged a sing-song to prevent the sounds of digging to the surface from reaching undesirable ears.

After two hours of darkness Angus re-appeared with the news that they had broken through but further from the edge of the woods than they had thought. There was no other option! The thirty men had to leave now. Straws had been used to determine who would follow Angus to freedom. Alexander was about in the middle of this band of tunneling men. Finally Alexander's turn came. In what seemed like an endless crawl he wiggled his way along the tunnel. He could hear curses from behind as ceiling dirt would find its way into unseeing eyes. About half-way Alexander's flight to freedom had been halted by someone in front of him. Had they been found out, he wondered? The sense of claustrophobia was made worse during these pauses. He could hear men whispering silent prayers during this journey through hell.

Finally he reached the upward stretch of the tunnel. His heart skipped a beat. Finally he was free!

It was a dark night, but now they were free. They just kept crawling on to the woods. Each man was now on his own. Some stopped to look back at their cage of damnation. Others, like Alexander, just kept moving to a place where they felt safe to stand and then move on carefully in a southern direction. By now a path had been made by the men who had already exited. Alexander headed for the darkest places he could find. Unfortunately this plan went awry and he had to back out of a grassy swamp. Every two or three minutes he stopped to listen for other escapees or worse still, Union guards. He heard neither. The route he followed was one which attempted to circle around the swamp and at the same time focus on where he thought 'south' would be. Muck from the shores of the swamp oozed up between his fingers turning his palms to soft mittens.

After what seemed like hours Alexander's path began to elevate and he found himself moving away from the swamp. Desperately he fought the temptation to just drop to the ground and sleep. He knew that distance from the prison camp was his only chance for safety. The rays of dawn's light started to break through the dark soon…soon he could rest. He thought he heard rustling off to his left. He stopped. He concluded it must be some night creature making its way to its daytime place of rest. The sun now rose and he was prepared to form some kind of resting place. Silently he twisted some branches from small tamarack trees and made a nest in an area that he had flattened from an area of scrub.

He woke to the sounds of soldiers marching toward him. He froze like a deer exposed to light.

"Michaels I want you to watch from this hill. We will try to eat quietly so you are able to hear the sounds of any of the escapees," ordered the gruff voice of a Northern officer. The soldier flopped quickly to the ground like some rag doll. So they are weary too…good.

At this juncture of his escape Alexander decided it was time to take rest.

Daylight and the presence of these soldiers made it impossible to do much else. He drifted off and had an amazingly good rest despite his condition. When he awoke all was silent. The soldiers were gone and he could rest. He had no idea how long he had been asleep but the sun was heading westward. It was a good sign for a man making his escape from hell. As the sun began to fall Alexander could feel the rumblings in his stomach. He was starving. But where would he find food? Continuing his push south he crossed roads of all conditions. After what seemed an eternity he came upon a small farm which he approached cautiously. But for a single light in a window he could not see any sign of activity. Suddenly he came upon a fence standing like a parade of soldiers opposing his movement.

Moving around the fence brought him a stroke of good fortune. Inside the fence was a garden and in the dwindling night he could see the neat rows of vegetables. They appeared in mature condition. Sifting among the rows he came upon a row of carrots. He looked for the tall leaves and began pulling a few. Wiping them off he knew they would make a fine start to his meal. They still had room for growth but there was no protest from Alexander. The particles of earth trapped in the crevices of the carrots failed to slow down his chewing. Beside them was a row of cabbages. Stripping off the first large leaves revealed the hard core of this find. He proceeded to take chunks out of the fresh cabbage. After living on scraps in the prison this was like a banquet. He thought it wise not to completely load his stomach. His stomach was not used to volumes of food. Feeling refreshed Alexander moved along on his goal to hit Southern land.

For two days he continued on, sleeping during the day, moving across fields during the night. He wished he could find some evidence that he had made it to southern soil. His first night's meal had done its work and again he felt the rumble of an angry stomach. It was time to take a chance. In the distance he could see the twinkling of a farmhouse. Approaching with caution he now heard the sound of a dog barking raising alarm. He continued toward the house.

"Who is out there?" came the base voice.

"Just a lost soldier without guns and near starved to death pleaded Alexander.

"Just step into the light of my lantern and don't try anything. There is a second gun trained on you from the window. Yankee or Reb?"

"Does it make a difference?"

"Not really," was the unusual response. In this war most people were loyal to one side or the other. Alexander mulled over the idea of standing and revealing himself. This approach might be a ruse to bring someone into view then shoot him. He thought about it and took the chance. He stood slowly and took minute paces toward the voice so as not to alarm the person with the gun. This approach worked and soon, through the elevation of the light, each man could see the other.

"Well you don't look particularly violent and don't seem to be armed." said the voice."

"I guarantee I have no intentions of harming you!" Alexander replied vehemently.

"Now don't get too excited there young fella. Come up on my porch and we'll get a better look at you."

Alexander mounted the porch. "My God fella you look terrible. Your clothes are torn, your hair looks like my shaggy dog and you downright stink. But you have an uppity kind of sound to you. Why is that?"

"Before I tell my story do you think I could be seated and have a drink of water?"

"Water! I can do better than that young fella. Come on indoors."

Both men ventured into the building. From the outside it had appeared rather worn. The inside was no better. There was a table, some chairs, and even an old rocking chair. Against the wall was a fireplace, with chunks of brick removed or fallen. Off to one side was a door, probably leading to a bedroom. Whoever lived here was not rich, that was for certain. The man looked to be in his sixties and his shoulders stooped. Suddenly another door opened from the back room and another man appeared. This man was in his early thirties and well muscled though not of large frame.

"This here is my son, Matthew, as good a young'un as there ever was. Pardon my rudeness. I'm Clayton, Clayton Archibald. Take a seat there young fella."

Alexander sat on the chair motioned to by Clayton.

"Pardon my manners. We southerners our known for our hospitality but these days you can never tell who is at your door. You from around these parts?"

"No I'm not." Alexander answered.

"Father not all people who pass through here are locals, particularly in these hard times." Alexander noted that the younger man's speech was more educated than the older man's. Meanwhile Clayton had taken a bottle down from one of the shelves and put it on the table.

"Just one minute while I find us some drinking utensils," muttered Clayton half-speaking to himself. The men, by this time, had put down their old flintlock guns, seeing that Alexander was of no threat to them. Alexander would have preferred some food. He was starved, but these two men did not look like they could spare much of what little they had.

"Pardon our manners again. We foolishly forgot to ask your name."

"Alexander Braithwaite." Alexander barely got out his name when his stomach growled loud enough for all to hear.

"My God man, when was the last time you had vittles?"

"It's been quite a while, two days perhaps."

Clayton retreated back to the cupboard and produced a large loaf of bread. "Here's some bread for you and here's the chicken left over from dinner. Matthew, go out to the garden and get some fresh vegetables for our friend here."

"No, No, this is fine Clayton."

"Do you mind us asking what you're doing around here Alexander?"

"I am an escaped prisoner of war. I was able to flee with a number of other Confederates through a tunnel. I have been moving south ever since my escape."

"What's your rank?"

"I am a colonel, if that makes any difference. Why do you ask?"

"Sheer curiosity; and you speak like them upper class folk colonel."

"Well now that I have answered your questions I have some of my own. Matthew, why are you not in uniform fighting the Yankees?"

"May I interrupt colonel because I hold the explanation for Matthew?" asked Clayton. Alexander nodded and Clayton went on.

"I see it this way colonel, I will fight, as Matthew would, to defend our land if it came down to that. But this war is being fought to protect slavery. Slavery has no impact on my life. Why, we have a free black man working for us tending the crops and we pay him what we can. Why would I fight to defend this slavery business?"

"But this war is also about our rights as a state to defend the rights of that state," added Alexander

"You can fool some of the small farmers like me but I just don't see that our rights are being violated. This war is being fought by ordinary white farmers like me. Too many rich folk have found ways to get around having to fight. Ever since conscription came in we've had to watch the men leave their farms and take up the musket. Now who is going to run that small farm? The wife and three small children? Not bloody likely. The longer this war drags on the more small farms like mine will begin to fall to ruin even without any invasion of Yankees. Your kind and the government in Richmond won't care as long as we fuel the front lines with bodies. And we will run out of bodies long before those northerners do. And what will we do then? Send children and old men?"

Alexander found that it was pointless to continue this discussion. He thanked Clayton and his son for the food and clothes and told them that he had to be on his way. He was well-rested and was needed elsewhere. He just didn't know where that elsewhere was!

"Before I leave I have one request to make. Is it possible that you have writing paper and a pen or pencil?"

"We look like backwoods folks but it doesn't mean we can't write. Of course we do and we would be proud if you would use our writing utensils. Do you want pen or pencil?"

"I would prefer pen if you don't mind, Clayton."

"Not all Alexander, not at all." And so Alexander began to write.


June 18, 1863
Dear Brother,


Much has happened since I last wrote you. I know you will want to express your ideas upon that which I write but make no mistake it is our only salvation. What I explain to you is premised on the assumption that the South will lose this war. I am sure you are certain of this as well. What will our plantation look like after the northerners are through with it? I am sure you can determine that outcome as well. Our organized and profitable system will be gone and all the reasoning behind what we have accomplished will be lost with the ages. Therefore I have come up with a plan. I will only outline it here because I hope to be home soon. I am finished with this war.

Brazil is the only country left in our hemisphere with legalized slavery. What I propose is that we pick up all the ideas inherent in our system and move them to Brazil. Our success is incumbent on two factors. First, that we can get a reasonable price in gold or Yankee currency for our plantation and secondly, that we are able to convince a majority of our blacks that they will be better off moving and rebuilding what we have. It is fortunate for our cause that they have or will become aware of the poor treatment at the hands of the northerners when they move to the cities.

Make no mistake, this will take us years of toil once again but Brazil is the only place we can apply our system. I hope that you will agree this is our only hope and that we should do so before the entire South is ransacked by the rapaciousness of the North and the dubious benefits of freeing the slaves. Stress this point to our blacks. Would they rather have the known or the unknown?

Please begin preparing the details surrounding the sale of our plantation. I will accept whatever you see as a fair price for our lands and buildings. Approach those you know who were pleased with what they saw when they visited us. I hope to see you soon.

Your Loving Brother,

Alexander

After he had penned these words to his brother he wondered when it was that he had reached this conclusion about the Confederacy. It was truly worse than losing a leg in combat, but it had to be so.

"I have one more request. Would you see that this letter is posted as soon as possible? I hope I haven't been too demanding."

Alexander waved a good-bye to the two men and started on his journey south to Richmond. First light was rising to his left as he marched along. It was then that he began to think.

For the first time in his life Alexander found that he did not have an answer and he discovered that he really hadn't any thought to the plight of the small farmer. It was they who had been fighting this war for the right of plantation owners to keep slaves. Why had he missed all this? His answer, like many plantation owners he lived in his own closed world. A plantation was like its own little economy with workers, bosses, rules, and different classes and food supplies. The only thing that tied them to the outside world was selling their goods. And if the only thing that made this system work was slavery how would it ever evolve and change? For in Alexander's mind change was a natural ingredient of improvement. He had proven that on his own plantation. He had fought for the South but what would be left after the war? Would everything return to the way it was before the war? It couldn't. Lincoln's Thirteenth Amendment, freeing the slaves in slave states put all of their southern social system in jeopardy. The slaves would simply walk away or worse still, burn and destroy what had taken years to build.

Alexander struck out on his journey to Louisiana, hoping to stay off main thoroughfares. He did not want to be taken by a local militia as a backslider who had escaped from the frontlines in the hope of finding safety. Again he did most of his traveling at night and moved into tall grass or leafy woods if he heard the sound of horses' hoofs. How grateful he was at the sight of a bubbling stream or a vegetable patch close to his route of travel. Clayton had provided him with a canteen and a sack for carrying vegetables. How handy they had been. For one stretch he had the good fortune to travel on the back of a buggy driven by a black man who had quietly approached him when he saw the limp in his gait.

"Welcome my friend let me take a burden off those legs!"

The black man whose name was Joshua was the winner in this situation.

Alexander had the chance to hear the history of his clan. But Alexander had grown angry as the poor man talked of whippings, the hanging of runaways, and the rape of young women. It convinced him further of the importance of their move to Brazil. After five or six hours the two men parted ways but it had brought a respite from the scuffling along primitive roads.

Then one morning the countryside began to look familiar to him. He noticed ponds that he had passed frequently on trips to town and trees that were like old friends for he assumed they had been there forever. He chanced taking the main road and after a few hours could see the gate to his plantation. He drew up to it and sat down and wept openly, not out of sadness but from the joy of reunion.

His first days home were spent visiting and discussing plans with many of his blacks, particularly those with whom he shared a common bond, about the proceeds of the sale and their ability to bring the plantation to its maximum production. It was this bond with the earth that did more than anything to create the human bond. These were equals sharing the same adventure of God's gifts, although this war had put thoughts in Alexander's mind about the sincerity of God's wishes. He had not had much time to spend with his brother, but they made a point of sitting together after one dinner.

"I feel badly to have commissioned you the task of finding a buyer for the plantation. I gave you no alternative it seems."

"Don't worry brother I have begun to question the chance of ever winning this war. The newspapers were full of the actions of the northerners on the Carolina coast and it was not a pleasant picture."

"Why? What has happened?" Alexander asked.

"It seems that the northerners who have taken this area have burned out fifty to sixty plantations, as well as freed the blacks. But they have not trained them, just used them as 'contraband' as they call them. It is just the Union using the blacks as servants to ply their trade of destruction in the coastal waterways."

"This makes me want to speed up the process of liquidating our holdings here before they are exploited."

"I have good news on that front Alexander. Thomas Filton has been here a number of times. You know that he has the greatest respect for you and what you have done. Well, he is putting together a group of like fellows who would be interested in making an offer. He only fears the price may be too great."

"Not to worry, if it is Thomas we could extend payment over a number of years. I dislike having to leave you with the business part of the plantation, but I feel that I should keep a low profile while I am here. It could be best to tell our men to keep my presence a secret. I am liable to be seen as a traitor by those who wish to take this war to its successful conclusion." Alexander had decided that it was time to put his plan into action and speed up the negotiations with Filton, if possible.

In the meantime he took long walks around the property and put out queries to the government of Brazil about a possible move there. His sojourns around the plantation tended to make him sad, however. He thought he would be rejuvenated by his walks but instead it made him realize how much time he had wasted fighting for the Confederacy.

August 2, 1863
Dear Alexander,

Thank you for your note notifying me of your presence back on the plantation and the tragic experiences you had fighting for this great Confederacy. While you and I can disagree about the efficacy of the Confederacy, I certainly agree with you about some of the so-called 'men' who are doing the fighting for us. I think sometimes, that if was not for the grand reputation of 'Marse' Lee our Confederacy would be in shambles. He is both a soldier and a humanitarian.

As to the sale of your property, you must realize what a drop has seen compared to pre-war prices. I have kept your name anonymous in negotiating with my partners. I am using your brother for business references. After much consideration we have come up with a figure. This will exclude, of course, all slaves and freedmen who wish to travel with you. The number we propose is $500,000 in Union greenbacks. We realize this might be seen as low but we have no other sales of properties like yours to offer as a comparison. I will leave you to dwell on this figure, and stay out of harm's way.

Yours in God,

Thomas Filton

Alexander was pleased that Thomas had kept his name out of the negotiations. Like Thomas, Alexander was unsure what a fair price would be in light of numerous factors. He would first have to get a quote from the Government of Brazil. He could begin to consider the cost of moving. It would probably be better to leave all the equipment behind and start afresh in Brazil. He would have to discover what crops could, best grown in the tropical soils. How much clearing would have to be done? Could he rely on the Government of Brazil for advice?

September 13,1863
Office of the Minister of the Interior,
Government of Brazil

Mr. Alexander Braithwaite:

We were pleased to receive your inquiry into the purchase of a large tract of land for the purpose of agricultural use. Let me assure you that we would be only too glad to have you purchase land from us. Such a venture brings mutual benefits to both sides. Judging from what you have told us about the size of your present plantation there are a number of good plots with sizeable tracts available for you to purchase.

You might be surprised to know that you are not the first Confederate plantation owner to seek information from us. We assume it is our use of slavery that offers you continuation of your way of life.

We have already divided many tracts near Sao Paulo to minimize your shipping needs. We try with each tract to include access to water, wooded tropical forests, and open land that can be easily worked. Included in this letter please find surveys of ten tracts that are presently divided according to my previous description. If the size of the tract is not large enough we can 'borrow' from another tract. We are reluctant, however, to reduce their size.

We are offering all of these tracts at the price of $5.00 American dollars per acre. We hope that the price is within your budget.

Mr. Juan Menendez

Assistant to the Minister of the Interior

Now Alexander had something concrete to work with. He could well afford a tract of land in Brazil and made arrangements with Thomas Filton to firm up his group's purchase of his land. But of equal importance, he had to sell his own workers on the idea. This would be harder now that Lincoln had freed the slaves in secessionist states. He decided to call a meeting of both his slaves and his freemen to find out where they stood on his idea.

He was glad he had built this all purpose meeting hall for his workers. They used it for religious meetings, dances, and other celebrations. Actions like this did not go unnoticed by his slaves and workers. The time had come for the meeting and they filed in by ones and twos, sometimes a small group would venture in laughing and talking as they made their way to the benches Alexander had arranged in a semi-circle so all could hear.

The meeting opened with a prayer for their own health and salvation and another for a quick end to this devastating war. And so Alexander began.

"My dear friends and workers, I am sure you have heard about my plan to move. I am here today to get your ideas, but first I want to tell you what I have in mind so far. I have been touch with the Brazilian government and it is possible for me to purchase a large tract of land near the coast. I propose that we leave our large equipment here and take with us only the basic working tools that are your own personal ones or ones that we would need as soon as we arrive. We'd best travel by wagon train and journey through Texas and Mexico to the Central American states and from there to Brazil. I know that this will be a long journey but we will benefit in the end. We can build our own wagons here. We have the facilities, including a wheelwright, to produce the wagons necessary for the trip. These will be purchased by me and given to families here. You may keep them when we arrive in Brazil. It remains to be seen what we will grow but we will take seeds with us to begin anew if it is possible.

"Your status, free and slave will remain the same but I will give a special allowance for slaves to allow them a quick opportunity to become freedmen. I know that there is great appeal to stay here or go north when the North eventually wins this war, but let me give you some advice. Freedom means little if it enslaves you to new owners. By this I mean the owners of large companies and the future landowners of the south. I have read that that there have been race riots already in the major Northern cities. White workers are beating and killing blacks because they believe their jobs are being lost to the 'niggers'. Beware my friends, the better world that you seek might not be found in this country. Going to Brazil might bring great changes to what we produce but it will not change the social order that you know well in your present state."

With these last words there were glances about the room and mumblings amongst the blacks, both free and slave. "Mr. Braithwaite may I speak?"

The voice in question was that of Abraham Wiley. He was a freedman and operator of the blacksmith shop on the plantation. He had been asked to speak by a number of the workers, both free and slave. His support would go a long way in making this venture a success. He had been trained at the school and was a powerful speaker. His large, muscular frame brought with it a powerful resonating voice that made people want to hear what he had to say. "Why certainly Abraham, go ahead."

"Mr. Braithwaite most of the folks I know on this plantation, know full well that we are a fortunate group of colored people. You have raised our condition above those on other plantations and our freedmen have more freedoms than those in the towns or those working their own land. We also respect the knowledge you have in making a plantation a success. You have proven that here. You probably don't know this but when we are off the plantation or visiting relatives on other plantations, those folk are always coming to us and asking us how it would be possible to get work on this plantation. We're a little selfish about this and tell them that we are already bursting at the seams and the 'massa' Braithwaite don't need mo' slaves'. His last phrase brought a chorus of laughter from the workers. First, because Alexander would not hear of the word 'massa' being spoken and secondly that he reverted to 'slave talk' at the end of his sentence.

Alexander could feel the positive, relaxed atmosphere that filled the room. He hoped that Abraham truly did represent the majority. Abraham spoke up once again.

"We have already taken a vote to determine who wants to leave with you and those who want to go north. Among the slaves sixty percent want to go with you and among the freedmen eighty per-cent want to go with you. We understand that there will be more discussions between us all but those results are strongly in favor of this move.""Thank- you for your support, and I would encourage the support of those of you who wish to stay here. I know that it would be a challenge into the unknown, but what will remain of the south?"

With those remarks the crowd dispersed and Alexander could hear the comments both pro and con, for leaving and staying. This would be a hard decision for his people. While he was thinking, Abraham, the black who had spoken to the assembled, asked if he could have a few words with Alexander.

"Of course Abraham, I encourage and welcome your input to our plans."

"Well sir, this might seem a small point to you, but for us it is an issue. We are concerned about your policy on firearms. We know that the freedmen are allowed to own guns, but that it is restricted among slaves."

"That's correct Abraham."

"Well sir, we have no knowledge of the dangers we would encounter on the trip there, nor would we know what we might encounter living there. We were wondering if that policy could be changed. We would need all the protection we could get and it might encourage more slaves to join us in this venture." Alexander mulled this thought over in his mind. While slaves were never allowed guns in the south for fear of rebellion, he had no such fears among his own slaves.

"Well, Abraham I think that is possible. Your fears are reasonable and if there were problems it would be good that we had as many males available who could fire guns. Let me have some time to think more upon your suggestion, but I don't see great problems with your idea in principle."

"Thank you, Mr. Braithwaite, I think your agreement would go a long way in reducing the fears that have been raised by some people." After that conversation Alexander returned to his home to reflect on what had just transpired.

****

The small group was ready to start on their northward adventure, still riding at night and resting during the day. They hoped to be on Federal soil within a few days. There were no untoward encounters and that seemed to make the trip go faster. The only problem was Ben's leg. It continued to drip pus and his leg was throbbing now with pain. He tried not to let it slow them down but he found that it was necessary to make extra stops to relieve some of the pain, temporarily at least. At times Ben felt weak and dizzy but he tried to live with it knowing that they would soon be 'home'.

Sergeant Chase had taken his responsibilities very seriously. He had served with Ben from the start and felt the bond that comes from continuous experience. He would see that Ben made it back alive. Suddenly a Union soldier stepped out from behind a tree. He must have been all of seventeen. He could tell by their uniforms that they were Union soldiers. He queried the men on their destination and seeing that the colonel was in distress directed them to the medical tent. They stayed on their horses until they reached the field hospital. Chase dismounted and asked to see the doctor. Fortunately he was not busy at the time.

"Doctor I need to get my colonel to a hospital in Washington as soon as possible, would you take a look at his wound?"

"Certainly soldier; just bring him directly into my tent."

The three men fussed over Ben, showing tender caution in helping him dismount and then carrying him into the tent and placing him on the doctor's examination table. One his assistants unwound the dressing that had been put around Ben's leg. The doctor could see that the shell had lodged somewhere in Ben's leg because there was no exit wound.

"Sergeant I think it best that I probe this wound and remove the ball that is inside. If I leave it, it is only going to make matters worse. Laudable pus has already begun to form."

The sergeant nodded to the doctor and Ben, who was semi-conscious, did the same. The assistant already appeared with cloth for the chloroform drip that would give Ben some unconscious moments free from pain.

The other assistant had brought out a clean set of probes and swabs. Ben was luckier than most soldiers. It was fortunate that this was not happening in the middle of a battle. The doctor cut away the infected skin and removed the pus from Ben's leg. He took his probe and soon felt the presence of the ball inside Ben's leg.

"The ball has lodged against a bone. It must have exhausted most of its firing power."

The doctor mumbled this to no one in particular and switched to his forceps to extract the ball. Deftly he worked. This was a man who had removed many a ball since the war began. Quickly he extracted the unwanted agent of death and with a sense of pride showed it to the men present.

The assistant cleaned the wound and surrounding are with a fresh cloth. Now the leg was wrapped carefully but firmly.

"There you are sergeant your colonel is almost as good as new. But I suspect it will take time to heal. Some doctors use different medications on top of wounds such as this, but frankly I don't believe that they do much good. Let's wait until he revives but I suggest giving him time. I gather you want to be on your way to Washington and one of their fifty or so hospitals." Ben was placed on one of the cots and the men moved outside until he recovered.

When Ben awoke he was groggy and nauseous. The doctor recommended they wait twelve hours before traveling. "Tomorrow I am sending one of our ambulance wagons to Washington with three other wounded officers who need hospitalization. Why don't we wait until then? That way he can travel more comfortably." Again Sergeant Chase gave his nod of approval.

Feeling that they had done the best they could for their colonel the three men asked if they could get some food and rest. The past few days had not permitted much of either. They were directed to the closest regimental headquarters and asked to speak to the colonel of the regiment.

"Colonel the three of us have been on a mission with our colonel who is in your hospital. Would it be possible to get some food and a place to rest?"

"Most certainly, sergeant. Orderly would you find a company that is eating now and find some worthy victuals for these men?" His orderly nodded and motioned for the three men to follow him. Soon Ben's spies were enjoying a beefsteak dinner and were engrossed in conversation with the men who served them this notable dinner.

The following morning as the three men walked into the field hospital they could see that their colonel was engrossed in conversation with the doctor. As they approached the doctor spoke first.

"Ah gentlemen, it is good to see you had a good night's rest. You definitely look more alert than you did yesterday, and you will see that your colonel is awake and alert but unable to hold any food down. That is not unusual. The ambulance will be leaving in an hour and you might want to travel along with it. It is one of the newer models and is equipped to handle four men lying down. All the soldiers I am sending will be in that position for medical reasons." They walked over to where Ben lay. He seemed rested. His men gathered his belongings and packed them in a valise.

"Well, are you fit for travel, colonel?" Chase enquired.

"Ready as I will ever be!" Ben uttered in a positive voice. But the men could detect an underlying sound, that of uncertainty, which he could not cover.

"We should be leaving shortly and we will make good time to Washington." They would be traveling singly rather than as a wagon train. Soon the litter bearers came by and picked up the handles at the ends of the litter. Carefully and deftly they placed Ben in the lower right section. The other three compartments were already occupied by soldiers in various states of ill health. Soon the wagon shook as the driver banged on the reins and took off.

They were starting from northern Virginia and had only a forty mile trek to make. Ben could have sworn this driver had learned every cussing word in the English language. He used it on the mules, the four patients, and his men when they pulled into view. Yes, he was a soldier, but of the lesser kind in terms of acquired social graces. The whole world was his enemy.

"Where is the colonel I am carrying?"

"I am down here, what can I do for you?"

"Well you could start by handing me your salary." This brought a cacophony of barked laughs from the driver, who was the only one to laugh.

Since no one else laughed the driver brought a torrent of vulgarity on the four victims. The man beside him was in great pain from the surgery to remove his leg. "My God driver, I am in constant pain, could you please slow down the wagon?"

"I am in charge of this wagon and how it is driven. When your leg heals you can get a job like mine and become miserable too." There was another burst of cackling laughter and again the driver laughed. Silence. That only lasted a half hour or so when the soldier above Ben began to moan. The more bumps they hit the louder the moaning became.

"Shut up you stupid arse. Do you think I enjoy this?" No answer followed.

Finally the last soldier decided to enter the discussion, if one could call it that.

"I understand we are headed for Carver Hospital."

"That's right my friend," he added in a mocking voice.

"Excuse me driver could I be let off at Harewood Hospital?" requested Ben.

"Hey bud, go where you are told. This ain't no private hospital wagon!"

The driver felt quite put upon by this request.

"How can I keep to a schedule if you want your private service?"

"I understand your argument but it will only add a few minutes to your journey."

"Forget it mister…oh, I forgot you are a colonel. Well, colonel if you come up with the money I will see that you get there.

"How much do you want?"

"I think fifty dollars will be just fine." Ben saw no point in resisting. He didn't have the physical or mental ability to do so. But he did make a mental note that it was not just the rich who were getting richer, the small man had his desire for a share of war profiteering. The springs on this wagon were well sprung making their bouncing greater. The man who had been moaning had stopped. Ben wondered if he had died. What they didn't know, there was an unwritten policy to send the serious cases to city hospitals.

Ben soon came to realize that this ride to the hospital might be the worst part of his experience. He tried to take his mind off the pain by thinking about Anna. After all she worked at Harewood Hospital and simply seeing her would bring some relief. After what seemed like an endless journey the ambulance stopped.

"Alright you heroes, it's time to take a rest, get some vittles into your stomachs, and prepare yourselves for a restful night. We should be in Washington by noon tomorrow."

The cooking utensils were kept under the wagon and the best Ben could do was listen to this cranky example of a man as he prepared their dinner. Ben was not shocked when he found out it would be salt pork and hardtack. He expected the worst. The salt pork he managed to swallow, gagging on the occasional piece. The hardtack needed something to soften it.

"Colonel how are you doing?" It was Sergeant Chase who, along with the other men had faithfully kept their word and followed the ambulance. Chase could see that Ben was in discomfort, confined as he was to the wagon.

"Could you ask this wretched driver if you and one of the men could remove me from the wagon to get some tea and soften this hardtack?"

"Certainly colonel."

Chase returned in a few minutes.

"Well sir you were correct about the disposition of that creature. I don't know how you put up with him. He said, or rather growled, that if we would lift you out and were responsible for you then we could do so."

"Fine, let's do that sergeant." Ben croaked in a voice Chase could barely recognize.

Two of the men began to slide Ben, ever so carefully, from the wagon.

The third man grabbed the other end as it slid gently over the wooden frame.

"Careful boys, let's place the colonel over here under the shade of that oak tree." With that accomplished Chase promised Ben that he would boil some water and make a cup of tea. Ben was able to sit up on one elbow and managed to move even further and lean against the tree. He was glad just to be looking at something other than the top of the ambulance. It was a pleasant July evening and a gentle breeze cooled Ben to the point where he almost felt comfortable. He enquired about the man above him who had mysteriously gone silent.

"He's dead!" exclaimed the emphatic voice of the unpleasant driver. Chase offered Ben tea. He was glad to get it so he could soak the hardtack and soften it.

"How's the leg colonel?" Chase enquired.

"Now that we are still I can feel the pain subsiding. It looks as if the bandage is oozing blood and pus, but I'll wait until we get to the hospital to get it cared for. Thanks for asking sergeant."

Ben nodded off to sleep and the three men hobbled their horses and prepared for a night of rest. The sound of snoring came from the driver who had put up his own small tent and was fast asleep.

Ben was awake before the others as the leg began to throb in earnest. Eventually the driver woke up and barked at the three men.

"It's time to get that colonel of yours into the wagon. I want to get going."

"Shouldn't we have some breakfast first?"

"No time for that, besides we are behind schedule."

"Well what about the men emptying their bladders?"

"Just let them piss themselves. They will be in hospital soon."

Chase had just about had enough of this gruff, miserable, uncaring man.

Now Chase understood why the men had said, "Better to die in the field hospital than in an ambulance".

Ben could make out the brightness of the sun pulsating its rays downward. They must be near Washington. No sooner had he made this observation than their 'keeper' yelled.

"There she is boys, Washington!"

The miserable driver almost sounded excited about their arrival. He must have been thinking of the fifty dollars. Ben and his fellow injured soldiers now found out what bumps were really like. The wheels of large cannon and heavy supply wagons had churned up the city's streets while recent rain had made the streets more treacherous. Ben found he had to use two hands to keep from rolling off the wagon. The side to side motion brought yelps of pain from him. He felt embarrassed doing this in the presence of his men.

The first three men were deposited in the city at the Carver Hospital. Now they headed for the outskirts of Washington and the roads became more tolerable again. They were almost in the country when Chase yelled out to him.

"I see the sign sir, Harewood Hospital." Ben tried to get a look and rolled onto his stomach so he could see where they were. The ambulance slowed down and Ben could see the canopy of flowers that covered the ground in symmetrical designs. Off to one side was a large vegetable garden where volunteers were caring for the bounty of early summer.

"Pay up Colonel. This is as far as you go."

Ben was able to roll over once more and rescue his money case from inside his coat pocket. He was careful doing this. He did not want the driver to see that he still had money left.

"You have cleaned me out soldier. Take your money and go."

Ben scowled out these words in mock derision of the driver, but the sloppy little man was too self-centered to get the message. Chase and the men pulled Ben out as he lay on the litter.

"Don't forget colonel, I want my litter back. Find yourself a comfortable bed and enjoy the luxuries of hospital life."

The man's sarcastic voice would be heard for the last time. For that Ben was thankful.

Chase followed the signs and waited until he found the building labeled

'Administration and Admissions'. The men walked over to the building and opened the door. There were three men on litters in front of them. They would have to wait. Ben gazed about the building which contained a variety of people. There were nurses, male and female made obvious by the blood on their white uniforms. He spotted some queer women who were dressed alike and wore hats that had two wings, one coming out each side of their heads.

Bearded doctors were also moving about, but less bloodied. Some seemed like clerks, sitting at desks and moving forms about as quickly as they appeared at their desks. Sergeant Chase managed to find a clerk who admitted the Colonel to Building 'B'.

Chase and another soldier carried their colonel into one of the long buildings. They had been directed to building 'B'. Upon entering the building their senses were attacked. The smell was a combination of infected wounds and urine. The activity was like the hurry-scurry of a family of mice. There were women with strange hoods on their heads who seemed to be helping the men. Doctors in suits seemed to be giving out orders to other women. Then what appeared to be family members, were sitting beside the beds talking and writing. Many of this group seemed to have baskets with them and were attempting to feed the wounded.

It was obvious from his expression that Ben was in pain. The jiggling of the trip up the stairs had been enough to aggravate the wound.

"Sergeant I want you to finish our trip by reporting to Colonel Winston at the war office. Give him the information about messages heading south from Richmond being in plain language. Ask him if any of our messengers made it back because none of the men returned to us."

"Yes, colonel."

"I want to thank you men for staying with me and keeping me from shooting that ambulance driver." The soldiers shared a good laugh with the last comment. With that the men left with Ben's encouragement. This scene was a shock, even for veteran soldiers.

"Ben!" Ben heard his named being called out by a female voice. He just could not find the source.

Suddenly Anna appeared in front of him looking very different from the way Ben had last seen her. She had her hair pulled back and covered with a cap. Her clothes were white, and stained with blood. Her appearance was almost plain. But those brown eyes were still there dancing and sparkling in their sockets.

"Anna, you are a dream come true! Someone I actually know in this place. I knew you worked at Harewood. I just didn't think I would run into you so soon."

"Let me help you Ben. I can get some water and wash your wound. It looks like your whole body needs a good washing down and some clean bed clothes would help. Oh Ben, I had hoped you would someday make it to take a tour. I didn't expect to see you this way."

"Believe me I wish you'd been right!"

Ben emphasized this response. He had come to understand what so many other soldiers had experienced.

"What am I doing in a hospital out in the country?"

"Do you really want to know?"

"It's my natural curiosity.""Ben let me go get some things you need and we can talk while I work."

Anna was gone before Ben could respond. He noticed his pain had seemed to disappear when he met Anna. His eyes gave him a partial tour of his new residence. It was a longish room perhaps forty feet by one hundred and fifty feet. A row of about twenty five beds were laid out in two rows. There was an aisle to be used as work space, and in the center, equally spaced, were three wood burning stoves, obviously for winter use. Ben looked at the ceiling. The walls must have been at least twelve or so feet high. A peaked ceiling ran the length of the building with the peaks coming to an end at the completion of each length. Ben could not see everything, but he gathered that there were rooms at one end of the long room. About ten windows were built into each of the walls giving the large room a reasonably bright appearance.

Anna returned and went to work on first washing and wrapping the oozing wound.

"So you want to know the history of Harewood? Just lay back and relax. The land was once farmland. It was acquired from a banker by the name of Corcoran. The government confiscated the land because he opposed the war. The first hospital I worked at here was a tent city. Soon, as the numbers grew, Harewood became surrounded by refuse and excrement. As a result mosquitoes and flies were in abundance. Soon malaria broke out among the patients. So those in charge used netting over the men's beds to try and deal with the problem. Many patients found it unbearably hot and uncomfortable. So they would just rip them down. It is no wonder that the men dreaded being sent to a hospital from the field hospitals.

"Finally the U.S. Sanitary Commission became involved and had the tent hospital closed. This resulted in what they call a 'pavilion' hospital being built. Some of them are built like the spokes of a wheel with a large central area. Others like Harewood are a collection of seven separate buildings. At one end there is a dining room for those who can move and rooms for the Sisters of Charity and the nurses along with all our supplies."

"Who are the Sisters of Charity Anna?"

"They are a nursing order of Catholic nuns who have given their lives to Christ in the service of men. They were highly sought after despite the absurd prejudice against Catholics in some hospitals. They make excellent nurses. I will see that you get to meet Sister Dorothy and Sister Florence, both are exceptional."

"Anna, I am still confused. What makes them exceptional?"

"As Catholic sisters they are required to take certain vows. These vows include poverty, chastity, and obedience. As a result they steal nothing and only give. They bring in whatever food they can. Chastity appealed to Dorothea Dix who was concerned about having bright and beautiful women helping the men. Because they are bound to obedience they do not get into squabbles with the lay nurses and listen to the orders of those above them."

"I see now why they would make such excellent nurses. Thank you for putting up with a nosy patient."

"I will always answer you Ben!"

With that the brown eyes glistened again, this time accompanied by a broad smile that transcended words. Ben felt he was looking at one of God's angels. He had to snap out of this mystical mode and ventured on with another question.

"What's the food like Anna?"

"I wished you hadn't asked. Cornmeal and hardtack fried in pork grease.

It is very uncommon that we receive any fresh fruit or vegetables. But I hope you did see our new vegetable garden.

It contains seasonal vegetables that will carry into the early winter, cabbages and carrots for example. Well-fed patients make for healthier patients!"

"We are far behind in so many things. There are practically no thermometers or stethoscopes available. They are widespread on the continent but our doctors are a conservative group of men. Before the Sanitary Commission entered the premises old dressings would be left on the floor, doctors would just wipe their instruments on their smocks, and even wet the suture strings by putting them in their mouths. I would swear these men have no understanding of correct medical practice."

"And why is that Anna?

"Most of these men only have two years of medical practice and no practical training. If they watch a poor quality doctor they pick up his bad habits."

"You are making Dr. O'Malley sound like a genius!" exclaimed Ben.

Anna just cocked her head. This was inside humor, so she just let it go.

"You will notice a number of women in street dress sitting with a patient. These are usually the wives, sisters, or mothers of some lucky patient who brought them their daily victuals. The negative side of this is that there will often be a soldier in the next bed that gets no visitors and suffers watching their well-fed brother patients. Oh, don't be surprised if you hear the voices of healthy visitors walking through the floor in search of a friend or relative. You will also see zealots who are more concerned with the souls of these men than bringing them back to health. Another organization that makes an appearance is the U.S. Christian Commission. They will help deal with the problems of the patients but mix in some religion and intellectual improvement. They will appear with books and magazines to stimulate the men's brains."

Just as Anna finished her last monologue she made contact with Ben's eyes.

"Will this leg be saved Anna?"

Her gaze moved away from his eyes.

"I honestly can't tell you Ben. The good news is that the doctor in the field hospital removed the ball from your leg. There is no instant remedy for it. But I can promise you that I will do everything in my power to see that you have a good chance that it will heal. I am going to promise to visit you at the end of each shift and bring in good food for you." A perky almost teasing look came over her face.

"Ben Halliday you are in the best hands a wounded soldier could have!"

"I believe you are right Anna."

"Oh, Ben one last suggestion. If they offer you opiates be very careful with their use. They can make the pain go away but there is the possibility of becoming addicted to them."

"Thank you for your advice, nurse I will listen to your every word."

Now Ben had a chance to play with Anna by putting on his serious face and saluting her.

Ben felt alone. He received more from Anna than she knew. Or maybe she did.

"Hey soldier you got one pretty looking nurse taking care of you."

"Oh she is a friend I met through the army. Ben did not want to indicate that he was getting any special attention from a nurse. That would be hard to cover in days to come.

Another nurse appeared in front of Ben's bed.

"Well, colonel, aren't you the lucky one."

"What do you mean?"

"You have your own personal nurse."

"That's simply not true!" Ben stated emphatically.

"Don't worry, colonel. I am only teasing you. I wish more of our nurses would use their own personal time to help out patients."

"You mean she wasn't even on duty?"

"Not when I saw her with you. Didn't you know? I would definitely consider you a very lucky patient. I hope she can bring a cure for that leg."

"Is there anything you can do for the pain?"

"I can give you some morphine. Just give me a minute or so while I visit another patient. Oh, has the doctor talked to you about surgery?"

"Surgery, for my leg? You can forget that idea nurse. I plan to keep this leg so I can return to active duty!" Ben exploded inside at the thought of losing his lower leg.

"It is possible that it could heal, but this is not the best place to be if you want to contain gangrene."

"The doctor in the field hospital told me the bone had not been damaged by the ball. Will that help?"

"Certainly. That is good news. I think I will get you a crutch as well. In a few days they might let you out to be in the fresh air. I have got to go now I will be back shortly."

True to her word the nurse returned with a crutch and some morphine.

"I am only going to give you a low dose. You are not in the same pain as some of these men."

The nurse, who Ben found out was named Nora, gave Ben the injection and went on her way. Within a few minutes Ben felt much better. A sense of euphoria overcame him. He felt like talking and taking in more of his environment.

Ben was near the end of the row and there was a man about his age in the next bed so he thought he would start up a conversation.

"Hello, friend how are you doing? My name is Colonel Ben Halliday."

The man looked over at Ben. At first he seemed reluctant to speak but he could see that Ben was not about to be harsh with him.

"My name is Captain Joshua Callahan, C.S.A."

Joshua had included his southern origins to see if that would shut Ben up.

"Really! You are the first Southern soldier I have ever spoken to. Otherwise I have would only have met you on the battlefield. How is it that you have wound up in a northern hospital?"

"I was captured at Antietem."

"That was over a year ago. Why haven't you been exchanged?"

"I was a courier for the division to which I belonged and when I burnt the papers I was carrying, they found an empty pouch. You Union boys just don't believe me when I tell the intelligence officers that I was carrying low level information. Your people think I have this secret locked away in my head."

"Well, Joshua I am not an intelligence officer so I will not even bother to ask you anything concerning your mission. But do tell me, what of your injury?"

"Fortunately I am not injured but I picked up a case of malaria while I was here caring for a wounded hip."

"The problem with these hospitals is that they are a breeding ground for disease. Now I have to take quinine for the malaria. They are in no hurry to exchange me. I hear that they are starting to set up prisons for captured soldiers. It's the damn loneliness that gets to me. I get no visitors and some of these boys aren't too pleased with having a Confederate near them.

I am able to write my family in Richmond but other than that the only visitors I receive are from the U.S. Christian Commission. I am thankful for them. They bring me books to read and believe me I have kept them busy."

Joshua was able to produce a chuckle and smile with that statement.

"I will see if I can get you some better food Joshua. Maybe that will brighten your day."

Ben continued with his visual tour of his immediate bed mates. Across from him was a young lad about seventeen or so. He was withdrawn with caved in cheeks and very pale skin.

"Hello, young man. I am Ben Halliday."

"Hello," came a laconic response.

"Why are you here?"

"Dysentery."

"Is your condition improving?"

"Not much. They have given me the 'blue mass', laudanum, calomel, but nothing seems to work."

Ben could tell that just these few words exhausted the young boy. He decided it was better to just leave him alone for the time being. Ben could feel the pain coming back to the leg. When a nurse came around he asked for some more morphine. She returned in about ten minutes and administered the medication. Again Ben had that sense of euphoria that deadened his senses to the pain.

Soon night time fell over the ward and Ben had his first experience with night on the ward. The sounds resembled an undisciplined orchestra. There were the wheezers who let out a whistling sound interjected with a quiet breath. Then there were the loggers who filled the air with a loud buzzing sound that reached its loudest as they finished their intake of air. They were the lucky ones who could find sleep. Some moaned in pain. The next group were the soldiers who relieved their battles in their dreams and would call out phrases or words exhorting their men on to victory or helping a wounded friend who had just been shot. These were some of the men for whom the war would never end.

The next day began with breakfast. This time some meat was added to the portions. Ben decided to go to the dining room at the other end of the room. It was a chance to rest his backside and stretch his unused muscles. For men who were ill there didn't seem to be anything wrong with their appetites.

This was followed by the washing and dressing of wounds for those that needed it. The staff, as one began the task of cleaning the bodies. All the nurses, regardless of their position took part. Male attendants cared for the private parts of the male anatomy.

Throughout the day doctors made their rounds. Ben had not introduced himself to the soldier on his left. He too had stayed very silent. When the doctor came Ben listened in on the conversation.

"Well soldier, I think we have given your leg enough time to heal and it isn't getting better. If we don't remove the leg your whole body will be poisoned. I think this afternoon would be a good time to do it."

"Will it be painful doctor?" The man asked softly.

"No. We have enough chloroform to put you to sleep. You won't feel a thing and when you wake up we will use opium to deaden the pain."

"Thank you doctor."

Ben got a sense from the articulation of his words that this could be an educated young man. The doctor had just left when the soldier addressed Ben.

"I am sorry if I don't behave very sociably. This leg has been such a worry and my parents have not yet arrived from Maryland. I hope their ongoing conflict over this war has not interfered with their arrival."

"What do you mean?" asked Ben.

"Well my father is a staunch pro-slavery advocate and my mother is an abolitionist. Does that give you an idea of the conflict that took place when one brother joined the Confederate army and I joined the Union?"

"I am sure there is much of that in the border states. Families have been ripped apart by questions of loyalty," added Ben.

"My name is Abraham. I understand you are a colonel."

"That's right. I've been in the military since I was eighteen."

"I don't know how you stand it." Abraham raised his voice in disbelief.

"Don't worry. I have lots of those days!" laughed Ben.

Just then he heard his name being called. There, with her omnipresent radiance stood Anna. This time she had Martha with her. Each had a basket in their hands.

"I came in early before I start work and this is Martha's volunteer day."

"What did you bring with you?"

Anna found a chair and brought it close to Ben's bed.

"Now you must keep an eye on these baskets. There are men who receive nothing and they will raid your food supplies during the night. Are you hungry now?"

"Yes I am. Breakfast was not inspiring so you are a godsend."

Anna brought out some freshly cooked chicken and started breaking off pieces for Ben. "Just open your mouth. There is no reason to get your hands all greasy."

What Ben was in for was a five course meal. "This is the first good food I have had since I visited your home for dinner."

"Ben you would be amazed what good food will do for the health of the body. We need to fatten you up. You have lost some weight."

Ben could not tell Anna why this was so. But she was used to the secretive side of the military. The basket of food included some bottles of jam, along with loaves of fresh baked bread. Ben passed a bottle over to Joshua who had been eyeing the food as it came from the basket.

"Thank you so much, Ben," was his grateful reply.

"Ben I have an idea, but we don't have to start it today. With your crutch you should be able to hobble outside and I can get you a wheelchair. I would like to take off your dressing and expose the sun to you leg. I hope that will speed up the healing process."

"Anna you are going to spoil me!" exclaimed Ben. Where is Rob?

"Oh away on one of those trips out west. But I do find that he has been around more. I think it has to do with Rose."

"What do you mean?"

"Ben I don't think you know the other side of Rob."

"And what would that be?"

"He is a relentless womanizer and he is taken a shine to Rose Green. I have tried to warn her but she can't see that part of him. It has made for some strained relations between Rose and me."

"They are both adults Anna. You can't tell them what to do."

"He is like his father and secretive as well. The women have to leave the house or go to the kitchen when Mr. Green comes over."

"What does Mr. Green do?"

"Oh, I thought you knew. He is the manager of one of the factories producing Springfield rifles for the war effort."

A bell went off in Ben's mind. He had no reason to suspect the three of any malfeasance, but something just sounded wrong about that relationship.

"Oh my, I have to get going. I'll see you at the end of my shift."

Martha and Anna went off in separate directions and Ben felt stuffed.

All was quiet at their end of the room and Ben's mind started to reflect. Why would Rob have anything to do with a manufacturer of Springfield rifles? He is an intelligence officer, or so he claims.

There was great excitement that afternoon. News that the Union had won victories at Gettysburg and Vicksburg came as a great lift for Union supporters who were used to the sounds of defeat. Ben wondered if this was an omen. Had the war turned a corner and future successes would occur? The effects of the morphine had relaxed him to the point where a good nap was in order.

True to her word, Anna returned and washed his wounds again. It seemed a natural thing to do so Ben took her hand

and, almost without thinking, gave it a gentle squeeze. If he had noticed, Ben would have seen a slight curl to the corners of her mouth. He had pleased her.

"Why don't I try taking a short walk outdoors Anna?"

Anna's first reaction was motherly and cautious, but then she knew that Ben had a great deal of common sense.

"Very well, let me find a wheelchair and you can sit in it while we are outside."

She returned in about five minutes with one that had seen better days.

"Sorry, but this is all I could find."

Anna muffled her laughter as she reconsidered the condition of this poor chair. Ben, for his part, was acquainting himself with his crutch. Anna watched him walk up and down the aisle two times and declared him fit for hobbling. The door was close by and nurse and patient exited through it. The sun felt good on Ben's face. It gradually spread warmth throughout his whole body. He had come to take the simple things of life for granted. Perhaps, he thought to himself, this would be a good time to refresh himself with the small and better pleasures of life.

"Ben, they have such a beautiful flower garden down by the main gate. Let's go sit by it."

Ben nodded in agreement and off they went, taking the first walk Ben had had in some time. Occasionally he would stop to readjust his armpit over the crutch or pull it out of some soft place in the ground wet with moisture from last night's rain.

"Anna let's stop by that large rock. You can have my cushion and I will just stay in the chair."

He thought to himself how naturally the two of them seemed to relate to one another. Anna's gentle and soft eyes only made it a joy to be with her. Neither spoke. Each other's presence was enough to please the other.

"Ben?"

"Yes?"

"What will you do after you are well enough to return to service?"

"I think this is a leading question, but nonetheless I'll give you a response. Military life is all I know. It comes naturally to me and I have made and lost some good friends in the service of this nation. Specifically I don't think I feel at my best in this 'cloak and dagger business' so I will probably ask for a command. I'll find out what my good friend Homer Ames is up to and see if he has need of my services."

"You have enough years of service to get a pension. Why not retire gracefully into business, or even a staff job like my brother?" Ben looked skyward, carefully forming a response for this question.

"Some of us are by nature born to a certain direction in life. Some are born to make money, some to govern. Some are born to protect. I think I fall into the latter Anna. Your brother's personality fit's the job he does."

If only Ben knew the truth of his statement. "Look at General Grant. He was a failure at everything he did in civilian life. It was so bad it drove him to drink. Now look at him. He's the Commander in Chief of Forces in the Field. I am but a shadow of the man, but it is where I feel I should be. Why do you ask?"

Now it was her turn to pause and reflect.

She opted to turn and stare into his eyes. "Because Ben Halliday, I would miss you greatly if anything happened to you on the field of war."

"I see." Ben was taken aback by her directness, but after all this was a new generation of females. They were outspoken and doing what had once been seen as men's work.

They sat silently. It seemed as if words were unnecessary. Instead they stared at the bounteous bouquets of flowers. How far away they seemed from the hospital, the war, the killing. Reality returned when they heard Martha's voice calling Anna to work. It had all seemed so simple. Without effort these two souls had fallen in love. But now it was time to depart. But never again would they claim to feel or be alone.

As they were returning Ben to his bed, they met the young man who had just had his leg amputated. Carefully attendants moved him onto his bed and waited for him to awake. Meanwhile Ben and Anna were saying their good-byes, until the next time they met.

Ben chose to sit up in his bed as those around him mounted a silent vigil for the man next to him. Finally a nurse decided it would be wise to check on him. She felt for a pulse.

"Doctor!" She called out with some anxiety in her voice. A doctor nearby turned and walked over. Repeating the actions of the nurse he stood up and quite clearly announced "He's dead."

There was no regret, no sense of loss, no emotion in his voice. It was simply another death, and he had attended far too many of those. The nurse pulled a sheet over his whole body while the other patients waited for the attendants to come and carry him off to the morgue.

When all awoke in the morning the bed was empty and another victim of the war was gone to his eternal rest. All returned to normal. Joshua was telling Ben how wonderful the raspberry jam was and how its taste reminded him of home. It was hospital chatter, common to all places where the sick and wounded tried to trivialize their ills and focus on whatever would offer a distraction from the great truth.

For Ben it was to be a day of puzzlement. At about two in the afternoon, a traditionally busy time for the arrival of visitors, Ben had his own guest. At first he did not recognize him when he stood at the end of his bed, but recognition dawned on him quickly. It was Colonel Winston, and judging by the stars on his epaulets, he was now General Winston. General Winston was known for his business-like delivery. As a result he was direct and to the point.

"Ben I wonder if we could have a quiet conversation?"

To Ben that meant getting the wheelchair and making a trip outside, which they did.

"Colonel Halliday, I have a question for you. It stems from your relationship with Colonel Macey. As you might or might not know, Colonel Macey had as one of his responsibilities the shipment of Springfield rifles to loyal Union supporters in northern Virginia. Well it appears that after the Battle at Gettysburg a number of unregistered rifles were gathered from the field of battle, particularly after Picket's charge. I am wondering if you know anything about this apparent irregularity."

"No, I'm sorry general I have no explanation for this situation. I am aware of the colonel's regular comings and goings but he is the epitome of the good secret service agent. He's quiet about his activities."

"I see, well I just thought you might have more information than I do. If you do hear anything surrounding this topic could you let me know? It would be much appreciated."

"Certainly, general."

"I have another area you might be interested in. I don't suppose you have heard anything about the results of our clandestine activities into your journey to the South. Overall it was quite successful. We have some improvements to make in how we go about gaining access to the Southern telegraph lines. All but three of the teams reported back. Some escaped with their lives but they made a point of hiding or destroying their equipment before engaging the enemy. We are concerned with the three that did not come back. We don't know whether they had the same chance or not. If their equipment was confiscated the Confederates will be guarding their lines more carefully and switch to code for transmitting messages. We feel that we can make one more foray into the South, but only let them stay one week. What I would like you to do is work on a team making suggestions. Seeing that you are recovering anyway, you can spend your time with the major making presentations to groups being sent out. What do you think of that suggestion? It will keep you out of trouble."

"Could I have a couple of days to think that one over general? I had planned to return to active duty as soon as possible."

"No problem, colonel. I know you are an active campaigner and God knows we need more men with your dedication to their duty and active service."

With that the general departed and Ben was left with his thoughts.

Ben began his reflections on Rob once more. He had no concrete information, but a continual chain of odd circumstances had him thinking. Now he had something new. He stopped in his mental processes and wondered, did the general know about the apparent ties between Rob's father and Mr. Green? He must have known the source of these guns or the war office would not have gotten involved in the first place. Just as he about to continue his mental ramblings about Rob, Anna made her daily appearance. She was her usual cheery self, but Ben sensed that she was fighting to keep up that appearance.

"I know something is wrong Anna. It is just a matter of time until you tell me."

"I guess I don't give you rural types enough credit for detecting peoples' inner thoughts, Ben. I just heard a story about one of my favorite doctors. Patients and other doctors weave fanciful and real stories about each other in these hospitals, Ben. There is a great deal of animosity between the volunteer doctors and the regular officers. The regulars claim the volunteers are disorganized and unable to take orders. At the same time, the volunteers consider the regulars arrogant and set in their ways in their treatment of patients. When things get serious it usually surrounds some doctor, along with a patient, claiming another doctor to be drunk while operating on patients. Oh, why can't they put aside their petty squabbles and see that there is so much more for us to do?"

"That is just human nature at work. We try to keep things the way they are and resent newcomers telling us how to do our jobs. Often it springs from a basic insecurity. That is what I have found."

"Thank you for listening, Ben."

With that the handkerchief was produced and a few tears rolled onto the red cheeks.

"Do you know something Anna?"

"What Ben?"

"You look just as beautiful when you are sad as when you are happy."

The tears started again. Ben made a point of dealing with one set of emotional conditions before moving on to the next one. She sat down beside him.

"Oh my leg, my leg!" Ben cried.

"I'm so sorry Ben.

He drew her to him. "It's the other leg Anna!"

"Oh Ben Halliday, how could you be so hurtful!"

This time she laughed along with him. All was forgiven. All was quiet and they spent some silent time just staring into each other's eyes. It was a silent and peaceful time.

Ben's convalescence moved along quickly. With high quality food from the Macey house and Anna's constant attentions, the infection was starting to heal nicely. Ben was even able to put some pressure on the leg to support his weight, but this usually got him in trouble with Anna so he discontinued his attempts to rush his recovery.

As he improved, Ben spent more time wandering about the ward, talking to soldiers, writing letters for them, and generally being his normal self. He found that he was spending more time thinking about Anna. It was on one of their outings in the hospital park that he decided to tell her how he felt. Untrained in such social skills he handled the situation the best way he knew how. He had just finished commenting on his good fortunes in this war when it spilled from his mouth.

"Anna I have something to confess to you."

"And what terrible thing have you done now, colonel?"

"I love you!" Ben blurted out.

Anna was stopped in her train of thought and was silent. To be truthful she felt the same way about Ben. He had just made it easier to tell him.

"I love you too, Ben."

Her head was facing away at the time, but she quickly turned to face him with her bright blue eyes and radiant smile. She threw her arms around him and drew him close to her and rubbed her nose against his in a playful manner.

"There! Now it is out! Now we can go back to acting our normal selves," Ben said

"My God Ben, is there no presence of the romantic in you?"

"Yes, but I don't know how to get it out. So I felt the best way was just to act my normal self. That is who you know."

"I have news for you Ben. I checked with the doctor and my parents and all are in agreement."

"About what?

"It would be healthier for you if you came and lived with us. You will recuperate even faster and now that it's official that you love me, it is the natural place for you to be."

"Did you think of consulting with me first?"

Anna appeared hurt.

"But I am glad you did it anyway Anna."

Ben pushed her away from him to get a better view of her beauty.

Now he felt romantic. He pulled her close to him and gave her a long, passionate kiss. Applause broke out from behind them. Three of the nurses Anna worked with were watching them. Their cheers gathered the attention of others who were walking near the garden. Ben went red. This was a part of life that was new to him. He was having feelings that he didn't know he had. He had spent so many years married to the military. The three nurses went on their way and Ben and Anna just sat there in silence, still in each other's arms.

"I am afraid I have to leave Ben, it is beginning to get late."

"Alright if you must leave me for another, I understand."

"Don't tease about this Ben. You are my first love and I just want to enjoy every moment."

"Very well, my dearest. But you should know that you will have trouble getting rid of me."

"And why is that?"

"I have accepted an offer to teach at the war department."

Without saying anything Anna embraced him in a powerful hug. Ben felt that he was having an eventful day.

# CHAPTER TWENTY FIVE:
# SOUTHWARD HO

The financial arrangements had all been made. All that was left to do was finish the preparations for their departure. They had had no idea how many wagons they would need. One was allotted per family, but that had not been enough. The final count would be somewhere around 550. The wagon making had been endless and the wheelwright had had to train more men to speed up production.

Alexander and his brother David, had some interesting decisions to make in the midst of all the arrangements. One of the more critical had been the question of guns. While the freedmen on the estate had always had the right to own guns, the slaves were restricted from possessing any firearms. Should those still classed as slaves be allowed to carry weapons? Giving weapons went against the grain of every slave owner, but these were exceptional times. Alexander's slaves were very loyal. He and David could not foresee a slave rebellion on the journey. They felt the added firepower the guns would give them was more important. No one saw this as an adventure without danger, particularly when they ventured into Mexico. In the end it was decided to arm the slaves with Winchesters and pistols. It had a dramatic effect. One well known slave named Elijah approached Alexander.

"Master we know this must been a difficult decision for you to make."

"No Elijah, in fact the discussion was very short. The reason for this is the trust we have in all our slaves. Particularly when they know that some day they will be free."

"Will we have to give them up when we reach Brazil?"

"No, they could be just as necessary when we reach our land."

"You can trust us master. You have always kept your word. There is no reason to believe you will change now."

"Thank you Elijah, it is good to hear that we have made the correct decision."

Both men departed from one another feeling that indeed, this trip would go well.

In total they would be carrying 80 adult male slaves, 150 freedmen, 213 women, and 87 children. Plans had been made to hold classes in two empty wagons so that school could go on as the wagons rolled along.

Food preparation would be centralized into three groups, and the wagons would be dedicated to carrying the actual food. Two wagons carried nothing but salted meats. Preserves had been made by the women and they were placed in crates to protect the glass jars. All of this took time. Also each family had to consider what items they would carry in their wagons, how much furniture they would carry and how what clothes. That decision was left to each family unit. One wagon would be dedicated to carrying water, and it needed extra springs to allow it to bear the extra load. Another wagon was dedicated to wheel repair equipment and extra wheels.

Alexander came to realize that this was not just a wagon trek. More had gone into its preparation than any person could have predicted. They set back the departure date another two months so that they would be leaving in the spring of 1864. Better to deal with the hot temperatures of summer than the cold of the winter months.

And so the day was approaching that a dream was to become a reality. Some were nervous and expressed this to Alexander, but this was only natural.

For himself, the only regret he felt was leaving the Confederacy while she still struggled in a futile war. As luck would have it word of the great adventure had leaked out. Reporters showed up from the newspapers. People wanting to join them made their way to the gates of the plantation only to be turned away. The greatest hurt Alexander and David felt came in the form of a letter.

February 24,1864
From the Office of the Confederacy.

Dear Mr. Braithwaite,

It is with mixed emotions that I have received information outlining your plans to emigrate to the safety of Brazil and take the soul of your plantation with you. We are engaged in a terrible and costly war and your people and your presence are a valuable asset to the success of this war.

I have received your letter of resignation from the Cavalry and have taken steps to incorporate your remaining battalion of troopers into General Bedford Forest's own cavalry. You could not have entrusted your men to a better general. They will be an asset to his command.

I am sure you can see the implications if you are successful. Thousands of other plantation owners will follow you to Brazil, as the last haven of slavery. It is this side of the argument that leaves me worried for the Confederacy. On the other hand, you have served this great Confederacy honorably and with nobility of purpose. The failed raid on Chicago was certainly not your fault. We know that there were traitors, but we have just not been able to catch them.

In ending this letter I hope that somehow you will be able to help us in our hour of need, particularly in the area of financial aid. Go in safety.

God save the Confederacy,

President Jefferson Davis
Commander -In -Chief CSA

When Alexander read this letter a single tear rolled down his cheek. He handed the letter to David, turned away, and faced Richmond.

There were still financial reserves available to him. With David's approval he sent $100,000 in gold to help the Confederate cause.

Finally the day arrived when all was ready. The wagons took their place in the column that extended for a mile. As a wagon's number was called out the driver would take his place in line. If one listened one could hear there was much crying amid the wagons. As humans it is hard to depart a place that has held good memories and such was the case with these people. It took a full two hours to get all the wagons onto the road that extended from the plantation to the local road.

Alexander rode at the front of the column as a leader should. Alexander too was having a hard time with this moment, but for another reason. This trip would take months and it would not be in a straight line. He only prayed that the journey would be a worthwhile one. After all, he had been the one who had told these people that their way of life would remain essentially intact if they came with him. He hoped that the military training he had given the men would not become necessary.

The best strategies for different circumstances would have to be practiced on the trip. Whenever they came to a wider road or were traveling over flat ground he would move into columns of two's. He used the marching technique for this and found it worked quite well. Every other wagon would move to the right or left and start a new column. The column would then begin to tighten up. It was a much safer traveling method. Whenever they neared a town, lists of items that they were consuming rapidly or had a short 'shelf' life were sought out so that they always had a fully replenished larder. When they used up their cattle a farm was sought out and sufficient, new cattle were added for beef and milk. He dreaded practicing the last drill on his list and that was encirclement in case of some kind of attack. For this the wagons would break every twentieth wagon and turn outward to start a new line. Every new break added five wagons so that they would meet at the end. The outside wagons were reinforced on the outside with an extra layer of wood. A variation on this was made in case they were able to use natural topographical features as protection, whether forest or mountain. This would take on the form of a semi-circle. Men were assigned positions to take in case of an attack. That would be their defense group. Alexander trained unmarried women to load the Winchesters thus doubling their rate of fire. All of this was in theory. It would depend on the nature of the enemy and the reaction of a group of men who had never had to kill other men to save their own lives. It was at times when they were practicing that Alexander was glad he had had the military experience to offer his people a chance of survival.

He had been particularly warned about the roving bands of Mexicans who fed off those who ventured into their land. Alexander had also prepared a map of large plantations. He did not want to be the one responsible for creating rebellions among slaves. When approaching these plantations they would try to take a more circuitous route.

Yes, he congratulated himself on his forethought to prevent problems and secure their safety on this venture to the south. While swamp areas had to be avoided he tried to keep his convoy to the southernmost route, crossing Georgia, Alabama, Mississippi, Louisiana, and Texas. He realized that the evenings had to be times of family meals followed by large or multiple singsongs and even prayer meetings for those so inclined. An 11:00 p.m. curfew was placed on all members of the group. Alternating crews kept guard so that no one would be tempted to steal their horses. A few horse thieves tried their luck but had successfully been driven off by the guards.

Occasionally they would be met by more newspaper reporters who were following the success of this first venture to Brazil. They had been pressured by other plantation owners who saw hope in Alexander's plan and recognized the demise of the Confederacy. No one would speak of defeat but reality was starting to sink in as the siege of Petersburg continued for months without any real chance of Confederate success. All of this led Alexander to the conclusion that he had made the right decision in leaving his plantation and following the only route open to his way of life as a plantation owner.

While traveling through Mississippi, they were stopped more frequently by blacks who would beg the travelers to take them away from their misery.

On one occasion the slaves were followed by a band of white bounty hunters who placed their horses between the wagon train and the slaves. The hunters started to drive the slaves back as if they were a herd of cattle. Cooperation was not forthcoming so a warning shot was fired over their heads. This did little to discourage the poor slaves. Five of the bounty hunters dropped their Spencer rifles to the level of the closest and simply shot him through the head. This caused the slaves to begin a return journey to their various plantations.

This event ate at the very fabric of Alexander's value system. He was helpless to do anything about this situation. To help the slaves would only have resulted in more slaves showing up, and they would be unequipped for such an adventure and so was he. To have helped would also result in the rapid diminution of their scarce resources. He had not planned on these encounters when he was organizing their trip. It cast a pall over the columns as they made their way westward.

The traveling was an adventure for his freedmen and slaves. Few had been more then five miles from the plantation and every new contact was, to them, recognition of life in the southern United States. Maybe the crops were different but the reality of plantation existence was a face all slaves knew. Their horizons had been expanded and they were heartened to rid themselves of this country.

Alexander's horizons had expanded too. He saw how close the children were to their parents, for the parents were the center of their young worlds. He noticed the open affection the parents and elders had for the young. He sensed too that the freedmen did not always relate well to the slaves. They had worked hard to raise themselves up to a higher social level and were not about to share all their advantages with those who had not won their freedom. The freedmen moved liberally through those who were their peers and could choose any time to ride ahead and converse with Alexander.

They were heard to comment on the fact that their benefactor still chose to wear his Confederate officer's uniform. They quizzed him on this point.

"Master Alexander we have a question for you. You are leaving the Confederacy but still wear your Colonel's uniform. We don't understand. Why is this so?"

"Some mantles, in a figurative sense, are hard to abandon. I had men serving me in the army as you serve me. I still feel a sense of allegiance when I see the battle ensign of the Confederacy. Many a good man has fallen to defend it. So I have not quite put away my allegiance to the 'cause'. It might also help us because when we meet whites they will believe that this column is under the protection of the Confederacy."

Alexander knew that this was a rather simple explanation but in the end he knew he did not have any reason to wear the uniform.

Fortunately the trip through the southern states went quickly. The roads were not encumbered with traffic and the humid air was made bearable by seasonally low temperatures. They also had little trouble finding spots to locate at the end of the day. Often plantation owners rode out to quiz the Braithwaites on their progress. They did not see his plan to head for Brazil and continue slavery as abandoning the Confederacy. In fact they offered them some comfort and solace in that they too would escape if the military situation foretold the collapse of the Confederacy.

The spirits of the travelers were high. So far two babies had been born on the trip, and more would be forthcoming. Mothers and babes were all doing well and it was fortunate that goats had been brought along to supplement the mothers' milk supply.

The nightly singing was an instrument of learning for Alexander. Black culture was revealed in the songs that they sung and their sounds were ones of consolation and hope, not the sorrowful songs of war that Alexander had heard around the campfires of the soldiers with whom he had traveled.

Crossing the Sabine River marked one of the highlights of the trip the travelers had planned. It now meant that they were in Texas. They stayed to the coastal plains. And as time passed they were introduced to new vegetation like pecan trees and the water oak. The land was generally very flat and grassy except when they encountered areas of dense shrubbery or spindly forests of the aforementioned trees.

One evening the wagon train, still traveling two abreast, stopped at one of these forested areas and placed the wagons in a semi-circle along the perimeter of these woods. Security had always been a part of Alexander's concerns. Every time they stopped for the night he would send out riders in every direction to keep their location secure for the night. At times Alexander thought that he was being silly. Safety seemed to be the least of his concerns. His military training once again had engrained in him this habit. The one thing these riders did not carry with them was any form of self-defense. Alexander felt a black with a rifle would be taken as hostile by any person or group of people. This was, after all, the South. This particular evening Alexander could see the dust rising from a rider heading directly for their encampment. As soon as the rider dismounted he searched out Alexander.

"Colonel, I came upon a column of riders about ten miles to the west and heading in our direction. They were carrying the standard of the Confederacy."

"Thank you for your information Luke."

At this point Alexander felt no urgency. The only action he took was to raise their own Confederate flag so the riders would know that they were friends.

Soon Alexander could see the dust rise from the approaching column which lay just over the horizon. The column grew closer and closer, to the point where Alexander could see the guidons of a military column. Suddenly the column broke into columns of fours. *How strange,* Alexander thought to himself. The column made a movement to the south and then turned to the north, bringing it directly in front of the bow that formed the center of the travelers' circled wagons. Alexander was beginning to have uneasy feelings about this movement. It was a military movement set for frontal attack. Some officer halted the column and they did a ninety degree turn to face the wagons. None of this was making Alex comfortable. David approached him.

"Alexander, I am not a military man but I would swear that this so-called Confederate column was preparing for an attack."

"Those are my sentiments as well David. Let's assume the worst and I will begin preparations for an attack. Find the bugler and send him to me."

When the young man arrived Alexander had the bugler call assembly in military language. The call sent men in all directions with various purposes.

Four wagons turned themselves inward and moved toward the center of the semi-circle. Quickly the backs were opened revealing two three inch parrot guns. They were rolled down from their place on the wagons and men worked feverishly to put them in position where they had been in the column. Two limbers were set up twenty paces away and then manned by a gun crew that quickly carried out all the movements of an artillery battery preparing to fire. Meanwhile columns of men lined up at the backs of the other two wagons and were handed Spencer rifles along with a cartridge box already loaded with ammunition. Each of the men went to their pre-assigned positions between the wagons. The women disembarked while various women placed themselves among the men. No one could ever say that Alexander Braithwaite was a man who had failed to make his preparations for the worst possible conditions. At its greatest estimate Alexander was putting 210 men along his defensive perimeter. In the meantime the newcomers had dismounted. There were about 200 men and their position put them in a skirmishing line facing the wagon train. The remaining cavalry stayed in their positions, yet to reveal their plans. There were about 200 riders. The numbers on both sides appeared about equal. He hoped the two cannons and Spencers would give them the advantage.

Who were these cavalrymen that they would take on a wagon train flying the same flag? There was a small group of men discussing tactics at the center of this group of men. If Alex had binoculars he would have recognized the shadowy shape of one Confederate Colonel named Fielding, Alexander's old 'teacher' of bushwhacking military tactics.

"My God, colonel they even have artillery!"

"Not a problem. We shall advance so rapidly that they will put a mere dent in our numbers."

So spoke the cocky Colonel.

Suddenly a cannonball exploded within twenty feet of Fielding, forcing him to calm his horse and watch as a whole space was empty where there had been ten men. They were lined up about three hundred yards from the artillerists who were making contact on their first shot. The second cannon barked out its flash of fire and hell and also made contact.

Meanwhile, Alexander was preparing his next tactic. The wagons holding the Spencers each had a hinged piece of thick wood flipped over the top of the side of the wagon providing excellent protection. Two rows of men were placed in the large wagons so that each wagon could hold twenty men. They were now returned to their place near the center of the semi circle. The Spencers needed the enemy to come closer to be effective. Fielding could do little with his dismounted cavalry but to try and reduce the distance between the two. The parrot rifles were doing their job now that they knew the distance of their targets. Each cannon was taking its toll on Fielding's men as they moved their guns to try and sweep both the cavalry and dismounted men. One of Fielding's captains now approached his colonel.

"Sir, how are we ever supposed to penetrate this wagon train with those parrot guns raking our men?"

"Keep your voice quiet. Do you want to scare off our own men?"

Fielding now tried to employ some Indian tactics. He had his mounted men form a single line. The line moved forward to the very end of the column then turned inward to bring them within rifle range of the wagon train. Now starting with the first rider they began to bring fire to bear on the wagons as they hurled themselves against the wagons. At a hundred yards distance they could effectively fire their rifles. As this column galloped across the line of wagons Alexander had his artillerists switch to case fire. The results were devastating for the attackers. The pellets from the case shot brought down a swath of a dozen riders each. Now Alexander could use the volley fire from the two wagons closest to the attackers. Again, unprepared for this, two more swaths were cut into the lines of the attackers.

It is axiomatic in military thinking that surprise always benefit's the side holding the surprise. Again and again Fielding sent his cavalry against the wagons. Each time fewer and fewer riders were returning for another dash into hell. Now his infantry were sent against the wagons with similar results. The accuracy of the defenders was enhanced by the fact that Fielding's men had no protection but grassland. Fielding gazed upon the battlefield and recognized that far too many of his dismounted cavalry had been shot. He could not afford many more losses. He had his bugler signal the retreat.

Fielding could not see that he was having an appreciable effect on the defenders. He called a withdrawal and immediately raised a white flag. Alexander did the same and both he and David rode out to meet their adversaries. Alexander was shocked at what he found.

"Fielding! What in God's name are you doing? We are both flying the same flag. Only from you would I expect such treacherous action as this. It is right and just that you are being thrashed to the ground by a group of settlers."

Fielding was enraged by this comment.

"Damn you to hell Braithwaite! You are using soldiers as well as your darkies!" Fielding had mistaken mulatttos as whites.

"Far from it colonel, these are trained blacks who know how to shoot."

Little did Alexander realize that he was revealing information to Fielding about the nature of his 'soldiers'. Alexander thought it was time to find out what Fielding wanted.

"Why were you attacking us?"

"I was aiding the Confederacy by acquiring spoils of war."

"I don't believe a single word of that. You are out of your territory for hunting supply columns. I think this has to do with vengeance for the soldiers you lost to my command when it was set up."

Alex had hit the nail on the head. Fielding's eyes glared into Alexander's and the look into them confirmed Alexander's suspicions.

"Our discussion is finished, Braithwaite. You will just have to wait for my next move." He grabbed his reins and yanked them hard to the right, causing his mare to rise up from the ground as it swung around and retreated back to where Fielding had been standing. And so the action had led to a siege. The wagon train was now surrounded in its semi-circle. Alexander moved his gelding more gently to the wagons.His men surrounded him to find out what had taken place.

"I fear I have gotten you men into a conflict that is basically between myself and the commander of those Confederate raiders. I also believe that he is here to wait and try to starve us into submission. Little does he know that we are well-equipped to handle a siege. We have enough food and water to outlast his own reserves. Let us take one hour at a time and see how his siege develops.

Unfortunately, Alexander did not see a rider heading out from the tent set up by Fielding to run this 'campaign'. If he had he would have been less confident as he presently felt. Alexander rode to an open space to view Fielding's deployment of troops. Fielding had left a mere skirmish line within firing distance from the wagons. Alexander's choices were two fold. First he could engage in a siege with Fielding knowing in the end he would win. His second choice was more risky and more immediate. He could take his wagons out of the half-circle formation and make a run for it, knowing that Fielding's troops would be emotionally down after this first engagement. He had had two of his men killed in the attack and a number with head and shoulder injuries that required attention and rest. Perhaps he could let them rest for four or five days and if nothing else had changed by then, try to make a break for it. Those most vulnerable were the horses. They needed food, water, and rest. This would probably be the determining factor. Even now men were taking turns leading the horses out of their trusses and walking them around and giving them food from the hay wagons. The problem was they could only manage to remove the harness two or three wagons at a time.

He had to consider the mood of his settlers. They knew that they had defeated an experienced cavalry battalion. They had the colonel's skills and preparations to thank for this success. A trade-off would be the best approach. They should be ready to leave by the next afternoon and thus the injured would be able to get some rest. But to make a successful break-out he would have to make some necessary changes.

****

Morning came. The skies were dark, which suggested possible rain. Alexander had not changed his mind. In fact it was reinforced by the fact that they had almost used up their supply of hay and the horses could only be given so much oats. The mood among the settlers was still good. Their spirits were reinforced by the dead Fielding left on the field.

About ten o'clock there was a stir in the cavalry camp. A line of about one hundred men in a single line and spaced about three feet apart approached the wagons. They stopped about one hundred and fifty yards, knelt down, and began with a volley against the wagons and any person moving in the open. Alexander responded with bursts of canister, but he had to conserve his supply. Even from this distance hits could be made with the Spencers. The colonel chose to use all of his men to make a further dent in Fielding's men and hopefully they would give up this pointless attack. The sound of rifles was constant but diminished after fifteen minutes, each side checking the other to see what damage they had inflicted.

What Alexander had failed to do was to place any guards at the line of trees backing onto the open end of the wagons. Without explanation the settlers were taking more hits than the skirmish line could inflict. Turning around Alexander discovered the source of this new enemy. Fielding had called up his reserve battalion, and silently like the criminal he was, somehow brought a number of men through the woods and were using the women and children hiding there as hostages.

"Don't shoot men! You will only kill the others!"

They were now effectively surrounded with no hope of defending against these new troopers who had been brought into the fray. Soon the settlers stopped firing, and so did the cavalry. Fielding now rode out onto the field and approached the wagons. He was alone. Arrogant as he was, he now believed no one would dare shoot him, so he just kept riding into the settlers' camp. Alexander came out to meet him.

"So you thought you were so smart Braithwaite, that your darkies could defeat us. How did you like my frontal diversion? Worked liked a charm."

Alexander said nothing. He just regretted not guarding his rear.

"I will dictate my terms to you. Your blacks will be treated as escaped slaves and sold at auction. Your wagons will be treated as bounty of war and be sold at public auction as well."

Alexander was boiling inside. David joined him and placed a hand on his shoulders.

"There is just one more thing I have to do Colonel Braithwaite."

Fielding took out his revolver and shot Alexander through the forehead. He slumped to the ground in a heap. Immediately a puddle of dark red blood mixed with grey matter began to form at the head of the slumped form of this heroic figure. David reached for his revolver and received the same treatment. The settlers were now leaderless. The blacks began wailing and screaming as they realized their predicament. The leader of the blacks approached Fielding and protested. He had heard the terms granted by Fielding.

"You have no right to turn over the freedmen in this group to a slave auction!"

For his audacity he too received a shot to the forehead. Fielding's men rounded up all the blacks who were able and spoke to them.

"You are considered as part of the spoils of war and as such must obey my commands. If this is done no one will be harmed. Stack your rifles in a pile at the front of where I am standing. Anyone caught not turning in a gun will be summarily executed. Is this clear?"

One could barely make out his words as the new conditions of their lives sunk into the heads of this blessed group.

"Can we at least bury the Colonel?" The blacks yelled out. "Certainly, feel free to do whatever you want with him."

A few of the settlers found their shovels and began digging graves for the three men while others found flat pieces of wood to make markers. The women prepared the three bodies for burial. They chose a spot near a clump of trees that would allow the graves to look out on the rising and setting sun.

The crying and wailing continued unabated as reality hit home to the settlers.

Fielding now faced a dilemma. What to do with the blacks? If he returned all, including the freemen, there would be a riot if he tried to take them to market. He had no time for this. The decision was made to free the non-slaves, send those that were still slaves to New Orleans for sale, and confiscate any of the wagons that provided him with lucrative spoils of war, although he expected little of value from freemen he knew the slaves would bring a good return. Being a man who saw his conquests as personal victories Fielding wanted to make sure that he was amply rewarded for his trials and tribulations.

They concocted a story that these were slaves found on the road as they made their way to New Orleans. And so this sad band of sullen slaves walked through the drizzle that had begun. Fielding started their calamitous journey back to slavery. Every step hurt, not from the soggy and rocky roads but from the dampening of a dream that had begun with so much promise. Even as the weather improved and the sun shone brightly, the slaves' burden could not be lifted from their shoulders. Friends had died in battle, their benefactor had died trying to save them, and their future was bleak.

When Fielding arrived it was a Friday morning. The word rapidly spread, like some infectious disease, that a large array of slaves was to be put to auction on the next day. Fielding, knowing the process, hurried to make them look as fetching as possible to squeeze every cent he could out of the local slaveholders. The bidding was brisk for the buyers could recognize quality slaves in good condition. Within an hour it was over. Fielding had come away with $11,900 for his troubles. Yes, he was glad that he had listened to the blacks that he had encountered on the road who had unwittingly doomed more of their own race to the agony of the unknown.

# CHAPTER TWENTY SIX:
# THE NEW RECOVERY

Ben sat at his side trying to comfort him. Luke was the boy across from him who had now been in Harewood for nine months with no sign of improvement.

"Luke let's write a letter to your mother today."

No response was forthcoming.

"Would you rather write to your father instead?"

"Yes, I think he would bear the stories I have to tell better. If I don't tell him they will have no understanding for the quiet times I feel inside. I used to be an active, humorous youngster but the war beat that out of me." And so Ben began to scribe for this sensitive youth. He wondered himself what could have caused his moodiness.

March 3, 1864
Harewood Hospital,
Washington D.C.

Dear Father,

I have directed this letter to you so that I can help you understand my state of mind when I return to home. In our company was another fellow who was the equal for my sense of humor. He would laugh uproariously when I told stories from my 'troubled' days as a student. He would even laugh at stories that were not particularly humorous. Some of the men thought of him as 'silly' but there was planned purpose to his laughter. He understood this war. He knew that it could often cripple how men viewed life generally and give them the feeling that they could never return home and be the same. They had seen too much tragedy and slaughter. It was his personal goal to keep up the men's spirits. The sergeant saw this in him and promoted him to corporal. He would lead with his humor.

Well this one night I was assigned guard duty for four hours. I always hated this duty because the time passed so slowly. I was hidden behind a tree that led down a gradual slope to a stream. I dozed off and fell into a deep sleep. This is a major offence in the lines. Suddenly I could hear whispered into my ear with a Georgia accent... "Put up your gun Yank!"

Without thinking I stabbed my bayonet into the night air. I hit home and could hear the gurgling sound of blood bubbling from the enemy's neck. I pulled out the bayonet and took my gun by the barrel and lashed out in club like fashion. Again I hit home. I called for help and two soldiers came running. I sent one back to get a lamp. When he brought it he shone it on the enemy's face. The problem was it was my friend Abraham. He had been up to his usual pranks and hadn't counted on my shocked reaction. We tried to save him but it was impossible. The blood flowed in all directions from his neck. I was in shock. My other friends tried to comfort me but to no avail. It was my fault. I should never have been sleeping.

As time passed, that event consumed more and more of my thoughts. I closed in on myself and rarely spoke to other soldiers. Finally I came down with this case of dysentery which could not be cured at the field hospital.

I know that you will find this story unsettling but if you are to understand me you must hear these words. I will write again.

Your Loving Son,

Luke

Ben found himself speechless and simply carried out the perfunctory deeds of putting the letter in an envelope, sealing it, writing the mailing address and promising Luke that he would mail it the next day.

Ben returned to his bed somewhat shaken by the letter he had just written for Luke. He couldn't imagine what it must have felt like to have killed a friend, and yes it was his fault. Ben tried to imagine the thoughts that must run through his brain. Would he have bayoneted the man if he had been awake? Might he have heard him coming? God, thought Ben, how could a man live with such an event and continue on? It must have helped to prevent him from recovering faster. Ben started to develop a plan.

The next day Ben appeared in front of Luke's bed with a wheelchair and a large smile.

"Come on Luke, we are going to wrap you up and give you some cool but fresh air. You need a change of venue."

Both were silent on the way out. The day was sunny and windless. The early signs of spring warmed even the dullest of spirits.

"Another month and the smells of spring will bring life to this place."Ben promised. He went directly to the point.

"Luke I have been seriously pondering the terrible story you revealed yesterday. At times I wonder how you bear it.

You are a hero for just living. I am sure if your friend was here today he would recognize his own foolishness." Silence.

"Can we go in, Ben?"

"Certainly Luke, whatever you want."

Again the re-entry was just as silent. Ben helped him to his bed. He had to leave him as Anna had arrived and she was full of the plans she had worked out to bring Ben to their parent's home.

"You will never guess what the final argument was that bought you time with us!"

"I have no idea," responded Ben, who still seemed befuddled.

"Rob!"

"Rob?" queried Ben.

"Yes! He has just returned from the West and when he heard about the plan he insisted that you be brought home to finish your recovery. Mother has always had a soft spot for Rob and could not argue any further. In the end she agreed it was a good idea. I will speak with the head nurse today and get you released to-morrow."

Ben was somewhat frozen by all these plans but he could not pass up a chance to get out of Harewood. Sleepless nights listening to the moaning and cries of the soldiers was starting to deteriorate his empathy for them.

****

Ben was dressed and ready to go. He just had to wait for Anna to finish her duty for the day. Rob was going to bring the carriage and take them home. The time passed like a snail making its way across a log, but eventually the time arrived and Anna appeared at the foot of his bed.

"Ben, we are going to have to get you a new uniform. That one looks like it has been in a war."

Rob rolled his eyes at Anna's lame attempt at humor. Ben still needed the cane to manage comfortably. He said his good-bye's to his fellow patients and walked, cane in hand, down the stairs and out into the windy March weather. Rob got down from the carriage and greeted Ben with a huge hug that took the wind out of him. His warm smile seemed genuine and he treated Ben like a brother.

"It's so good to see you Ben. You look like you have lost some weight. Not to worry. Our cook will get you fit quickly. We will have to get you to the tailor and fit you out with a new uniform."

Sometimes the Maceys' annoyed Ben with their need to be clothed in their best. Ben had not forgotten his humble rural origins.

****

"Now that was a fine dinner, Mrs. Macey!" Ben exclaimed after gorging himself on the roast of beef that had been the centerpiece of the meal. Soon after the meal Ben began to feel weary. He was not fit yet and it was an effort to manage his way around. He was still taking morphine for the pain that would shoot up his leg from time to time. Anna was fussing over him and soon had him placed in his bedroom.

"It's fine, Anna, I can make my own way when comes to dressing and undressing. You can visit me after I am in bed. I am used to your visits from the hospital." Anna blushed at the thought of being in Ben's room by herself. She would have to learn to overcome her family traditions. "Before you go to sleep I would like to change the dressing on that wound, Ben."

Ben nodded his approval. It made him feel like a patient again. Anna left and he put on the bedclothes that he'd borrowed from Rob. A knock on the door indicated Anna's return. She looked at the wound and commented on how it was just about healed.

"You know that you will always have a scar on this leg and you could be left with a small limp."

"I'm just glad I have my leg so that I can return to duty."

Anna's head popped up.

"You mean you aren't going to retire from the military, Ben?"

Her question took him off guard. He just assumed he would be returning to regular line duty after his leg was improved and that healing could contine while he taught at the war department. Anna went silent. She raised herself up and sat on the edge of his bed.

"Ben you served your country with gallantry. What else do you have to prove?"

"I don't have anything to prove but I still have a duty to my country."

Anna went silent and expressionless. Ben could see that she was holding back tears.

"Anna look me in the eyes." Their intense gaze froze both of them. "I love you Anna and I won't take unnecessary chances in the field."

"I love you too Ben, but I think I am being selfish. I don't want you away from me."

Her head dropped but quickly she resumed eye contact. Ben gently took her two hands and held them in his. He looked down at them and realized the differences in their backgrounds. His hands were gnarly and covered in healed scars, the product of farm life and a lengthy stay in the military. Hers were soft and smooth with finely trimmed nails and missing the hair that covered the tops of his manly hands. He smiled at her and blew her a kiss which she grasped, in play, with her hand and put to her mouth. They were young lovers, but not so young. Ben was now thirty and Anna twenty-four. They were not young, foolish, and without common sense. They were made for each other.

Ben let his hand softly caress the curls that hung from the top of her head. He moved her to him with the back of his hand and ever so gently pressed her to his chest. If only time could be frozen and entwined hearts remain at rest together. He felt her gently reach to his mouth with the delicate fingers and now it was her turn to take command. She drew back from Ben and placed her open lips against his.

"Well, young lovers how are doing tonight?"

It was Rob and he was enjoying the romantic interlude they provided. "I'll leave you two lovebirds to finish off your evening and have a pleasant one."

Both Anna and Ben were left speechless and finally just laughed to each other like two lovers who had the confidence to handle public display of affections. Now it was time for Ben to sleep.

****

Over the next two weeks Ben spent his days walking around the Macey house. Martha and her parents had become used to his travels and joked about it at dinner. Ben began watching his timepiece as the day wore on, knowing that his love would soon be returning to him. As the two weeks were coming to a close he found himself becoming restless. He had discarded the cane and pushed himself to live with the pain. When it became constant he took some morphine to make the pain disappear. It was time to move on, but where?

Then one day he received a note from Colonel Winston asking him to pay him a visit on the following Thursday.

This caught Ben's attention but he just assumed the Colonel wanted to gather more information about his adventures in the south. How wrong he was.

When the day came, Ben was up early and borrowed one of the Maceys' carriages to travel to the war department. Mounting the stairs reminded Ben that he had to work harder at climbing, for his leg was screaming at him. He remembered the directions to the colonel's office, found it, knocked on the door and entered. The first thing he noticed was the single star on colonel's epaulets. He was now a brigadier-general. Ben saluted crisply and General Winston returned the salute.

"I can tell that life at the Macey's agrees with you. You are looking fit and in good spirits."

The general slapped his hands on his desk and asked Ben to take a seat.

"Well, general what can I do for you?"

"I think it is the other way around Ben. You see I have received a request for your services in the field."

Ben's body was almost lifted from the chair.

"Yes, it seems one major-general by the name of Homer Ames has asked for your presence at Petersburg to take command of a brigade. Let me be the first to announce your promotion to the rank of brigadier-general. Congratulations, general."

Ben was dumbstruck. "But …but I have been out of the field for so long and I thought you wanted me here to teach at the war department." "We can handle the teaching job at this end but there is a dearth of field commanders of your quality." Ben had the conversation with Anna in the back of his mind, she would be distressed. But the thought of a promotion to a brigade commander stirred the blood in his veins. This war must end soon. He found it hard to part with Anna however. General Winston wished Ben success in his new command. Ben stood and shook hands with General Winston knowing he was about to meet up with his good friend Homer. He found his way to the carriage and on the trip 'home' pondered how he was going to break the news to Anna.

# CHAPTER TWENTY SEVEN:
# WHAT WEBS WE WEAVE

Rob rode, without conscious thought, to Rose's home. His mind was wrapped up in the affairs in which he found himself, and he was afraid that he had lived the life of the 'gay vivant' without any real thought of anyone else or the consequences that could befall him. Was he so sure of himself that in the wink of an eye his life could turn to shame and even death?

The letter he had just received from Hobart described a plan falling apart. Their cotton smuggling escapades were about to be discovered. He could accept this. Others had been caught and escaped justice's wrath. What was more worrisome was the knowledge that General Winston had been to Harewood to visit Ben. What could be brewing in that corner? He did feel safe that the two necessary murders would forever be kept hidden through the ages. Or so he thought. What bothered him most was the realization that as his relationship with Rose blossomed, so did the remnants of a hidden conscience. He struggled mightily with this paradox, that as his hidden and honorable love for Rose increased so did his questioning of all those callous and criminal actions which pecked at his conscience like a maddened woodpecker.

As he drove up the Woods' driveway he tried, almost successfully, to put these thoughts about all of his nefarious activities to rest. He had a pleasant evening to look forward to. He stepped down from the carriage, after replacing the winter blanket from his legs to its spot in the back of the carriage. His arrival was met by their horseman who doubled as the butler, for after all the Greens had not acquired that quality of life war could bring those who sought its riches. They were still a social step down from the Macey's. Rose was anxiously awaiting Rob at the door.

"How are you, my beauty, you are a pleasant vision in this maddening world!"

As usual he was dramatic to the point of being insufferable. It did not even produce a twinge of a reaction from Rose. This was a man who suffered more than others knew and had all but been ostracized by his two sisters. Rose held to the view that men, particularly well-to-do men who happened to be handsome as well, were held in deep suspicion by those who had not done as well. That oft they were seen as lotharios who preyed on the innocent.

As her parents weren't immediately at hand she touched his face ever so softly and gave him a warm, wet kiss. Rob knew Rose loved him, but not like those other women and girls with whom he had liaisons. She was a woman of a different ilk. She looked beyond what others said and did and trusted her own judgment. After all Rob had always been nothing less than a gentleman with her. She liked to think that she had been responsible for the conversion of Rob to that condition.

"Rob, how would you like to visit in the library? In my father's absence we can take advantage of his well-stocked winery."

Rob was impressed. Rose's father had accumulated a plethora of grape that would equal any Southern, well-to-do gentleman. Rose seemed to know her way around the bar and did not see a need to send Rob to do what was traditionally a man's job.

"Rob, the other day I found a curious note that fell from my father's desk. In it, he describes the need of certain men to cease and desist their arms shipments to the South. The author had gained knowledge of General Winston's awareness of the gathering of unnumbered Springfield's left on the field of battle. The location of these guns seemed to indicate that they had been dropped by Confederates. I think you already know the author of the note. So far I have done nothing with this note, but I have showed it to your sister Anna. We are both of the opinion that it is a damning piece of evidence that could put ropes around the necks of the traitors."

Rose had simply thrown this piece of information out to see how Rob reacted, but she had been careful not accuse anyone. Rose walked behind a chair and placed her two hands firmly on its back rest. She fell silent and waited for a response. But there wasn't one. Rob wanted to hear more.

"Anna, Martha and I have always suspected that something was amiss between our two fathers. We made inquiries and even visited the factory, but it appears that loyalty abounds among conspirators."

For the first time in his life Rob felt terribly ill at ease. He knew this was no bluff.

"Anna, Martha, and I discussed the issue at great length and finally found a solution that pleased all of us. We are going to ask you to volunteer to serve on the front lines, wherever that might be. I think you will be awed by our reasoning powers. The observation we made was that you had made every effort to stay out of harm's way. Now we want you to serve directly in front of it. We want you to feel the fears and decisions that officers have to make. You will encourage others to instantly put an end to the gun running. That we took for granted. This method would also save our families' names which seem important to the male members of this family. Most importantly, it left the mothers of both families out of the situation. They would forever remain ignorant of the three of you. In return, the three of us would be bound to silence and destroy the note in question."

Rob was completely taken aback and unprepared for this attack on their monetary successes. He had nothing to say.

"Oh I forgot Rob. We also want both families to donate $100,000 to the soldiers' hospitals in Washington. It would be set up as a trust administered by the three of us."

"But…but stammered Rob."

The only question in his mind was whether this was all a bluff; that too many dinner parties and rounds of drinks had left alert ears on guard that something was amiss. He did not think so.

"And where did you expect me to serve?"

"We thought that question would be left up to Ben. He is a friend of yours and I know he can't wait to get back into action."

To Rob, Roses' eyes had lost their natural glitter and had become slits that glared down at his half-hearted responses.

"Do you have any questions Rob?"

"None whatsoever," was the laconic response.

"I feel this is a test of the strength of our relationship Rob. It will tell me who or what you truly love."

"You drive a hard bargain Rose, but I suspect that, in the end, I am deserving of such treatment."

"Fine, let's us make the best of a difficult situation and enjoy the roast prepared by our maid. She is an excellent cook you know."

Rose finished the last sentence with a flippant quip, as if nothing had taken place.

The dinner was held in virtual silence. Rose was seeing a side of Rob that few ever saw. Inside, Rob's thoughts were flashing like lightening in a storm.

He tried to think of schemes to silence these three women but nothing short of murder would work. The only card he could play would be to make himself into a superb officer, one whose actions would make it hard for such a heinous story to be credible. Yes, that was it… become a hero for the Union!

He gave no hint of his inner self to Rose. When dinner was finished Rob begged an early exit thus avoiding the consumption of an aperitif and cigar, a rarity for him. Good-byes were fragile, but at least separated the two so each could go off and analyze their reactions to the aforementioned meeting.

When she closed the door Rose was smiling from ear to ear. At the same time her hands trembled uncontrollably. She had never believed she could carry off this assault on Rob's ego. She had to remind herself of the nobility of their cause and that it brought some justice to an unforgivable act of treason. She had tested his love for her. Now it was up to him to make the next move.

# CHAPTER TWENTY EIGHT:
# OLD FRIENDS AT WAR

March 15,1864
General Ben Halliday
c/o Harewood Hospital,
Washington, D.C.

Dear Ben,

It has taken a devil of a time to track you down. I had feared you had expired in some God-for-saken hospital. I sent a request to General Winston asking for your whereabouts, along with a request. I have been asked by the powers that be to build a new division using what is left of the men you knew and the men I had inherited as a brigadier. This new division will place you at the head of one of the brigades with a greater number of the soldiers coming from New York. It seems the rioting was appeased by the financial rewards for joining. This has been aided of course by compulsory military service. They will only receive about four weeks of training. God knows that isn't enough but we will have to make do. I have also asked that Emile Lacroix be made a brigadier-general. He will command the other brigade. I am sure you will concur with my decision. Perhaps you can make some suggestions for colonels. We will let the New Yorkers offer suggestions for lieutenant-colonels and majors.

I received a curious letter from Rob Macey the other day asking for appointment as a staff officer. That boy has seen enough of the hind quarters of charging soldiers, so I have offered him a position as a colonel in charge of a regiment under your command. I am sure the irony is lost on no one in this case. I have elevated Lieutenant O'Malley and given him the rank of major and assigned him as a personal surgeon to me. But I know O'Malley as you do. He will be out in the field hospitals doing what he does so well.

I know that you have been out of touch with line command, serving General Winston as you did and then suffering that nagging injury to your leg. But the good cream rises to the top of the cup and you will have no trouble adjusting to your new command. I will be seeing you soon and hope that your leg will be just fine.

Yours Truly in God,

Major-General Homer Ames

April 2,1864

Dear Homer,

It is a pleasure to hear from you and I am quite willing to accept your offer to serve as a brigadier in charge of these New Yorkers. I am under no delusions. Many devastating battles have been fought since I served at the front during Shiloh. In the east the calamities of Fredericksburg and Chancellorsville left the North reeling in confusion. Fortunately we were successful at Gettysburg and I have met some veteran officers who served there on those three days. They speak of that battle as a high point in the war for the Federal cause, but also a time when the best of the best on both sides got to fight and tore at each other for three days.

The good news of all this is the appointment of General Grant to the position of commander-in- chief of the army. While General Meade will control the Army of the Potomac you can be assured it will be General Grant who will direct the overall campaign.

Giving Rob a regiment will turn some heads and I guess we will find out the mettle of the man. He is intelligent and sociable. Hopefully these qualities will serve him well when he is in command.

I understand that we are to be trained at different facilities. My four New York regiments are going to Camp Stockton in New Jersey. Emile's regiments will compress what is left of your old brigade into a full regiment, including the old Twentieth. He will train at Camp Chase in Ohio and most of his new regiments will come from that state. We should continue to correspond so that we, or the army, can set a date for our placement in the lines. Until I hear from you again, good fortune.

God Save the Republic,

Ben

****

Ben was pleased with the fact that they would be sent away from the bordellos of Washington for training. His only regret was that he had had so little time with Anna. She had been so kind to him. Her caring ways had overwhelmed him and left him with a special place in his heart for her.

It was a dreary overcast day when he arrived at camp Stockton located on the Dickinson farm just south of

Woodbury, New Jersey. A lieutenant was waiting for him with a steed that was to be his if he so wished. He was taken to the camp that would be his headquarters during their stay. Here he was met by First Lieutenant Aaron Bolger, who would be his personal staff aide. Such were the luxuries of promotion, he thought to himself as introductions were made. The lieutenant had seen action with the Fifty-fourth Mass. and was familiar with the handling of colored troops. It seemed his superiors had failed to inform him that one of his regiments would be colored. But no matter, the reports on them had been excellent.

As his mind rambled in no particular order he saw out of the corner of his eye four officers heading toward him. The eldest of the four had taken on the responsibility of introductions. The only thing he knew was that one of them would be Colonel Robert Macey.

"Good day, general I would like to let these officers introduce themselves to you. I am Colonel James Barrington and I come to you from the Fifty-first Ohio Volunteers. Next to me is Lieutenant-Colonel Edward Greg of the Thirty-fifth New York Volunteers. Next to him is Colonel Lucius MaCreary of the Fiftieth Mass. Volunteers. Our last commander is apparently well-known to you, and comes to us from General Staff, Colonel Robert Macey."

All present knew of the close relationship between the two and were waiting to see how this new situation would be handled.

"Gentlemen it is a pleasure to serve with you battle hardened veterans and I assure you that what Colonel Macey lacks in front line experience he makes up for with his wealth of knowledge and brilliant mind."

What had been a stoic face up to this point broke out in the Macey smile with Ben's remarks.

Both men had handled their first greetings sincerely and to the point. It was a good way to start off their new relationship.

"Gentlemen, I will get right to the heart of the challenge before us…green recruits, but a different brand of recruit. We first began this war with men who wanted to be defend the Republic. Little did they know what they would face and the emotional scars this war would create. The men we face today come from a different situation. They are conscripts. They don't necessarily want to be here. Additionally, they are mainly city boys, unused to the handling of firearms. They have also been exposed to a press that has not treated the Union leaders well. They have read of the horrors of war and the racism that still exists in this great state. The riots against the blacks will offer proof of this fact. I should explain to you that Colonel MaCreary has had considerable time working with colored troops and will be called upon at times to educate us in what we should do in the event problems occur. I am sure that you have received your regiment numbers, but just in case I shall review the assignments. Colonel MaCreary you will be assigned to the 210th, Colonel Greg the 211th, Lt. Barrington the 212[th,] Colonel Macey the 213th.

Ben nodded toward Colonel MaCreary as an act of deference to his experience. Ben wanted to keep this meeting brief and concluded it with the good news that staff had hand-picked the sergeants who would be drilling these recruits. Their soldiers would arrive the morrow. Ben planned to have five officers meet them as they marched, if you could call it that, through the gates of Camp Stockton. Ben dismissed his four colonels with the affirmation that they would leave this camp prepared and motivated to fight. Ben made a point of welcoming Rob to his new job. Whatever reservations he had of Rob, he knew that he would give his best.

"Well Rob, did you ever think you would see the day when you would be serving on the front lines?"

"To be honest Ben, I did not. I had spent time doing patrols in the west but had never seen action."

"I have no doubt of your ability to command and handle men. You might want to brush up on Hardee's Manual, just in case some obscure command is issued. To change the topic, your sister has been a great moral and physical support to me during my stay at Harewood. Not only did she gain my admiration but it made me realize how difficult it was to be a patient in that hospital. Some men had no friends, or visitors, and quite frankly not much to look forward to in this life. My prayers are with them."

"Yes, Anna is a special person, strong minded and sensitive at the same time. I wouldn't be amiss to say that she has a special place in her heart for one certain brigadier-general."

"Well Rob, I must be about my new duties. In the meantime find us the nearest bar in Woodbury. The camp is attached to the southern end of the town and we can take an evening walk and gain another view of our men."

Little did Ben know that Rob's behavior was very much the result of Rose's ultimatum. But Rob was a good actor.

May 8, 1864
Camp Stockton, New Jersey.

Dear Homer,

I have almost made it through this first day of command and with enough savoir faire to convince even my worst critics. Granted it was only introductions but I found I had to exude that confidence of command that comes naturally to you. As one goes further up the chain of command I find myself more alone. I am not sure why that occurs. My association with Rob went well and I hope for the both of this that this experiment goes well. I thought his resentment from removal of staff would show through but it didn't. My other three colonels seem like fine chaps, experienced and confident to command. I know this is a short note, but be prepared for more.

Trusting in God,

Ben

May 15,1864
Washington D.C.

Dear Ben,

I know how you feel. Now you have finely experienced the loneliness of command. It will lessen as time goes on and you are with your men, but remember there will always be a necessary distance. There will be a time when your men must not know your thoughts or emotions. Only then can you command successfully. Just take the many skills you acquired as a colonel and raise them to a higher level. What will be new, in a larger sense, is the knowledge of your place on the field of battle. You must take in more and relate to those commanders to your right and left. Don't worry, it will be like all else. It comes in time.

Up the Republic,

Homer

****

How strange it felt, sitting atop a horse marching to and fro and having no active part to play. Ben had always been in the middle of the action. Now his promotion cast him to the sidelines as an observer. The sergeants sent to train these men knew their drills and had the men both exhausted and grumbling after a day's worth of 'shoulder, arms', 'present arms', 'form columns of fours', and 'left oblique at the double quick'. As boring and repetitive as it seemed, Ben now knew the value of disciplined men. It would help them to march into hell. He paid close attention to the four colonels and how they behaved, particularly Rob, who seemed to revel in his role as leader of a regiment. Did they help make corrections? Did they communicate with their officers? Were the officers in complete control of their men? All seemed to be developing, as it should. Then one day it happened. Two soldiers from different regiments had taken flight but it seems they had holed up in the town of Woodbury, not fully knowing what to do next. They managed to elude the provost company sent out to find them, but with such ill-made plans it was only a matter of time until they were apprehended.

Both were brought before Ben who was now forced to make his first real military decision. He knew he had to make an example of them. Each was to receive fifteen lashes of the whip while tied to a wheel. A sergeant-major would administer the punishment. One man held his own during the whipping but managed to bite through his lower gums. The second man wailed and begged for mercy by the second lash of the whip. This was something new for Ben. It had been extreme but was intended to send a message to the brigade. No shirkers would be tolerated.

This message was repeated by Ben to the assembled mass of the four regiments. He rode his stallion in and out of the assembled soldiers, directing his eyes downward so that each man felt the personal wrath of their general concerning this issue. One of the soldiers had been in Rob's regiment. Rob asked to see Ben and presented his strong opposition to how one of his soldiers had been treated. Ben sat back listening in silence, watching the rapid transition from traitor to leader. Who was the real Rob Macey?

Camp Stockton did what it had to do and thus after a brief training period, they were deemed by the powers to be, fit for war.

June 15, 1864
Camp Stockton New Jersey,

Major-General Homer Ames,
It is with pride and conviction that I declare my brigade fit to fuel the furnace of this bloody cruel war. These men show no ambition to meet the enemy quickly, nor is there an esprit about the success of their training period. These are a different kind of soldier. I will assume that you have made plans for my brigade to meet up with General Lacroix' brigade so that we can begin our obligations to the Great Union which we all serve.

I wait anxiously for your further instructions.

God Save the Union

Brigadier-General Ben Holliday

P.S. I hope you will see that I am provided with the best of whiskey upon my arrival.

June 20, 1864
Washington, D.C.

Memo to: General Ben Halliday

From: General Homer Ames

Your last letter tells me that your men are prepared for war. You and your two brigades are to move immediately to Petersburg, Virginia and take up positions in the trenches that continue to be constructed around the city of Petersburg. This will be a crucial campaign as this city is responsible for supplying goods to Richmond. If Petersburg falls, so will Richmond. This could well be the last campaign of the war. The Confederates know this and are digging in, constructing elaborate trench systems south of the city of Petersburg.

Your transportation has already been arranged and together with your second brigade will meet you in the South. I will be traveling from Washington so that we can form this new division.

Yours in God,

Major-General Homer Ames.

# CHAPTER TWENTY NINE:
# THE PETERSBURG CAMPAIGN

It was like old friends meeting after a prolonged absence. There they were dressed as generals and trying to carry themselves with military bearing. Homer, Emile, and Ben met behind the major trench system that stretched for thirty miles in front of Petersburg. After handshakes and hugs Homer was the first to speak.

"We have already been given our first assignment. We are to circumvent the city and move to a location twenty miles from Petersburg. Union reconnaissance has found that a division of Confederates are forming there as well. Their task will be to put a stop to the Union engineering regiment that is spending its time tearing up and destroying an important railroad, The Southside Railroad. Our task will be to build defenses to keep these Confederate forces at bay. Don't bother to make camps. We will be leaving on a forced march first thing in the morning. I suspect you will want to pass these commands on to your regimental commanders. We will be helped by a cavalry screen to protect us. Remember we are fighting in Secesh territory and irregulars are trying to harass any movements we make. The division will also have a battery of three inch parrots along for support. Any questions?"

Ben and Emile looked at each other and said nothing. Homer had done a thorough job of outlining their orders.

"Fine, then I will give you time to address concerns within your brigades."

****

Morning came early and quick. The order to march was given. Ben's brigade would form first and march in ranks of four. Soldiers filled their water cans for the day. It was a warm spring day in the South and men would need respites from their marching. Ben had received a second aide, another lieutenant, John Grogan. Ben gave the order to send out flankers and skirmishers. Lt. Bolger carried this order to the first regiment in line which was commanded by Colonel Greg.

The march proved uneventful and gave Ben time to look around the countryside. In the distance to north and south of them the smoke from burning fires filled the air and wafted lazily upward on this windless day. Homer was marching at the front of the column so Ben thought to ask him if he knew what they were. Homer responded.

"I would imagine that these are farms and fields being razed by Union troops."

"Since when did we start making war upon civilians?" Ben queried. Homer caught Ben up on the changing face of war.

"I suppose the first concerted effort was at Vicksburg back in 1863. General Sherman is shaping military policy these days and it is his belief that war is intended to attack anyone or anything that aids the Confederate cause. Even the Confederates do the same thing. They don't want to leave anything that we can use to fight the war. It certainly is a long way from the military beliefs at the start of this war. Then it was supposed to be battles between the opposing forces that determined the nature of warfare. Times and circumstances have changed the thinking."

Ben nodded, obviously in agreement with Homer. While Ben was dwelling upon the effects this type of warfare must have on civilians, Homer sent one of his own aides to ask General Lacroix to join them. Within minutes cantering horses could be heard from behind. Homer placed his two commanders beside him and laid out his plans for the coming action.

"It appears that the Confederate division we may face will come from the north. My thinking is to build a set of fortifications north of where these engineers are working. It will take the shape of the end of a right angle so as to fend off attempts at flanking by the Confederates. Plus, the cavalry support and cannon will be placed near the two open ends to further support our flanks. The total length of the earth works we build will be about one quarter of a mile. We will fight in single ranks and try to stretch our defenses as far as is practical."

Both generals agreed and were satisfied that they knew what was to be done. The day wore on as the march continued without event. As soldiers sloshed through bubbling springs they took time to fill up their canteens. The clear day offered a hot sun beating down on these men in blue.

At about 4:00 p.m. those at the front of the line could make out fires near the railroad tracks that had just come into view. The sounds of clanging steel and squeaking nails could be heard even from this distance. Within half an hour most of the division was up to or close behind those in the lead. Both generals gave the command to form the beginning of the apex of the angle.

For this division, made up as it was of new recruits, many a man turned to watch the engineers lifting the nails that bound the rails to the ties below. Huge fires raced skyward and were being constantly stoked. On these fires were lengths of train track red hot at the centers where the section met the fires. The heat from these fires reached out to warm the men. Each regiment was given its place in the formation and after half an hour's rest began the task of building the earthen fortifications that were topped and reinforced with logs taken from the woods near-by. The light from the fires gave the soldiers the chance to complete their defenses during the night. So during the evening hours this new division spent the cool evening mounding earth logs while watching the engineers toil in the heat of the fire.

The soldiers got to watch the engineers carefully lift these superheated rails then take them over to a near-by tree and bend them manually or with the simple leverage of other logs. The rails were now permanently crippled for further use by the Confederates.

By 2:00 a.m. the soldiers for the most part, were ready for a good sleep. Few bothered to put up tents but collapsed on oilskins under the twinkle of stars.

General Ames set reveille for an hour later. The division had done a thorough job. Let them revel in extra sleep. Reveille was sounded at 8:00 a.m. Grumbles of burst blisters and aching muscles provided the main topics of conversation. Officer's call had been one hour earlier. Those present included Homer, Ben, Emile, their staffs, and the eight regimental colonels who would be responsible for making this plan work. Homer spoke.

"Good morning. I hope you all had a good rest. I feel today will be a solid test of our mettle. I want to comment on tactics that you will likely use today. If the Confederates make a traditional frontal charge, maintain your places. But there is a good chance that they might choose to veer off and take on but one of our wings. We must react quickly and with expectations of such a tactic. If this should occur the two regiments closest to the apex of our angle will slide along to help the wing under attack. The rest of the men on that wing will shift along on orders from lieutenants and captains. This will reinforce the attacked side. The two remaining regiments will climb the breastworks and form a single line forming to the north. They will then engage the left wing of the enemy with a left oblique. This maneuver has not been practiced and will require a movement by one of the flag bearer units. All companies should perform an oblique on their movement. I suggest that those regimental commanders make that decision. Are there any questions?"

A youngish looking colonel from Emile's brigade raised his hand.

"Yes, what is it colonel?"

"I question whether they will follow the flag bearers closely. There is no the desire to be bearers like there was at the start of the war. While once these men were considered the elite and frowned on shooting that this has now disappeared. Men are shunning the duty. They no longer believe that there is any courage or honor attached to being one of these men. The soldiers now believe one should shoot the bravest and help demoralize the enemy. The honor has been lost. What I am saying in summary is that courage is not an honor it itself."

Colonel Barrington now raised his hand. Homer nodded for him to proceed.

"While we don't make a ritual of prayer it seems that men are less concerned with it. Soldiers used to pray openly but in conversation with my lieutenants, they claim that prayer does not act as a protector of soldiers. Men die regardless of whether or not they have prayed."

More hands were raised. Colonel Greg added his name to the list.

"General, we are seeing an increase in the number of those shot for desertion. The men claim there is a blurring in what constitutes a coward. If a man honorably decided to do his best but is caught up in the hell of battle and runs away, is he the same as a man who skulks off from his company without anyone knowing? There seems to be a difference."

"Gentlemen I think we have lost sight of the purpose of this strategy meeting. But I do hear you and will address your concerns in a later meeting. You have all made valid statements and asked reasonable questions."

Amos was frustrated with these statements. They needed to be addressed but so did a possible upcoming battle. Just as he had concluded his last statement a rider galloped to the command tent.

"General a column of Confederates was spotted by our cavalry coming in our direction about three miles distant. Sir, they will be here in an hour or so!"

The rider was out of breath and obviously frightened.

"Colonels go be with your regiments. Oh by the way you have the option to have a regimental prayer."

The officers laughed as the general poked fun with his own absurdity.

"Generals Lacroix and Halliday, please remain behind."

He waited until the others were out of earshot.

"Gentlemen you must understand I do not have the time to teach a war college lesson on honor. We must ready ourselves. We will be pitting novice soldiers against Confederate veterans and we are light on artillery."

****

This was like the battle of The Ridge with the Twentieth Regulars, fought when they were for the most part totally green soldiers. How well would they stand up to the howling banshee cry of the Confederates? Ben sat on his horse surrounded by his two aides. He paid close attention to the movements of his four colonels. Each stopped to give a company captain a few words of advice and a pat on the back. Time raced like the journey of a turtle. Soon however, over the crests of a hill one could see the waving battle flag of the Rebs. They were still a mile away but within artillery range. He sent Bolger and Grogan to instruct the officers in charge of artillery to commence firing at will until they heard his order to cease fire.

Within minutes the first shot rang out as it blasted its way toward the approaching Confederates. It was hard to tell how accurate the firing was. He would have to wait until they closed to five hundred yards. Ben moved closer to Rob's regiment. He was charging up and down giving his men all the encouragement he could. Now Ben moved to the apex where the first action would probably occur. In the distance he spotted an officer on a large grey horse raise his sword. The gleam from their fixed bayonets reflected back by the sun told him that they were making a right oblique. Carried out so early this would surely place the Rebs around the left flank of the division. He scribbled a note to General Ames to see if he could verify his observations. This time he sent Bolger. Soon he returned and the general concurred. He instantly scribbled another note suggesting they pull the artillery on the right to join the guns on the left. Message sent. Again Homer concurred and a courier was sent to inform the artillery lieutenant to move his guns immediately. Ben now hoped that this was not a ruse to produce movement among the Federals.

Fortunately it wasn't. The Confederates marched on and the occasional sound of exploding ordnance and the sight of flying bodies told Ben that they had the correct distance on these Rebels. He could see his colonels looking back at him, wondering when to fire. He had decided he would wait until 100 yards had been reached. These were novices to the trials of battle.

The Confederates fired their first volley. Occasional screams were heard as men took head and shoulder hits. Ben felt a strange detachment from these events. He had larger concerns. Ben sent out a message to his colonels that volley fire should commence when he pointed his saber to the ground. He had to learn to give time for these orders to be received. He needed the discipline of this action as a brigade general.

The Rebels stopped their oblique and were on course to challenge the center-left of their position. Instinctively he dropped his saber and a large whoosh went up along with a cloud of white smoke. Immediately he looked to the rebels and could see them falling. He raised his saber again hoping for one more volley. Again he dropped it and the whooshing sound was repeated. This time with the smoke from the guns hanging in the air he could not ascertain the effects of their volley. A courier came in and the General advised him to prepare to make his shift to the left and send his two regiments into the field. Ben waited until he could see that the last oblique had put the enemy head on with the left side of the angle and probably overlapping their earthworks.

Homer had issued commands for the cannons to switch to canister fire. Ben decided to keep his two regiments back until he could get a clear view. He wanted to know exactly what Homer was thinking. With his guidon waving in the breeze and followed by his two aides Ben found Homer in the thick of battle racing up and down on his horse encouraging men to fight. He watched as one group of men began to pull back from the earthworks. The General was right there with pistol in hand daring one soldier to retreat. They returned to their place in the line.

"General Ames, can you see how far over their soldiers are from the end of our earthworks?"

"Probably fifty yards as I see it. We have accommodated for that."

Homer sounded irritated with the question. Ben knew when to back off from the general and returned to the apex. He sent a note to Emile advising him that he should command Ben's two regiments that had been pushed to the left, while he would go out on the field and command the other two regiments. Ben gave the order and sergeants and officers dressed on the apex while Ben grabbed a flag and placed it to the north furthest from the apex.

The infantry advancing on them had no artillery and that had been a large error on their part. It would have traumatized his soldiers even more. He placed the flag about 300 yards northward and ended the line there. What was developing was a Union defensive position that was beginning to envelop the attempted obliques of the Confederates. These soldiers caught the idea and Ben noticed no lack of interest in color guards putting themselves in harm's way. About 150 yards from the earthworks the Rebels stopped and prepared their own volley fire. Men in blue could be seen holding their faces as lead crushed their heads. Ben's two regiments had a clear chance to attack the left wing of the Confederates and lay down enfilade fire upon them. The Union soldiers repeated this fire again and again, creating huge holes in the Confederate left wing. The Reb commander could now see that they were the ones being encircled. His use of obliques had failed. The canister fire and constant rifle fire from front and left flanks were enough to discourage the Confederates from proceeding further. To their credit as soldiers, they made a controlled retreat, taking with them their walking wounded.

Within an hour an officer appeared with a white flag of truce asking that they be allowed to attend to their dead and wounded. Ben sent the officer over to Homer for that decision.

The victors were ecstatic. Sounds of 'Hurrah, Hurrah' encompassed the earthworks. Ames' division fought a good battle and their reward was victory. Their elation was diminished when they too looked around from their place of battle to see the dead and wounded soldiers of the Union that had been lost to them that day.

The regimental aid stations soon became overwhelmed as soldiers with all sorts of injuries, from twisted ankles to stomach wounds, appeared at their doorstep. Now the reality of war hit these men as it had hit those of the Twentieth Regulars. There was a large price to be paid for victory.

Fearing the possible return of these Confederates, the three generals conferred quickly on their priorities. First, care for the wounded. Second, get some food into these men who had not had breakfast. Third, bury their dead, and lastly, fix the earthworks in case of a second attack. By standards of the day their casualties were light, 230 had been killed while the number injured was double that figure. It was a total of 700 casualties out of a division of 4,000 and in a well-defended location.

During the truce Ben decided to ride out on the field of battle where many a rebel had fallen. He noted how many of the dead and wounded were shabbily dressed. Uniforms could not be replaced in these difficult times for the South. Some had no shoes while others had both shoes and pants that had been stripped from a dead Union soldier in another battle. The ages of these men varied greatly. There were some who looked like they could barely carry a rifle while others were old and emaciated. There, leaning against a tree was a wounded Rebel of about thirty who had taken a Minnie ball through the calf of his leg. He was waiting for transport back to his regiment. Ben thought he would start up a conversation with this soldier and try to find out more about conditions from this man.

"Morning soldier, care for a drink of water?"

The soldier looked at him with a wary eye, wondering what a general could want with an ordinary soldier. "Don't mind if I do general, much appreciated."

Ben climbed down from his mount and proceeded to hand his canteen to the Rebel soldier. The soldier was indeed thirsty and gulped down most of the contents of the canteen.

"I have some biscuits with me. Care for them?"

The soldier nodded emphatically. "We had no food before our attack on your position. It's tough fighting on an empty stomach." The soldier managed a smile after his comment.

"Who is your commander?

"We're a part of Beauregard's Corp."

The soldier took a liking to Ben and started in with his personal narrative of the war as he saw it. He claimed to be a small farmer from Virginia who wished he was home.

Letters from his wife begged him to leave the army and return home for the spring planting. It seemed that this was not uncommon among his chums. He felt that both soldiers and families back home had tired of the war and grown weary of 'the cause'. It was a cause that had little impact on his way of life. Food was so scarce that they had been forced to scrounge what they could find from Virginian farms.

"One wonders what's become of our military strength when we have to steal from our own citizens in order to survive. These people have barely enough food for themselves, let alone feed us. We look forward to the raids when one of our 'irregular' cavalry brigades can capture one of your Union wagon trains loaded with provisions or the occasional victory when we can strip your dead and wounded of whatever supplies they are carrying. This battle was a break from the tedium of being in the trenches. It's a rare day any unit gets a respite from duty in the trenches."

Ben fed him the rest of his biscuits and hoped that would tide him over for a few hours.

"You get well now Reb. I have to return to my troops."

With that information mulling over in his mind, Ben trotted back to the breastworks where the litter carriers were finishing up their task of retrieving the injured and taking them to regimental aid stations. He gazed around for Homer's Division flag bearer. Spotting it, he cantered over to the general where a cluster of officers had gathered.

"Ah, General Halliday, we thought we had had lost you to the enemy. Did you have a good visit with the enemy?"

"Most certainly, general. Am I holding back discussion?"

"Not at all. We were just making plans for our next assignment. We have been given a position holding one of the sections of trenches in front of Petersburg. They are using us to give relief to a division that needs some rest. As soon as the burial detail is finished we will begin our march back to the Petersburg trenches."

This was Ben's brigade's first battle and they had handled themselves well. Now it was their turn to experience the loss of friends to death and injury. Ben watched as soldiers could be seen kneeling over a fresh burial where a friend had been buried. Occasionally he would spot an officer or sergeant comforting a soldier sobbing uncontrollably. Ben had almost forgotten this part of war. He had become used to death and for a long-serving soldier it was to be expected. He let his subalterns handle these situations. Instead, he went about praising his men for their success this day. Now they would have something to write about to their loved ones. Homer had decided before marching a meal was in order, so soldiers just sat where they were and proceeded to crunch on hardtack and salt pork. Washed down with some water it was enough to control hunger's pangs. A call from Homer's bugler told Ben it was time to get into marching order. He would take the lead again and sent his aides out to find his colonels and form up.

Soon they were on their way and could already feel the heat of the mid-day sun beating on their backs like some uncaring sun god. As he headed out to the road, Homer galloped over, followed by his aides, to get things moving. The injured would remain behind to be cared for by the medical staffs of each regiment. A company from Rob's regiment was left to offer some protection in the event they encountered any irregulars. As they marched, the men could see that the battle had not slowed down the progress of the engineers who were intent on making this rail line irreparable for the Confederates.

And so his men had met the 'elephant' and performed well. He rode up and down the column, greeting men and handling questions when possible, but mainly he was listening for grumbling and complaints. Some asked for food and water but that was the limit of their comments.

This was a far cry from the officers he talked to who had warned him of this new breed of soldier. They were, after all, conscripts, men who had been forced into war rather than the rush of patriots that filled the ranks in 1861 and 1862. There were more substitutes as well, men who had been paid anywhere from three hundred to five hundred dollars to replace a man who did not wish to fight. Talk was cheap among these so-called 'loyal Unionists'. When it came to actual action their money replaced their loyalty.

Ben continued to ponder the comments that he had heard about this 'new' war, in which terror among civilians was the logical path to bring this war to a more rapid closure.

****

Ben had finally settled himself into his quarters, if that was the word to use. It had taken a few days to get acclimated to living underground. His headquarters had been dug out of the side of a hill and planks were used to shore up the sides and ceiling. He decided he had to share his life in a trench system with someone other than Anna. He chose his father.

June7, 1864
Petersburg, Va.

Dear Father,

Excuse my tardiness once again but I need at this time to burden someone with the turn in the nature of war that has taken place. For the common soldier the war has turned into a constant hell. Both sides in this war have seen fit to settle into what we call trench warfare. Continual trenches have been dug into the ground and run approximately thirty miles along a front to the south of the city of Petersburg. Each side has dug secondary and even tertiary lines behind the most foreword trenches. They are about six feet deep and four feet wide. Most are lined with logs which have been given the name abates with stakes of wood placed in the ground with a pointed end facing the enemy. These are called cheveaux de fres.

If it rains the men are up to their knees in muck and they must try to defend their position despite the weather. Their lives are in constant danger. This is due to new tactics and weapons used in this style of warfare.

I had occasion to run into Doctor O'Malley again. He is acting as 'chief of doctors'. Homer had the wisdom to use such a learned man to try to educate regimental surgeons. I spent some time with him and apart from the usual diseases he had noticed a new one that he called 'battle fatigue '. This he saw as the by-product of having to stand at arms for long periods of time. The men would appear totally exhausted and claim that they could not go on. He accepted their word. He said it was sad to see how many officers could not comprehend this new addition to the trials and tribulations of warfare. Eventually after a good rest many could return to duty.

Your loving son,

Ben

June 8, 1864
Washington, D.C.
Dear Ben,

I hope that your life in the trenches of Petersburg is going well. Life here has taken a turn for the worse.

Just yesterday the provost guards came to take father away. The same has happened to Mr. Green. From what we can understand they are being charged with treason for selling Winchester muskets to the Confederacy. If they are tried and convicted it could mean that they will be hung.

Now Rob's past actions have caught up with him. Mother is so distraught over these proceedings she is unable to speak. All she does is mutter to herself. Today I will try to gather my senses and call father's lawyer so that he can have him released on bail. They are going to need time to prepare a defense. I think I will call the doctor and have mother put on some medication to help her cope.

I will have to take a leave from the hospital so that I can find out more about this situation.

I miss you so much and wish you were here. You would know what to do!

Yours Always,

Anna

Ben's jaw dropped in shock when he read the letter. It could only lead to terrible consequences. He could identify water stains on the writing paper and took them as tears that must have rolled down Anna's face as she wrote the letter. He tried to think what to do. This probably meant that Rob had received the same news but to be certain he would wait until Rob raised the issue himself. It was time to write and try and help Anna, if that was necessary.

June 25,1864
Petersburg, Va.

Dear Anna,

What terrible news this is for you and your family. I will assume that General Ames will grant a leave to Rob so that he can go home and try and put these affairs in order. If there is anything I can do please let me know.

This will be just a short note to let you know that I received your letter. Try and stay calm and say nothing to the military until you have talked to your attorney. My prayers are with you.

Love,

Ben

Ben hurried his response to the quartermaster to make sure it would reach Anna as soon as possible. Now he would have to sit and wait until Rob came to him with the news.

But in the meantime he thought to pay a visit to his soldiers in the rear taking their two day rest. Ben had to admit what drew him to the rear was the smell of chicken cooking over fires. When he arrived at the source he discovered four small groups each roasting skewered chickens over open fires. He could tell by their faces that the soldiers were almost drooling while waiting for their dinners to be ready. Around the edges of the fires potatoes were roasting. The men were turning them to keep them from burning.

"How are you tonight men? It looks like you are celebrating Christmas early."

"No sir, just enjoying our just rewards for the hard work we do every day."

The soldiers laughed loudly with that remark.

"It's amazing general, what you can find when you put your minds to the task."

"Would this task involve liberating these animals from some Confederate farm?"

"We would be lying if we said otherwise general."

Ben had come to accept that scrounging was now a part of army 'policy'. It lightened the burden for these soldiers stuck in the trenches. If it improved their morale, so be it, thought Ben to himself. He wondered what he would have done if he'd found his men doing this in the early years of the war, back in Mississippi. He knew the answer.

Ben continued his wanderings and came upon a group of soldiers singing to the strings of a talented violinist. But times had changed and he heard this song more often around the campfires.

"We're tenting tonight on the old camp ground; give us a song to cheer.

Our weary hearts, a song of home, and friends we love so dear.

Many are the hearts that are weary tonight, wishing for the war to cease.

Many are the hearts that are looking for the right to see the dawn of peace.

Tenting tonight, tenting tonight, tenting on the old camp ground.

We are tired of war on the old camp ground, many are the dead and gone.

Of the brave and true who've left their homes, others been wounded long.

Many are the hearts that are weary tonight, wishing for the war to cease.

Many are the hearts that are looking for the right to see the dawn of peace.

Tenting tonight, tenting tonight, tenting on the old camp ground."

Ben listened carefully to these lyrics and found himself thinking of his family back in Illinois and Anna. Anna, who had cared for him and gave of herself freely to mend him back to health. He turned away without saying anything but he could see these men also having similar thoughts of loved ones. How much longer would they have to put up with this cursed war?

Suddenly musket fire came from the front trenches in front of where he was standing. He walked quickly, passing through the reserve trenches and into the front line. Soldiers were holding lanterns down low caring for three wounded soldiers.

"What happened here?"

"Another damn trench raid. Took us off guard."

"Any reason why they picked this location?"

"Probably because we've been doing a fair bit of sharpshooting in this area. We must have hit some of their men, general."

"Just watch those lanterns so that you don't get hit men."

"We'll be careful. But the Rebs are probably through for the night, now that they got their revenge."

Again Ben wheeled on his heels and this time retreated to his protective hole. He had seen enough for one evening.

Morning came early for Ben and his brigade. The Confederates decided to test out their new coehorns. These were short tubes made of cast iron and fastened to a wood base. The angle of their barrel allowed an artillerist to lob shells from close range. These were new to Ben and he watched the results of their destructive abilities when a direct hit occurred. The closeness of the trench system at Petersburg made them an ideal weapon for destruction.

# CHAPTER THIRTY:
# THE CHAOS AT THE CRATER

This was a war that allowed men to bring many of the skills that they had acquired at home to battles among brothers. No one was more of an asset to the fray than engineers. The building of bridges was one such skill. Less in demand were the miners from Pennsylvania. That is until a group of them approached their commanding officer, Lt. Colonel Henry Pleasants, who was a skilled engineer.

Pleasants grabbed at the idea like a painter to canvas. Petersburg would be a place to apply the skills he had mastered. He knew he would have to convince his commanders that the idea was viable. They would lay explosives in quantity below the Confederate trenches and push forward to roll up the remnants of the explosion. His research suggested a spot known as Elliot's Salient, a mere 140 yards from the trenches, held by the Union Ninth Corps. First the idea was given to their divisional commander, Brigadier General Potter who then passed the plan on to Ninth Corps commander Major-General Ambrose Burnside. While Burnside knew he needed approval higher up the chain of command, actual permission for the venture grew less enthusiastic. In the end, however, it was given.

Digging began 120 yards behind the trenches of the Forty-eighth Pennsylvania Volunteer infantry. Lacking in proper equipment and supplies, the men of the Fortieth-eighth used everything from empty crates to a broken down bridge. The earth removed was to be carried out in cracker boxes to avoid its disposal being observed by the Confederates.

Fresh air posed a problem for the miners. To solve this dilemma they sunk vertical shafts from the trenches down to the tunnel. A small stove was placed at the bottom of the vertical shaft and the ascending air would pull with it the foul air created by the miners. Wooden pipes were then placed in the shaft to allow fresh air from the opening to be brought into the shaft.

At mid-point in the excavation the miners hit upon a thick layer of clay. This was overcome by tunneling at an upward incline to the next layer. The tunnel was then returned to parallel tunneling. Secrecy was of the utmost importance and the soldiers were told not to tell these plans to friends or in letters home to parents.

After three weeks of tunneling they had dug a shaft five hundred feet long. At this point chambers were dug parallel to the Confederate trenches making a 'T'. These were about forty feet in length. Debate ensued about the volume of the charge but it was finally set at 8,000 pounds of powder.

The main attack would come from the Fourth Division Ninth Corp commanded by Brigadier General Edward Ferraro. Included among the attackers were two regiments of Afro-American troops who had not seen much action but were highly trained. Ferraro was to create two tight columns of his two brigades. They were to make a breach through the crater. The two brigades were then to spread out in opposite directions and consolidate the area surrounding their point of breakthrough. Lined up to join in the carnage with The Ninth Corp were 8,000 men of The Eighteenth Corps, a division The Tenth Corp, 5,000 men from The Fifth Corp, and lastly Ames' division.

For those not aware that such an explosion was going to take place, this event must have seemed like an earthquake. At 4:45 a.m. on July 30, the earth spewed into the sky in a plume such as none of these men had seen. Into the cauldron of earth and rocks were added the pieces of about four hundred Confederate soldiers. Along with that were the slivers of what was left of various carts, caissons, and cannon. After the onslaught from below, the first Union men looked into a hole that measured 28 feet deep, 65 feet wide and 180 feet in length. Half of the salient had been churned into the adjoining area or fell back into the hole itself.

The landscape added a ghoulish humor to it. Protruding from it were men's' legs, torsos, or even a mere hand. Only two cannon were lost but they had been dispersed to give an allusion of greater destruction. The two brigades that first arrived on the scene were so mesmerized by the need to gawk at the remains they forgot their main objectives and soon became mixed together with no hope of retrieving any semblance of order. Men slid, tumbled, or were pushed down the bank on the Union side, waded through the carnage of the bottom of the pit, and tried to ascend the Confederate side. It was then that many realized no thought had been given to the manner in which the men in blue would ascend from the cauldron.

Having regained their senses, the men of the South Carolina regiments manned what was left of the trench system and poured fire down upon the Union men. Additionally, the Confederates still in the trenches that formed part of the salient were able to bring fire to bear on those pouring into the confusion forming below. It wasn't until 7:30 a.m. that permission was given for the Fourth Division to advance. This included the colored troops who successfully made the crest of the Confederate side, reached as far as their support trenches, and captured a number of Rebs along with their colors. For the most part, little advance was made. Charging men mixed with charging men in the midst of a withering Confederate fire that was now backed by reserves brought to aid their fellows.

What made this carnage even more frightful was the excessive bayoneting of retreating men and the killing of men who tried to surrender, particularly colored troops. By 9:00 a.m. Major-General Burnside called a halt to the debacle and ordered Union men back to their lines.

Ames' Division was at the end of the column and had never been called upon to attack. For the first time in his military career Ben felt glad not to have taken part. It was indeed a strange reaction for him. He wondered what it meant. On returning to his command bunker, Ben found a letter waiting for him. He hurried to open it....

July 20, 1864
Washington, D.C.

Dearest Ben,

I finally have some good news for a change. My father and Mr. Green have been released pending a larger investigation by The Committee on the Conduct of the War. It seems that they were allowed to visit north Virginia, under guard of course and procure depositions from many men who were serving as Union Militia in the north and informed the officers accompanying my father that they had indeed received guns without registration numbers. Many of the men even produced the weapons to convince the Union officers that they were indeed sent by Mr. Macey and Mr. Green.

This seems to have quieted down the first attacks upon their character and any malfeasance in this matter. However the war office will continue to investigate as the total number is unknown. Father has said he will find the shipping bills for these guns and this will clear them completely. Let us pray all will go well for them.

I Love You,

Anna

Ben felt a wave of relief spread over him, particularly for Anna and the rest of her family.

"General Halliday, are you available?"

The voice came from the front of his domicile. He put down his drink, put on his boots and went outside to see who was calling him. About thirty feet from the entrance sat Rob, sitting comfortably on his fine mare. Ben looked around. How unusual, neither of his aides were available. He would have to speak with them.

"Glad to see you, Rob."

"I haven't had much time for visiting lately. Come and have a drink with me."

As he spoke, Ben walked over to Rob's horse. He was standing on the right side of the horse and that would be the first boot to dislodge itself from the stirrup. Strange thought Rob, the rounded end of his spur was still broken. He thought he should mention that fact to Rob.

"I know Ben, I have had to use this old pair I carry with me. My good ones have disappeared."

Rob secured his mount and the two men each took a chair and sat just outside the entrance to his headquarters. No point in having all his men thinking he was an all day drinker. The two officers raised their glasses and each took a good mouthful of hard liquor. Both savored the warmth it brought to their throats, parched from a day of doing nothing.

"Well, that was a grand waste of time, but it did offer a great show."

Rob laughed. Ben could not take it so lightly. He had heard from one of Homer's aides that casualties would be in the thousands. Rob talked on about the problems at home, but he had heard the good news. Ben could barely focus on that spur. Why was he even thinking about it? Then it triggered. He still carried that piece of spur from Addy's tent with him. He wanted to find it. Suddenly Ben could stand it no longer and told Rob he had orders to give and paperwork to do. Rob said he understood, and left noticing that Ben seemed very distracted.

Ben walked Rob to his horse and made time for a future get together. Ben had to sit down for a minute. He realized where his line of thinking was taking him. Could Rob have been the one who killed Addy? But why?

He leapt up and went over to his personal case that held everything that he had gathered over the years as well as his uniforms.

Finally he found the frock coat that he had worn before being promoted to General. He searched nervously through the pockets until he felt something metal in his inside coat pocket. He compared this piece with his own. It was the same shape and size. He sat frozen to his chair. What else did he have? Suddenly he remembered Addy's sketchbook. He kept rummaging through the traveling case and near the bottom came upon the sketchbook that he had hidden away as if to blot out that day of infamy. Ben started to look through the book. Addy sketched everything from flowers, to animals, to the faces of many of the men she knew. The last sketch he came upon was one of an officer that appeared to be walking up a hill. She had finished all of the officer except for his face. Whoever it was wore a staff officer's hat and there was only one man in camp at that time who was at staff level....Rob Macey.

My God, what have I discovered? Ben wondered to himself. It took some time to sink in. He looked at the sketch again and realized she had been meticulous about this person and the person in question obviously took pride in being carefully dressed.

Ben took the bottle of whiskey from his trunk and took a hard swig of the auburn colored liquid. He could feel it burn as it trickled down to his stomach. What was he to do? Were his observations leading him away from Addy's real killer? What possible motive did Rob have for the killing? Ben knew he needed a sounding board, someone else who could test his conclusion. That could only be Homer. It had to happen immediately! If he was right he could scare Rob off and allow him time to prepare logical excuses for all of Ben's questions.

****

The walk to Homer's headquarters was numbing. Here he was about to accuse one of his friends of a most heinous crime. How would Homer receive Ben's story? Would he agree with Ben's logic? Would he be alarmed that Ben could turn on one of his friends with so little evidence?

When he arrived there was a gaggle of officers hanging about Homer's headquarters. Ben recognized one of Homer's aides and bade him to come to him.

"A hectic and deadly day. Would you agree General?"

"Yes it certainly is, major."

If only the officer knew the reason for his presence he would be even more alarmed.

"Is it possible to speak with the general presently?"

Ben could feel his stomach fluttering. The officer looked over his shoulder and saw that the General was writing at his desk.

"Let me see how pressing his work is at this moment."

Ben waited, hoping to get his accusations aired as soon as possible. The officer returned.

"Yes, the general can see you now."

Homer's headquarters was a larger version of Ben's, except it was stacked with even more boxes of files and personal belongings.

"Ben, it's so good to see you. Our busy days keep us apart."

The expressionless look on Ben's countenance, told Homer that something was not right. He reached over to where a bottle of bourbon sat. He produced two glasses and filled them. It looked like Ben was bringing a serious matter to him.

"It's about Rob, Homer."

Ben stumbled through these few words. He took a hard swig of bourbon and explained the details and his conclusions to Homer. He even mentioned the use of the Macey name that had appeared when he was spying at his telegraph post. Typically of Homer, he sat with his elbows on his knees and brought his two hands together to form a church steeple. He stood, walked over to the door and closed the heavy cloth that hung from it. Then there was silence. Homer had to absorb the shock the same way Ben had. He began......

"Ben I am sure this has occurred to you but what would his motive have been for killing Addy?"

Ben tried to make sense of the situation and suggested that Addy had possibly stumbled upon Rob doing something or even saying something that jeopardized Rob's situation. Ben emphasized how he had never been convinced that Hal was the killer, but at the time he had no better explanation. What would the next step be? To confront Rob here would scare him off. Would this be better handled by someone like General Winston? Did this have something to do with all the turmoil surrounding Mr. Macey and the gun smuggling? Now Homer sat back in the same manner that Ben had, trying to make sense of this information and what to do with it. Both men were at a loss.

****

Ironically, as these two generals scratched their heads for an idea, Rob was busy planning another secret meeting with a Confederate agent. He had not met the man before and could only hope that things would go well. In the meantime, the best that the two men could think of was to send Ben on a snooping mission by raising the issues surrounding Addy's murder and showing Rob the picture from her scrapbook. If it was indeed Rob he would recognize himself and perhaps let something slip. They had to get across the idea that he was a suspect without directly accusing him. Both men were satisfied with this first step. Ben felt more confident knowing someone else agreed with him and so he took his leave of Homer, making a point to head directly to Rob's headquarters. He mulled over in his mind what he would say. He had come within one hundred yards of Rob's tent when he spied the colonel heading out from his tent. Ben jogged ahead. He wanted to talk to Rob before he changed his mind.

As he approached Rob's headquarters he stopped and asked his orderly if he knew where the colonel was going. The orderly did not know. Ben made a split decision to follow Rob. Call it instinct or call it foolishness, he felt any action might help at this point. He let Rob stay a good 75 yards away from him. What was curious was the fact that Rob's walk was taking him away from the camp near a wooded area. Suddenly Rob disappeared into the trees. Ben was afraid he would lose him so he picked up his pace.

Ben found the same entrance to the woods that Rob had taken. He had lost sight of him, but decided it would be better if he remained out of view. He walked for about ten minutes when the path suddenly broke into two sections. What should he do now? He bent over to look for fresh boot marks.  None were visible. He went further down the path that turned to the right and found a puddle of water. Knowing Rob he knew he would not want to dirty his boots. He must have jumped over. Sure enough, on the opposite side of the puddle was a fresh boot mark. Luck was with him this evening. Fortunately, this path was cleared of branches and twigs so Ben could proceed in silence.

Suddenly he could hear men's voices. He stopped. His approach was slow and methodical. He felt uneasy. Should he draw his pistol? Carefully he unbuttoned his holster and crept forward in silence. There they stood, in front of him, not thirty feet away. He knew that the cocking of his pistol would be distinctly heard in the gloomy silence of this woods.

Nonetheless he did it. He stepped out into the path as both of the men wheeled to the sound of his gun.

"Ben, is that you? I can barely make you out in this light."

Rob was as cool as ever. Ben could see the other man's hand slide down to his pistol.

"Stay where you are and take your hand away from that gun!" Barked Ben, hoping his voice would be enough. It wasn't. The stranger continued to reach for his pistol and Ben let loose a volley toward the man. The Minnie ball struck him in the stomach and he crumpled to the ground. While this was taking place Rob had reached for his pistol in an attempt to halt Ben's actions. Ben had never seen Rob use a gun, but he was very capable as a Minnie ball hurled its way toward Ben, hitting him in the left arm. Ben took a second shot and it hit Rob in his gun hand causing him to drop his pistol. Ben was now in command.

He ignored the blood streaming down his left arm, but kept a good aim on Rob with his right hand. He approached closer to the two men. The man on the ground was writhing in pain but neither man could pay attention to his obvious need for help.

"Ben!" Rob yelled. "What has come over you? I had a meeting with my good friend Mr. Kehoe. Don't you remember meeting him from Corinth? Explain yourself!"

Rob was putting himself on the offensive to try and dislodge Ben's train of thought and gain the opportunity to reach his pistol with his good hand.

Suddenly the sound of men's boots could be heard coming from the camp. Both were carrying their muskets. Again Rob tried to outmaneuver Ben.

"Sergeant, take this general and put him under your guard. He has become deranged and tried to kill my friend and I."

"Sergeant, I have a better idea. One of you go immediately and find General Ames and bring him here."

It appeared the sergeant was cool under fire and moved so that he could fire on either man if necessary. The sergeant followed Ben's idea and turned to the other soldier.

"Go find General Ames. I will stay here and keep an eye on both of these officers."

The other soldier did not hesitate. He twirled on his right foot and headed back up the path.

"General, I am going to have to ask you to place your pistol on the ground."

Ben did so reluctantly.

"Now move over beside the colonel so that I can keep a good eye on the both of you."

Ben moved cautiously so he wouldn't alarm the sergeant, who was now the man in charge.

"Both of you keep your hands in the air."

The sergeant was as cool as Rob. Suddenly Rob leapt behind Ben and in one motion put his wounded arm around his throat and with the other hand drew a derringer from inside his coat.

"Now sergeant, it is my turn to be in charge. Frankly, I don't care which of you I kill so I suggest you put your musket down on the ground."

Ben knew Rob meant what he said. He had to act quickly. He took both his hands and lifted them over his head breaking Rob's hold on his neck and managed to fall off to the right side as he did so. Before Rob could bring his derringer back to bear on the sergeant, the sergeant took a shot that hit Rob in the hip bringing him to the ground. In the meantime, Ben had rolled out of gunshot range and picked himself up from the ground. The sergeant now drew his pistol and kept it on both Ben and Rob but worried more about Rob after what he had said.

"Sergeant could you let me look at his wound?"

The sergeant felt that Ben was less of a danger than Rob and let him do so.

Rob was prone on his back. The Minnie ball had been fired at close range, shattering the hip.

Again the sound of men running broke the macabre silence and four men appeared, one of them was Homer.

"My God what is going on here?"

Ben took the offensive this time. "General, I found these two men conducting a business transaction. You might want to see what is in the two pouches that each man was carrying."

Without saying a word Homer opened the first. It contained U.S. currency. The second contained a map showing the command positions of various officers. Homer's first thought was that Rob had made Ben's and his own job much easier. Homer turned his attention to the wounded men and addressed one of the soldiers.

"I want you to find Doctor O'Malley. You can locate him at Colonel Macey's medical tent. Have him bring two stretchers and the men to carry them."

Ben's mind was spinning, partly due to his injury, but mainly because Rob had simplified the task of trying to prove him a murderer and traitor. Homer stayed silent through this all of this.

In about ten minutes Doctor O'Malley arrived with the required stretchers and men.

"My God what has gone on here?

"Don't worry about that right now doctor, just try and care for these three men and prepare them for transfer to your tent."

O'Malley moved quickly from man to man and realized that the stranger was the one who most needed his aid. He had the soldiers with him lift Colonel Macey to a stretcher. He determined that little could be done on a path so he suggested to General Ames that they move quickly to his hospital tent. He put a guard on each of the officers. At this time he did not want to show any favoritism toward Ben.

"Medical attention comes first, gentlemen. We will try and sort out the facts of this incident after that."

Ben was the walking wounded in this small column of men that trundled its way back to the camp. All three of the shooting victims were triaged at the hospital and Ben was placed in wait as his was the least serious of the wounds. Close attention was being focused on the Confederate spy as his stomach wound was serious and needed prompt attention. In the meantime, Ben mulled over in his mind what had just taken place. He had gone hunting for a murderer and instead found a spy. Either crime carried the death penalty but the spying incident probably carried the best chance of providing a desired outcome. Ben mentally slapped himself. Here he was thinking about a man's fate in a negative manner and at the same time the person was a friend. Rob had always treated Ben with integrity, respect, and provided good company and conversation on more than one occasion. But like the chameleon, Rob was able to change his colors quickly. In addition, Ben was becoming very serious about Anna. How would she receive all this? Ben would be a prime witness in the establishment of Rob's guilt. He started to feel like a traitor to the Macey family. What to do? He would write a letter to Anna and deal with this mess at the personal and emotional level. Ben still wanted to make very sure that this relationship continued. He had no idea how she would feel knowing her possible future husband was the hangman in her brother's life.

Finally Doctor O'Malley made his way to care for Ben. So far O'Malley had been dealing with medical matters. He knew nothing of what had transpired. He spoke quietly to Ben as he worked on his arm.

"What the hell is going on here Ben?"

Ben responded by giving him a summary of the events that had just transpired.

"Whew!" O'Malley whispered. "Who would have thought that we counted a double agent as one of our friends?"

"War does strange thing to men. But in this case I think the seeds for his behavior were already present. If you knew more about his father you would know what I mean."

"There you are as good as new. You will need to wear a sling for awhile so get used to it. Come to my tent every day and get that bandage changed. We don't want any infections setting in."

Ben thanked the doctor and caught Homer's eye as he too was getting ready to leave.

"We need to meet Ben. I want a full written report of the events on my desk by to-morrow afternoon."

It had been a long day. It had started with the battle at the crater and ended with catching a spy. Ben would give himself a good shot of Bourbon and try and get some sleep.

****

July 30, 1864
Petersburg, Virginia

Dearest Anna,

I hope this letter finds you in good spirits. It was good to hear Mr. Macey and Mr. Green have been temporarily freed. I am afraid that I have some bad news and because I was involved I would rather you hear it from me. Rob has been caught selling Union documents to the Confederates. He was also shot in the process of being captured. He has not been formally charged yet but I fear for his future.

Unfortunately I was the one that discovered the transaction going on between Rob and a Confederate agent. At present he is in the worthy hands of Doctor O'Malley.

Say nothing to your parents and wait until they are informed through regular channels or from Rob.

I hope that this event will in no way alter our relationship. If we stay the course it will strengthen the bonds between the two of us. Remember Rob was my friend as well.

With All My Love,

Ben

# CHAPTER THIRTY ONE: CLOSING THE DOOR

They embraced tightly, their bodies swaying back and forth. Finally they were together and for the moment could put all of the distractions of life from their minds. Ben and Anna were together. They did not speak. The silence spoke volumes. Rob was on the same train but in shackles. Anna's hands went to her wide open mouth. He looked weathered, unkempt, and had a discernable limp. She almost felt sympathy for him. But then it all came flooding back. The man was a traitor. He hobbled by Anna without saying a word.

"Ben you must come and stay at our house. Father is quite humbled and won't present any problem. We need someone who is strong."

"Very well, I will do this for you. But if there is any chance of Rob being released I would have to leave."

The couple found the carriage Anna had used to get to the station and the two took a quiet ride back to the Macey residence. It was a warm night in Washington and the slight breeze was a welcome relief. When Ben and Anna arrived Francis and Martha were at the front door. Again Ben felt there was nothing to be said. He used his strong arms to envelop the two women. He could tell that this was what they needed, some honest male contact.

All moved to the library. Ben took charge and poured himself a strong whiskey. The burning effect was relaxing.

"Well Francis how can I help you?"

"The lawyers for Steven have matters in hand."

She paused to produce her handkerchief, Ben could see her eyes beginning to tear as she spoke. I know that this must be very hard for you too Ben. You have become as well, a victim of the transgressions of the males of this family. Ben turned to Anna to enquire about Rose.

"I am afraid she is another of the victims of this affair. She and Rob had become quite close and in my conversations with her it seemed that Rob was able to show a completely different part of his character."

All looked exhausted and Anna suggested all head to bed and try and get some sleep. She reminded her mother about her medication and Francis nodded in appreciation of Anna's concern.

****

Steven had been out late that night so he was incapacitated for breakfast.

Ben had known Rob and associated with him, but Steven was a different case. Ben knew little of the circumstances surrounding the gun shipments and even less about Steven as a man. When he made his appearance Ben felt very ill at ease. His cheeks were sallow, his body hunched over as if he had gained twenty years in age. His supposed involvement had already taken a toll on this Macey. Ben said nothing to Anna about his condition but he was certain she would have noticed this marked change in her father. Steven announced that he had to go to his lawyers this morning and would be gone most of the day.

Ben tucked the three females under his wing, spoke to the maid and had her prepare a picnic lunch for the four of them. He announced in a faked voice the destination…

"We are going to a place that is quiet and peaceful. Where the flowers bloom almost all year round and all of you have been there. The women looked at each other with a shock. How had Ben gathered just a rapid knowledge of Washington. It was no wonder that they broke out in laughter when the carriage stopped in front of Harewood Hospital. Fortunately for Ben all the females appreciated the thought and proceeded to spend an afternoon away from their memories of misfortune. At the end of the day Anna walked Ben down the familiar road and wrapped her two arms around his right arm.

All good things must come to an end and so the little party made its way back through Washington to the Macey residence. There seemed to be a cluster of men standing around the front door and Francis identified their priest as one of the members. They climbed down and approached the men, all showing grim faces.

"Mrs. Macey I am afraid we have some bad news." Spoke the priest.

"This afternoon your husband suffered a fatal heart attack while at a meeting with the lawyers. We offer you our condolences and may your souls be filled with the grace our 'Good Lord' has given us to deal with these tribulations."

Ben said a quiet 'thanks be to God', as well, but for different reasons.

A messy and probably fateful court process had been avoided for one of the Macey's. Now it was time for Ben to take the lead again and take the organization of the funeral under his wing. Francis was only too thankful.

\*\*\*\*

The next day Ben spent most of his time at the undertaker's. Francis had told him to spare no expense and like an obedient son followed her directions. The funeral would be held the following day.

Many of Washington's civil, social and military leaders made their way through the Macey drawing room where the wake was held. It was a noisy affair, as most funerals are, even when old friends meet in solemn conditions. The hum of subdued voices and well-intended condolences was enough to keep Francis and the girls both active and vocal. The family rallied around their mother. When all had departed after the traditional sandwiches and tea, one last viewing was to take place.

There appeared at the door Rob Macey, unshackled, with Rose holding his arm and two large men following them. Rob had nothing to say. He walked over to the three females and whispered in their ears. His stay could only be brief. He walked over to his where his father lay in his casket and mumbled something no one could decipher. He looked at Ben, raised himself and gave a salute…Ben returned the salute and Rob departed.

Ben and Anna walked around the gardens which were in full bloom. Anna spoke "I am glad Rob had a chance to see father, they were two of a kind."

Ben meanwhile heaved a silent sigh of relief. Both of them were exhausted.

****

The first trial was that of Thaddeus Green. Ben and the Macey women came to the courthouse every day to give support to Ann and Rose Green. Mr. Green it seems caught a break. No soldier could be found who admitted moving the guns or exchanging any money. The case strengthened for Thaddeus when General Winston made an appearance and testified that he was fully aware of what was going on in the shipping of guns to the south. As well, no books could be found to act as a record of criminal wrong-doing. In the end the Military tribunal exonerated Mr. Green from any wrong doing. There were tears on the part of both families when this decision was rendered.

****

About two weeks later the trial of Rob began. This was a lengthier affair. Numerous character witnesses heralded Rob Macey's military career and Ben began to feel like as he was to be the prosecution's main witness.

Rob's lawyers tried every means to confuse, implicate, and generally demoralize Ben while he was under oath. But to no avail. Ben saw the two pouches as did the two soldiers. Information for money and that was it!

Rob was being tried for treason and there was no escape.

After what felt like a lifetime the generals came back with their ruling.

Guilty! The sentencing could not be lenient. This was a high profile case and there could be but one sentence. Death by a firing squad. Rose Green collapsed on the floor distracting attention away from Rob, who looked amazingly calm under the circumstances. Reporters ran to their carriages to be the first to report on this tawdry affair.

The shackled Rob was led away by the guards, taken down the stairs of the courthouse and promptly taken back to jail. There was only one problem.

The return route to the jail was the same as the route which had brought Rob to the court house. About half-way back a band of men stopped the hapless guards and demanded their keys. The lead guard refused and was quickly struck on the head for his troubles. He fell from the wagon and with him his set of keys. The guards were tied with rope and placed in the wagon. Rob was ushered to a waiting horse and the small band disappeared before anyone had a clue of what had taken place.

News reached the Macey family and there were mixed reactions. They spoke of justice and Rob's life in the same sentence. As a result undercover Pinkerton men were placed around both the Macey household and that of the Green's.

****

Three months later and life in both residences was beginning to resemble some degree of normalcy. There was no word from Rob. He had disappeared. Both Thaddeus and Steven had made legitimate funds and that, coupled with the selling of all business ties, left the two women with a tidy sum of money. Rose hoped for the day that she would see Rob…but this seemed too much to ask. Ben had resigned his commission in the military but felt kind of 'lost', military life was all he knew. At dinner, one night, Ben and his 'five women' were eating dinner when, out of no-when Francis uttered the following.

"You know we don't really belong in this society any more. Oh, people are friendly enough but their little 'whispers' tell a different story. We need to change our lives dramatically. I have been doing some research into this plan I have and I would like you all to consider it. We move to the west and become cattle ranchers!"

Heads turned abruptly Francis' direction.

"And why would you suggest this idea Francis? Queried Anna.

"Well in the first place our reputations are ruined. Even moving to another city would not stop our sullied family history from following us."

We need a fresh start in a part of this country where we are unknown, besides I have heard that there is good money to be made, particularly if we had a large herd. Eyes went from one to another. They were searching for reasons to counter Francis' idea and none could be found. The idea of a new life appealed to them.

When Ben and Anna had the chance they aired their own views about the plan Francis had put forth.

"Ben, you would come with us if we went, wouldn't you?"

"Yes, of course Anna came the robotic answer." This was not the time to offer any thoughts that could harm their relationship. It had been a long time since Ben had seen a smile as broad as the one from Anna's face. He had made the right decision.

LaVergne, TN USA
21 April 2010

180082LV00002B/1/P